MORAVIA, ALBERTO
TIME OF DESECRATION   ($10.95)

FC

Time of Desecration

Also by Alberto Moravia

FICTION

The Woman of Rome
The Conformist
Two Adolescents (Agostino and Disobedience)
The Fancy Dress Party
The Time of Indifference
Conjugal Love
Roman Tales
A Ghost at Noon
Bitter Honeymoon
Two Women
The Wayward Wife
The Empty Canvas
More Roman Tales
The Fetish
The Lie
Command and I Will Obey You
Paradise
The Two of Us
Lady Godiva
The Voice of the Sea

GENERAL

Man as an End
The Red Book and the Great Wall
Which Tribe Do You Belong To?

PLAY

Beatrice Cenci

Time of Desecration

ALBERTO MORAVIA

Translated from the Italian by
Angus Davidson

FARRAR · STRAUS · GIROUX
NEW YORK

Library of Congress Cataloging in Publication Data
Moravia, Alberto.   Time of Desecration.
Translation of *La Vita Interiore.*   I. Title.
LC 80-14438

This novel consists of an interview given by the character indicated by the name of Desideria to the author, indicated by the pronoun 'I', during the seven years of the drafting of the book. Like those of all the other characters, Desideria's story is not told by the novelist; she tells her own story.

THE HOUSE OF ILL FAME

CHAPTER ONE

Desideria: My name is Desideria. And I have experienced a Voice.
I: A Voice? What Voice?
Desideria: I will answer you with a passage from a book.
I: What book?
Desideria: *The Life of Joan of Arc*. She too had a Voice. Here is the passage: 'This Voice reached me about the time of midday, one summer day, in my father's garden. The day before, I had fasted. Rarely did I hear it without seeing a brightness from the direction from whence the Voice made itself heard. The first time I heard the Voice, I vowed my virginity for as long as it should please God.'
I: Why Joan of Arc? What has Joan of Arc to do with you?
Desideria: In that passage there is mention of two things that I have had in common with Joan of Arc: the Voice and virginity. For some years a Voice has spoken to me, has guided me, has commanded me. And, at the same time, I have wished, like Joan of Arc, to take a vow of virginity until a certain event came about. Indeed, as with Joan of Arc, in me Voice and virginity were closely bound; one justified the other, the one existed because the other existed.
I: But this virginity – you had not vowed it to God, had you?
Desideria: No, I vowed it to something different, something which is still a kind of divinity, today, for many people.
I: What is that?
Desideria: I prefer not to tell you. It will become clear from my story.

3

I: Are you still a virgin now?

Desideria: No, I no longer am.

I: So that means that that particular event for which you vowed your virginity has come about.

Desideria: No, it has not come about.

I: And the Voice?

Desideria: The Voice has vanished.

I: So you are no longer a virgin and the Voice has left you?

Desideria: Yes, it's like that. I am going to tell you the story of precisely how I lost, at the same time, both my virginity and the Voice.

I: That is, the story of your vow?

Desideria: Call it that, then: the story of my vow.

I: How did it happen that you heard the Voice for the first time?

Desideria: It all began one night when I was very hungry and got up to get something to eat in the kitchen.

I: Where did this happen?

Desideria: In a big expensive penthouse that occupied the whole of the top floor of a villa in the Parioli quarter of Rome, where I lived with my mother, Viola.

I: How old were you?

Desideria: Twelve. I was very different from what I am now.

I: Different?

Desideria: I was a fat girl.

I: A fat girl?

Desideria: Yes, I was one of those corpulent children in whom the fat is equally distributed over the whole body and seems to cancel out every incipient feminine form. Have you ever seen the case in which a double-bass is kept? Such was the envelope of fat in which, like the musical instrument in its case, my body was enclosed and made unrecognizable. I had no behind, I had no belly, I had no hips, I had no bosom, nothing but fat. I remember – like something that happened to another person – that when I walked my thighs rubbed against one another; a humiliating sensa-

4

tion that I could not manage to get accustomed to and which filled me with a feeling of obscure unhappiness, as though it were the sign of an irreparable degradation. I was, in fact, conscious that, with every gesture I made, I produced a caricature of the graceful movements of the feminine body. And as though that were not enough, I was afflicted with a continual hunger.

I: Perhaps you were fat because you ate too much.

Desideria: No, on the contrary, I ate too much because I was fat. That is, I ate in order to console myself, by means of food, for my unhappiness. And in fact I ate even when I was not hungry, owing to a kind of nervous stimulus rather like the stimulus which urges smokers to light one cigarette after another. For example, when I was doing my homework, I might happen to notice an itching between my legs, or under my breast. So I would put my hand to the place where I was itching. I would feel that enormous fatness which for a moment I had forgotten, and immediately after scratching myself I would reach with the same hand for a packet of sweets that I always kept ready in the drawer and would put one in my mouth; in that way, by eating, I would forget that I was fat, in that I was doing precisely something that would increase my fatness. Or again, I would perhaps get up and go into the kitchen, open the refrigerator and lay my hands on whatever I found there, remains of cold meat or vegetables, fragments of pudding, pieces of cheese, pots of honey or jam. I would stuff myself haphazardly and in great haste, and then, with my mouth still full, go back to my room. In the morning, before going to school, although I had only just had breakfast, I would go into a confectioner's and buy cakes to keep in my desk and eat gradually during lessons. My own room was full of boxes and bags hidden all over the place; on my desk and in the drawers there were always crumbs and remains of food. At the same time, besides being a glutton, I had also become a drunkard. Above all I liked wine, which I gulped down in big mouthfuls straight out of the bottle, smacking my lips; but I was also fond of the small bottles of strong liquor

5

which stood in a row on the shelves of the bar, at the far end of the living room. I drank in order to get drunk; then, as soon as I felt I was drunk, I would go and shut myself up in my room, turn the key in the door, throw myself on the bed, and masturbate.

I: You masturbated?

Desideria: Yes, furiously.

I: When did you start masturbating?

Desideria: I don't know: I've always done it.

I: Did you think of anything special while you were masturbating?

Desideria: No, nothing. It was a mechanical thing which nevertheless made me forget my fatness for a few minutes.

I: Always that fatness!

Desideria: Fatness, in my eyes, was a symbol of all that I was and would not have wished to be. Besides, gluttony brought with it other – how shall I say? – *lateral* characteristics. All that eating and drinking, always done in a frantic hurry and with an obscure feeling of guilt, had caused me to become furtive, false, untruthful, hypocritical, deceitful. I was conscious of this, too, as I was of my gluttony; but it was an inactive, impotent consciousness which served only to make me more unhappy. Furthermore, my unhappiness was doubly increased by the fact that I was not the only person to be conscious of my fatness; above all, my mother was conscious of it.

I: You mean that your mother saw you as you were?

Desideria: As even worse than I was. Her consciousness of my fatness was not gloomy and unhappy, like mine; but angry, disappointed, irritated, impatient. In this consciousness of hers I saw reflected, as in a pitiless mirror, my own guilt at not being beautiful. By way of comparison she, seeing me so ugly, was furious in the same way and for the same reasons as a trainer who, having bought a well-bred colt at a high price, sees it, in time, become mere butcher's meat.

I: Why, what aim, in your mother's view, ought you to have contested and achieved?

6

Desideria: All the aims in life in which she had been defeated, the races in which she had come in last.

I: Tell me about your mother, tell me what she was, what sort of person.

Desideria: At the moment when my story begins, she was about forty years old. She was Italian-American and she had married a Greek-American called Papas. For many years she had been with her husband in the Middle East; he was a builder, he created entire quarters of Eastern towns; then they had come to Rome, the husband had died, and she was left alone with me, a child of three. But, at this point, there is something you must know: Viola was not really my mother. Viola and her husband had adopted me soon after they established themselves in Rome. Of course I did not know that I was an adopted daughter. I came to know it rather late, in the way I am going to tell you.

I: Who was your real mother?

Desideria: A working-class woman who, so it seems, got rid of me in order to be freer to lead the life she liked. I have a suspicion that this woman had been a maid in our house; and that, even if Viola was not my mother, her husband was really my father. But it's only a suspicion. In any case, I never bothered to clarify the rather uninteresting mystery of my origins; what was important to me, as you will see, was not to know who were my real parents but to what class they belonged. In fact, somehow or other, I avoided going back to the personality of my mother; all I wanted was to be sure that she was of the working class. But you wished to know what my adoptive mother was like. In the first place, she was rich.

I: Wealth is not an individual characteristic.

Desideria: In her, it was. She was rich first of all. Just as other women are first of all dark or fair, so she was first of all rich.

I: Was she very rich?

Desideria: Yes, she was extremely rich; but that is not the point.

I: What is the point?

7

Desideria: She was 'only' rich.

I: Only?

Desideria: I mean that, for many reasons, she had nothing in life to fall back upon, except money.

I: What d'you mean by 'fall back upon'?

Desideria: Viola was a sort of 'stateless' person, but not in the sense usually given to that word. In a much more complete sense, if I may put it like that. She was stateless not merely as regards her native land, since she was at the same time American, Greek, and Italian; but also as regards society and family, because, just as she had a native land from the purely legal point of view, that is, inscribed in her passport (she was an American citizen), she had merely a semblance of a family and took part in what was no more than an outward appearance of society. She was, in fact, the most fantastically rootless person I have ever known. And just imagine, she did not speak any language.

I: A person always speaks some language, even if he speaks it badly.

Desideria: Perhaps I did not explain myself very well. Viola did not express herself in any language: all she did was to make herself understood, like tourists travelling in a foreign land.

I: What languages did she speak?

Desideria: English, but the English of an emigrant, poor and slangy, for though she had been born in the United States she had had little in the way of education; Italian, but this too in a summary sort of way, with an admixture of dialect words (her parents had emigrated to America from Calabria); a little French, a little Greek, a little Arabic. Normally, at home, she expressed herself in Italian. When she was angry and wanted to be harsh and haughty, then, curiously, it was English that emerged. French, Greek, and Arabic were limited to a few words that came up now and then to the surface of her speech, like jetsam from a shipwreck after a storm. She was, in fact, stateless even linguistically: a real genuine monster, in her own way.

I: So then, what you mean is that wealth was a kind of

8

fatherland for her. That her roots were in money and in the well-being which money secured to her. The world is full of people like that.

Desideria: You are wrong. She did not actually attach any importance to money. Instead, she was obsessed by the things she had not got, especially by family and society.

I: You mean that her life hinged on the fact of having an adopted daughter and of belonging to Roman society.

Desideria: Again you are wrong; her life hinged on sex. Perhaps there had been a time, when she first came to Rome, in which family life and a position in society had been her chief preoccupations. But that time was now distant; nothing was left for her now but a kind of pig-headed longing, of stubborn hope.

I: Longing and hope for what?

Desideria: That she might someday, by some miracle, have everything that she had not succeeded in obtaining by will-power. Meanwhile, however, with her full but helpless consciousness, sex had become the centre of her life.

I: What was she? A sex maniac?

Desideria: She was not so in the sense of someone who had made a final choice; she was so for lack of anything better, so to speak, or, if you prefer, for lack of what she obstinately considered to be better. She would have preferred to be a good mother of a family, a respectable bourgeois lady; but these two things unfortunately displayed themselves to her as two conventions, or rather, as two roles to be acted rather than experienced. On the contrary, sex, to her despair, was the real, true, genuine thing which she felt urged to perform spontaneously.

I: How do you come to know so many things about your adoptive mother's past?

Desideria: I have already told you that there continually cropped up in her mind the hope of some sort of miracle which would tear her away from sex and restore her, or rather enclose her, truly and for the first time, in a reality of a different standard. It sometimes happened that she took action to favour voluntarily such a step. For example,

9

as regards her social ambition, I have retained a precise though remote and almost incredible memory of a kind of social catastrophe which occurred when I was still a child.

I: A castastrophe?

Desideria: Yes, a great, solemn reception to which she had invited let us say a hundred people and – as though they had come to an agreement among themselves – nobody turned up.

I: Nobody?

Desideria: Yes, incredible as it may seem, really nobody. I remember the preparations, above all the immense dishes arranged on two big tables and full to the brim with cakes and other victuals. I also remember Viola in an extraordinary 'reception' garment.

I: Why extraordinary?

Desideria: You know those covers that are put over teapots so that the tea should not get cold? Or those immense dresses supported on wicker frameworks, worn by women in pictures by Velázquez? Well, Viola, for the occasion of this reception, had acquired a similar dress. I was present, full of admiration and astonishment, at the dressing of my adoptive mother. In the first place, her maid helped her to fix the crinoline round her waist, that is, a kind of cage inside which Viola's body looked to me unexpectedly slim, like the body of an adolescent girl, in contrast with the enormous width of the framework; then she slipped the dress over her head and pulled the skirt, with its flounces and festoons, down to her feet. The dress had a very deep opening at the back; it reached right down to her loins and showed off her back, which was Viola's best feature. In front, on the other hand, her skimpy bosom was enclosed in a tight bodice. I was left in no doubt that this dress was extremely elegant, that Viola was the most beautiful woman in the world, and that her party would be a great success; I remember that I skipped around her, repeating: 'Mummy, you'll be the most beautiful of all of them.' Alas, I did not foresee that such a competition would not take place, since, as I have told you, it was as if the

10

guests had passed the word round and no one, absolutely no one, came to the reception. Viola, after she had finished dressing, moved majestically but with some awkwardness; in order to pass through the door she had to go sideways; then, walking slowly and with the crinoline swaying at every step, she went and sat down in the living room, in front of the buffet tables, on a divan which was immediately covered, almost entirely, by her immense skirt; and there she sat and waited. Behind the buffet tables stood waiters, trying to occupy their time by moving the bottles and the dishes: from the far end of the living room came the arpeggios of a group of instrumentalists mounted on a sort of platform; Viola sat still, her arms wide apart and spread out over her skirt, her bust erect, her eyes fixed on one of the dishes in which was enthroned a large roast turkey. An hour passed in this way, and it could still be supposed that the guests, as often happens in Rome, were merely late. But when a second hour had gone past without anyone coming, and the two waiters, tired of standing, had sat down behind the buffet table, smoking and chattering in low voices, and no sound came from the far end of the living room, as though the instrumentalists had gone to sleep, all five of them, over their instruments, then Viola told one of the servants to bring her a whisky. I do not know why, but this whisky, drunk in solitude in front of the untouched buffet, in the silence of the big, illuminated, deserted room, made me realize, all at once, that the reception was a failure, that nobody would come, that nobody wished to have anything to do with my mother and myself. I had remained until that moment, sitting on one of the immense armchairs in the living room; but when I saw Viola carry the glass to her mouth and empty it in one single draught, and then immediately afterwards signal to the waiter to bring her another, I ran away to my own room, threw myself down on the bed, and started sobbing from an obscure feeling of humiliation and outrage. It was not I who had been humiliated and outraged but my mother; and precisely because of this my feeling of bitterness and shame was all the greater.

11

Then I remained on my bed, in the dark, without the courage to get up. From time to time I listened carefully to see if any sound of people arriving could be heard; but all was silence. Finally, I fell asleep, and slept for perhaps a couple of hours. Then I awoke with a start and, without delay, almost mechanically, pressing back my hair and smoothing my crumpled dress with my hands, I went back into the living room. Dismissed no doubt by Viola, the waiters and the instrumentalists had vanished. But Viola was still sitting on the divan in her incredible dress, in front of a small table on which I at once saw the glass again half full and the bottle almost completely empty. She was looking straight in front of her, as she had been two hours before, her eyes fixed on the enormous, ironical turkey enthroned on the buffet dish; it was as though she were trying to evoke, with that staring gaze, the absent crowd of the party guests. I went up to her and said in a low voice: 'Nobody came, Mummy. Perhaps you made a mistake and it should have been tomorrow'; and for reply I received a most violent backhanded blow on the mouth and cheek, all the more painful owing to the massive rings on her fingers. Then she rose and, staggering in her immense, swaying dress, went off towards the far end of the room. She walked in an uncertain manner; one could see that she was drunk. In spite of the pain of the blow, I had a strong feeling of compassion when I saw her moving away like that, with that enormous crooked skirt. Then she reached the door, opened one leaf of it, placed herself sideways to make a passage for her dress, and . . . fell to the floor and remained there, motionless, like a gigantic doll with broken joints. I ran out and gave a loud call, and four people arrived, the cook, the governess, the maid, the chauffeur. With an effort they pulled Viola up from the floor, where she was lying, put her back on her feet, and led her off into her bedroom. She was so drunk that she promptly went to sleep, while we were still undressing her. We put her to bed, threw her dress onto an armchair and then went away. Next day all trace of the party had disappeared; Viola was normal again. But for

12

some time there was no further talk of parties, at least of parties of that kind. From that day onwards Viola invited to our house only those few people who she was sure would come.

I: Sure – why?

Desideria: Because they were socially inferior, or dependent upon her: her lawyer, her man of business, her doctor, her dentist, her architect, a few married or unmarried women friends of her youth, a few of her or her husband's relations, a few Greek or Italian-American businessmen who were passing through Rome, and so on. After the failure of the reception these were the people whom my adoptive mother frequented. And it was from that time, also, that Viola acquired the habit, at least three times a week, of transforming our living-room into a kind of gambling den, with a lot of little green card tables drawn up in a row beside the windows. As I have told you, they were rather a haphazard collection of people, and those evenings, or rather nights, produced a casual, squalid, even rather sinister atmosphere. But they came, no doubt of that. When the guests left in the early hours of the morning, the air was clouded with cigarette smoke; cards and counters were strewn in disorder over the tables; the buffet looked completely devastated. From my room, where I barricaded myself, I used to hear, half asleep, the buzz of conversation until very late. But the success of these evenings devoted to gambling produced in me the same feeling of compassion for Viola which I had once felt after the failure of the party. I knew, in fact, that Viola despised these makeshift guests; and I could not help sharing this feeling.

I: Did you ever understand why no one, absolutely no one, had come to the reception?

Desideria: No, how could I? I was a child, Viola was my mother, I had scarcely yet been outside my own home and I knew nothing of the world. So I ended up by attributing the failure of the party to some mysterious taint or defect that applied not merely to Viola but to myself also and, indeed, to our family. I remember that, a few days after the

13

party, when we were expecting a guest to lunch, a certain Tiberi who was Viola's man of business, I said suddenly: 'D'you think, Mummy, that he too won't come, like the reception people?'

I: And what was her answer?

Desideria: She threw me a look full of irritation and impatience and then muttered between her teeth: 'Don't talk nonsense.' Now you must know that this Tiberi, an antique dealer who was also her man of business, was then her lover.

I: And you didn't know?

Desideria: Of course not.

I: I now know a good many things about Viola, but not what she was like. Tell me what she looked like, physically.

Desideria: She was . . . two-sided.

I: Two-sided?

Desideria: Yes, she was different when seen from the front or the back. If you looked at her from in front, you saw a mature woman with a wasted, deteriorated, worn-out body. Her neck looked decrepit, with two or three circles of wrinkles all round it; on her chest, her breasts hung down like two brown bags, deflated and flabby; her belly, possibly because of an interrupted pregnancy, was a regular network of thin folds. But if you told her to turn round, you then saw the back of a young woman, a woman of less than thirty. Her shoulders, her back, her buttocks, her thighs looked mysteriously yet eloquently graceful, sensual, provoking.

I: Mysteriously, why mysteriously?

Desideria: Because it was a mysterious fact that a woman of her age should have so youthful a back.

I: Eloquently, why eloquently?

Desideria: Because, apart from the mysteriousness of its youthful look, as soon as Viola moved, her back became eloquent owing to the appeal that emanated from it.

I: Appeal? What sort of appeal?

Desideria: Perhaps a detailed description will make you understand what I mean. Viola had the most beautiful be-

14

hind you've ever seen. It combined the perfection of forms that are proper to youth with the softness of maturity. Onto this behind, at the point of the waist, was grafted the slim, as it were delicate, back of an adolescent girl. The simultaneous movements of her back and her behind produced the appeal that I have called eloquent. In reality what was eloquent was the kind of provocation originated by these movements. A provocation – how shall I say? – which implied and suggested an invitation to violence.

I: You mean that Viola, without realizing it, had a tendency towards masochism.

Desideria: If you like to put it that way.

I: We've had a full enough account of Viola, let's now turn to you. And so, in the middle of the night, you felt hungry; you left your room and went into the kitchen to find something to eat.

Desideria: Wait. I still have to tell you how Viola judged my gluttony.

I: How she *judged* it?

Desideria: Finally, when all was said and done, Viola was an American puritan. She judged it in a moralistic way, as if it had been something guilty, a sin; and not, as it certainly was, the effect of a physical disadvantage.

I: What, for instance?

Desideria: Knowing me to be a glutton, she watched me. So it might happen that she would descend upon me in my room when, though I was studying, I was furtively munching what I had managed to find in the refrigerator or had acquired outside. Then she would make very unpleasant scenes in which she expressed her disappointment at seeing me becoming so very different from what she had hoped.

I: What did she say?

Desideria: I remember that she surprised me one day when, with my elbows on the desk, I was looking out of the window in front of me and demurely eating a cake that I had bought in the morning, when I came out of school. Perhaps what especially irritated her was the fact that we had risen from table barely half an hour before. She came

15

in, saw that I was eating the cake, threw herself upon me, snatched it out of my hand, opened the window and threw it out into the garden. Then she attacked me with these words: 'Don't you realize that, if you go on like this, you'll become like a circus monster? Don't you ever look in the glass? There it is, the looking glass; look at yourself; you have no eyes, you have no nose, you have no mouth, you have nothing, you have nothing but fat!' As she said this, she opened the wardrobe, made me get up, dragged me to the mirror that was fixed inside the cupboard door. However, this was not so much a gesture of cool demonstration as an irresistible outburst of her fury. Her nails were sticking into my shoulders as she held me fast in front of the glass; her voice was jarring and strident. 'Don't you see that, at thirteen, you look as if you were forty? Don't you see? The fat has gone to your head, it has gone to your brain, you're the stupidest child I've ever known. You know what the cook says? "It would be better if Signorina Desideria would decide once and for all that she wants a meal every two hours. Then I would take a meal to her in her room every two hours and so she would no longer be coming into the kitchen, opening my fridge, and taking the lids off my saucepans."

I: Mortifying words!

Desideria: Especially for me. I was morbidly sensitive about everything that concerned my fatness. And then I passionately loved the woman I believed to be my mother. Again, I remember that one day, in the morning before I went to school, I went into her room to greet her. She was in bed, she had her breakfast tray on her knees, she was reading the newspaper. In a sudden explosion of affection I rushed at her and embraced her with such impulsiveness that I upset the coffeepot. She repelled me violently and exclaimed in a rage: 'Be careful, you idiot, you're just a mass of lard and nothing else.' I said in a low voice: 'I'm sorry, I'm sorry, I'm sorry'; then, hopping and skipping as though it were a game invented on the spot, I left the room, went and shut myself in my bathroom, and there, sitting on

16

the lavatory bowl, I cried for some time, and still crying, I masturbated, so that in the end I no longer knew whether I was lamenting with sorrow or moaning with pleasure.

I: For you, everything ended with masturbation.

Desideria: Yes, masturbation was, I believe, a way of reassuring myself, of rediscovering an identity in moments of bewilderment. Not being able to have any relationship with others, I tried, through masturbation, to have one with myself.

I: But did your mother have nothing but rude words for you? Was she never affectionate?

Desideria: I have already told you that she was left with a longing for a family that she had never succeeded in having and the hope that, some day, she would be capable of creating one for herself. Sometimes this fantasy of a family seemed to take shape, to be materialized as if by a miracle: in the evening, Viola would be watching television, sitting in an armchair in the living room, and I would be watching it with her, squatting on the floor leaning my back against her legs, with her hand on my shoulder, a hand which I would take in mine and turn to kiss. Or else, in the afternoon, I would have to do my homework for the next day; Viola would come in, would sit down beside me at the desk, would find me stuck in front of an arithmetical problem, and, there and then (she was very good at mathematics), would solve the problem. While she, with bowed head, rapidly set down her calculations in the exercise book, I would put my arm round her shoulders, press myself against her; and I was happy. In such moments her aspiration to create a family for herself seemed to be fused with my illusion that she really had one, in a sweetness in which there was nothing of the sentimental, in the debasing sense which is usually given to that word. It was the sweetness of what should have been the normal condition of our life; but which, on the other hand, for reasons independent of our wishes, was so abnormal as to appear positively miraculous. At such moments I did not so much love Viola as adore her; you must understand the word 'adore' in its

17

literal, traditional sense. I recall that when, in the evening, she came to kiss me good night, I very often thought that I saw an aureole round her head, like the halo surrounding the figures of saints in the churches. It may be that this impression of an aureole was due to the fact that my room was in darkness and that she left the door open when she came in, so that her dark figure stood out against the luminous background. After she had gone away, I curled up in bed in the darkness and said to myself aloud: 'I have a saint for a mother.'

I: But was it only your mother who looked after you? Didn't you have a governess?

Desideria: I was going to speak to you about my governess, or rather my governesses. Yes, for the whole of my childhood I had governesses and continued to have one up till the day when, without my noticing it and in spite of myself, I took the place of these governesses in Viola's life.

I: What's the meaning of that? What is it? A riddle?

Desideria: It is something of which I must speak, even if only in a summary way, before I embark upon the story of that fatal night when I got out of bed and intended to go to the kitchen. You must know that when I go back in my memory I at once see, between myself and Viola, the figure of another woman, a young, robust, cheerful woman, more or less good-looking, but nevertheless with foreign, exotic good looks – the governess of the moment.

I: The governess of the moment? Why 'of the moment'?

Desideria: Because they never lasted more than a year, or perhaps even less, three months, one month; only one or two of them held out for a little longer. They were French, English, Scandinavian, German, Swiss girls whom Viola managed to find through employment agencies, advertisements in the papers, and other similar channels. They were rarely governesses by profession. For the most part they were students, girls who wanted to see the world. They all of them had, however, one distinctive characteristic: they were young, or even very young, with that youthfulness which is free and adventurous, ambiguous and thoughtless,

18

and which does not seem to give importance to anything except itself. Looking back, I see all these governesses as being fair-haired, tall, and well-built, with splendid complexions, shining eyes, mouths that were prompt to laugh, dissolute and sensual. The fact that, as I have said, they lasted only a short time in our house, at this distance in years nullifies their variety, unifies the whole lot of them into a single physical type. It seems to me that it was always the same girl; and this is so, either because Viola seemed always to have the same relationship with them, or because the last of these governesses, for reasons you shall now know, is the one who has remained the most deeply impressed on my memory and who was, in fact, tall, well-built, and fair, with a splendid complexion and blue eyes.

I: What relationship had Viola with these girls?

Desideria: What would you say of a relationship between two people which begins with liking, attraction, transport, infatuation, passion; which continues with sweetness, tenderness, intimacy; and which then, all of a sudden, for obscure, inexplicable reasons, collapses into coldness, into hostility, into cruelty, into hatred?

I: I should say what you have said: that it was a love relationship. But did you know that Viola made love with your governesses?

Desideria: How could I have known it? Everything went on under my eyes and in spite of that, because of my innocence, or rather, of my obtuseness, everything remained outside the field of my observation; or rather, I continually made mistakes, of which later, when I knew the truth, I was angrily ashamed. For instance, in Viola's lesbian squabbles I sometimes took *her* side, sometimes that of the governess. Sometimes it seemed to me that Viola was unkind and unjust with the governess, and I went and told her so; sometimes, on the other hand, I attributed the unkindness and injustice to the governess, and then I reproached her and defended Viola.

I: How did Viola and the governesses receive these interventions of yours?

Desideria: The governesses, for the most part, with mysterious tolerance and embarrassed explanations; Viola with impatience and disdain. She told me brusquely that I was a busybody, a Nosey Parker, that I was interfering in things that did not concern me. Her relationship with the governesses, moreover, was often very explicit: at the onset of passion she would go so far as to caress them and even to give them a light kiss before my eyes, as though compelled by an irresistible temptation and at the same time deluded into thinking that I did not notice; finally, when love had turned to hatred, she did not hesitate, in my presence, to make scenes with them and, at least in a couple of cases, to resort to blows. All this upset me, more as one who cannot help taking sides in a quarrel, being bound by affection to both sides, than as one who understands what is concealed behind the quarrel itself. With regard to this, I remember the reply that one of those girls, to whom I had become especially attached, made to me on the very day of her departure, as she was packing her bag after being summarily dismissed by Viola. 'My poor Desideria,' she said, 'someday you will understand a whole lot of things. For the moment, I tell you merely that your mother is an unhappy woman who makes both herself and others unhappy. Who can possibly get on with a sadist like her?' At this, when I timidily asked what the word 'sadist' meant, the girl, giving me a caress, explained: 'It means unkind, cruel, somebody who takes pleasure in making others suffer. But it is also true that your mother is a masochist of the first order, that is, one who likes being made to suffer. In fact, just the type of person with whom I don't get on. And she, it must be admitted, has understood this and has asked me to leave.'

I: Did you realize the truth, this time?

Desideria: No, I did not understand anything; and partly because of that the sentence has remained impressed in my memory: the idea of a kind of suffering which it gave pleasure to inflict and, at the same time, to undergo, was entirely new to me and, in some way, fascinated me as an obscure enigma which might even concern myself. In any case, the girl's remark, although it did not explain the basis of the question, coincided with my own direct observation. When, at table (meals were Viola's favourite moment for discussing the affairs of the heart), she attacked, and caused herself to be attacked, in an allusive, veiled language, by the governess of the moment, I was fully aware, but without explaining the reason to myself, that one of the two, invariably, was causing pain to the other, and vice versa.

I: So they allowed you to open the door of the room at night and look into the living room with the intention of going to the kitchen to find something to eat. By the way, what time was it?

Desideria: It was not so very late; I looked at my wristwatch and saw that it was barely eleven. Now I knew that Viola had gone out with Tiberi, her man of business and lover (but, mind you, I did not then know that he was her lover), to go to the cinema, and that she would not be back before midnight. The governess, a Frenchwoman called Chantal, had gone out with them, after an explicit invitation that Viola had given her at table; and she had accepted, I remember, with these two precise words: 'avec joie'. And so, knowing that Viola was still out of the house, I scarcely hesitated and, without turning on any lights, I went confidently through the living room towards the door of Viola's bedroom.

I: But didn't you intend to go to the kitchen?

Desideria: Yes, but you must know that Viola, for some time, in order to prevent my secret eating, had got into the habit, in the evening, of locking up the refrigerator and taking the key away to her room. It was a small flat key with a label, on which was written FRIDGE. I knew that she put the key in a drawer of the commode in her room – always the same drawer and always in the same place, the left-hand corner, under certain pieces of junk of her own. I had already been several times to carry off this key in her absence, which I then put back in the drawer after I had thoroughly

21

stuffed myself: so I had no hesitations; I went with complete confidence.

I: Did the door of Viola's room open directly into the living room?

Desideria: No, it opened into a little private passage. I went into the passage and walked towards the door of Viola's room. There was a light in the passage; for this reason I did not see the streak of light under the door, from which I could have deduced that Viola was at home. I took hold of the door handle and opened the door brusquely, as one does when one is sure there is no one in the room. When I saw that there was a light in the room and that the three whom I believed to be at the cinema were there, it was too late for me to draw back. So I stopped in the doorway, more perhaps from curiosity than from fear, long enough to have a good look.

I: What did you see?

Desideria: The bed, low and wide, was opposite me. Viola, completely naked, was on her hands and knees on the bed, her head bent down towards the pillow, her bottom higher than her head. Chantal, also naked, was standing erect at the head of the bed, in a calm, natural attitude of patient contemplation, leaning with one hand on the head of the bed, her other hand hanging down over her hip, her long, fair hair hanging loosely to one side, over her left shoulder, her big blue eyes turned towards Viola with a curiously attentive look, as of one who watches a difficult operation and follows its outcome with interest. Finally, Tiberi, also naked, was standing behind Viola, his two hands on her hips, his belly thrust forward so that it was in close contact with her buttocks.

I: What did you think, when you saw them?

Desideria: I didn't think anything; the sight I saw, which usually goes by the name of 'orgy', was quite new to me, incomprehensible, and, in a way, even comic. At the same time, however, I had the strange impression that it was something I had already seen, had already experienced.

I: Already seen?

Desideria: Some years before, Viola had taken a trip to Japan together with Tiberi, and had brought back an album of antique erotic prints, hand-coloured. It was one of those albums which, in traditional Japan, mothers used to give to their daughters on the eve of their marriage, to give them instruction on the different positions in which the sexual embrace might be practised. Viola kept this album in a drawer of the same commode in which she hid the keys of the refrigerator; in fact, it was actually when looking for the keys that I had found the album. And so, when Viola was not at home, it was not unusual for me, after I had eaten all I wanted in the kitchen, to go into the bedroom to put back the keys and then occupy myself in looking at the album, print by print. I did not very well understand what was going on in those exotic rooms, on the disordered beds, amongst screens painted with representations of bamboo and herons; what struck me most forcibly was the contrast between the eager, almost hilarious impassiveness of the faces and the violence that I could not help noticing both in the flushed colour of their faces and in the acrobatics of the intertwined bodies. When I saw Viola on hands and knees, Tiberi standing behind her and Chantal at the head of the bed, very naturally I remembered those prints.

I: Why, was there a similar scene in the prints?

Desideria: No, the prints, as I said, pictured merely, for the use of the bride, the positions of love-making between man and woman. But these three resembled the characters in the prints in the singular, unnatural impassiveness of their faces. I have already mentioned the expression of eager, attentive expectation on the face of Chantal. As for Viola, although she was on all fours, she was sticking out her head, in the way dogs sometimes do, from behind her shoulder; she too was looking with curiosity and attention in the direction of Tiberi. And the latter, his eyes fixed on Viola's hips, upon which he had placed his two open palms, had on his face the careful, calculating expression of one who is preparing to undertake something difficult.

23

I: But how did you contrive to look Tiberi in the face, seeing that he had his back turned towards you?

Desideria: I looked up and saw him in a mirror which was placed, rather oddly, above the bed, in a position where no one could look at himself, that is, hanging in the corner formed by the wall and the ceiling. I was accustomed, practically every day of my life, to seeing this mirror slanting, above the head of Viola's bed; but only now, when I saw the reflections of Viola on all fours and Tiberi standing behind her, did the unusual and significant character of the place where it hung dawn upon me. It was, in fact, one of those mirrors which are usually to be found in houses of ill fame and which allow one to see oneself during the act of love; together with the album of Japanese prints, it showed the degree to which the obsession with sex had infiltrated into the daily life of my adoptive mother. And now Tiberi's face, which I could see reflected in the mirror, was not merely impassive like the faces of the characters in the Japanese prints, but, curiously, its features had something Japanese about them.

I: Japanese?

Desideria: Yes, Tiberi had a high, bald brow surrounded by scanty hair, glossy and brilliantined, his eyebrows were arched and at a distance from his eyes; his eyelids were heavy and slightly oblique. His nose was hooked and narrow at the base, with markedly curled nostrils; his mouth, its lower lip more fleshy than the upper one, was set in an expression of disgust and sullenness. He was truly reminiscent of the samurai that are to be seen in Japanese prints, in kimonos with a sabre in the belt. Except that the samurai in the antique Japanese prints have white, flour-dusted faces like actors; whereas Tiberi was a rosy, or rather a red, samurai, owing to the continuous blood-red flush that lit up his face and slightly recalled those paper lanterns, also Japanese, with the purplish flush of flames visible through their transparency. This Japanese head was set between two shoulders in the shape of a sack, that is, at the same time both sloping and massive. Tiberi knew that

24

he had a Japanese look, and often he purposely assumed an enigmatic expression, raising his eyebrows high up and lowering his eyelids. Viola called him 'Sam', short for 'samurai'; this nickname lasted for the duration of their love relationship; then the sudden return, on Viola's side, to the surname of Tiberi showed me that the relationship was finished and that Tiberi, for Viola, was now nothing more than her man of business.

I: You stood in the doorway and looked. What happened then?

Desideria: Suddenly it happened as in the cinema when, for reasons of the production, a picture remains fixed for some time on the screen, with the characters motionless in the most diverse positions; and then, all of a sudden, the film starts running again and the characters are abruptly released from their immobility. Thus, with the same slightly comic suddenness, the whole scene finally started moving, and all four of us (for I too, though only as a spectator, formed part of the scene) began to take action. Tiberi made a brisk forward movement with his hips and belly, while, in the deep silence, his voice, in a low, intense tone, uttered this extraordinary and to me incomprehensible remark: 'Give me America.' At the same moment Viola, who, as I said, was sticking her head out, in curiosity, from behind her shoulder, screwed up her face in a grimace of pain, opening her mouth and her eyes wide; and then she replied breathlessly, in the same low, intense tone as Tiberi's: 'Take it.' Finally Chantal, who was watching them and seemed to be waiting for some sort of signal to take action herself, slowly brought the arm that was hanging down her hip, diagonally across her own body, till she plunged her hand deeply between her legs. As for me, I opened the door wide and almost ran towards the commode.

I: Why did you go in? You might have retreated without any noise; no one would have noticed.

Desideria: No, Tiberi had seen me. Our eyes had met in that mirror hanging over the head of the bed. Besides, I hadn't understood anything of what was going on in front

25

of my eyes, and therefore I still clung, mechanically, to my first decision to take the keys, go into the kitchen, open the fridge and satisfy my hunger. The foreseen, in fact, showed itself stronger than the unexpected.

I: Did you say anything to justify your irruption into the bedroom?

Desideria: Yes, I said in a loud and clear voice: 'Mummy, I've come to fetch the key of the fridge'; at the same time I rushed to the commode, pulled out the drawer, without hesitation seized the key, knowing exactly where it was, and then ran away. All this could not have taken more than ten seconds.

I: And they?

Desideria: I don't know what they did after my departure. There must have been great confusion and then – how shall I say? – a council of war. Certainly all I know is that next morning Chantal had gone; she had left that same night.

I: And you – what did you do?

Desideria: I went into the kitchen, opened the refrigerator, looked inside it. On a dish there was half a cheese pie, so I took out the dish, placed it on the table, and ate the pie standing up, breaking off bits that held together with my fingers, and putting them into my mouth without appetite and without enjoyment, with a mixed feeling of defiance and disgust. Meanwhile, I was looking at the door, almost hoping that Viola would come in and surprise me at my vicious habits, just as I, shortly before, had surprised her at hers.

I: And then – did Viola really come?

Desideria: No, she did not come. But I wanted her to come, and so I prolonged my nocturnal meal as long as possible. In order to prolong it, I had had to eat the whole of the pie, piece by piece, something like half a kilo of stuff; this I did sadly and scrupulously, as though seeking to surpass the excess of what I had seen by the excess of what I was doing. In the end the dish was empty; but Viola had not come. So then I went back to my room.

26

I: What did you do in your room?

Desideria: I went to sleep almost at once. After an hour, however, I woke up, feeling a great weight in my stomach; I got up, went into the bathroom, and vomited. All this in my sleep, or, at any rate, with a minimum of consciousness. I think I also masturbated before going to sleep.

I: Why did you masturbate?

Desideria: I masturbated in order to re-establish my disturbed equilibrium: I have already told you, for me masturbation was a means of communication with somebody; I was alone and could only communicate with myself. After masturbating, I think I went back into the bathroom and washed myself, then I went back again to bed. But again this time my sleep did not last long. I awoke for the second time and masturbated for the second time. I went to sleep again and then woke up again and masturbated and went back to wash in the bathroom for the third time. It was, in fact, a night full of repetitions, a kind of reiterated nightmare, during which I alternated between dreams and awakenings, without clearly distinguishing one from the other. Even what I had seen in Viola's room probably, in the morning, would have had the effect of a dream for me if Viola herself, next day, had not taken steps to dissipate all my doubts on the subject.

I: Viola alluded next day to what had happened during the night?

Desideria: Yes, but with characteristic puritanical hypocrisy she tried to put me in the wrong, by substituting my vice for hers. At table, at a moment when the maid had gone out and we were alone, she said to me suddenly: 'So last night you came to my room to fetch the key of the refrigerator. Goodness knows how long this story has been going on, goodness knows how much longer it would have gone on if we hadn't found, yesterday evening, that the cinema had changed programmes, and so we came back home. Why, aren't you ashamed? Don't you realize that at this rate you'll become a mere barrel of lard? A fat person from whom everyone will keep away in disgust?' She went

27

on for some time in this inflexible and, in a way, reckless tone, for she could not but realize that it would have been easy for me to make her keep her mouth shut, by taunting her in turn with the orgy in which I had surprised her. But I did not speak. I was paralysed by reflecting almost admiringly on the fact that Viola replaced the reproach, for her impossible, of my having spied upon her while she was making love *à trois*, by the other reproach, apparently dictated by maternal love, of my being an incurable and repugnant glutton. Thus, her lechery came to be obliterated by my greediness, and the picture of her on all fours, offering her buttocks to penetration by her lover, beneath the attentive, collusive eyes of the governess, was replaced by that of myself standing in front of the refrigerator furtively guzzling the cheese pie. I said that this reflection paralysed me. It was, in fact, the first time that I had observed Viola objectively, without any veil of affection and in what I may call a critical way; and just because it was the first time, it seemed to me that I was already sufficiently vindicated for the hypocritical injustice of her reproaches in looking at her like this, no longer as a daughter, but as a stranger. Nevertheless, I had to say something, if only to stop this torrent of cruel rebuke. So I exclaimed: 'But, Mummy, what can I do if I wake up and realize that I am hungry?' Then suddenly Viola's disappointment at seeing me so different from what she would have liked me to be exploded with violence, like a spring too long compressed: 'Don't call me Mummy. You're not my daughter and I'm not your mother. It's high time that you knew it. I adopted you, you're the daughter of a prostitute who did not know what to do with you and was very pleased to palm you off. If I could only do so now; unfortunately, I can't and I must continue to keep you with me. I had adopted you because I had such a strong desire to create a normal family, with a husband and children. Instead of which, disaster has struck me, first of all with the death of my husband and then with your transformation from the very beautiful child you were when I adopted you into the monster you are now. I had so hoped to have a daughter who was beautiful, intelligent, and brilliant; whereas I find myself confronted by a fat, stupid glutton who fills me with horror and never does anything right. So don't call me Mummy; we're two complete strangers and it's right that you should know it and that you should behave towards me precisely as a stranger.'

I: What effect did this revelation have upon you?

Desideria: I felt an acute pain, the most acute I had ever felt in my life. This pain, too, like Viola's rage, was like a too long compressed spring and the revelation released it. I looked at Viola for a moment and then I burst into tears, clasping my face between my hands. I sobbed with a violence that was vaguely frightening to me because I felt in it the sign of an ancient, profound unhappiness. Through my sobs I kept repeating: 'Don't say that, Mummy, it's not true, it can't be true, I beg you, I beseech you, Mummy, don't say that.' I repeated that word 'Mummy' especially because I realized it was the last time I should utter it with the tender affection I had hitherto felt for Viola.

I: What was Viola doing while you were crying?

Desideria: The silliest thing that can be imagined, perhaps out of nervousness: she was picking her nose.

I: Picking her nose?

Desideria: Yes, she was one of those people who continually do things of that kind, that is, things that are repugnant and intimate, without any attempt to hide it; not so much from shamelessness, however, as because they imagine they are not observed. She would rummage in her nostrils with her fingers and put what she found there into her mouth; she would squeeze pimples; she would pick her teeth with a toothpick; she would fumble in her ear with the nail of her little finger; she would feel any part of her body with her hand and then sniff at her fingers to see if any smell resulted. Her face was pale, with an exhausted, bloodless pallor, with two large black eyes in which, behind the rather dreamy expression that belongs to short sight, was the clear, inextinguishable flame, impure and devouring, of

29

desire. It was a beautiful face, or rather, there lingered in it a reflection of former beauty; but this romantic look was contradicted in a significant way by a quantity of red spots on her skin, caused by her continual, coercive pressing and scratching and squeezing. Now, as I have said, while I was sobbing noisily, she was frenziedly fumbling in her nostrils. Then, still weeping, I stammered, with profound bitterness: 'Today, this very day, I shall leave this house. I want to go away from here, I want to live with my real mother; you must tell me where she is, I shall go and look for her and you will never see me again.' Of course, it was not in the least true that I wished to go away; I knew perfectly well, as I spoke, that I was threatening to leave in order to provoke an affectionate outburst on Viola's part. But Viola did not have an intuitive mind, even if now, according to her usual alternation between eroticism and family, she probably wished to re-establish the mother-and-daughter relationship which the revelation of the adoption had compromised. And so, foolishly, she thought I was speaking in earnest, and she answered with resentment: 'Go on, go on, go away, then. But I warn you that it will be a change for the worse, a great deal worse. The woman whom you call your real mother gave you away because she could not afford to keep you, not even with the profession she was practising. Go on then, *bon voyage*. But instead of remaining here, in this house, and having the best education that money can buy in Italy today, I'll tell you where your real mother will place you: in the street, to earn your living on the pavement, like her. But no, I was forgetting that, ugly and fat as you are, nobody would want you, even on the streets.'

I: And what did *you* say?

Desideria: I did not answer. Every one of her words had a double effect: giving a death blow to my surviving affection for her and providing me with information about the woman who had brought me into the world. Besides, I was blinded by tears, I seemed to be drowning in them as in a pitiless and very bitter sea. I was breathless and incapable

30

of speech. Suddenly I rose and went and shut myself in my room.

I: And then?

Desideria: Then nothing. That day I did not go in to dinner. I said I was not well. Viola did not appear; all she did was to send and ask me whether I wished to have dinner in my room, and I answered that I was not hungry. All this took place through our old maid; Chantal, as I said, had departed, and after her I had no more governesses. But that same night Viola, who had gone to the cinema with Tiberi, came into my room with him. I had dozed off. I awoke with a start; he had stayed standing by the door, whereas she was standing in the dark with a plate in her hand. She told me that it was an extremely good sort of pudding, that the cook had made it specially for me, knowing that it was my favourite sweet; I had had no dinner; I could eat it without fear and it would take the place of dinner. She did not wait for my reply, she put down the plate on the night table, bent down and touched my brow with a light kiss, and then went out. I waited a little; then I turned on the light, got up from the bed, went into the bathroom, and threw the sweet down the lavatory.

I: What happened next day?

Desideria: We met at table, as usual, for lunch; neither I myself nor she spoke of what had happened, but Viola seemed now to have decided to play, for some time, the part of affectionate mother. And so, two days later, she got the family doctor to come to the house and had me minutely examined, explaining to him that she wished to make a last effort to get the better of my obesity and that she was ready to face any expense to have me turned into a normal child; and so on, in the same tone, that is, an ostentatiously and, without doubt, sincerely maternal tone. 'She was the most beautiful baby I have ever seen,' she concluded, looking at me fixedly as though to retrace, beneath the envelope of my fatness, the vanished features of my past beauty. 'Why should she not go back to being what she was?'

I: What did the doctor say?

31

Desideria: He prescribed water treatments, he jotted down a few recipes, he advised gymnastic exercises, sport. The usual things, in fact.

I: And what was the end of it all? What I mean is, how did you manage to transform yourself from the fatty that you were into the exceptionally beautiful woman that you are today?

Desideria: Perhaps it was the remark that Viola made to me: 'Ugly and fat as you are, nobody would want you, even on the streets,' which made me turn into what I am today. In reality I had not become, I had 'wished' to become, fat. Now, after that remark, I 'wished', with the same unconscious determination, to become thin, and so I did.

I: Tell me how you did it.

Desideria: To answer you, I want to relate a little dialogue which took place during the summer of that same year, that is, a few months after my nocturnal irruption into Viola's room. Imagine a bathing establishment, at Fregene, in the month of June. It is two in the afternoon; Viola has gone to the restaurant with Tiberi; she has left me alone; before going away, she has given me, for my lunch, according to the diet prescribed by the doctor, a ham sandwich. Slowly I eat the sandwich, sitting in the hut, looking at the beach and the sea. Few big umbrellas, since this is only the beginning of summer, are distributed over the clean beach, which still bears traces of the rakes with which the attendants have combed the sand in the morning. The huts, for the most part untenanted, stand in a clear, bright-coloured line facing the yellow beach and the blue sea. A light breeze has arisen, as happens every afternoon; it ruffles the sea and raises numbers of small, sparkling waves with white crests. I finish eating my sandwich and then get up and go behind the hut. Here, stretched out face downwards in the shade, I am awaited by a fair-haired little girl with slightly prominent blue eyes, and with a prudent, fussy expression in the nostrils of her aquiline nose and at the corners of her mouth. Two locks of hair hang down on her shoulders; she wears a two-piece bathing suit on her thin

32

body, which is entirely devoid of feminine shapes. This girl is called Delfina; she is the daughter of a doctor and is, at this moment, my best friend. I will relate our conversation, exactly as it took place during that sleepy hour of early afternoon, in the shade of the hut. 'If I tell you something very important, will you be capable of keeping it to yourself?' 'Who d'you think I should go and tell it to?' 'How do I know? You might tell your Mum.' 'Do you know of my ever telling my Mum of something you've confided in me?' 'Not so far, but one never knows.' 'Why then, d'you see how feeble you are?' 'Well, now I want to tell you the secret of my life.' 'What, you had a secret and you haven't told me yet – a nice kind of friend you are!' 'It's something I got to know not so very long ago. Listen then, now: the lady I live with and whom I call Mummy is not my mother.' 'And who is she, then?' 'She's just an ordinary lady who had no children and who wanted some and so she adopted me.' 'What does it mean, "adopted"?' 'You see how half-witted you are. It means that this lady went to my real mother and bought me, that is, she gave her some money and carried me off in exchange.' 'How much did she give her?' 'I don't know: a lot.' 'But your real mother, why did she sell you?' 'Because she was a working-class woman and was very poor, like all people of that kind, and so she had need of money. If she hadn't needed money, she certainly wouldn't have sold me, because she was very, very fond of me.' 'What job did your real mother have?' 'She was a prostitute.' 'But then, if she was a prostitute, why did she sell you? Don't you know that prostitutes earn lots of money? With the money she earned by working as a prostitute, she could perfectly well have kept you.' 'Obviously she didn't earn enough. How much d'you think prostitutes earn?' 'I don't know; millions.' 'You see, you don't know anything. If they earned millions, all women would work as prostitutes, even those who behave like ladies, like your mother and the lady I call Mummy. Whereas my real mother, even working as a prostitute, remained poor to such a degree that she gave me away to the lady who wished to adopt me. And

33

now I want to tell you another thing: as soon as I'm grown-up I also want to be a prostitute like my real mother. I'll be a prostitute and save up the money I make. You know why? To repay to the lady who adopted me all the money she has spent on me, down to the last centesimo. I shall save up, put the money aside, and when it seems to me that I have a sufficient sum I shall go to the lady whom I now call Mummy and I shall say to her: "How much have you spent on me so far? So much? Well, here is the money you've spent, neither more nor less. Now we're quits, I don't owe you anything more. Thank you for everything and I bid you goodbye." 'But when d'you think you'll be able to work as a prostitute?' 'I think I will first pass my school-leaving examination and then I will come to a decision.' 'But prostitutes have to be beautiful. In my opinion, you're too fat to be a prostitute.' In fact, she said the same thing that Viola had said; and I could not help noticing it. And then, I don't know where from, the certainty came to me that it would not always be like this; that Viola and Delfina would infallibly be proved wrong. And I answered confidently: 'I shall not always be fat. In a year or two, at most, I shall be thin like you.'

I: How did you manage then, in reality, to get rid of your fatness?

Desideria: It happened as though of its own accord, that is precisely because I had unconsciously wished it to, by instinct of survival. Once I was back in town, in the autumn, I began to get thin, and in a few months, even before I had foreseen it myself, I had become as I am now.

I: Do you remember when you realized for the first time that you had got thin?

Desideria: One morning, not much more than a year after the events of which I have told you, I went into the bathroom, took a shower, and then, without drying myself, went to the looking-glass and looked at myself. I had a long lock of wet hair across my forehead; big drops of water, clear and brilliant, sprinkled my face, my chest, my belly, my legs, looking like dewdrops; and then, all of a sudden, I

34

realized that I was no longer fat and that I was beautiful. As I looked at myself, it crossed my mind that, with my face and body all sprinkled with drops, I was like an antique amphora that I had once seen fished up from the bottom of the sea by a diver. Yes, I had been for a long time at the bottom of a sea of unhappiness, and now I was emerging from it, all dripping and beautiful and desirable, at last worthy of my name of Desideria.

I: How did Viola take this transformation of yours?

Desideria: It happened to be a moment when what I may call the pendulum of her life, in its continual oscillation between eroticism and family, was directed towards the latter. And so her joy was sincere and profound and would have moved anybody except me. Unfortunately, I could no longer feel anything for her and, what was worse, I was conscious of this. So all I could do was coldly acknowledge her change of humour towards myself.

I: You say that Viola's life oscillated continually between eroticism and the family. You also said that Chantal had left the house and that you had no more governesses after her. Viola, then, had renounced her eroticism?

Desideria: No, she hadn't renounced it at all.

I: So what, then?

Desideria: Then, when the pendulum started oscillating again in the direction of eroticism, she simply fell in love with me.

I: Fell in love with *you*?

Desideria: Yes, fell in love, there is no other word for it. By that time I was fifteen; we were no longer mother and daughter; there were no more governesses; to make up for that, there was myself, and I, providentially, after I had become slim, had taken on an appearance, physically, that was not so very different from that of the governesses. I imagine that the idea of substituting me for the governesses came naturally and spontaneously to Viola.

I: Did you immediately notice Viola's falling in love with you?

Desideria: I didn't notice anything. I had only one

35

thought, a fixed, dominant thought: I must work as a prostitute, I must make a lot of money, I must save it up. Then I would go to Viola and say to her: 'Here is your money. Goodbye.'

I: And yet Viola had to some extent shown her feeling?

Desideria: Yes, that's true; she looked at me in a new way.

I: In what way?

Desideria: As though she did not recognize me. And then she joked with me.

I: She joked?

Desideria: Yes, as some mothers do with their daughters, but with an added weight of uncontrollable sensuality which she deluded herself into thinking she controlled and concealed. Indeed, under any pretext, and more and more frequently, she kept stroking me, fondling me, touching me, even as it were by chance and casually. Finally, for the first time in ages, she gave me presents.

I: What effect did these attentions have upon you?

Desideria: None. I've already told you: my fixed idea was that I should prostitute myself, set aside a certain sum, and repay Viola for her expenses in keeping me.

I: Did you then make any investigation on the subject of your real mother?

Desideria: No, I didn't even think about it; fundamentally I did not want to look for her. Sometimes, in passing along certain suburban avenues, I looked at the street-walkers standing under the lamp posts and thought: There, my mother might be one of them. But that was all.

I: I should think the moment has come for you to tell me when you heard the Voice for the first time.

Desideria: It all began one hot day in June, towards one o'clock, as I cáme out of the French school in Piazzale Flaminio. In a sweater and a miniskirt (it was the year in which that type of garment was in fashion) and riding boots, with my hair loose and falling over my chest and shoulders, hot and sweaty (I remember that I had two dark circles of sweat round my armpits and trickles of sweat that made my sweater stick to my chest), I walked off towards the Tiber embankment, where Viola's car was waiting to take me home. Now you must know that outside the school, at the time when we came out, there were always a certain number of governesses and parents awaiting the pupils. For some days I had noticed a particular woman amongst them. She stood a little to one side, near the sign of the bus stop; but it had at once become clear to me that she was waiting, not for the bus, but for me. In fact, as soon as I appeared, she started to look at me, as, making my way slowly towards the Tiber embankment, I drew nearer to her. I passed in front of her, almost touching her, but she said nothing; all she did was to look at me in her particular insistent manner. Then, after I had gone past, she left the bus stop and followed me at a distance. I was conscious of this attention on her part and I walked slowly on purpose; I did not know why; perhaps it was because I was vain and it gave me pleasure to be looked at. But it was also true, on the other hand, that there was something in her gaze that made me uneasy.

I: What was that?

Desideria: I should now term it an evaluation followed by a calculation.

I: She was estimating your value?

Desideria: Yes, like that of an object which is not one's property but might become so.

I: This evaluation – was it high or low?

Desideria: It was high, very high, and that was the reason why I felt flattered and walked slowly on purpose, so that she might look at me at her leisure, piece by piece.

I: And the calculation – what did the calculation consist of?

Desideria: For that woman, not merely was I an object that had a value, but also I did not belong to anyone, that is, I was at the disposal of anyone who took possession of me. So, while the evaluation related to my physical personality, the calculation was concerned with my psychological availability.

I: What a lot of things you were able to see in one look!

Desideria: I did not see them, I felt them.

I: What was she like, this woman?

Desideria: She was small, with a big, prominent bosom, very broad hips, and very crooked legs. She had fair hair, which was pulled back so as to expose her low, hard brow; her eyes were of a washed-out blue; she had a small, turned-up nose, a wide mouth with thick, curving lips. She was wearing a light-blue cloth dress and her jacket was open so that you could see her pink blouse.

I: You passed in front of her, you almost touched her; what then?

Desideria: Then, as I told you, she followed me at a distance until I reached Viola's car, which was waiting for me on the Tiber embankment. The chauffeur got out to open the door for me; as I was getting in, I saw that she was still looking at me, as she stood on the pavement opposite.

I: Did she finally speak to you?

Desideria: It was I who spoke to her first. Or rather, the Voice.

I: The Voice? So it was then that you heard it for the first time?

Desideria: Yes.

38

I: You compared it with Joan of Arc's Voices. Was it like that with you, too?

Desideria: I made the comparison so that you would understand that I really had heard the Voice, that it came from outside, that is, it was not an hallucination. But in any case, it was different. For me the Voice was, so to speak, an expansion, a prolongation of masturbation.

I: A prolongation? What does it mean?

Desideria: As I told you, I masturbated regularly, twice a day, early in the morning as soon as I woke up, and at night before I went to sleep. Sometimes I did it also during the day. For instance, while I was studying, the desire would come upon me; then I would go and turn the key in the door, go back and sit down again at my desk, put my hand between my legs, and, while still continuing to read and write, quietly achieve an orgasm. I had always done it; it was a habitual thing of which I was almost unconscious. Now one day, or rather one night, for the whole thing happened at night, the masturbation unexpectedly prolonged itself in a Voice which spoke to me from the darkness. What I mean is, that I had not reached the orgasm; I heard the Voice, so I stopped masturbating and listened to what the Voice was saying.

I: The Voice came from outside?

Desideria: Yes, from a corner of the room.

I: What was the Voice like?

Desideria: What d'you mean, what was it like?

I: What accent did it have?

Desideria: Normal, I should say.

I: What do you mean by 'normal'?

Desideria: I mean, no particular accent.

I: But there are various ways of speaking, not only according to one's place of birth, but also according to sex, class, profession, and so on. Incidentally, was it the voice of a man or a woman?

Desideria: Of a woman.

I: Of a young or an old woman?

Desideria: Older than me, perhaps, but not much.

39

I: Working-class, bourgeois, aristocratic?

Desideria: Without any special class.

I: What was it like, from the point of view of profession? I mean, did it speak as a secretary would speak, or a woman professor, or what?

Desideria: It spoke like a governess.

I: Like *your* governesses?

Desideria: My governesses were not real governesses, they were girls that Viola chose so as to make love with them. The Voice was truly a governess. The first of my life.

I: What type of governess?

Desideria: A rather special governess. To make you understand, all that's needed is to tell you the first words with which she apostrophized me from the darkness: 'Little swine from the Parioli quarter.'

I: What was it, an angry voice?

Desideria: No, not exactly angry, severe if anything; the tone was exactly that of a governess who catches her pupil in the act of doing something that is forbidden.

I: And then what followed this apostrophizing?

Desideria: I think it was: 'instead of masturbating, stop and listen to me.' But I don't remember the precise words, perhaps because I was too astonished and still incredulous. In short, it explained to me that the woman who waited for me outside school and looked at me so insistently was my real mother, she who had brought me into the world and then, for money, had sold me to Viola. According to the Voice, this woman came to look at me every day because she was proud of having such a beautiful daughter and had regretted having sold me, and it gave her pleasure, since she could not live with me, at least to look at me from a distance.

I: But how did the Voice come to know all this?

Desideria: It did not tell me. All it did was to order me to approach the woman and say to her: 'I am Desideria. You are my mother, aren't you?'

I: Just like that?

Desideria: Yes, just in those very words.

I: And you, what did you do?

Desideria: I obeyed.

I: Why?

Desideria: I don't know. There was something irresistible about the Voice, at least at the beginning. I hadn't the courage to disobey it.

I: And yet its assertion that this woman was your mother was improbable; you could have made some objection, dictated, so to speak, by common sense.

Desideria: I did so. I said I could not believe it, that it did not seem to me possible, et cetera, et cetera. But the Voice immediately reduced me to silence with a terrifying threat.

I: What threat?

Desideria: 'If you don't obey, you will never hear me again.'

I: Why terrifying?

Desideria: There again I don't know what to say. I only know that the threat frightened me and that I at once replied that I would do as it said.

I: At least you can tell me what sort of terror you felt.

Desideria: The terror of losing something that I considered an acquisition, a progress, a privilege.

I: So it gave you pleasure to have this Voice speaking to you, guiding you, commanding you?

Desideria: Yes, it gave me pleasure, above all, it inspired me with security. I felt more sure of myself. To lose it then, at any rate, would have meant that I should have gone back to the state in which I was before hearing it that night, in the dark, in my room.

I: What state did you fear to return to?

Desideria: The Voice told me in this way: 'If you don't obey me, you will never hear me again; you will go back to being what you were before: a piece of flesh, inanimate but frenzied, a hole surrounded by a body, a holothurian or sea cucumber.'

I: A holothurian?

Desideria: Yes, a holothurian, precisely so. The holothurian is a sea creature; I had read about it at that time in a book of mine on zoology, and had been struck by its description. It said: 'The holothurian is a marine organism intermediate between animals and plants; it has an elongated body in which can be distinguished a forward extremity in which there is the opening of the mouth, a backward extremity in which there is the opening of the anus.' A kind of cucumber, in fact. That is, a creature of cylindrical shape, compact, massive, deaf, obtuse, blind, nothing but a tube capable of digestion and clothed with flesh, endowed with vitality, of a frenzied kind, consisting of purely physical contractions and spasms. It was this creature, this holothurian, that I myself should have been, according to the Voice, before it made itself heard.

I: So you didn't want to go back to being a holothurian. And that was why its threat of abandoning you terrified you.

Desideria: Yes, that was how it was.

I: So you obeyed the Voice. What did you do?

Desideria: That same day, when I came out of school, I immediately looked towards the bus stop to see if the woman was there. I saw she was there, so I walked with my usual slow, absent-minded step to see whether she was looking at me as on the other days, and I saw that she *was* looking at me. I went a short distance past her, then, as though changing my mind, I turned and went up to her and said the exact words that the Voice had ordered me to say to her.

I: What, precisely?

Desideria: 'I am Desideria and you are my mother, are you not?'

I: And she?

Desideria: I saw distinctly that I had taken her unaware. In her hard, washed-out blue eyes the pupils were for a moment dilated, as if with astonishment. Then there was a change of expression such as comes about after a lucid lightning flash of reflection.

I: What sort of expression?

42

Desideria: An expression of understanding, of agreement, of approval. All this accompanied by a strange look, between compassion and satisfaction.

I: Compassion and satisfaction?

Desideria: It was as much as to say: 'The poor young thing is crazy; very good, let's take advantage of it.' She did in fact answer in a hurried way: 'But of course, certainly I am your mother, your mother who is so very fond of you, who adores you, your mother who has been looking for you for such a long time and has finally found you.' She had a strident, discordant, shrill voice with a curious accent, as of someone who is accustomed to speak in dialect and is trying to express herself in proper language.

I: She assumed her role immediately, in fact. Recognition scene and all the rest of it. And you?

Desideria: I felt myself to be completely detached, just as always happened later every time I acted on account of, or at the suggestion of, the Voice. This is equivalent to saying that there were, at that moment, two persons inside me: one who watched and one who acted. The one who watched was, so to speak, the holothurian, that is, the person I had been hitherto, before the arrival of the Voice. This person judged according to common sense and told me that I was behaving like an idiot and that the woman, who of course was not my real mother, was taking advantage of my idiocy for her own ends, which I could not manage to understand. The other person, on the contrary, was acting according to the instructions and orders of the Voice and was, in fact, practically indistinguishable from the Voice, was the Voice itself translated into action.

I: What do you mean? That your so-called Voice was nothing more, when all was said and done, than one of the two persons in whom you felt yourself to be detached at that moment? That the Voice, in fact, came not from outside but from inside?

Desideria: No, that's not what I meant. It is true that I felt detached in two separate persons, one who acted and one who watched. But the Voice always spoke to me from outside. And so, in reality, I was detached into two persons, one of whom obeyed the Voice and the other who obeyed me.

I: Obeyed common sense, that is?

Desideria: Put it like that, then.

I: Common sense was opposed to the Voice?

Desideria: Not altogether, anyhow that day. But it judged its handiwork with relative lucidity.

I: Relative?

Desideria: Yes, because it was an impotent, paralysed, intimidated lucidity.

I: Let's go back to Piazzale Flaminio. What happened then?

Desideria: The woman recovered completely from her astonishment and entered definitively into what you have called her role. She took me by the arm and said enthusiastically: 'Yes, I'm your mother who is so very fond of you, who will give you a lovely present if you will come with her to her house, for a moment, just for one moment. Come, let's go, my precious daughter, you'll see what your mum will give you in a moment, something that will give you so much pleasure, something so very lovely, my precious daughter, so really lovely. Come, let's go, I have my car just behind here, give me your books, I'll carry them for you, come with your mother who looked for you for so long and who has now found you, at last! Come, the car's just here, only two steps away, and then in ten minutes we shall be at home and you'll see the lovely present your mummy is going to give you there, a present that you'll remember all your life.' As she said this, she took the bundle of books that I was carrying in my arms and put it into an enormous bag, which was hanging from her shoulder. Meanwhile she was pressing my arm very high up, near my armpit, holding me up and guiding me as though I had been lame or handicapped and making me almost fly over the flagstones of the pavement. At this point I could not help saying to her: 'But I have a car waiting for me on the embankment.'

44

I: And she?

Desideria: By now she was positively elated. She asked me what time we had lunch at my home; I told her that we ate very late, about half past two; she burst out into a big, joyous laugh and exclaimed that it was barely one o'clock, so I had plenty of time to go to her house, receive my present, and then be back home at half past two. An hour and a half. I did not know that one could do so many things in an hour and a half! I must go to the chauffeur therefore, and tell him he must go back without me because I was going home with a friend, here in Piazzale Flaminio, to re-do my homework. Then my friend would see to getting me taken home.

I: A real proper plan already prearranged! And you?

Desideria: The Voice told me to do as the woman told me, and once again I obeyed. We were on the Tiber embankment: I crossed the road; Viola's big car waited in the shade of the plane trees; the chauffeur was reading the newspaper with his arm bent outside the window. As soon as he saw me, he threw down the paper and made a movement as if to get out and open the door for me. I told him exactly what the woman had suggested to me; he replied that it was all right; I turned away from him and went back across the road, slowly, towards the woman who was watching my approach with, as I realized, visible anxiety, and whose face, when she was sure that I was coming back to her, lit up with an expression of almost savage joy. She took me by the arm again, up under the armpit, and started to make me run, in fact to fly, in the direction, this time, of her car. All the time she was running, she continued speaking to me hurriedly, as though she feared that I would recover from my madness and that for this reason it was necessary to bewilder me with her chatter, so as not to allow me time to reflect on what was happening to me. Here is a sample, so to speak, of her breathlessly uttered monologue as, after making me get in beside her into a minute utility car, she drove it through the Roman traffic: 'It's only one o'clock, precious daughter, we have plenty of time – and besides, even if you arrive at home a little late, what does it matter? You can always say you have been to the dressmaker and the dressmaker kept you waiting – which, after all, would be the truth, my precious daughter, because your mum *is* a dressmaker, yes, she really is a dressmaker, and so you've no need to tell a lie, you'd be telling the truth, and everybody will believe you because the truth, as everyone knows, is convincing. Yes, your mum is a dressmaker and, if you like, this very day we'll take the measurements for a nice little dress and then, my precious daughter, you'll come and try it on, and you'll always find your mum waiting for you and making you some lovely present. Yes, your mum will make a whole lot of nice little dresses for her precious daughter, so that the people in the street will turn round and say: "Why, who is that beautiful girl, I wonder where she found such a splendid mother to make her such lovely little dresses?" Yes, my precious daughter, you're very lucky to have a mother who, besides giving you a fine present every time you come to see her, will also make you a lot of dresses which will suit you so very well and will help to attract attention to your figure, which, though perhaps you don't know it – but you do know it, because there are certain things that women *do* know at the bottom of their hearts – is exceptional and should be made use of; otherwise, what's the good of being beautiful? Yes, you are beautiful, really beautiful, and your mum, who is so very fond of you, wants everybody to know it, everybody to see it. Well, well, I'm saying things that you already know perfectly well; all I needed when you became aware that I was looking at you was to see how you moved, how you walked, how you made first one gesture and then another as if to ask me: "Haven't I a beautiful body? Am I not in fact a really beautiful girl?" – that was all I needed in order to understand that you know it and that you are one of those quiet ones who seem to be all innocence and reserve but who secretly think of only one thing – and you know what that is. But there's nothing wrong about it, precious girl, nothing wrong, it's just a matter of age; you

46

would be a monster if you didn't think about it, it's a matter of age and it's right that you should think about it. And your loving mum will do this, too; she will relieve your curiosity about men, she will introduce you to not only one but lots of men, as many as you like. Yes, your mum wants her precious daughter to satisfy all her wishes, all her caprices, otherwise what sort of a mum would she be? She wants her precious daughter to be amused and contented, and since she knows that the best way of being amused at her age is to go with a man one likes, she will introduce this man to her precious girl, she will introduce him as soon as possible, perhaps even this very day, in a short time,' et cetera, et cetera. As you see, it was a monologue that was in no sort of way casual and spontaneous but that was directed, with lucid intention, towards a very precise aim, even if that purpose was hidden by the blah blah of an affected, melting motherly love.

I: And what did you do, what did you think, while she was delivering this monologue?

Desideria: I sat still, with my hands clasped in my lap, my eyes turned towards the street, and I listened to what the Voice was saying to me.

I: What was it saying to you?

Desideria: I had by now understood, even if only in an obtuse and, as it were, fascinated manner, that the woman was a procuress and that she was taking me to a house of ill fame or some such place, where, in accordance with her own words, she would get me to meet one or more men. And I was afraid. But the Voice, on the other hand, said that this fear derived from my bourgeois upbringing, that this was a unique opportunity for me to earn the money that would go towards repaying Viola for the expenses she had hitherto had on my account, and that I must not allow myself to be put off by an absurd, unjustified fear and, even less, by ridiculous considerations of morality.

I: I don't understand whether the Voice realized that the woman was not your mother, or not.

Desideria: It's difficult to say. Certainly it believed it. At

47

the same time, however, it encouraged me to keep my eyes open and, mother or no mother, to get paid as much as I could, once I was in the house of ill fame. So, fundamentally, the Voice sought to replace the fear of prostitution by the fear of not being paid, or, at least, of not being paid enough.

I: Did it succeed?

· *Desideria*: I should say it did. I recall that that day I was carrying, hanging from my belt, a hunting knife in a leather sheath, of the Boy Scout type. The Voice explained to me that, if the woman did not pay me enough, I must not hesitate one single moment to make her fork out the money under the threat of the knife. This thought reassured me; I no longer had any fear of prostituting myself, which was precisely what the Voice desired.

I: You were thinking these thoughts; the woman was driving the car and chattering. What happened then?

Desideria: At a certain point, whether perhaps so as not to let herself say too much and thus frighten me before we reached her house, or whether perhaps she had nothing more to say and would have to repeat herself, the woman fell silent and turned on the radio. I even remember the music; it was a cello suite by Bach. So it was through that slow, grave music that I saw the last part of our journey. It had a strange effect upon me, which for a moment even distracted me from the consciousness of the situation in which I knew I found myself.

I: What was the effect?

Desideria: I suddenly had the feeling which is inspired by an action which one knows one has to take even if one foresees that it will not serve any purpose. It was not a disagreeable feeling, in fact, in a way, it was pleasant. For a moment I saw myself as a heroine.

I: A heroine? Why a heroine? Where was the heroism?

Desideria: Is a hero not perhaps a man who devotes himself to a dangerous undertaking that is foreordained to failure and who nevertheless goes forward intrepidly, right to the end? For a moment I had this feeling and I seemed to

48

see that it was derived, precisely, from the double consciousness both of the action itself and of its vanity. Then, as
suddenly as it had begun, the music came to an end and,
after a moment's silence, the announcer gave the information that that particular cello suite by Bach had been performed. At this announcement I immediately ceased to feel
a heroine and went back to being the young girl I really was.
At the same time, it was as though my eyes had been opened
after a long sleep: for the first time, I saw the place where
I found myself.

I: Where were you?

Desideria: In a neighbourhood that I did not know; I
have now come to the conclusion that we were not far from
Piazza delle Muse. A rather old-fashioned quarter, with a
lot of winding streets, tree-lined, and with old houses and
villas hidden in gardens. We turned into one of these streets;
I remember that there were trees, willows perhaps, their
branches laden with tiny leaves bending over towards the
centre of the street and forming a kind of tunnel of foliage.
The little houses and villas could sometimes be seen, sometimes not, beyond the gates and amongst the trees in the
garden. We drove on for a short distance along this street,
then came to a stop against the pavement; the woman got
out and said jubilantly: 'Here we are!' Together we went
over to a gate with two white pillars; the woman continued
to hold me tightly by the arm, as though fearing that I
might run away, while with the other hand she fumbled in
furious haste in her bag, took out a bunch of keys, opened
the gate, and urged me to enter in front of her, with a
curious push as though with her knee in my back. I went in
and stood still, in uncertainty, while she closed the gate. I
looked round; it was an old garden, narrow and much over-
grown, and at the back rose a white villa of three storeys,
with a projecting roof of iron and glass above the doorway.
The woman approached and said to me again: 'Come on,
my precious daughter, here we are; this is the house in
which your mother lives who loves you so much.' She went
on talking to me in an affectionate, motherly tone; but, now,

49

as a matter of form more than anything else, as if she were distracted by other thoughts. We entered the house – there was neither porter nor lift – and started up a white marble, spiral staircase with wrought-iron banisters. At the second floor we found ourselves in front of a door with a brass plate on which was written: DIOMIRA, DRESSMAKER.

I: Without any surname?

Desideria: Yes, without any surname. Still holding my arm tightly, the woman, whom henceforth I shall call Diomira, led me through an entrance hall, guided me to the end of a passage, opened a door, and introduced me into a large room with two windows. There was a double bed, the white curtains at the windows diffused a quiet light, and a small door, wide open, revealed the bathroom. I looked at the bed and saw it was covered with a quilt of shrill yellow. At the head of the bed, with legs outspread, sat a doll dressed as a Spanish lady, with a comb and a black mantilla.

I: How did Diomira explain to you the fact that she had brought you straight into the bedroom?

Desideria: It was I who spoke first, or rather the Voice through my mouth. The Voice had instructed me first of all to get quite clear the question of money and I, naturally, obeyed. I sat down sideways on the bed and said in a clear, precise voice: 'Well then, Mother, how much will you give me for making love with the man you are shortly going to introduce me to?'

I: Very explicit. And she?

Desideria: She was surprised for possibly a fraction of a second, during which she threw me a penetrating look. My question had in some way proved that I was not as scatterbrained as she had hitherto thought; but the word 'Mother' confirmed that I was not altogether normal. So she answered almost at once, with remarkable promptness, accepting my allusion to the client, but at the same time avoiding all reference to money: 'Precious daughter, I don't promise you anything. It's late, at this time of day men go home, they have more desire to sit down at table than to make love. But now I'll make two or three telephone calls; you'll see, I'll

50

find what suits you. I don't say all of them; but there are some men who would skip lunch, dinner, and other things too for a girl like you. Meanwhile, lie down here, lie down on the bed and relax. Don't you see what a lovely bed-cover it is? It's absolutely new, I bought it a month ago. And look what a lovely doll! Your mum will take away the doll so that you can rest your head on the pillow. Yes, precious daughter, lie down and let your mum make her telephone calls.'

I: And you – what did *you* do?'

Desideria: You mean, what did the Voice make me do? I did not lie down and I replied harshly: 'Yes, Mum, but first of all I want to know how much you will give me.' She looked at me again with that experienced look of hers and then started laughing with indulgent, boisterous laughter: 'My precious daughter doesn't trust her mum, eh? But she ought to trust her, because her mum loves her and knows what is needed for her. As to how much you will take, how much I will give you, precious girl, I might tell you one sum of money or another and yet be wrong. However, I'm your mother, who knows you well and who tells you that, luckily, you are not one of those girls who do it for money. No, money doesn't matter to you, you're a rich girl, you even have a chauffeur waiting for you with a car outside the school; like all the girls of your class you are not interested in money. I'll tell you what you are: you're a vicious girl and you'll do it because you like it, because you think about men all the time and you'd almost go so far as to pay money yourself to the strong man who takes you, so much do you want it. But now, luckily, you've met with your mother, who understands you thoroughly, and just because she knows you're not a poor girl who does it from necessity, but a dirty-minded creature who does it out of curiosity, she'll introduce a man to you and you'll at last be able to realize your desire, to see what a male is like, a big, handsome male of the kind that is so attractive to vicious girls of your class. You're fortunate, my precious daughter, because in a moment I'll telephone the man who is just what you

51

want, a man who has been saying to me for some time: "Diomira, find me a young girl who really *is* a young girl, a schoolgirl who knows nothing about anything and is doing it for the first time." Now I'll go and telephone him at once; you'll see, he's a refined, distinguished man, a real gentleman, and a handsome man into the bargain, a man who is never tiresome, who is at the ideal age, between forty and fifty; he's just what's required for you, as you'll see for yourself, anyhow. And then, why shouldn't I tell you? You must know that from *that* point of view he's a real phenomenon, just what's needed for a novice like you; he does everything at a stroke with his big cock so that you don't even notice it, just a little passing pain and then it's over and you can amuse yourself and be as vicious as you like; it's now broken and you can give it to anyone you please. But when you ask me how much I shall give you, then your mum, for all that she's so fond of you, really has to scold you. Why, I do you the favour of letting you give rein to the vice that's eating you up and then you ask how much you will receive! But it's you who ought to be paying me, my precious daughter, you should be saying to me: "Mum, you keep the whole lot; even if you don't give me anything, I shall still be in your debt," ' et cetera, et cetera. She had now switched over to the language of the brothel; seeing that since she had now got me into her house, there was no further need of precautions. But I was not the vicious girl she thought I was; and the Voice insisted that I should come to clear agreements and earn as much money as possible, so as to be later in a position to pay Viola and leave the house. So it made me persist, in a cold, obstinate tone of voice: 'First of all, you must tell me how much you will give me. Otherwise, nothing.' Then she looked at me with eyes that were genuinely astonished; she had not expected such tenacity; she opened her mouth and began: 'But, my precious girl . . .' But I interrupted her harshly: 'Mum, you've got to tell me not only how much you'll give for making love but how much I shall be paid for my virginity. They are two distinct things, aren't they? Love-

52

making is one thing, virginity another. It is right that both should be paid for. Don't you think so?'

I: Really you were very cold and obstinate.

Desideria: I was so in what I said: in reality I was deeply troubled, and it seemed to me that I was walking precariously poised, on tiptoe, on the edge of a deep ravine. Diomira must have noticed that underneath this intransigent bargaining on my part there was nothing but ingenuousness and lack of experience, for suddenly she burst out again into that boisterous laughter and exclaimed: 'Well, my precious daughter, it seems that you know more about it than your mum. Tell me, then, how much you want. Your mum will satisfy you as far as possible!' Now I knew nothing about anything; all I had to go on was the childish calculations I had heard from Delfina three years before, when she had talked about the earnings of prostitutes. But I guessed that Delfina, too, was inexperienced in such matters; and so, mainly to satisfy the Voice, I halved the figure of a million which Delfina had indicated as being the most probable, and murmured: 'At least half a million,' thinking privately that it was still an excessive amount. From Diomira's look and from her disconcerted expression I realized, nevertheless, that I was not very far from the truth. Then she exclaimed: 'But, my precious daughter, you have no feeling for money; anyhow, that's understandable: anybody who has money doesn't know what it is. But, precious daughter, the thing that you think is so valuable in reality is worth nothing, all women have it at a certain age and give it away for nothing, just like that, to the first comer, and they're actually even grateful to him, my goodness, because afterwards, as I told you, they can make love as much as they like. But never mind. My precious daughter wants to know how much she'll receive; and her mum who is so fond of her wants to satisfy her in this, too. So it's understood, don't worry, you'll get half – all right – half of whatever amount your mum manages to get paid. Yes, precious daughter, half; because while you yourself give nothing, absolutely nothing, since all women have that thing and give it away for nothing, there won't be much left for your mum when everything has been paid – I mean the rent, the light, the telephone, the heating, the maid, the maintenance expenses. But all I want is for you to be content, that you should give expression to your vice, thoroughly and to your full satisfaction, so that later on, whenever you feel the desire, you can come back here and always find your mum ready to fulfil all your caprices. Yes, my precious daughter, half, neither more nor less. I'm not saying how much this half will be, because one can't know in advance. It depends on the client; there are some who are generous and who would give you even more than you ask; and there are some mean ones who argue and, so to speak, want a discount. But don't worry, leave it to your mum. So we're agreed, aren't we?' I had listened to her rigmarole, expecting all the time that she would give an exact figure. I was on the point of insisting further when the Voice stopped me: 'Accept, she relies on your coming back, don't worry, she will give you the half now, and then, when you come back, you'll be able to ask her for more.' So I answered in a barely audible voice: 'Yes, that's agreed.' Immediately, with enthusiasm, she said: 'I knew we'd understand one another, you and I; you're my precious daughter and I'm your mum: mother and daughter may possibly quarrel a little but they always end up by coming to an agreement. Isn't that so?' It was odd how she believed and at the same time didn't believe in the fiction of her being my mother; it was almost as though she were really convinced, at moments, that it was not fiction but reality, even though it was a reality more symbolic, so to speak, than effective.

I: What did she do then? Did she go and telephone?

Desideria: Yes, she went out, but she left the door open. The telephone was on a small shelf in the passage right opposite the door; so that I was present, so to speak, at the telephone call and heard every word that she said to the unknown client. D'you want me to repeat the telephone conversation? It is registered in my memory as on a tape-

54

recorder; it's necessary for you to know it because it had great importance in successive events.

I: All right, tell me.

Desideria: Here, then: 'Who is speaking? Who? Ah, you? Forgive me, I didn't recognize your voice, I thought I had the wrong number. Now prick up your ears, listen carefully; I have something for you; leave everything, get into your car, and come here at once. I repeat again: I have what you have so often asked me for, yes, really that, neither more nor less, I repeat it again, exactly the thing that you've asked me for every time you've come here, I mean that absolutely brand-new thing, so beautiful and so rare, that when someone like me manages to get her hands on it there are then a thousand people ready to pay any sort of price in order to get it. Yes, I have it here, at your disposal, all ready and entirely for you. And then, while we're speaking of it, I want to tell you another thing, to prove that you're a fortunate man. This is not only the thing you wanted, but it's also of a special kind, rare, in fact extremely rare. I mean, it's not of what I may call the everyday type that is to be found everywhere; instead, it's something very refined, exceptional. D'you understand? Exceptional. This, in fact, is a case of an object of value, not merely because it's new, that is, only just come from the factory, but also because it's not mass-produced, but made, so to speak, by hand, one at a time. What d'you say? Like last time? No, no, that time it wasn't my fault, I had been cheated and fell into the trap before you did. I had been too trusting; and I can't tell you how sorry I was because you're a serious client and I should never have allowed myself to tell you something that wasn't true. But this time it's quite safe. There's no deception; it's just as it should be, in fact: even better. And into the bargain, let me tell you again, it's an exceptional article, rare, extremely rare; it happened through a combination of circumstances, a stroke of luck, I got it by a chance that never occurs; these are things in fact that happen only once in a lifetime. So get into your car at once and come here. What did you say, you don't trust me? But how am I to

55

explain to you that this is a safe piece of goods, guaranteed brand-new, of the kind that tradesmen put aside for their most important customers. If there's any danger? Why, what danger? This isn't contraband stuff, I got it perfectly legally, spontaneously, freely. It's true, it's a product that came from the factory only about a dozen years ago, a product not yet tested, but you can be sure that it works wonderfully well. You'll have it at your entire disposal, you'll be able to do what you like with it, even to break it if you like, then it will go home and the rest is my affair. Yes, break it; after all, it's your own thing, you pay for it, and you have the entire right to do what you like, without being accountable to anyone. How? What? Whether it's a light or dark specimen? My dear sir, what a lot of things you want to know! I guarantee you that this product is new and has never been used. But how can I get to know whether it's light or dark? In any case, it only arrived this morning, an hour ago, and it's still packed, shut up in its box; I haven't taken it out yet or examined it closely. At a glance it would appear to be light, not very light, however, but light. What? Now? You're very curious, you know. All right, wait, stay on the telephone while I look for a moment and then I'll be straight back.'

I: What did she do?

Desideria: She put down the receiver on the shelf, came in a great hurry into the room towards me where I was still sitting on the edge of the bed. I was almost frightened when I saw the expression on her face.

I: What expression was it?

Desideria: Now, after the bargaining, she felt sure of herself and she had almost given up the mother-fiction. So that her expression no longer had anything affectionate in it; it was the expression of a professional engaged without any reserve in a job that concerned her passionately; only this job concerned the transformation of my person into an object of commerce and therefore was obscurely frightening to me. Then she came close to me and said, in a fussy, eager way: 'Why, d'you know that I still don't know whether

56

you're fair or dark? This gentleman wishes to know at all costs; otherwise, he says, he won't stir from his own home. Now, let me see, don't worry; after all, it's he who pays and he has the right to know.' Then, without more ado, she seized hold of the edge of my skirt, turned it back over my belly and bent down to look. Then, all of a sudden, something happened that I ought to have foreseen but which, in the unexpected circumstances into which the Voice had forced me, I had completely forgotten.

I: What was that?

Desideria: I happened to be in the period of my monthly disturbance. The flow of blood had not yet occurred, but I expected it any day. Now obviously the emotions of that morning had brought it on. And so, when Diomira uncovered my legs to see whether I was fair or dark, the first thing she saw was a red stain, not very large but perfectly visible, on the white cotton of my pants.

I: What was Diomira's reaction?

Desideria: Very bad indeed. Like somebody – to make use of the metaphor she used on the telephone – somebody who goes to open a box that has contained some fragile, precious object and finds it all in pieces.

I: What did she say?

Desideria: She said nothing, she tried to overcome her disappointment and succeeded. She stepped back, shook her head with an air of perplexity, then – as a matter of form, so to speak – with a strange look, she slightly pulled back the edge of my pants till she uncovered the brown curls of my pubic hair: in spite of everything, she still had to provide her client with the information he had requested. Then she ran off again to the telephone, took up the receiver, and said, in a much less joyful and triumphant tone: 'Well, I've opened the box and had a look. Let us say she is brown, not black, brown. And now what will you do? Either you come at once and take her, or I offer her to someone else. There's really no lack of admirers.' There must have been a positive reply from the other end of the line, for she added immediately: 'All right, then I'll expect

57

you. But be quick.' Then she put down the receiver and came back into the bedroom.

I: What did she do?

Desideria: She came over to me, planted herself at the head of the bed her hands on her hips, and stared at me, shaking her head slightly, as much as to say: 'D'you realize what a disaster you've let me in for?' Her look aroused a kind of shame in me; I made as if to pull down my skirt, which was still turned back over my stomach, but she stopped me with a movement of her hand. 'It's useless now for you to try and cover yourself up. It's not from me that you must hide it, but from this gentleman who will be here shortly. You tell me, then, what I am to say to him, you tell me, now that I've summoned him and he's coming here very pleased and quite sure of having a virgin. And what will he find instead of a virgin? A pack of sanitary towels.'

I: Brutal, wasn't it?

Desideria: Yes, exactly like a tradesman who hasn't managed to bring off a deal. I suffered unspeakably at that moment, in spite of the Voice telling me I was an idiot. I was ashamed, I was afraid, I felt I had been guilty of madness in recognizing Diomira as my real mother and allowing myself to be carried off to this house of ill fame. But the Voice consoled me in this way: 'You absolutely must not deviate from your purpose, which is to extract as much money as possible from this adventure, so as to be able finally to repay Viola and leave the house. Therefore, keep calm and don't on any account relinquish the conduct you have so far maintained. Diomira depends on you, she's experienced and you'll see that she'll find a way of putting things straight.' It was right. Diomira, after a moment's contemplative reflection, herself pulled my skirt down and said: 'There's not much blood, however, just a few drops. Perhaps it's the beginning. Do as I tell you: go now into the bathroom, wash yourself thoroughly, then lie down on the bed and stay still, calm and quiet, without agitating yourself. And, above all, in the dark. Yes, in the dark, because he mustn't notice that there is blood in that place. If

58

he notices it, it's goodbye, he'll go away and never be seen again. We all know that men are disgusted by that particular thing, they can't endure it. When he comes, I will tell him that you're embarrassed and that you want it all to take place in the dark, and he won't say a word, because he knows you're a young girl and to him it's logical that a young girl should be ashamed the first time. So you'll do everything in the dark and then, blood or no blood, he won't discover anything and everything will go smoothly. And now, hurry up, go and wash, be quick, because this man lives not far away. Meanwhile, I'll put a towel on the bed, so that you won't mess up the coverlet, which is new. Come on, the bathroom is there, hurry up, be quick!'

I: She had, in fact, recovered from her confusion.

Desideria: Completely. She had her feet again on the solid ground of her profession and her action was based on experience. I did as she told me, partly because the Voice encouraged me to do it; I got off the bed and went into the bathroom. From there, while I was washing, I looked at her as she fussed about: she went hither and thither, she took from the cupboard a big strawberry-pink Turkish towel, which she spread over the bed, she rearranged the pillows, she went to the windows and lowered the roller-blinds. For a moment the room was left in darkness; then Diomira lit a small lamp with a red shade on the night table. In the mean time, I had finished washing. I went back into the bedroom and looked in embarrassment at the bed, without deciding to lie down on it. Then a curious thing happened. As though the surprise of my menstruation had unnerved her and made her lose control of herself, Diomira suddenly treated me to a whole speech of – what can I call it? – moral justification of her own profession.

I: Moral justification?

Desideria: Yes, now listen carefully. This new monologue of hers, I can relate it to you almost exactly, because at the time it struck me very forcibly. 'Now don't stand there like that, looking as if you wanted to go away. Lie down on the bed; I've put the towel there so that you won't dirty my coverlet. But lie down fully dressed, just as you are, because men get half their pleasure from undressing women, it's one of their passions; some of them want a woman not merely fully dressed in every detail but with her most serious, most formal clothes; the ideal for them, so to speak, would be to find themselves faced by a bride, with white veil and orange-blossom, so as then to undress her very slowly, until he even has her quite naked, but still with flowers on her head and a veil on her shoulders. Oh yes, I know men and not only from today, with their caprices and their fixations. And I tell you that a young girl like you, with your school books, your ink-stained fingers, your look of a schoolgirl who, nevertheless, at the same time is a woman in every respect, drives them mad, and if for a beautiful woman they are ready to pay ten, for someone like you they are ready to disburse a hundred. And now – I can read it in your eyes – you're convinced that I shall start thinking about the money again and perhaps you may even be afraid that, because you've got your trouble, I shall no longer give you the half as I promised. But I *will* give you the half and no less; once I have made a promise, I keep it; indeed I want to tell you something so that you shall understand that your mum has not only never thought of robbing you but also has other reasons, apart from interest, for doing what she does. Yes, my precious daughter, I want you to know what sort of a person your mum is. Of course, I want to earn money, it's my trade, and who doesn't want to earn money by his own trade? But one doesn't have a trade simply in order to earn money. If that were so, I might perhaps give it up and look for another job. No, I do what I do for another reason as well, and for this reason I think I should do it in any case, even if possibly I didn't earn anything. And d'you want to know what that reason is? The reason is that I am angry with women, yes, with all women, without exception, whores all of them, one may say, from the very cradle; at home they pretend to be respectful, serious, obedient to their parents, submissive to their betrothed, faithful to their husbands, and woe if they leave it

60

in doubt; and then, on the other hand, when they allow themselves to be persuaded, by fair means or foul, to come here, then they let fly and no one can hold them any more, and they throw themselves on the man as if they were starving and, in fact, show themselves in their true light, which is, as I said, that they are whores to the bottom of their hearts. Yes, I'm angry with women, for it's not right to make believe that you're one thing when you're really another. So my greatest pleasure is to unmask them, to make them feel that they're not what they claim to be. To fulfil this purpose I act positively with a passion that I should not feel if I did it merely for self-interest. For example, when I come across a woman whom you can see, clear as light, wants to do it but hasn't the courage, then I persecute her, I never leave her in peace, I pester her with telephone calls, I make use of my job as a dressmaker to go and see her even in her own home and remind her that on such and such a day she must come and try on her dress – and all this in the presence and under the very nose of her husband, her betrothed, her parents. Well, you may not believe it, but there's not one of them, not a single one, I say, who, seeing me arrive unexpectedly at her home, protests, rebels, tells me to my face that she has no dress to try on, that I'm not a dressmaker but something else, that my purpose is different and my trade different, too. All of them, I tell you, all of them, accept there and then the charade of the dress to be tried on, they say they will come, they fix an appointment. Then, if they regretted it, who would force them to it? But, once they've accepted, once they've fixed the day of the visit, it's as though something inside them has given way, it's as though they can no longer bear to resist the desire that's eating them up. And so they hurry here, punctual and impatient; one would think they hadn't made love for years. You ought to see them then, how they hurl themselves upon the man. They scarcely wait until I've gone away and shut the door before they've pulled it out and engulfed it completely, starving and frantic as they are; I'm telling you the truth; sometimes, in spite of my having seen so many of them in my life, I'm almost ashamed for them. Well, well, my precious daughter, if you don't understand that women are all whores, you don't understand anything. Yes, they're all whores right to the bottom of their hearts, and once they feel secure and realize that it suits them, there's no knowing what they're not capable of. And then, as I told you, I feel some sort of moral satisfaction, so to speak, in bringing them here, in introducing them to men, in seeing how, here in this room, once they're on this bed, they throw off the mask and reveal their true natures. So, when they finally get dressed again and I give them the money and they put it in their handbags and say to me: "Diomira, if you have anyone, why, even tomorrow, I would come back at the same time" – well, you know what I feel like answering: "But aren't you the one who once told me that you loved your man, husband or fiancé, whoever it was? Weren't you the one who was so haughty, who claimed to be so innocent and virtuous?" No, it's not right that a woman goes about putting on the airs of a saint when she's really a whore like all the others. Yes, I like to unmask them, so much so that sometimes I have a sort of dream – of them on this bed, with the client, and then, all of a sudden, the wall falls down and everybody in the street can see what they're doing. Now then, tell me: is this self-interest? Isn't it, rather, indignation over woman's hypocrisy?'

I: Interesting, this moral justification of hers for her profession. And you, what did you reply to her?'

Desideria: Nothing. Something terrible was happening to me and I couldn't wait for her to go away and leave me alone.

I: What was this terrible thing?

Desideria: The Voice had disappeared; it no longer answered, was no longer there.

I: What did this mean?

Desideria: What I'm telling you. Suddenly a great anguish came over me; I turned to it to be reassured, to be given courage. And it did not reply. Where previously I

62

had felt its presence, there was now an obtuse, dumb, massive silence.

I: What had happened?

Desideria: Simply, it had gone away.

I: But had it warned you it might ever happen that it would absent itself?

Desideria: No, it had not told me. Later on, I discovered that the Voice did this often and I became accustomed to it. But at that moment I hardly knew anything about it and I was truly frightened.

I: What did you do?

Desideria: Diomira went out, saying that she had to do something or other in the kitchen. I think she had potatoes boiling on the stove; and I, then at last left alone, at once started searching for the Voice. At first I called it by name, then, since it did not reply, I begged and implored it. All this, of course, in my mind, in the most complete silence. Nothing. Then, just imagine, I recollected that it had made itself heard the first time while I was masturbating, I turned out the light and, there and then, although I had no special inclination for it and did not in the least wish to do it, I started titillating myself with desperate frenzy, calling upon it at the same time, in a subdued voice, so as not to be heard by Diomira. Again nothing. All at once I turned on the light again, got up, went to the window, and pulled up the blind.

I: What did you mean to do?

Desideria: Throw myself out of the window.

I: You mean, to kill yourself?

Desideria: Yes.

I: Why?

Desideria: Because the Voice was no longer to be heard and I could not bear the feeling that it was no longer there.

I: What sort of feeling was it?

Desideria: The feeling of having gone back to what I was before it made itself heard. A massive, mute lump of flesh, a holothurian.

I: Had it happened to you before, the temptation to kill yourself?

63

Desideria: Of course, more or less. I had it at least once a day.

I: Once a day; and why?

Desideria: There was no *why* about it. It was like the ebb and flow of the sea: at one moment I liked living, and then I wanted to die.

I: So you opened the window. And then what did you do?

Desideria: I leant forward and looked down.

I: And what did you see?

Desideria: The window looked onto the part of the garden that was behind the house. There was a cement pavement, all broken up. Then there was a gravel path, full of weeds, then a surrounding wall over which rose the branches of some big trees in the next-door garden. I looked at the trees and then I looked downwards; I saw the pavement and reflected that I would throw myself down and would land half on the pavement and half on the path, and there I would remain, dead, with my legs on the cement and my body on the gravel, my arms flung out and my hair spread out round my head and a pool of blood underneath my hair; and suddenly I felt pity for myself and I thought: I'm barely fifteen and I've got to die, and I hesitated. Then, at that precise moment, the Voice suddenly spoke.

I: It had come back?

Desideria: It appeared that it had.

I: What did it say?

Desideria: Just these words: 'So why are you waiting to throw yourself out?'

I: Only that?

Desideria: Yes.

I: And you?

Desideria: I was terrified and could not help asking: 'You wish me to kill myself?' You know what it answered? 'At this point there's really nothing else left for you to do.' Then I said to it: 'But it was actually you who convinced me that Diomira was my real mother; actually you who made me come here, and now you wish me to kill myself?'

I: What did it answer?

Desideria: It answered dryly that, just as it had had its own good reasons for making me go to the house of ill fame, so now it had reasons for urging me to suicide. Finally it concluded: 'Get on with it, then, throw yourself out and let's make an end of it.'

I: Did it really want you to kill yourself?

Desideria: No, it didn't want me to kill myself; it wanted me really to desire to do so – that is, to obey it.

I: What's the difference?

Desideria: Now you'll see. Well, at those words, inflexible as they seemed, I made up my mind, seized the edge of the window-sill with both hands, and with a single thrust, closing my eyes – just as one does when one throws oneself from the springboard at the swimming-pool – I made as if to throw myself into the void. But in the fraction of a second in which I thrust the whole upper part of my body over the window-sill, all at once the Voice broke into a strange laugh and said to me: 'That's enough now, stop! You've shown that you really wanted to kill yourself because you thought I had abandoned you; now shut the window, go back to the bed, and listen carefully to what I'm going to say to you.' Of course I obeyed, with a mind full of joyful goodwill, happy to have found the Voice again and happy not to have to die. I shut the window, went to the bed, and lay down again on my back. After a little the Voice started speaking again: 'Now open your ears and do exactly what I tell you. Now lie on your side with your back towards the door, as though you were reading a book by the light of the lamp on the night table. Attached to your belt you are carrying a hunting knife. Lie in such a position that the knife's handle is towards your lap and its blade turned outwards, as though it were a penis in a state of erection. Then call Diomira, who won't be far off and will hear you at once. When she comes in, say to her, without turning round: "Come here, Mum, I want to show you something." Diomira, naturally, hurries round the bed, full of curiosity. Now she's standing in front of you, asking what you wish to show her. Then you say: "Now look at this, Mum"; and at the same time you grasp the handle of the knife and pull the blade out of its sheath, gradually, so that she has plenty of time to see how compact and sharp and pointed it is. When you've withdrawn two-thirds of the blade, suddenly you unsheath the whole of the knife and you shout: "I'm going to kill you"; and you throw yourself upon Diomira with the knife raised.'

I: A precise and detailed programme. And what did you do?

Desideria: I obeyed. What else could I do?

I: And so what then?

Desideria: I did exactly what the voice ordered me to do. I lay down on the bed on my side, I placed the knife in such a way that the sheath was turned towards my stomach and the blade outwards, then I cried: 'Mum, Mum!' Diomira heard me, she opened the door, and I said: 'Come here a moment, Mum, I want to show you something.' She exclaimed, just as the Voice had foreseen: 'What is it, my precious daughter, what is it? D'you feel ill again, is there some more blood – let me see.' As she spoke she walked round the bed and hastened to see. I did not look at her but at the knife I was clasping. I said in a thoughtful voice: 'Look at this, Mum; what d'you say to it?' And at the same time I displayed the massive, shining blade, withdrawing it from its rough leather sheath. The knife slid gradually out, and I went on: 'What d'you think of it, eh?'; and then, all of a sudden, following the promptings of the Voice, I jumped up like a madwoman, with the knife in my fist, crying: 'I'm going to kill you, I'm going to kill you.'

I: Did you really wish to strike her?

Desideria: Without the shadow of a doubt. I had even selected the point into which I would plunge the blade. Diomira, owing to the heat, had taken off her blouse and was left in only her brassière, with her shoulders and arms bare. She had enormous milky breasts, thick, soft arms; in her armpits grew tufts of hair of a dull blond veiled, as it were, with coagulated sweat. Well, I meant to strike her just

66

there, near the armpit, then, with all my strength, thrusting the blade down and down, in the direction of her heart. As a child, in the country, I had been present at the killing of a pig and I had retained the memory of the long blade which the peasant, with one single blow, had thrust into the animal's neck, going straight to its heart.

I: So you were striking to kill. What happened then?

Desideria: When she saw me jump to my feet with the knife in my fist, she let out a scream of terror and, at the same time – how shall I express it? – of sudden consciousness not only of her danger but also of *my* transformation from a piece of goods to be put on sale into a free and active person. She managed to make a backward jump, narrowly avoiding the knife, and rushed off to the door, still screaming. I pursued her; but she was quicker than me, partly because I did not know the layout of the rooms, and so I wasted a few seconds in the doorway, facing the passage. She had disappeared, but I did not know whether she had gone to the right or to the left. Suddenly I heard the sound of a key being turned in a lock and I rushed in that direction, only to come up against a door locked from the inside, probably the door of the kitchen. I knocked loudly, angrily, several times; then I stopped and looked down at the floor.

I: Why?

Desideria: Because I now felt blood trickling down the inside of my thighs. And indeed I saw some wide, dark red marks appearing on the old grey floor tiles. Then the Voice spoke again.

I: What did it say?

Desideria: I don't remember the exact words. I only remember their sense. It said, to put it briefly, that, just as previously it had been satisfied with my really desiring to kill myself, so now it was enough that I should really have had the intention of killing Diomira. The seriousness of these two attempts, one of murder and the other of suicide, guaranteed their genuinely symbolical character.

I: Genuinely symbolical?

67

Desideria: Yes, just as genuinely symbolical as – to give an example – the traditional banknote which has its equivalent in gold in the safes of the bank that has issued it. The Voice, in fact, held the opinion that there is no need to act to the bitter end if one acts with genuineness and sincerity. In such a case, the action acquires a symbolic character just like that of the banknote, whose value in gold can be redeemed at any moment. It was, therefore, the inner character which was of supreme importance to the Voice.

I: And how did you yourself react to this invitation to be satisfied with a symbol?

Desideria: Once again I obeyed. The Voice also told me what I ought to do and I carried out its instructions.

I: What did it make you do?

Desideria: It told me that I ought now to go back to being the ingenuous, innocent young girl that I was in everyday reality. It also suggested to me a kind of teasing refrain to be hummed, in lieu of goodbye, to Diomira, who, without doubt, frightened to death and still gasping, was at that moment listening close to the door.

I: A refrain? What refrain?

Desideria: It was the conclusion of a fairy story that I had read as a child. It was sung by the protagonist of the story, a little girl like me, in order to tease the bad witch who had tried in vain to steal the magic wand which she had received as a gift from a good fairy. I put my mouth close to the door and sang in my most silvery voice:

> *Fai fai fai*
> *non l'hai avuta*
> *e non l'avrai.*

I: What was it that Diomira had not succeeded in having?

Desideria: That's clear, isn't it? My virginity.

I: What was Diomira's response to your refrain?

Desideria: Nothing, or rather a profound and total silence, a silence as of terror. I waited a little longer, then I went away. I went into the entrance hall on tiptoe, opened and closed the front door without any noise, went down the stairs, out into the garden, and thence into the street. I found a taxi in Piazza delle Muse. Ten minutes later I was at home.

THE CRIMINAL YEARS

I: So far you have told me in what way the Voice made its first appearance in your life. But there are two or three obscure points on which I should like you to enlighten me. For example: the Voice ordered you to go to the house of ill fame. But once there it ordered you to kill Diomira. Is there not a contradiction between the first order and the second?

Desideria: In appearance, there is. But think: the first order meant that I was to rebel against Viola and her world, into which, by adopting me, she had introduced me without asking my consent and without my knowledge. The second order, on the other hand, meant that I must rebel against Diomira, who wished to sell me to her client. It looks as though there were a contradiction between the two orders; in reality, they were united by a similar motive.

I: What motive?

Desideria: That of revolt. Which gradually changes its object and, in spite of that – in fact, for that very reason – remains always equal to itself. And then, as I have already mentioned, there is the question of symbolism.

I: Ah yes, symbolism.

Desideria: Since everything happened, not in the world outside me, but inside me, between it and me, according to the Voice it was not necessary to develop the revolt to its bitter end. It sufficed to have had the intention of it, seriously and sincerely. In practical life one acts realistically; but in the inner life everything happens symbolically.

I: Was it not, so to speak, rather convenient, this way of acting that you call symbolic?

Desideria: It would have been so had it not produced any effect. In fact, it did. For instance, after I had gone to the house of ill fame and had tried, sincerely and seriously, to prostitute myself, the effect, inside me, was as though I had really done so.

I: At what point, in your opinion, did symbolism come into the question?

Desideria: In the discussion between Diomira and myself about the price of virginity. That discussion symbolized the complete, irreversible experience of prostitution.

I: Another obscure point. Why did the Voice want you to remain a virgin?

Desideria: It explained this to me the night following my visit to Diomira's house. According to the Voice, I was to preserve my virginity for a man worthy of me.

I: Worthy of you? What does that mean?

Desideria: It meant worthy of *it*. But the Voice did not explain itself otherwise. It merely gave me to understand that he too must be a rebel, like me. Until I came across this man, the Voice wished me to keep myself a virgin. That was why I told you, at the beginning, that I had made a vow like Joan of Arc. Actually, it was a question of a kind of vow.

I: To what cause had you vowed your virginity? To revolt?

Desideria: Put it like that, if you wish.

I: Then, after your visit to the house of ill fame, what happened?

Desideria: That was the beginning of my criminal years.

I: Criminal?

Desideria: What I mean is that, from the age of fifteen to the age of eighteen, I was, or – which comes to the same thing – I considered myself to be, a criminal.

I: Come now, let's take things in order. You're a girl, as they say, of good family. That is, of the middle class.

Desideria: Say, rather, of the upper middle class.

I: Of the upper middle class, with a rich mother ...

Desideria: A very rich mother.

I: ... who doesn't let you lack for anything and has given you, and continues to give you, a good education ...

74

Desideria: According to Viola's own words: the best education that money can buy.

I: From what I understand, you are studious . . .

Desideria: Very studious. And then, from the moment when the Voice made its appearance, it has been as if I studied twice as hard.

I: Why?

Desideria: Because the Voice was – how shall I say? – omniscient, that is, it knew everything, it had had experience of everything, it found an explanation for everything. So I was learning outwardly, at school, and inwardly, from the Voice.

I: Very studious, in fact. Besides that, did you go in for sports?

Desideria: Yes, I did, but in a certain very precise way.

I: What way?

Desideria: Viola had made me practise only those sports from which I might derive something socially useful, such as tennis, riding, golf, swimming . . .

I: Socially useful?

Desideria: Yes, the sports for which you have to go to gymnasiums, clubs, swimming-pools, riding-schools, and so on, that is, places where you may be able to make so-called acquaintances.

I: After all, you're attractive.

Desideria: You might as well call me beautiful.

I: Yes, you are beautiful. Now, tell me how you combine this picture which is so positive – positive in a conventional, bourgeois sense – with something as negative as criminality.

Desideria: I don't know. I only know that the combination has been there, quiet and complete, from the very beginning.

I: The combination of normality and criminality?

Desideria: Yes.

I: But then, what kind of criminal were you?

Desideria: A dissociated kind. Externally, at home, at school, in the neighbourhood, in the houses of friends, I

75

was a girl of good family, as they say. Internally I was what, in the ordinary sense, is usually called a criminal.

I: I see. Let us continue, then. How did they start, the criminal years?

Desideria: That same year in which I got thin and became as I am now. After the exams were over Viola took me to Switzerland, to Zermatt. It's a famous tourist locality, at the foot of the Matterhorn. We stayed in an old hotel; we had a big room with a double bed, in which Viola and I slept together. There was a french window onto the balcony; from this balcony one saw the Matterhorn like an enormous triangular diamond, faceted and scintillating, rising luminous into the blue of the sky, with the wider part immersed in the dark green of the forests. One day Viola said she wanted to take a walk; we dressed, left the bedroom, and went down into the hall of the hotel. In the hall Viola discovered that she had left her camera behind in the bedroom, and since she wished to take some photographs of me during our walk, she asked me to go and fetch the camera from the bedroom. Obediently I went up in the lift to the second floor, went into the bedroom, took the camera, and went out into the corridor. The door of the bedroom next to ours was open, a trolley with cleaning apparatus was standing on the threshold, but the housemaid was not to be seen. I glanced into the room; then suddenly I heard the Voice saying to me: 'Look, there on the table near the window is something that shines in the sun, a gold compact. Go into the room, take it, and put it in your pocket.' Naturally I objected that this would be stealing, and the Voice, as it were, impatiently, confirmed: 'Precisely.' I was still in the period when I blindly obeyed the Voice; I went into the room and crossed over to the table. I saw then that the compact was not of gold but of some kind of yellow metal, and before taking it, I said to the Voice: 'It's not made of gold, it's of some yellow metal, it's not worth anything.' And the Voice, again in a tone of impatience like a governess with an unintelligent pupil: 'What does it matter whether it's gold or not? Take it and have done with it.' I

76

took the compact, put it in my pocket, left the room hurriedly, ran along the corridor to the lift, and went down to the hall where Viola was waiting for me. We went for a walk along the stream that flows at the bottom of the Zermatt valley. The path wound along on a steep slope above the stream, in the shade of fir trees, in the shelter of the mountainside. Viola walked in front and I followed some distance behind. Viola, as often happened during these walks, talked to me, without turning round, about the people staying in the hotel and about the fact that I, by opening a conversation or being willing to listen, should make friends with some of my contemporaries, through which she, in turn, could meet their mothers and make friends with them: she was always thinking about our social position, it was a kind of obsession. We reached a little bridge of fir-tree trunks that crossed the stream; on the other side of the bridge the path continued round the mountainside. Viola, still chattering without turning round, started across the bridge and I followed her. But barely had I taken the first step than the Voice instructed me: 'Stop now and throw the compact into the stream.' I asked why in the world I should get rid in this way of an object that I had only just stolen. And the Voice, for the third time impatiently: 'Because now that you've stolen it, it serves no further purpose.' I did not have the courage to enquire what purpose my stealing it had served; I went to the parapet and dropped the compact into the foaming water of the torrent. Then I rejoined Viola, who was now calling me in order to take a photograph of me with the background of the bridge and the fir trees.

I: What, in your opinion, was the reason why the Voice made you steal the compact and then made you throw it into the stream?

Desideria: The compact was not so much a compact as a symbol of property. Stealing it meant not so much stealing it as challenging property. But I'll talk to you about all this in a moment. For the present you must be content to know that the Voice had made me act symbolically.

I: How was Viola behaving towards you now?

Desideria: I've already told you that, when I got thin and became beautiful, she had fallen in love with me; but I did not know it. She was openly very affectionate, almost zealously so, as if to ask forgiveness for her previous harshness; and when she thought I was not aware of it, she brooded over me with a curious, insistent look, both surprised and searching, as though disbelieving that I could have changed to such a degree. This look vaguely embarrassed me. I felt it was not a maternal look; mothers look in a different manner. But I was reassured by telling myself that my embarrassment perhaps derived from the fact that, whereas I now considered Viola a stranger, Viola, on her side, still considered herself my mother.

I: But what did you feel for her? Antipathy? Aversion?

Desideria: No, I still even retained a certain affection for her. The Voice, on the other hand, was violently against Viola.

I: What did the Voice say about your adoptive mother?

Desideria: The worst possible things: that she was avaricious, a sex maniac, stupid, snobbish, ignorant, conventional, and so on and so forth. And all these things were gathered together in one single word: bourgeois.

I: The Voice was anti-bourgeois?

Desideria: Yes, passionately so.

I: But up till now the actual word 'bourgeois' has not made its appearance in your story. When was it that the Voice began to call the class to which you belonged the 'bourgeoisie'?

Desideria: At first it said *'pariolina'*, from the quarter where I live, the Parioli quarter. D'you remember? The first three words that it said to me were: 'Dirty little *pariolina*.' Then it replaced 'pariolina' with 'bourgeois'. Finally it began to designate as bourgeois everything against which, in its opinion, I ought to rebel. It was, as they say, a crescendo, from the scattered and fragmentary allusions of the beginning to a coherent discourse, an obsession. By now, when the Voice said 'bourgeois', I knew immediately that this word had a negative significance.

I: Let's go back to your walk. Viola took a photograph of you. Was this another novelty in her attitude towards you? Or had she taken others before?

Desideria: It was a novelty. Before leaving for Zermatt, she had purposely bought a Polaroid. From the time when we arrived she had done nothing but photograph me, everywhere, at every moment, in all sorts of poses. That morning, for instance, she had already photographed me several times, naked, as I was taking a shower; then while I was dressing; then, fully dressed, on the balcony. Finally on the open space in front of the hotel. She took her photographs with great care, seriously and with close attention; regarded the photograph with complacency as it came out of the camera when the mechanism was released, like an irreverent tongue from a mocking mouth; she would wait for the photograph to emerge gradually from the mist of indistinctness, with all its contours and colours; and then, jubilantly, she would come and show it to me.

I: What did she say to you while she was taking your photograph?

Desideria: She was embarrassing, as when she looked at me. She would say: 'Let me take your breasts again, you have such lovely ones'; or 'Place yourself there, in such a way that your belly catches the light; it's your most beautiful point'; or again: 'Stay like that, three-quarters length, I want to photograph your back, which is so beautiful', et cetera, et cetera. The word 'beautiful' was continually repeated, pronounced in a strange manner.

I: Strange?

Desideria: Yes, because I felt in it an attempt at aesthetic objectivity that did not manage to conceal the agitation of desire. She spoke the word 'beautiful' almost with regret, as though this word were not sufficient to express the quality and intensity of her feeling and as though she were continually tempted to communicate it to me in a non-verbal and more direct way.

79

I: More direct and non-verbal?

Desideria: Yes, physically, with caresses.

I: Well, the photographs were taken, and then you went back to the hotel; what happened next?

Desideria: After lunch we went to our bedroom. Viola lay down on the bed to rest; I went and sat on the balcony, facing the Matterhorn. I have already told you that I had the habit of masturbating at least twice a day, as soon as I woke up in the morning and at night before going to sleep. But the fact that, at the Zermatt hotel, I slept in the same bed as Viola had altered this habit; I was afraid that the movement of my hand would make the bed tremble and that in the end Viola would become aware of it. So you must not wonder that on this day I devoted myself to my auto-eroticism in the sleepy hour of early afternoon, on the balcony: I was sure that Viola was asleep and that she would neither hear me nor see me. I pulled my skirt halfway up my thighs, slid my hand under my pants, pressed the palm of my hand against my groin, and started masturbating, at first gently and, as it were, distractedly, and then harder and with a steadily quickening movement. I was looking, meanwhile, at the Matterhorn, which rose, gigantic and sparkling, into the blue sky; I was panting gently and between one gasping breath and another I was repeating: 'Yes, yes, yes, yes,' and I did not quite know whether I was talking to myself or to the wonderful mountain that rose before my eyes: it was as if I were approving them both. Finally I had an orgasm, a profound, violent orgasm; I threw my head back, far back, and then for a moment I saw behind me, standing on the threshold of the open french window, Viola, looking at me and holding the Polaroid against her chest. At the same moment she must have taken the photograph, for I was dazzled by the magnesium flash and immediately afterwards she had already vanished, so that I was left in doubt as to whether I had really seen her or not. Nevertheless, I did not interrupt my masturbation and continued to titillate myself beyond the first orgasm, until I had a second and then a third. I wished to demonstrate to

80

myself that it did not matter to me in the least that Viola, by now a complete stranger, should have seen and photographed me.

I: Was it you who thought this about Viola, or was it the Voice?

Desideria: The Voice, of course. We must be in agreement on this point. Every time I attribute thoughts of this kind to myself, that is, thoughts hostile to Viola, you must understand that these thoughts were suggested to me, or rather, imposed upon me, by the Voice, and that I myself had nothing to do with them.

I: What else happened?

Desideria: I remained for perhaps a few seconds in a kind of astonishment, my eyes turned back towards the Matterhorn; then, exactly like the first time it had spoken to me – that is, as though it had been a prolongation of the dissociation belonging to auto-eroticism – suddenly the Voice made itself heard.

I: What did it say?

Desideria: It ordered me to seat myself at the little table there on the veranda and to write down what it was going to dictate to me. Obedient and filled with curiosity, I rose from the armchair and sat down at the table. I was in the habit of revising the subjects for a couple of exams that I had to take again in October. So on the table there was everything necessary for writing· a couple of school exercise books, pencils, a pen. Without further ado I started transcribing in one of the exercise books everything that the Voice dictated to me.

I: What did it dictate to you?

Desideria: The programme for life in the years to come.

I: What does that mean? Why the programme?

Desideria: According to the Voice, henceforward, since it had entered into my life, I must no longer live in a casual way, day by day, but rather by putting an ideological plan into action.

I: Ideological?

Desideria: Yes; it said ideological.

81

I: It had never said that before, had it?

Desideria: No, it was the first time. But the Voice always behaved like that: suddenly it would introduce into its remarks a word that was entirely new and, into the bargain, to me incomprehensible, as if it had been the most natural thing in the world. Strangely, after it had been using this word for a short time, I grasped the sense of it without any need for explanations, and used it in my turn with the greatest ease. So it was with 'ideological'. At first I pretended to understand, but in reality I had no idea of what it meant. Then, somehow or other, the significance of the word became clear to me of its own accord, so to speak, and I began using it myself. So then, I was no longer to live in a casual way but according to an ideological plan.

I: What was this plan? I mean: how was it formulated?

Desideria: With a recapitulatory title and a series of dialectic slogans.

I: Dialectic slogans? What sort of thing are they?

Desideria: More words from the language of the Voice, adopted almost at once by me.

I: What was the recapitulatory title?

Desideria: The recapitulatory title was: 'Plan for transgression and desecration.'

I: 'Transgression and desecration'? Did you know what that meant?

Desideria: No, at that moment, not in the least. It was the first time I had heard these words. Why should a young girl of fifteen know two such words?

I: But the Voice – it knew them?

Desideria: Certainly, seeing that it was the Voice that said them to me. It knew them perfectly well and had no doubt about their meaning.

I: Well, what were the dialectical slogans?

Desideria: For instance: property theft.

I: Why should property theft be dialectical?

Desideria: According to the Voice, property was an institution which was precisely negated by theft. In short, what the Voice wanted was that I, by so many transgres-

82

sions and desecrations, should oppose the laws, the rules, the institutions and habits and regulations, the prohibitions and taboos of morality. The first thing the Voice made me write down was: property theft, because that very morning, without yet knowing it, I had already put into action the plan of transgression and desecration, by stealing the compact from the room in the hotel. I have already explained to you that it was a symbolical theft. In reality, therefore, though without knowing it, I had put into action, for the first time, the plan of transgression and desecration.

I: What else did you write down?

Desideria: I continued in the same way to write down, on the left, what I may call the positive value, and on the right the negation of this value. Thus: religion–impiety; love–prostitution; culture–rejection of culture; respect for human life–murder. As for this last slogan, the Voice made me underline it, as being the most important.

I: Why the most important?

Desideria: What is there more sacred than human life? According to the Voice, once human life was desecrated, all the other desecrations followed logically from it, without difficulty.

I: How much did you write?

Desideria: Not so very much. It's wonderful how social life, whether bourgeois or not, is founded on such a restricted number of fundamental values. I wrote barely a page and a half.

I: Well, you wrote. And then what did you do?

Desideria: I closed the exercise book and looked at the Matterhorn, so exalted, so luminous, so pure, and I had a feeling of elation. It was as though, in that page of my exercise book, equally exalted, luminous, and pure, there were an infallible plan for my future life. My eyes filled with tears. It seemed to me that I had an invincible force inside me; I realized that I owed this force to the Voice.

I: How long did this elation last?

Desideria: Some few minutes. Then I was unexpectedly brought back to reality by an unforeseen incident.

I: An incident?

Desideria: Yes, Viola appeared in front of me in a dressing-gown, with her long black hair loose over her shoulders instead of being gathered into a bun as it usually was, and with a pale face devoid of make-up. In her hand she held a photograph from the Polaroid and she gave it to me without speaking. Before taking the photograph, I took a hasty glance at her face: it wore a curious expression of, as it were, excited jealousy, both unsure and severe. I lowered my eyes: the photograph showed my head seen from behind, then, beyond my shoulders, foreshortened, my legs well apart below my short skirt, my arm thrown diagonally across my belly with the hand thrust up between my thighs. I looked at it and could not help having a feeling of shame, even though the Voice reassured me in this way: 'You mustn't feel ashamed; anyhow, there's nothing wrong in it, and besides, she's not your mother, she's a stranger, and that's that.' Then I heard Viola's voice, faltering but aggressive, torn between authority and jealousy, saying: 'Was it pleasant, then? From the noise you made with the armchair, one would say it must have been.'

I: And how did you answer?

Desideria: The Voice made me answer with sudden, unforeseen brutality: 'Better to masturbate than to get it stuck up your bottom, like you.' Then I threw the photograph on the floor and made a movement to get up. As though excited and encouraged by my violence, Viola exclaimed: 'Let us see what you wrote to make you masturbate – some sort of filth, I suppose'; and she snatched the exercise book out of my hand. With sudden fury, I cried: 'Don't touch my exercise book, I forbid you to touch it.' But Viola had already opened it; another moment and she would have read about the 'transgression and desecration' plan which the Voice had just dictated to me. I saw her retreat, saying as she did so in a tone of derision: 'Ho, ho, you forbid me!'; and I threw myself upon her. For a moment we struggled; Viola took advantage of this to squeeze my breast, not really violently, rather, in fact, with

84

a fumbling, trembling hand; I, on my side, bent down and bit her hand, but again, not so very hard, and without any intention of hurting her. She immediately abandoned her grip, exclaiming in a tone more of surprise than of malice: 'You're biting!' I said nothing, I hugged the exercise book to my breast, escaped into the bedroom, and from there went down into the hall of the hotel.

I: What were the consequences of this quarrel?

Desideria: None at all. In order to calm down, I went for a short walk, by myself, in the wood behind the hotel; then I went and sat down at the tennis courts and watched a couple of games. Later I went back into the hotel and found Viola quite normal. In fact, if anything, more affectionate than usual. So we went on for a few days. I thought continually of the plan that the Voice had dictated to me; I said to myself that it ought to begin to be put into action as quickly as possible and that, for a number of reasons, it could only be started in Rome. But we were only at the beginning of our stay at Zermatt; we were supposed to stay until the end of August; how could I remain for so many more days in that dull holiday resort, playing the part of a young girl spending the summer in Switzerland with her mother? The more I thought about it, the more I was tormented with impatience. At this point the Voice suggested to me a way of getting away from Zermatt and escaping to Rome.

I: What did it make you do?

Desideria: It made me go to Emilio.

I: Who was Emilio?

Desideria: A boy I had got to know at the hotel. He was two or three years older than me and was at Zermatt with his mother, a mature and still handsome woman, wife of an industrialist. Emilio used to accompany us on our walks through the woods of Zermatt; and of course, according to his own candid admission, he wanted to get me into bed. Equally naturally, I did not take him seriously; but I had turned to him so as not to be left alone with Viola.

I: What was Emilio like?

85

Desideria: He was a rather short young man, with red hair and a freckled face, slightly protruding eyes of an ugly sort of blue like cheap crockery, a beak-like nose, a mouth full of teeth and saliva. With the thick lenses of short sight and a bad stammer. He read a great deal and studied a great deal; he was what is called a 'swot'. But at the same time he seemed curiously endowed with practical sense, with a capacity for independence, because he was rich, perhaps, and already, even at his age, possessed a lot of money. We came to an agreement at once. We would go in the little local train as far as the nearest town and thence, in the normal train, to Milan. I would stay in Milan with him for some days, and then leave again for Rome.

I: Why Milan?

Desideria: Because the Voice said I ought to make use of Emilio in order to put the plan to the test. That is, to experiment on him with a certain number of transgressions and desecrations to see how I got on.

I: How did you manage to escape?

Desideria: We made an appointment for eight in the morning on the *Ferragosto* holiday, at the local station. But vestiges of affection for Viola still made me hesitate, in spite of the assurances of the Voice. Providentially, on the evening before our departure, something happened of which I made use in order to justify the escape to myself.

I: What happened?

Desideria: It was like this: the evening before the day fixed for our flight I went for a walk with Emilio; we were late and night had almost fallen when we got back to the hotel. Viola had already dined and had gone up to our bedroom. I had dinner in the hotel dining-room with Emilio and his mother; then I delayed so as to dance, still with Emilio, in the bar; finally, rather late, I went in due course to the bedroom. I found the room in darkness; a slight movement in the bed, at the moment when I entered the room, made me realize that Viola had not yet gone to sleep. Without putting on any lights, I undressed and felt my way into bed, raising the covers on my own side and being careful not to touch Viola. I was very tired and very soon fell asleep. I slept for I don't know how long, an hour perhaps, then I woke up, but not with a start; very slowly and gradually, just as the thing that was causing my awakening was slow and gradual. At first I lay with my eyes shut, without deciding to open them, still uncertain whether I was dreaming or awake; then I opened them, and I listened. There was black darkness; a slight sound of troubled breathing came from the side of the bed where Viola lay; this sound of breathing was accompanied by a rustling sound, also barely perceptible, of something moving inside the entanglement of the sheets. I strained my ears; the sound of breathing came nearer, then the rustling sound ceased, but immediately afterwards I felt the pressure, precise even though light, of a hand on my groin: Viola's hand which, after insinuating itself very, very slowly beneath the bed-covers, had now landed on the part of my body which constituted its goal. Then I waited without very well understanding, as yet, what was Viola's intention; I was obscurely aware that she had insinuated this hand to reach my belly in order to caress me; but I was too surprised and at the same time confused by sleep to go beyond this uncertain, idle conclusion. It was probably owing to the uncertainty caused by drowsiness and by the novelty of the situation that I did not move; I awaited some clearer, more decided movement; I thought it might even be one of those unconscious gestures that one makes during sleep. So I waited a long time for the hand to start moving again; but nothing happened; the hand remained resting on my groin, but it did not move; I felt its palm lightly pressing on my pubic hair, but that was all. How long did I wait in that vague state of semi-sleep, between incredulity and curiosity? I do not know, I had lost the sense of time; in the end I fell asleep again. During my sleep I do not know what occurred. Perhaps Viola summoned up courage and caressed me gently until she made me arrive at an orgasm, without waking me. Or perhaps she contented herself with keeping her hand on my groin and then, at a certain moment, she withdrew it and

87

I, excited even in sleep by her timid, unfinished caress, myself brought it to a conclusion, mechanically, without waking up. Certain it is, however, that suddenly, in the depth of the night, I awoke and discovered that my nightdress was pulled up and carefully rolled halfway up my belly, and I had a feeling of wetness between my legs. I put my hand to my right, under the covers, and found that the bed was empty. This time I awoke completely, opened my eyes wide, and saw that on the far side of the room, in front of me, beyond the bed, the french window giving onto the balcony was half open, in a dim light that appeared to come from the street. Making no noise, I rose and went to the window, and exactly as Viola had done on the previous day when she had photographed me with her Polaroid, I looked through the pane of glass towards that part of the balcony where I supposed Viola would be. I was not mistaken, I saw her at once; wrapped in a big coat, she was sitting in the same wicker armchair in which she had photographed me that afternoon; in front of her on the little table was a half-full glass and an almost empty whisky bottle; her back was towards me and she seemed to be contemplating the Matterhorn, which, directly in front of her, raised its enormous and vaguely white shadow into the moonless but clear sky. I looked first at her as she showed her back to me, then at the Matterhorn in front of her, and I asked myself whether that wonderful mountain, symbol for me of sublimity and purity, was inspiring in her the same feeling of exaltation and hope that I had felt in the afternoon. Then I remembered that Viola, at that moment, was the mother, even if only the adoptive mother, who, shortly before, had stretched out her hand under the bed-covers to bestow an incestuous caress on her own daughter; and I saw that it was precisely the sublimity and the purity of the Matterhorn that should provide for her a kind of silent condemnation which she could not escape, even through drunkenness. Furthermore, as I knew, Viola's remorse was not due only to the consciousness of having committed a forbidden act; but also, and above all, to the realization that she had further frustrated the substantiation of her dreams of family normality. Thus, the inaccessibility of the Matterhorn provided, as it were, a symbolic but precise allusion to the inaccessibility of her mirages of normality. To tell the truth, this reflection aroused in me a feeling of pity for her; for a moment I was tempted to go out onto the balcony, throw myself at Viola's feet, embrace her knees, and then, without speaking, lay my face in her lap, as I had been accustomed to do when a child. But the Voice stopped me with these cruel words: 'No, don't do it; she might mistake it for an invitation on your part to renew the caress of a short time ago. Besides, isn't what happened last night an excellent justification for your flight tomorrow?' So then, albeit unwillingly, I renounced my feeling of pity, left Viola to her desperate, drunken contemplation of the Matterhorn, and went back to bed, where I very soon fell asleep.

I: What happened next day? Did you get up in time and go to the station where Emilio was expecting you?

Desideria: Yes, I had taken care, during the evening, to set the alarm for an early hour. It rang punctually and I got up. Viola did not hear the alarm; more likely, she pretended not to hear it. She was huddled up at the edge of the bed, her head wrapped in the sheet, as far from me as she could be and with her back towards me. Being careful not to make any noise, I went into the bathroom, took a shower, then dressed, took up a small suitcase, which I had packed the day before, left the room on tiptoe, and went down in the lift to the ground floor. Here I did everything with the somehow systematic calm that came to me from the knowledge of now having a precise plan to carry out: I had breakfast in the hotel dining-room; then I wrote a note for Viola, in which I told her that I was going away with Emilio and that there was no need for me to tell her the reasons for my flight, because she could easily imagine them; in any case, we should see one another in Rome in September. I took up my little suitcase, handed the note to the porter and left the hotel.

I: You wrote that you would see her in Rome in September. But you said that it was the day of the August holiday. Where did you expect to spend the next two weeks?

Desideria: I didn't know; I had written that phrase mainly in order to add ambiguity to a letter which was already in itself ambiguous. In reality, I couldn't very easily imagine what I would do, once I was in Milan. I thought vaguely that I would spend two weeks there with Emilio, trying to experiment upon him, as upon a kind of guinea pig, with the so-called plan of transgression and desecration that the Voice had dictated to me. But if Emilio, for some reason, withdrew from this role of experimental animal, then I knew already for certain that I should go straight to Rome, there to await Viola's return.

I: But weren't you afraid that Viola, as soon as she received your letter, would also rush off to Milan?

Desideria: There had been that incestuous caress during the night: Viola, fundamentally, would have been grateful to me for having run away, thus giving her time to recover herself and think things over. Besides, I was running away with Emilio, don't forget that: Viola, as I knew, often foolishly indulged hopes of this kind; doubtless she hoped that Emilio, during our escape together, would make love to me and would then tie himself to me to the point of a so-called engagement and to a possible future marriage. For all these reasons, I was a hundred per cent sure that Viola would not come to Milan.

I: You went to the station, found Emilio awaiting you, you got into the train, and the train started. What else?

Desideria: I sat in a corner by the window and looked out at the thick forest of fir trees which, more and more rapidly as the train gathered speed, slipped past in front of my eyes. And then, suddenly, I had a wonderful feeling of joy.

I: Of joy? What kind of joy?

Desideria: What shall I say? – a *destructive* joy.

I: Destructive?

Desideria: Yes, I had the exact feeling of running downhill.

I: It was, in fact, precisely that: Zermatt lies at a height of almost two thousand metres and you were indeed going downhill.

Desideria: Yes, but the words 'going downhill' must be understood in a historical sense.

I: Historical?

Desideria: Yes, at school I had read in my history book phrases like this: 'The barbarians, with the fall of the Roman empire, started to descend more and more often upon Italy.' Or: 'Descent of the barbarians upon Italy: causes and effects.' Now, as the train rapidly descended the Zermatt valley, I had the impression of doing as the barbarians did: descending upon Italy to put into action a plan of overthrow and destruction.

I: Did the barbarians have a plan?

Desideria: They did not have one, but it was as though they had. Of course, these were stupidities and schoolgirl pedantries; but they can give you an idea of my state of mind that day. It was a grey, damp morning, as often happens in high mountain country; it was raining slightly, with an almost imperceptible, silent drizzle. I kept the window open, in spite of the rain which wet my face, and I greedily breathed in the smells of the mountainside, the odour of the undergrowth, thick with ferns, the odour of resin trickling and coagulating on the trunks of the fir trees, the odour of tree trunks recently cut down, the odour of damp, moss-covered earth. These smells suddenly aroused in me the strange, confusing sensation that I was experiencing a unique moment, a moment which, just because it was unique, was in some way immortal and eternal. I thought, as I looked at the grassy bank beside which the carriages of the train were gliding swiftly and smoothly: 'Never again shall I feel this sensation. I must cling to it as long as I can. I must savour it as deeply as possible, for a moment like this will never be repeated.' Then my exaltation became too strong and I started to cry with joy, trying not to be noticed by Emilio and keeping my face firmly turned towards the window.

I: You used often to cry with joy then, didn't you?

Desideria: Yes, I used to become elated with my thoughts, with the thoughts, I mean, suggested to me from time to time by the Voice, and then I used to cry.

I: While you were crying, what was Emilio doing?

Desideria: As long as I didn't turn towards him, he read a book which he had brought with him.

I: What was the book?

Desideria: A book on Marx.

I: And then, when you'd stopped crying, and at last turned towards him, what did he do?

Desideria: He talked to me about the book he was reading.

I: What was Emilio? A revolutionary?

Desideria: No, he was a boy of seventeen, the son of rich Milanese parents. But he was the first person to talk to me of revolution, the first by whom I heard the name of Marx mentioned.

I: You didn't know who Marx was?

Desideria: No, I didn't know. It will seem to you strange, but it is not really so if you think of Viola and of the surroundings in which she had brought me up and the type of school I attended.

I: What did Emilio say about Marx?

Desideria: He tried to convince me that Marx had really existed.

I: Why, did you doubt his existence?

Desideria: Not only was I ignorant but also presumptuous. Everything I did not know I was led to think did not exist. In addition, I was infatuated with my plan and I did not attribute any importance to Emilio, whom I despised and of whom I intended to make use solely as a guinea pig. And so, between me and my travelling companion, there began a comic dialogue in which I, annoyed by Emilio's tone of pretentious superiority, openly made fun of him, saying I had never heard of this person Marx and who was he? Perhaps he had entirely invented him or he was someone altogether obscure and unknown to whom he gave a

92

capricious and disproportionate importance, and other
similar nonsense of which, remembering it, I am ashamed
even today; and there was Emilio, who, knowing more or
less who Marx was and seeing himself so unjustly made
fun of, was trying, stammering and stuttering and splashing
saliva, to explain that I was wrong, that Marx was truly
famous, that I ought to read him and that, without Marx, I
could not hope to start a revolution.

I: Emilio wanted to start a revolution?

Desideria: I think I understood that Emilio started from
the prejudiced premise that it was impossible *not* to have
a revolution. Now, I did not know who Marx was, perhaps
not even what revolution was; but while the name of Marx
meant nothing to me, the word 'revolution' was – how shall
I say? – sympathetic to me. And so, offended, I answered
Emilio that I would start a revolution even without his
friend Marx, whom I did not know what to make of. Emilio
burst into a loud, sarcastic laugh and replied that, without
Marx, the revolution could not take place. At this, irritated,
I told him that in any case, between us two, I myself was
the revolutionary and not he.

I: What did you mean by this assertion?

Desideria: I did not know precisely. It was the Voice
that made me speak like that.

I: And Emilio?

Desideria: He was deeply offended. Still stuttering and
splashing saliva, he said that, in any case, in order to start
a revolution, it was necessary to take account of class differences. Revolution, in fact, was based on class consciousness
and on the consequent class struggle.

I: What did you do?

Desideria: These were all things which I had never heard
mentioned; I was disconcerted and began to guess that perhaps Emilio was right, after all, and that I had much to
learn from him. But at the same time, I could not help
despising him because he was so awkward and so ugly, and
for that reason I made an effort to confront him and not to
be outdone by him, seeking desperately for something to

oppose to his bookish pedantry. Then the Voice intervened, suggesting to me that I should allude in some way to the plan for transgression and desecration.

I: Why?

Desideria: According to the Voice, Emilio might perhaps know more about it on the theoretical level; to make up for that, however, I was superior to him precisely because I possessed the plan.

I: What did you say to Emilio?

Desideria: I refuted him scornfully: 'Perhaps I may know less about it than you, I haven't read the books you've read; but, to make up for that, I shall act.'

I: What did he say?

Desideria: For a moment he was perplexed, uncomprehending; then he exclaimed: 'You will act? And what will you do?' I answered him ambiguously that I did not intend to tell him; all I wanted was that he should know that I had a plan. What plan? At this point the Voice forbade me to say any more. So I answered him, shrugging my shoulders: 'I have a plan; more than that I can't say.' Then he, making fun of me, said: 'What is it, a five-year plan?' I did not understand the allusion to the Soviet plan-making, but I realized obscurely that once again he was getting the better of me through his theoretical knowledge, and I said hurriedly: 'I have a plan and that's enough. In fact, I know perfectly well what I shall do, but I'm certainly not going to tell you. Meanwhile, leave me in peace with your Marx. Who is this Marx; can you tell me what he did?' Emilio, at this perfectly frank question, lost his temper and started stammering: 'Marx is a grea ... great man. He wrote *Ca* ... *Ca* ... *Ca* ... *pi* ... *pi* ... *pi* ...' And I, still with my presumptuous, infuriated ingenuousness: 'Caca and pipi, pipi and caca: I understand, your friend Marx has written a book about caca and pipi.'

I: How did Emilio react to what I may call this scatological teasing?

Desideria: He did something which was at the same time childish and masculine, in which there was a mixture of

94

rage at seeing himself so unjustly contradicted and of the attraction that I exercised over him. Suddenly he jumped upon me, seized me by the hair, and tried to slap me; then, as if changing his mind, he took hold of my breast and squeezed it cruelly and at the same time tried to kiss me. So I gave him a blow in the chest with my knee, scratched his face, and pushed him away from me.

I: Where did all this happen?

Desideria: We were alone in the compartment. It was the day of the August holiday; many people were arriving at Zermatt but no one was leaving it. Seeing himself thwarted with such violence, Emilio retreated, passed his hand over his scratched face, and looked at it to see if there was any blood, and finally said, breathlessly: 'You're stupid, ignorant, presumptuous. Now, as soon as we get to Milan, I shall telephone to your mother to come and fetch you.'

I: How did you, in turn, react to this threat?

Desideria: I didn't react. All of a sudden the Voice intervened in an unexpected way.

I: How?

Desideria: By saying to me that Emilio was right, that I was ignorant and presumptuous, that Marx was really important and that I ought to get Emilio to explain to me who Marx was.

I: The Voice knew who Marx was and you didn't?

Desideria: The Voice knew everything.

I: Very well: and then?

Desideria: Then I obeyed the Voice, as usual. Trying to hide my discomfiture by pretending it had all been a joke, I said: 'Come on, then, tell me who your friend Marx was and what he said in his book on caca-pipi.'

I: And he? Was he offended again?

Desideria: No, he calmed down at once. With great emphasis, and swelling himself out like a turkey-cock, he replied that he would not only explain to me in detail who Marx was but he would also give me books by Marx or which described Marx. And, in fact, he began there and then to deliver a kind of lesson on Marxism. It may have been that he did not know much about the subject; but, to make up for that, what he did know he had learned recently and, therefore, he had all the enthusiasm of a neophyte. So, to the accompaniment of this sort of lecture on Marx, which I, obeying the Voice, listened to demurely, we finished our journey in the little local train and boarded the train for Milan. This time, however, we were not alone in the compartment; there was also a family – father, mother, and two children. The father was middle-aged with a placid face and a slight paunch – something in the nature of a private employee or public official; the mother was a little fragile woman with a pale, anxious face; the children were two little boys about five or six years old, petulant and fretful from the journey. But then, in front of this obtuse, bored audience, Emilio actually continued his lesson on Marxism; and I, with a kind of stupid, pretentious coquettishness, started answering him in my own way, that is, in a rude, sharp manner. All this, moreover, was undertaken consciously by both of us, in order to provide a spectacle for the bewildered little family, as we sent the ball of the discussion from one end of the compartment to the other, dealing blow for blow.

I: Did you go on all the way to Milan in this manner?

Desideria: No, by this time it was midday and the family had its revenge.

I: In what way?

Desideria: They took out of a basket a quantity of packages of things to eat. Like us, who a short time before had been exchanging obscure, pretentious remarks about Marxism, so now they began, from one end of the compartment to the other, exchanging things to eat. We had excluded them from our dialogue and forced them to act as spectators; so now they excluded us from their luncheon and forced us to be present with empty mouths. Our remarks on plus value, on alienation, on the expropriation of the expropriators were succeeded by theirs on the subject of cheeses, on ham, on hard-boiled eggs, on wine. Emilio tried to continue the dialogue with me, but in the end he

96

had to give it up, overcome by the gastronomic fervour of the hungry family. As for myself, I remained silent and mortified, for the Voice was now reproving me for my silly exhibitionism, to which, moreover, it had itself urged me. But it was my fate that the Voice made me do things and then their opposite. After about an hour we arrived in Milan. Imagine, it was the first time I had been there.

I: You say it as if it had made a special impression upon you.

Desideria: It's true, it did. It was the day of the August holiday and there was emptiness and silence everywhere. Empty and silent was the big open space in front of the station, empty and silent the streets. The houses looked uninhabited, with all the windows closed and the front doors tightly shut. Only one or two cars and a few bicycles stopped at the traffic lights. Nobody but tourists with shirtsleeves rolled up, crumpled trousers, and cameras hung round their necks walked the pavements. I said to Emilio that Milan appeared to be a dead city; and he replied with revolutionary fervour: 'It's not dead, just as capitalism, of which it is the fortress, is not dead. But the revolution will finish it off, and before very long, too; then only to make it rise again, greater, richer and freer than ever.'

I: Very fanatical, Emilio! But he came of a rich family, didn't he?

Desideria: Certainly, very rich. I knew that, because Viola was always talking to me about their wealth. His wealth was confirmed to me by the house, as soon as we arrived.

I: What was this house like?

Desideria: A very spacious apartment which occupied a whole floor of a big old palazzo, in the neighbourhood of Via Manzoni.

I: What happened between you, once you were in the apartment?

Desideria: Instigated by the Voice, I was now thinking of nothing but what I may call the general test of the transgression and desecration plan.

I: The general test?

Desideria: Yes, as I have already told you, I wished to make Emilio do, experimentally, the thing which I then reserved for myself to do, seriously, once I had returned to Rome.

I: And what was that?

Desideria: No sooner had he closed the door and we found ourselves alone in the apartment than I began to make fun of him: he was so keen a revolutionary and yet he was living comfortably with his family, in an apartment like this, which stank of capitalism a mile off! He desired revolution and yet he lived in a home like this, very far from being proletarian!

I: You had very quickly mastered the jargon of the Left.

Desideria: Nothing easier. Besides, as I've already told you, I knew nothing; but the Voice knew everything: it was as though it had been a professional revolutionary in another life.

I: How did Emilio take your mockery?

Desideria: Very badly. He defended himself by saying that, until he was very well up in the theory, he would not leave his family. First of all he would have to become thoroughly conscious of his class situation; then he would proceed to action. I asked him what this action would consist of. He answered with assurance, as if he were astonished that I should ask such a question: 'Revolutionary action, of course.' Then I wanted to put him to the proof, pursuant to my plan. We were in the kitchen, a very spacious room, all white tiles, with stoves as big as those of an hotel, a gigantic refrigerator, a crowded collection of pots and pans, a row of painted cupboards, an enormous table with a marble top. I opened one of the cupboards. It contained a large number of glasses arranged in three rows, and I said to him: 'Well, why don't you start the revolution in your home this evening? I bet you're not even capable of taking these glasses, one by one, throwing them on the floor, and breaking the whole lot to pieces.' You won't believe it. He seemed almost frightened, perhaps more by the expression of my face than by my challenge.

I: What was your expression like?

Desideria: It was probably one of serious, even if sarcastic, elation.

I: What did he do?

Desideria: He began stammering and stuttering that revolution did not mean breaking crockery. In any case, somehow or other, this crockery did not belong to his family but to the people, and it was his duty to preserve it until the day of the revolution. I started laughing and said to him cruelly: 'What d'you mean, the people? Be truthful, you're afraid that your mother, when she comes back from Zermatt and finds all her glasses broken, may turn you out of the house.' He went red in the face, answered me angrily that I was an idiot and that he would now show me that he was not afraid of anybody and less than ever of his mother. As he said this, he went up to the cupboard, took a glass, and hurled it to the floor. Then something comic occurred. The glass was unbreakable; it bounced back from the floor without breaking and then rolled under the table. I commented spitefully: 'There's your revolution! You throw a glass on the floor, but at the same time you're careful to choose an unbreakable glass.' Stung to the quick, Emilio gave me a stammering reply: 'You who talk so much, what are you finally? A nice young girl, respectful and attached to her mother's apron-strings, who thinks she has done goodness knows what by going alone, without her, from Zermatt to Milan.'

I: What did *you* say?

Desideria: It was the Voice which suggested my reply: 'I may be a young girl, but I've already done things you've never dreamt of.' 'What can you have done? You're a girl of good family – what do they call you in Rome? A "*pariolina*", because you live in the Parioli district. What can a *pariolina* do?' 'I may be a *pariolina* but one particular thing I *have* done.' 'What?' 'I went to a house of ill fame and lost my virginity to a man for a sum of money.'

99

I: Why do you think the Voice suggested this boast to you, which was inexact into the bargain?

Desideria: I don't know; perhaps to compel Emilio to accept the challenge and to make him do what he would otherwise have been afraid to do.

I: What impression did your remark make upon him?

Desideria: At first I saw an immense astonishment written on his face, to be succeeded by agitation and calculation.

I: Calculation? Agitation?

Desideria: Yes, probably he was agitated at the thought that I had lost my virginity in a house of ill fame; but at the same time he could not help calculating that, if things stood like that, he would no longer encounter any difficulty in getting me into bed. Finally, he had second thoughts and was afraid I had told him a tall story.

I: As in fact you had done.

Desideria: And he asked me for details. For example – just imagine – he asked how far the man's member had penetrated into the vagina. I knew nothing about this, but I indicated the distance on my index finger and added a phrase that I had heard at school, from a boy: 'Right up to the balls.' I did not know precisely what this meant, but I presumed that it meant 'up to the limit'.

I: Did Emilio believe you?

Desideria: This time he did. He again asked whether it had hurt me. He was visibly agitated: red in the face and with his eyes shining behind their thick lenses. Recalling Diomira's words, I answered that it had stung me for a little but that then it had passed. And the blood? The blood, I explained, had made a large stain on the towel which the proprietress of the house of ill fame had had the forethought to spread on the bed. A towel? Yes, a towel laid over the bedspread; in the end it was all soaked with blood, and I had more blood on the insides of my thighs, on this side and on that. At this point Emilio's agitation had a new focus: in a voice so thick that pronunciation seemed difficult, he wanted to know how much they had given me, whether the

100

money had been paid to me directly by the man or had been handed over to the proprietress. My reply was what seemed to me logical that he should wish me to reply: directly to me, in fact, the man had made a gesture that was both special and significant. What was that? He had placed the banknotes on my belly, saying: 'I'm putting them here because you've earned them very well and precisely with that thing there.' At these words, Emilio suddenly fell silent, as though I had dealt a decisive blow to what remained of his incredulity. Then he said: 'This means that I am face to face with a prostitute.'

I: Logical even if not flattering. And you?

Desideria: I felt that I was blushing; but the Voice immediately reproved me, saying that I ought not to be ashamed of the only act of courage that I had so far performed in my life. Indeed, with a sudden increase of feeling, it suggested to me that I should mention my theft at Zermatt. I obeyed willingly, being above all anxious to change my form of boasting. 'Yes, on one occasion I played the whore. But that's not all: I've been a thief, too. I went into a bedroom in our hotel at Zermatt and stole a massive gold compact with a diamond clasp.'

I: This again was not true. In reality you stole a compact of yellow metal, of no value.

Desideria: Yes, but I wanted to make him believe I had stolen an object of great value, just as, shortly before, I had made him believe that I had lost my virginity.

I: Why?

Desideria: For the usual question of symbolism. For me, by now, the theft and the visit to the house of ill fame had a significance, as the Voice said, of transgression and desecration; thus, all I had to do to have a full right to proclaim myself a prostitute and a thief was to set foot in a house of ill fame and to steal an object of no value. But for Emilio the symbolic meaning did not exist; and so I had to make him believe that I had truly and without any symbolism, and in a, so to speak, material way, prostituted myself and stolen.

101

I: How did Emilio react to the news that, besides being a prostitute, you were also a thief?

Desideria: He was now looking at me with an expression at the same time both undecided and frightening, as if oscillating between two opposite feelings.

I: What feelings?

Desideria: Fear aroused in him by the thief and desire aroused by the whore.

I: Which of these two feelings prevailed?

Desideria: The second, but with some reservations. He said: 'I should like to make love with you. But I warn you at once that I can't give you any money: I haven't any. I left Zermatt with barely enough money for the journey.'

I: So Emilio is miserly, too!

Desideria: Possibly. Or else, as is probable, he was telling the truth. The Voice, however, at once made me pursue relentlessly: 'Well, you won't give me anything; to make up for that, however, we'll make love in your parents' room, actually in their bed.'

I: You wished to put him to the test?

Desideria: Goodness knows what I wanted. It was the Voice that directed me. And what the Voice wanted was not clear to me. But Emilio, unexpectedly, lost his temper at the idea of his parents' bedroom. He stuttered: 'My parents' bedroom is locked and I haven't the key. What does it matter to you? We'll go into *my* room; there's a bed there, too; what difference does it make?'

I: What did you say?

Desideria: At this juncture the Voice decided to transfer Emilio from a dimension that still had some character of reality to another, a dimension of dream.

I: Of dream?

Desideria: Yes; the masculine dream of universal prostitution.

I: What does that mean?

Desideria: I did not say anything. I raised my two hands to my blouse, unbuttoned it, and pulled the edges wide apart so as to uncover my breasts. I was not wearing a

102

brassière, I never do; my breasts were, as they still are, one of my best features. I realized, however, that this exhibition was still not enough to create the dream which the Voice wanted Emilio to dream with his eyes open. And so, as if taking a running jump, I asked him, with a constrained, awkward hopefulness: 'Do you like my breasts?' and at the same moment, ostentatiously, clumsily, I winked at him. And then I at last saw on his face the expression of incredulity that I had sought to arouse in him by my gesture.

I: Incredulity?

Desideria: Yes: not the incredulity of someone who does not believe, but of one who marvels at seeing and thinks he is dreaming and finds it hard to believe in what he sees. He thought, in fact: hitherto I had been a young girl of fifteen; suddenly I had become, beneath his eyes, a shameless streetwalker; and this although I was still a young girl and still only fifteen. It was, in fact, the masculine dream of the uninhibited, promiscuous woman who, by that gesture of showing him her breasts, had become, for him, a credible even if improbable reality. And now Emilio no longer resisted. He stammered: 'I'll take you into my parents' bedroom, but you must promise me that we shan't touch anything. It's nothing, but I shouldn't like them to get to know that in their absence I bring women into the house.'

I: He was still frightened.

Desideria: Yes, he was frightened of everything. I buttoned up my blouse, saying: 'Let's go, then.' But he opened the kitchen door and stood aside – a movement that I did not immediately understand, because Emilio was in his own home and I had no idea where his parents' room was. But as soon as I had crossed the threshold and found myself in a long, dark corridor, the real reason of all this ceremony was revealed to me.

I: What was revealed?

Desideria: Emilio was still experiencing the masculine dream into which I had purposely introduced him. He made me go forward a few steps, then gave me a caress on my

103

behind, as a man does to a woman with whom he is preparing to make love.

I: And you?

Desideria: The Voice was not in time to stop me. I turned round in a flash, and gave him a violent slap on the hand, saying furiously: 'Hands off!'

I: How did Emilio react?

Desideria: Very badly indeed. But then the Voice came to the rescue and made me say: 'I'm sorry, but after all, you know, I've only done it once. This is the second time; I've got to get accustomed to it.' I saw him shake his head, as though to say, 'It doesn't matter.' We were standing in front of a door, which he opened and led me across a huge dining-room: a big marble table occupied the centre: the chairs ranged round it were provided with light summer covers. From the dining-room we went into a solemn drawing-room full of pictures and antique furniture, a room plunged in grey shadow, with groups of armchairs and sofas also swaddled in summer covers. Finally, along a narrow passage, we entered his parents' bedroom. It was in the same style as the other rooms, rich and solid. There was a big double bed with a damask coverlet; a big antique cupboard, dark with embossed doors; a big dressing-table with an oval mirror, laden with bottles and boxes: everything was big, massive, imposing, solemn. My eyes rested first of all on the head of the bed, upon which were enthroned two enormous pillows adorned with lace and ribbons; then they moved to the two night tables, which also were monumental; and then I noticed that, on the left-hand night table, which presumably was that of the mother, there was a framed photograph of the father, and on the right-hand one, which was the father's, a photograph of the mother. Suddenly the Voice spoke through my mouth and made me say: 'I agree, you can't give me any money because you haven't got any. Instead of the money, I ask you to do something. You see those two pillows into which your papa and mamma sink their heads each night? Well, stand up on the bed and perform your natural functions on them.

I don't ask you for money. I ask you only this. Do like your friend Marx: caca and pipi.'

I: What were you thinking while the Voice spoke through your mouth like this?

Desideria: I was horrified, but above all I didn't understand.

I: What didn't you understand?

Desideria: I didn't understand why I was asking Emilio for a proof of love of that sort.

I: And he – how did he react to the suggestion?

Desideria: He implored me to spare him the proof. He brought out a rather comic reason.

I: What?

Desideria: That he had already performed his natural functions, both of them, in the lavatory on the train. He said this in such a comic fashion, with a good faith that was so desperate, that I could not help bursting out laughing, internally.

I: Internally?

Desideria: Yes, I hadn't the courage to contradict the Voice with an inopportune burst of laughter in the very midst of this sort of revolutionary rite. The Voice pretended not to notice that Emilio was comic; or it really did fail to notice. And it caused me to have recourse to a proof of love which was just as cruel, even if different.

I: What was that?

Desideria: It made me say: 'In the train you evidently exhausted your reserves of caca and pipi, but not of saliva. At any rate, to judge by the splashes that you send into my face, you have saliva enough and to spare. Well then, spit on each of those two photographs and let us say no more about it.'

I: Truly pitiless, the Voice!

Desideria: It will seem strange to you, but perhaps the very tension of his desire may have unnerved Emilio. Anyhow, all of a sudden, he took his face between his hands and burst out crying. Through his tears he kept repeating that he was ready to explain Marx and Marxism to me and to love me even for ever, but that was all I must ask of him.

I: Very moving, wasn't it?

Desideria: Yes, it really was; and I can't deny that, somehow or other, in spite of the sarcasm of the Voice ('There's nothing to be done, you will always be the usual *pariolina* doll, sentimental and idiotic'), in my heart I didn't think he was right. But I did not even attempt to express my feeling: the Voice gave me no respite, it was like a wind at sea blowing stiffly and incessantly, for days and days, over stormy water. So, almost to my surprise, I heard my lips uttering this relentless remark: 'You want to start a revolution and yet you haven't the courage to spit on a photograph; is this your revolution?' While I was speaking, I was leaning against the bed and I could see myself in the dressing-table mirror; I could hardly recognize myself in the girl who faced Emilio with a hard, direct look, smiling in a way that was sarcastic and full of hatred. Where did this girl come from? Who had substituted her for me, without my being aware of it? Now she was leaving the bed and going towards Emilio. The photograph of Emilio's mother stood on his father's night table and bore, at the bottom, an affectionate dedication that appeared to allude to the love relationship which still existed between the husband and wife. This dedication, written in a regular, cursive handwriting beneath the smiling, well-curled head of the woman, said, in fact: 'Think of me, my darling, when you fall asleep, as I too think of you. Thus we shall both sleep better.' The pitiless, hate-filled girl into whom I realized that the Voice had now transformed me took up the photograph from the bed-table, read the dedication aloud slowly, commented: 'Very moving!' and then incited Emilio in this fashion: 'Come on then, spit on it!' Emilio looked at me with a dazed expression as though he had not understood, then made a movement like that of a puppet suddenly and clumsily jerked by a secret mechanism. He seized hold of the photograph, bent his head stiffly, and spat. The jet of saliva fell on the upper part of the glass and began trickling towards the bottom. Emilio was holding the photo-

106

graph in his hand and appeared to be sorrowfully watching the saliva as it descended slowly towards his hand. But in reality this was not so. He had given me proof of his love; his mind was now directed towards the thing I had promised him in exchange for this proof. On the other hand, however, his desire seemed to have been turned aside and weakened by the effort he had made to overcome the resistance of his filial love. So he did what he thought he had the right to do in the most awkward and least attractive way that can be imagined. He stood with his legs apart, the photograph in his hand; then he lowered his other hand to his trousers, pulled down the catch of the zip fastener, put his hand inside, and gave me a glimpse, between two fingers, of something purplish in colour, soft, wrinkled, and swollen. Filled with repugnance, I asked the Voice what I should do; and it answered promptly, with absolute assurance: 'That's enough. Give him a good shove and run away.'

I: Did you run away?

Desideria: Yes, I shoved Emilio aside and ran towards the door. I remembered that at the end of the corridor there was the antechamber; I reached it breathless, opened the door, rushed down the magnificent marble staircase. It was enveloped in half-darkness; the entire palazzo appeared, on that August holiday, to be completely uninhabited. I reached the ground floor, opened, with an effort, the heavy leaf of the main door, and went out into the street.

I. What did you do then?

Desideria: I had with me about a hundred thousand lire, put aside out of the money that Viola gave me every month; I went straight to a taxi rank and had myself driven to the airport. I had already travelled by plane with Viola; I had no difficulty in paying for the ticket and, after waiting for little more than an hour, in embarking on the plane for Rome. I arrived there at night, tired and hungry. I went home, and immediately telephoned Zermatt. With some surprise I did not notice any anxiety in Viola's voice, any relief, any joy. To tell the truth, in spite of the hostility of the Voice, secretly I had counted on it. Perhaps it was for

107

that reason that I paid attention once again to the Voice, in my reply to Viola's unexpected recriminations.

I: Recriminations?

Desideria: Yes, as soon as I told her that I was in Rome and that Emilio and I had quarrelled, that I had fled from Milan and would certainly never see Emilio again, Viola could not help showing her own disappointment: as I had foreseen. Like the good mother that every now and then she would have liked to be, she had hoped that our flight would end in an engagement; and now, instead, I was disappointing her. She exclaimed in vexation: 'And now what am I going to say to Emilio's mother? *You* tell me what I should say.' I hesitated and then accepted the phrase which the Voice, in a precise application of our plan, was suggesting to me: 'Tell her that her son is impotent. Tell her that he has a tiny little cock, red and wrinkled like the face of a new-born baby.'

I: Transgression and desecration, then? But of what?

Desideria: Of good breeding. Or, if you prefer, of so-called polite language.

I: What did Viola answer?

Desideria: There was a long silence at the other end of the line, during which I seemed to see Viola again, in person, as I had noticed her so many times while she was sitting at the card table, taking a long, scrutinizing look at her opponent before playing her own card. I don't think, in any case, that my rude words had made any particular impression upon her; if anything, she must have wondered, after the night during which she had given way to her desire to caress me, just as lovers do when faced with any sort of novelty deriving from the beloved, what sort of meaning, for her and merely for her, was implied in my recourse to the language of the brothel. Finally, I heard her voice asking me, in a perfectly normal tone, what I intended to do now, stay in Rome or return to Zermatt. I answered her at once, with a certain measure of violence: 'I'm not even thinking of returning to Zermatt. It's too boring.' With those words I spoke exactly what I thought, neither more nor less.

So, when the Voice made me add: 'And besides, you must realize that, after what happened the night before my departure, I should have to take a room in which I could sleep alone,' I had the strange, ambiguous feeling of something very like a piece of coquettishness. Again this time a brief silence ensued; then Viola said that perhaps it was better like this, that I should remain in Rome; she would be staying on at Zermatt until the twentieth of August, and then, after a short trip to Geneva for certain business affairs, would in turn be coming back to Rome. The telephone call ended with the usual recommendations to be made by an affectionate mother, of the most conventional type, to a fifteen-year-old daughter who is alone in the house. I threw down the telephone, stretched out on the bed, and asked the Voice, with all possible seriousness, why it had made me utter the remark about the room in which I would have to sleep alone. You know what it answered? This was it: 'That night Viola did something of which you will be able to make use henceforth in order to destroy your mother-and-daughter relationship. Viola would like to have a traditional family, to be tied to you by an affection that is simply and solely maternal. But now you know for certain that this is not so. Well, this certainty will serve to make Viola's efforts go up in smoke.'

I: And did you make any objection?

Desideria: None. I realized that all this derived from the logic of the transgression-desecration plan; and I was aware that for me, that summer, a new period of my life had begun.

I: Now – according to your very own metaphor – you had 'descended' upon Rome like the barbarians in your secondary-school history books. And furnished, into the bargain, with something which the barbarians certainly did not have at their disposal: a so-called plan of transgression and desecration to be systematically brought into action. Your criminal years were really beginning. What happened then?

Desideria: The Voice explained to me that the barbarians, being pagans or else forming part of some heretical sect, did not hesitate to devastate churches and other places dedicated to religious observance. According to the Voice, this way of acting on the part of the barbarians could be described as desecratory precisely because the places that they devastated were sacred. But what did it really mean – desecratory? It meant that the barbarians with their devastations did not so much destroy churches as despoil them, once and for all, of their sacred character. Before the devastation, the church was a place which one entered bare-headed, in a spirit of reverence, walking slowly and speaking in a low voice; after the devastation, it was nothing more than a warehouse, a big shed, in fact a structure possibly intact but devoid of any sacred character. Thus had it happened and thus it would continue to happen until I should have finished applying the plan, in my own case, too. Every transgression on my part would be desecration and vice versa. In fact, just to give an example, the theft of the compact in the hotel at Zermatt was not a real, genuine theft – that is, the appropriation of an object that did not belong to me; either because the object, with its low value, did not justify the appropriation itself, or because my intention, in stealing, had been different. What had been my

110

intention, or rather, that of the Voice? It had been on the one hand to transgress that law which forbids theft; on the other, to remove from the stolen object the somehow sacred character conferred upon it by the law itself. And indeed, even more than a compact, the object was a piece of property; by stealing it, not to appropriate it for myself but to demonstrate to myself that it was merely an object and nothing more, I deprived not only the compact but all the objects in the world of the sacred halo of property. Thus, by means of this minute theft, I had desecrated all pieces of property, from the yellow metal compact worth only a few thousand lire to the palaces of a multi-millionaire.

I: Is that what the Voice said to you?

Desideria: Yes, more or less.

I: But you had become convinced of the truth of these ideas of the Voice?

Desideria: Not altogether. It seemed to me too convenient to steal a compact worth very little money and then to proclaim, as the Voice did, that, thanks to the symbolic significance of this theft, I had, fundamentally, *also* robbed the palace of a multi-millionaire. Besides, symbolism seemed to me to reduce experience to a purely interior phenomenon. If anything this meant that, in time, I should be favouring, more and more, my inner life in contrast to what may be called the 'external' life; with the result, in effect, that I should no longer be alive.

I: What reply did the Voice make to these objections?

Desideria: As usual, nothing. It went ahead with its own ideas, but gave no answer to my objections.

I: Well then, what happened in Rome?

Desideria: The Voice gave me to understand that, first of all, I must desecrate precisely that thing which lay at the origin of so many other things which are generally considered sacred: to be exact, the family.

I: But had you not already performed this desecration? By going to the house of ill fame, by running away from Zermatt with Emilio?

Desideria: According to the Voice, I still continued,

111

fundamentally, to nourish a filial affection for Viola, that is,
I continued to consider her my mother. Now, as long as this
filial feeling existed, the family, according to the Voice,
would not be truly desecrated. In order to attain this object
I must make use, said the Voice, of the perfectly suitable
means which, without intending it or knowing it, Viola had
put at my disposal.

I: What means?

Desideria: Her incestuous passion, now declared and
undeniable.

I: What ought you to do, in the opinion of the Voice?

Desideria: Not leave Viola with any illusions as to the
possibility, for her, of restoring the tottering edifice of the
family.

I: In what way?

Desideria: By recalling to her, whenever necessary, the
reality of her passion for me.

I: But what would you have to do: flirt with her, flatter
her, even encourage her with a few caresses, a few looks, a
few allusions?

Desideria: Encourage her, yes, but in the same way as
the brutal, ingenuous girl who had telephoned her at Zermatt from Rome and had told her that Emilio had 'a tiny
little cock, red and wrinkled like the face of a new-born
baby'.

I: So what?

Desideria: The Voice wanted me to encourage Viola
with rude words.

I: Rude words – why?

Desideria: Because this fitted in with the plan as an
element of transgression and desecration of bourgeois
language. At the same time, it placed the daughter–mother
relationship in a state of crisis; it encouraged another
relationship of an opposite nature.

I: Then let us hear how you went about encouraging
Viola with rude words.

Desideria: It happened one morning at table, some days
after Viola's return from Switzerland. You know that Viola

112

oscillated continually between eroticism and maternal affection. Now, after the nocturnal caresses at Zermatt, the pendulum had had a violent swing in the direction of the family. That morning Viola had spent some money in a women's fashion shop and, after buying what she wanted for herself, had decided to buy something for me also – a magnificent scarf which she had placed, folded, on my plate, in place of a napkin. I sat down, saw the scarf and, without thinking, unfolded it and exclaimed: 'Ooh, how lovely! Is it for me?' Viola, who was following my movements with a maternal anxiety which was, in its way, sincere, immediately answered jubilantly, adopting the third person, which was in her a sign of special tenderness: 'Your mother did some shopping this morning, and bought this scarf for you. As you see, your mother never forgets you.' She appeared moved; but the Voice explained to me that she was moved more by the fact of having been capable of behaving like a traditional mother than by a genuine maternal feeling; and it concluded: 'Give her a lesson. Remind her that what she really wants is to make love with you. But say it to her with rude words, d'you see?' There was a moment's pause. Then I said drily: 'Thank you. But stop talking about yourself as a mother, and in the third person into the bargain. Have you forgotten that at Zermatt, while I was asleep, you caressed me in the groin?' When I expressed myself in this way, I felt myself blushing deeply, since it is one thing to say obscene words with one's girl friends at school, and another thing at home, with one's own mother. Moreover, I could not help thinking that this blushing confirmed the Voice's idea that the family, in my innermost self, had not been desecrated and that I still nourished a filial feeling for Viola.

I: How did Viola take your remark?

Desideria: She behaved as she had done when, on the telephone, I had described Emilio's penis to her. She remained silent for a long moment, examining me uncertainly. And I, again, thought of the look with which, during the evenings at cards in our house, she used to examine the face

113

of her opponent before showing her own card. This gesture on her part, so innocuous and so habitual, brought her closer to me; suddenly her silence seemed intolerable to me. So I disobeyed the Voice and said to her: 'I'm sorry, I had no intention of offending you. But it was too strong for me. And so, from now on, in order to avoid painful scenes, I beg you no longer to consider me as a daughter, even an adopted daughter, but as a guest, a boarder, a complete stranger, in fact.'

I: How did she respond?

Desideria: What had not happened with my rude words suddenly happened with my affectionate tone, perhaps because Viola was no longer accustomed to it and thus did not expect it. I saw her stiffen yet further, with her bust erect and her head pulled back. Then I realized that she was crying and that, with this movement of the head, she was seeking to prevent the tears from overflowing. But the tears burst forth just the same, sparse but large, and slid hesitantly down the thin cheeks that were tinted with too vivid a rouge, until they were finally lost in her neck. Then, yielding to her usual vice of chasing the secretions of her own body, Viola put out part of her large, pointed tongue and licked away a tear. Immediately afterwards, however, she became aware that this licking was not in accord with the sincere grief that was overcoming her; she put down her napkin on the table, rose to her feet, and left the room. Left alone, I also rose, after a moment's reflection, and followed her. I was conscious, as I walked after her, that I was again disobeying the Voice, that I was again acting in accordance with the respect for other people's sorrow that had been instilled into me ever since I was a child. I went straight to Viola's bedroom and found her weeping without any further restraint, huddled up now in the armchair at the foot of the bed. Not knowing what to do, I sat down on the arm of the chair with my side against her face, my arm round her shoulder; and I asked her why she was crying. Then she took her handkerchief from her face, looked in front of her for a moment, and said slowly: 'I cannot con-

114

sider you a stranger. You're my daughter, I love you as one loves a daughter, you're everything to me. If I had to consider you a stranger, I don't think I could endure life any more.' Her tone was sincere; but the words ambiguous. Yes, it was possible, in fact probable, that I was everything to her; but everything, in what sense? In that of being a daughter loved with a tender, pure affection? Or in the sense of being, on the other hand, a woman all the more desirable inasmuch as I was present in her life in the role of a daughter? As though to confirm this doubt on my part, Viola suddenly took the hand which rested on her shoulder and carried it to her lips. Although somewhat embarrassed, I allowed her to do it; and she, sniffing and rubbing her eyes with her free hand, started passing the palm of *my* hand across her face. Then something happened which, to tell the truth, not even the Voice, although so violent against Viola, could have foreseen. Viola stopped sniffing and passing the palm of my hand across her face; she became motionless, with staring eyes and a strangely half-open mouth, still grasping my hand but holding it suspended in mid-air, with an intent but vague expression; she seemed to be reflecting upon, or rather examining, the rise of some kind of sudden feeling within herself. Then, at last, she made up her mind: that same big, dark, pointed tongue which shortly before I had seen drinking up a tear, stuck out between her lips: Viola held up my hand to her mouth, but turned it over, as though she wanted me to muzzle her mouth with my palm; then I felt her tongue moving about inside my hand, advancing towards my fingers, darting into the space between one finger and another. This time the Voice was successful in encouraging me: 'You see! But let her do it, we'll see what she does.' So I obeyed the Voice and allowed Viola carefully to lick my hand; it made one think of a dog, partly because the sensuality of the act was mingled with a sort of devotion consisting of pathetic, servile remorse for having formerly despised and hated me so much. However, my passivity and my silence in the end aroused Viola's suspicions; it was as though they had been

115

a dumb, inert way of repelling and condemning her. With an unforeseen, clumsy change of attention, she stopped licking my hand; in fact, she thrust it away from her mouth, like some forbidden fruit that had suddenly revealed a disgusting flavour; she looked at it for a moment as though she wanted to examine it, and then uttered this incredible remark, no less clumsy than the gesture which inspired it: 'D'you know, you have an extraordinarily long life-line? I'm sure you'll live to be at least a hundred.' I answered sharply: 'Well, we'll talk about the lines in my hand another time. Now let us go and eat.' And she, half comforted, half ashamed, rose from the armchair and followed me into the other room. The Voice said to me triumphantly: 'Who was right?' And I answered: 'You, as usual.'

I: Did you ever again say rude words to Viola?

Desideria: From that day onwards I had no more scruples about saying them.

I: What rude words?

Desideria: The usual ones. First of all, what we may call the two fundamental ones that designate the male and female sex. Then I replaced the current euphemisms by the equivalent obscene terms: 'bottom' with 'arse'; 'to make love' with 'to fuck'; 'sodomitical relationship' with 'buggery', and so on. With regard to this last word, one day, again at table, I was speaking of a woman friend of Viola's and I said that she had 'an enlarged arsehole because she made her lover stick it into her'. Viola, this time, reacted: 'I beg you not to speak like that about a person I'm fond of.' Then, with a sudden impulse, the Voice made me retort: 'You defend her because you too, for goodness knows how long, have been getting yourself buggered by Tiberi.'

I: How did Viola take that?

Desideria: She looked at me and as usual was silent for a moment. I persisted: 'You say nothing because you know that it's true.' Then, for the first time, she alluded to her relationship with her antique-dealer-administrator-lover in a curious manner, half pathetic and half calculated, half-

116

way between a mother who knows she has behaved badly to her daughter and recognizes it and wants to be forgiven, and a lesbian seeking to reassure her jealous companion. 'You're always thinking of that night, I know,' she said. 'But at least you ought to know this: next day I not only sacked Chantal, who in fact left that same morning, but I also told Tiberi that everything was over between us and that thenceforward he must limit himself to being our man of business. This is the absolute truth, I swear it. There has been nothing between me and Tiberi for at least three years – that is, in fact, ever since that miserable night.'

I: How did you receive this explanation; or rather, this revelation?

Desideria: The Voice made me say: 'I don't care a damn about your Tiberi.' But it wasn't true.

I: Why wasn't it true?

Desideria: Because her words, in some way, had made me test the intensity and force of her aspiration towards family normality. After all, Tiberi had been her lover for years; Chantal was the woman whom she loved at that period; yet she had not hesitated to break with them both on my account. And it could not even be said that she had done so because she had fallen in love with me. At the moment of her rupture with Chantal and Tiberi, I was still the colt that had turned out to be a worn-out horse, the fat, stupid adopted daughter from whom nothing good could be expected.

I: As to Chantal, it can be admitted that she was summarily dismissed. But Tiberi? He continued to be her business manager; why in the world should he have ceased to be her lover, too? She could have seen him away from the house, that's all.

Desideria: I haven't told you that I was upset by the news of her break with Tiberi; I have told you that it was the tone with which she gave me the news that upset me. The fact is that you are right: Viola did not break with Tiberi then, but three years later; meanwhile, she continued

117

to meet him and a third woman – the woman on duty, so to speak – away from the house.

I: Where?

Desideria: At a place which I will tell you about later. For the moment be content to know that the precise fact that at that moment she was lying to me gave sincerity to the tone with which she lavished her lie upon me.

I: What did the Voice think of all this?

Desideria: The Voice had no pity for Viola. It said that I must not give way to sentimentality.

I: Did you still continue for some time to say rude words to Viola, or did you stop?

Desideria: I stopped. I did not like saying them; even more than they offended Viola, they offended that part of myself which the Voice called bourgeois but which was, on the other hand, simply the part of me that was alien to violence, even the verbal kind. And so one day I asked the Voice whether it was really necessary for me to continue using brothel language. To my surprise it replied that I could stop: by now I had proved to myself, and above all to the Voice itself, that I was capable of breaking the taboo concerning rude words and I could therefore quietly resume my usual manner of speaking, which did not entirely exclude them, yet did not base itself uniquely upon them. I must admit that this decision gave me enormous relief.

I: You were still, after all, a well-brought-up girl.

Desideria: No, I was a sensitive girl, whether I obeyed the Voice or whether I disobeyed it.

I: Let us go back to the plan. What was the transgression–desecration that you undertook after that of language?

Desideria: That of culture.

I: This is something important: what culture?

Desideria: At the age of fifteen, what one understands by culture is mostly what is taught at school. Thus desecration was childish and external, and it never even occurred to me that culture should be transgressed and desecrated by means of another culture or, as they say nowadays, by means of a

118

counter-culture. Instead, I organized a kind of scatological rite by means of which I deluded myself into thinking that I rejected once and for all the culture of all periods and all places, from its origins until today.

I: A scatological rite?

Desideria: Yes, scatological, excremental. One afternoon Viola had gone out and I was left alone in the house to do my homework. I took a fine thin-paper edition of the *Promessi Sposi*, went into the bathroom, placed the book on the edge of the washbasin, pulled down my trousers, sat down on the lavatory seat and defecated. Then I placed the book on my knees, opened it at a previously chosen passage, tore out the page, wiped my bottom with it, looked for a moment at the page all crumpled and dirtied, threw it onto the excrement at the bottom of the lavatory bowl, and then urinated on it.

I: Why exactly the *Promessi Sposi*?

Desideria: Possibly because at school they attributed a great importance to this novel; but possibly also because of what was written on the page I had torn out.

I: What page was it?

Desideria: The last page, where the character of Renzo says: 'I have learned not to get involved in tumults, I have learned not to preach in the piazza, I have learned not to lift my elbow too much,' et cetera, et cetera.

I: Who had chosen this page, you or the Voice?

Desideria: The Voice, of course. I knew nothing of tumults, of piazzas, of lifting one's elbow; this page left me indifferent. But the Voice seemed intensely irritated by this page. 'Wipe your bottom thoroughly with that page,' it said to me in a furious tone, 'and get it thoroughly into your mind that, at the very moment when you are wiping your bottom with that page, it is with the whole of their damned culture that you're wiping it, in a definitive, irreversible manner.'

I: *Their* culture – whose?

Desideria: They – that is Viola, the people of the Parioli quarter, the school, the teachers, et cetera, et cetera.

119

I: And you had the impression that this had really happened?

Desideria: This? What?

I: I mean that that page of the *Promessi Sposi* really symbolized the whole of culture from its origins until the present day?

Desideria: I had no impression at all because I was not cultured. The Voice, on the other hand, *was* cultured and for it the symbolic operation I have just described to you, did function. As I pressed the handle and released the jet of water on the dirtied page, the Voice exclaimed: 'Don't you feel better now?'

I: Let us continue. What was the next desecration?

Desideria: Practically no day passed without my putting some sort of desecration into action. Well then, let us take, say, religion.

I: In that case one not only can but one must speak of desecration.

Desideria: No, not at all. What claims to be sacred is not always so. It seemed to me, for instance, that I accomplished a much more effective sacrilege in wiping my bottom with the page of the *Promessi Sposi* than in putting into action the same type of desecration in the church where I went with Viola to Mass every Sunday morning.

I: Why?

Desideria: I imagine it was because culture seemed to me more alive and more important than religion. That was my feeling, though obscure and unjustified.

I: Unjustified? I should think that the Voice, which, according to you, was omniscient, would have explained to you why culture, in its opinion, was more alive and more important than religion.

Desideria: The Voice rarely explained to me the reasons for the desecrations. It was omniscient in that it behaved with the assurance of one who knows everything and has had experience of everything, not because it explained things to me. The Voice wanted me to act, not to acquire

120

consciousness. According to it, consciousness should not come before action, but after it.

I: Now describe your sacrilege.

Desideria: I'll describe it to you in the third person, as though it were something that did not happen to me but to someone else.

I: Why?

Desideria: Because on that day I was really another person. The sacrilege did not seem to stir a single fibre inside me, even the most secret and unconscious, and I obeyed the Voice like an automaton, that is, just exactly as if I had been absent and my body had been a puppet manipulated from outside.

I: Are you sure that the use of the third person and the fact that during the sacrilege you seemed to be an automaton do not stand to indicate instead a religious feeling all the stronger, all the more outraged, in that it was repulsed and also hidden from your own consciousness?

Desideria: I am sure that all the religious feeling of which I was capable was – how shall I say? – commandeered, mobilized by the Voice. In church, during the Mass, it seemed to me that I was a complete stranger, I felt nothing, absolutely nothing, just as though I had found myself witnessing the incomprehensible rites of a religion that was not mine.

I: You felt nothing; why, then, the desecration?

Desideria: Because it was the religion in which Viola and the people like Viola believed, or rather pretended to believe.

I: I understand. Now tell me how things went.

Desideria: One morning, a Sunday morning, a big, funereal black car stops in front of a church in the Parioli quarter; out of it get a very elegant middle-aged lady with a wasted, mature face and a youthful figure, and a pretty girl of about fifteen in a sweater, miniskirt, and boots, with her hair loose on her shoulders and a sly, quiet expression on her face. The lady walks in front of the girl through the crowd in Sunday clothes that fills the square in front of the

121

church; they go in together; the lady dips her fingers in the holy-water stoup and crosses herself; the girl does not dip her fingers and does not cross herself. The lady goes to a pew in the back rows and sits down; the girl sits down beside her. The Mass proceeds in the normal way, except that the girl, like a wrongly assembled automaton, does things mechanically and, into the bargain, the wrong way round; she sits down when the other people rise; she rises when the others sit down; she kneels and lowers her eyes as though she were praying when the others are standing up with their eyes wide open and fixed on the altar. Furthermore, her genuflection at the moment of the elevation would seem not without strangeness to a close observer. Because, for instance, she kneels with her legs wide apart, her knees as far apart as possible – a position, in any case, highly uncomfortable. Would it not be more practical to kneel with knees together, like everybody else? And then, at the moment of the elevation, when the bell gives its silvery tinkle, why does the girl begin, with bowed head, to make a rustling sound with her lips, a sound like running water, the same sound that mothers use to encourage their babies when they won't make up their minds to perform their natural functions? The noise is heard by the lady, who turns anxiously, gives a sign to the girl to be quiet, her finger on her lips. But the girl pays no attention to her, she continues to produce that subdued rustling sound with her lips, while the bell, shaken forcibly by the priest, rings loudly up at the altar, with shrill, prolonged tinklings, in the silence of the church. Finally, there is a last peal; all cross themselves, but not the girl who, on the contrary, inserts her hand under her miniskirt, as if to arrange something. Now all the people sit down again; the girl, however, remains on her knees and nudges the lady with her elbow. The lady turns, then the girl seats herself too and, with a clearly indicative gesture of her hand, points out to her, down on the floor of the pew, a little pool of transparent liquid, of a faintly yellow transparency. The lady looks in astonishment, uncomprehending, incredulous; the girl, with

122

sudden decision, bends down, dips two fingers in the little pool, and makes the sign of the cross. The lady rises hurriedly to her feet, seizes the girl by the arm, makes her get up from her seat, with her steps quickly across the central nave, and pushes her out of the church. The car is there, waiting beside the pavement. The two women, one holding the other by the arm, hurry to the car, wake the driver, who was asleep, and get in. The car moves off.

I: This is the story in the third person and the present tense. Afterwards, what happened in the first person and the immediate past?

Desideria: Nothing of importance. Viola was silent for quite a long time as the car moved in the direction of where we lived. Finally she said: 'Tomorrow we go to see my psychoanalyst.'

I: Viola believed in psychoanalysis?

Desideria: Viola was an American, she believed in science, in any kind of science. Besides, in the past she had had treatment for a couple of years.

I: What for?

Desideria: Probably for the usual reason that she could not manage to overcome the contradiction between eroticism and the aspiration towards a normal family life.

I: And with what result?

Desideria: None. The treatment did not succeed either in making her accept eroticism *in toto*, or in restoring her *in toto* to family life.

I: What answer did you give her when she told you she wanted to take you to the psychoanalyst?

Desideria: Personally, I should have been in favour; if only because it was a novelty. Besides, I didn't dislike the idea of talking about myself and of hearing myself talked about: perhaps I needed treatment even more than Viola. But the Voice immediately showed itself completely hostile.

I: Why?

Desideria: I imagine because it was convinced that I was neurotic; and it had need of the neurosis in order to

123

dominate me. The treatment, on the other hand, might have cured me and thus nullified its influence over me.

I: What did the Voice make you answer?

Desideria: I was silent for a moment and then, without looking at Viola, my eyes fixed on the driver's back, I said: 'No, I'm not going to the psychoanalyst.' Viola looked at me sideways, without moving, remaining in profile; then she murmured between her teeth: 'You did pipi in church, you made the sign of the cross with the pipi; it seems to me that there is more than enough to make one think that something in your psyche doesn't function.' To which I, in a low voice and taking advantage of a jolt of the car that made me fall on top of Viola: 'If you take me to the psychoanalyst, I'll tell him what happened that night at Zermatt.'

I: And she?

Desideria: She made a movement of her head in the direction of the driver and said in a low voice: 'Be careful, he might hear; that is a thing that must remain between the two of us, nobody must know about it'; and then she gave me a little slap on the hand, as if to advise me to be good.

I: And you?

Desideria: For a moment I was absolutely furious. What impertinence! As though there were by now a long-standing complicity between us, as though we had been lovers and I was not bothering to keep it secret, whereas she did not wish anybody to know! I told the Voice I wanted to protest, to tell her that she was shameless; but the Voice ordered me not to do anything, with its usual argument that, as long as Viola behaved like a lover, there was no danger that she would hinder the success of the plan by behaving instead, like a mother.

I: So you said nothing?

Desideria: Nothing; I bit my lips and remained silent.

I: But did you think that the Voice was right?

Desideria: No, I thought it was wrong because, from the very fact of considering herself my mother, Viola derived the incestuous impulse to wish to make me her lover. But the Voice understood nothing of psychology; or rather,

124

it did not think that one should attribute any importance to it.

I: Did you then go to the psychoanalyst?

Desideria: No, there was no more mention of it. Nor yet of going to church, to Mass, on Sunday morning.

I: You have desecrated – even if only symbolically – property, culture, religion, good manners, the family; what still remains? Don't you think it's enough?

Desideria: There remain all sorts of things. We don't realize how many things there are which we respect without any valid reason. But the moment we give the matter our attention, we discover an infinite number of them. Practically the whole of our life is a tissue of unreasoned respects, of unfounded taboos.

I: Very well. Then tell me the first thing that entered your mind to be desecrated after religion.

Desideria: Money.

I: Money was sacred to you?

Desideria: No, but it was for Viola. Religion, too, was not sacred to me; but it was for the people in the quarter where I lived.

I: How did you come to be aware that money was sacred to Viola?

Desideria: In all sorts of circumstances. I remember one incident especially, at table.

I: At table?

Desideria: We had an old parlourmaid, very fond of me, who was called Luigia. She was already in the house when Viola adopted me; by now she formed part of the family and I thought of her almost as a relation. You must know that Viola had caused to be built, on the flat roof of our palazzo, a little top-floor flat above our penthouse. It was an investment of the great amount, of the superfluous amount of money which Viola did not know what to do with; one of her favourite investments, because it allowed her, as long as the building of it went on, to have an occupation of some sort in a life that was otherwise completely

126

idle. With regard to this top-floor flat – always with the idea of reinforcing her maternal and non-maternal ties with me – she had asked me to receive the people who came to inspect it and, in the event of their enquiring, to tell them the very high price that she was asking for the lease. I had accepted the job, at the suggestion, especially, of the Voice, which wanted me to continue being slightly flirtatious with Viola, so as to lead her to believe that I was not entirely insensible to her passion. Now one evening at dinner I told Viola that three people had come during the afternoon; they had looked at the flat but had found it too expensive. As we discussed the question, it so happened that I mentioned the price of the lease; then I saw that Viola was making me an understanding glance in the direction of Luigia, who was serving at table. I did not understand, but continued my remarks about the lease; Viola changed the subject in so contrived a manner that the Voice felt it its duty to warn me sarcastically: 'I don't know, but one would think you had made a *faux pas*.' I remained silent; Luigia went out at last, and Viola said: 'One doesn't speak of money in front of the servants.' 'But Luigia isn't a servant, she's more like a relation. And then, why shouldn't one speak of money in front of servants?' 'Luigia is a parlourmaid; one shouldn't speak about money in front of her because we have plenty of it and she very little indeed.' 'But why? Is money perhaps such a sacred thing that one can't even name it?' As no doubt you have guessed, this question was suggested to me directly by the Voice, as though to get Viola to confirm what it was teaching me all the time. And Viola, in fact, replied with cynical gravity: 'Yes, for many people it is sacred.' 'Is it sacred for you too?' I noticed her hesitate, then she said: 'I am under no illusions. What should I be without money? Yes, from that point of view, it is sacred for me, too.'

I: Was it then that the Voice decided to make you desecrate money?

Desideria: Not exactly; but, as you can imagine, it made unscrupulous use of that remark of Viola's about servants.

127

After that day, it never stopped telling me that Viola was a horrible Parioli lady; that one of the fingernails of Luigia, a woman of the people, was worth more than the whole of the bourgeois multi-millionaire Viola; that I, myself, also belonged to the people, whether by birth, or whether, now, by the influence of consciousness that it had been able to inspire in me; that I ought as soon as possible to desecrate money, proving by deeds, not by words, that I was not only not its slave but also that I intended to take it away from Viola and place it at the service of the poor, exploited people.

I: Did the Voice speak like that?

Desideria: Yes, like that.

I: Where did it learn this language of the Left?

Desideria: Didn't I tell you that the Voice had had all possible experiences and was omniscient?

I: Yes, you told me, but how can one manage to believe it? I mean, how can one manage to believe that you knew nothing and that the Voice knew everything?

Desideria: And yet, whether you believe it or not, it was exactly like that. At any rate, one day the Voice's propaganda against Viola bore fruit.

I: How was that?

Desideria: One morning I came back from school two hours earlier than usual because the Italian lesson had been skipped owing to the illness of the teacher. I reached home, asked the manservant who opened the door to me where Viola was. Innocently the man answered me that she was in the study with Doctor Tiberi.

I: Innocently?

Desideria: Yes, because, as I have told you, ever since that night when I surprised Tiberi in the act of sodomizing Viola, the latter, though she continued to employ him as business manager, had always contrived that I should not meet him. She saw him during the hours in which I was at school, in her own house, or else, when she wanted to make love *à trois*, together with the call-girl who, on the occasion, replaced Chantal, in the flat designed for that purpose

128

which I have already mentioned to you. As soon as it heard the name of Tiberi, the Voice, for some reason, caused me to become pugnacious, aggressive. I rushed to the study . . .

I: The study? Who studied there?

Desideria: Viola called it the study, but neither she nor anyone else ever studied there. It was a room in the English style, with mahogany furniture and bookcases, sofa and armchairs upholstered in black leather, a desk with bronze ornaments, a big revolving chair, and a lamp with a green shade: everything as in a study, but without any studying. Actually Viola received there the people who looked after her affairs, the builders and architects who built or restored the apartments in which she invested her money and, to be precise, Tiberi and the lawyers and rent-collectors who were managing her business. So the Voice made me throw the door open with something of the same impetuosity with which I opened it on the night when I had caught Viola, Tiberi, and Chantal at their love-making *à trois*. It will seem strange to you, but this time again I had the same sensation as on that distant night, that is, of catching my adoptive mother and her businessman in the act of doing something sinful and forbidden.

I: Why, were they making love?

Desideria: No, not at all, and that is why I said that my sensation of catching them in the act of committing some sinful act might seem strange to you.

I: What were they doing?

Desideria: They were composedly sitting opposite one another, on the two sides of the desk. Tiberi had his back turned to me, Viola was facing me. On the desk I saw a small, flat suitcase. It was open and I saw that it contained a number of small cylinders or rolls wrapped in paper. Beside the armchair in which Viola was sitting one shelf of the bookcase was open like a small door and showed the grey, shining surface of the polished metal of a safe. Perhaps it was precisely this safe which gave me the feeling that something secret and forbidden was occurring in that room, either because it was the first time I had seen it and had

129

never known that it existed, or because, at my abrupt
entry, Viola had made the gesture of putting the shelf back
in place; but her gesture stopped halfway as soon as she
saw that it was I. In the mean time, however, I had seen
something else which was presented to my eyes for the
first time: gold.

I: Gold?

Desideria: Yes, for again on the desk, beside the suitcase,
there was a little heap, yellow and shining; this was a heap
of gold coins. Then I realized that more gold coins were
enclosed in the little rolls wrapped in paper that filled the
suitcase. Reconstructing the matter later on, I realized that
Tiberi had broken open one of the rolls in order to show
Viola how many coins it contained and so give her an
account of the total sum that she would finally have to pay
him for the gold.

I: Nothing sinful, then: Viola, like all rich people at
that time and always, was investing her own money in gold.

Desideria: That was what I thought, too. However, the
Voice made me behave as if I had caught them in the act of
doing something ugly and shameful.

I: Ugly and shameful?

Desideria: Judge for yourself. I stopped abruptly in the
middle of the study, and exclaimed in an ironically well-
bred tone: 'I'm sorry, Mum, I'm sorry, I'm sorry, I didn't
know you had visitors.' Then I went close to them and, before the two of them had recovered from their astonishment,
I shouted with all the voice I had in me: 'Bourgeois, you
loathsome bourgeois, so you're counting your gold, you're
counting your gold that you've robbed from the people; in
time we'll make you vomit it out right to the last coin, you
can be sure of that.'

I: A remark suitable for a rally! Or like one of those
that you see written on walls with a paint-spray. Where did
you get it from?

Desideria: From the Voice, obviously. If it had depended
on me, I should certainly never have uttered it. Anyhow,
those brilliant little coins, of yellow, glossy metal, so small

130

and so bright, seemed to me to be something beautiful, something fascinating and precious.

I: How did Viola and Tiberi react to your invective?

Desideria: All Tiberi did was to look up at me with a glance of cold surprise and astonished appreciation.

I: Appreciation?

Desideria: Yes, of my beauty, I suppose. As for Viola, she said in a disconcerted tone of voice: 'Desideria, what's come over you? These coins belong to you as well.'

I: And what did *you* say?

Desideria: Still at the suggestion of the Voice, I cried: 'They're not mine, because I'm not your daughter, I'm the daughter of a whore from whom you bought me, perhaps even with two or three rolls of those same coins. They are not and they never will be mine – and in fact, look! I spit upon them.' As I said this, I went up and spat on the coins, but the spittle fell on the hand that Viola had placed on the shining heap as if to protect it. Then I turned my back, feeling all the time upon me Tiberi's heavy look of appreciation; and I went away.

I: Where did you go?

Desideria: I went to my room and threw myself on the bed. I was now angry with the Voice, and I said to it: 'I should like to know why you made me make that ridiculous scene.'

I: And what did the Voice reply?

Desideria: As usual, nothing. It said to me: 'You do what I tell you to do and don't ask for explanations.'

I: Was there any sequel to the scene?

Desideria: Yes, but not immediately. In a way I hoped that Viola would desert Tiberi and run after me . . .

I: You hoped?

Desideria: Yes, I felt remorse and shame on account of the scene, and I should have liked at least to let Viola know that I had not intended it and that it had all been the fault of the Voice.

I: Speaking to her of the Voice?

Desideria: That I should never have done. But Viola

131

ought to have been made to understand that my scene had been – how shall I say? – involuntary. That is, due to an impulse of my unconscious.

I: Very convenient and opportune, the unconscious! And what comment had the Voice to make on your remorse and shame?

Desideria: In its characteristic way, it said: 'You're a little bourgeois whore, sentimental and lascivious. Yes, you're sorry you made that scene, you want to apologize to Viola. But at the same time you perhaps even secretly hope that she may lavish a few caresses upon you, of the kind that you allowed in your sleep, at Zermatt.'

I: But didn't you say that the Voice encouraged you to flirt with Viola, even for the opposite purpose? Why the sudden change?

Desideria: The Voice had not changed. When I flirted with Viola, at its suggestion, with the opposite purpose in view, as you say, it approved; when I flirted on my own account, possibly even from an occasional, transitory impulse of sensuality, then it said that I was vicious and bourgeois.

I: Well, what did you do? Did you wait for Viola?

Desideria: I waited for a little; finally I realized that Viola, even if she came, would not come so soon because first of all she would have to complete her business with Tiberi and send him away; and I felt a certain annoyance. I rose from the bed, undressed, went into the bathroom, and took a shower. I did not do this in the morning because I got up early to go to school, so I washed the evening before in order to be able to sleep a little longer in the morning. Beneath the jet of hot water the desire came upon me to masturbate, thinking of Viola and of the way she had caressed me at Zermatt while I was asleep. It was the Voice, with its reproof of my being a vicious, bourgeois little whore, that had reminded me of it and made me desire it. So I put on a dressing-gown and slowly and gravely went back to my room, lay down on my back on the bed, my legs spread out, with the dressing-gown open; and I began to

132

caress myself, thinking meanwhile of Viola and of what she had done to me while I was asleep, that night at Zermatt.

I: What did you imagine she had done to you?

Desideria: I had always imagined a light, prolonged caress of the hand. But lately the memory of my nightdress rolled back with great care over my belly, as though in preparation for a caress of a different type, has made me think of oral sex.

I: What did you feel while you were masturbating with this new interpretation?

Desideria: I had a profound, ambiguous feeling, oscillating between profanation and rebellion.

I: Profanation of what?

Desideria: Of what still remained of a filial quality in my relationship with Viola.

I: Did much of that still remain?

Desideria: Perhaps so – who knows?

I: And rebellion?

Desideria: For once, rebellion against the Voice, which wished to impose its will on me.

I: By the way, how did the Voice behave during your auto-eroticism?

Desideria: Strangely, it was silent. Perhaps it thought that, when all was said and done, I was desecrating the family, even if in a vicious and bourgeois manner.

I: And then?

Desideria: Then I was on the point of reaching orgasm, and I stammered breathlessly: 'Viola, Viola' – perhaps for the first time in my life; for usually in my thoughts I called her 'Mum'; and then the name I had invoked acted, so to speak: the door opened and Viola came in – so suddenly that I had no time to recompose myself, and remained as I was, lying on my back with my legs apart and my dressing-gown open.

I: What did Viola do?

Desideria: She saw me, understood what I was doing, and was visibly troubled. But she controlled herself and,

133

without saying a word, came and sat on my bed, sideways, close to me. We looked at one another fixedly, for a moment, in silence. Viola was holding in her hand two of those little paper-wrapped rolls of gold coins that I had seen in Tiberi's little suitcase. Finally, she spoke in a voice that appeared to be making a rather useless effort to seem calm and reasonable: 'I should like to know what's got hold of you. Tiberi was upset, too; he asked me whether by any chance you hadn't gone mad.'

I: And what did you say?

Desideria: At that moment, somehow or other, there was a kind of fusion of the two kinds of coquettishness, the negative one of the Voice and the incestuous one on my own part. I answered in a capricious, mournful, sensual, listless tone: 'You told me you had broken with Tiberi. Instead of which, I come into the study and find you with him. Seeing him there with you, I confess, made me lose my head.'

I: What was it – a way of telling her that you were jealous of Tiberi?

Desideria: Perhaps it was. In any case, she understood it like that. She was agitated; the customary impure, burning blush rose from her neck to her cheeks, and she said with vivacity and relief: 'But you must not think that. I told you the genuine truth: for at least three years Tiberi has been nothing to me. I see him for our business, that's all; why don't you believe me, foolish little thing that you are? I had instructed him to procure me some gold coins for the purpose of investment, he brought them to me and at that moment was counting the coins as he had to do; it was his strict duty, yet you have to come and make that scene!'

I: Foolish little thing that you are? It sounds like a caress, even if only with words!

Desideria: Not only with words. She had placed her hand on my knee and had made a sort of movement to edge it upwards. Then she corrected herself and added: 'Look, I swear to you, I haven't any men; and Tiberi, ever since that night three years ago, has been positively repugnant to me.'

I: It wasn't true – at least you told me so.

Desideria: Certainly it wasn't true. She was lying, but perhaps, as sometimes happens, it was also true. Then she went on: 'I don't think about men; I want now to devote myself entirely to you,' which was a profoundly ambiguous remark; one did not see clearly whether it was dictated by incestuous lesbian feeling or by maternal affection or even – as was more probable – by both, mingled and fused together. I said nothing, and she concluded: 'Look, I've brought you two of those little rolls of Queen Elizabeth gold coins; they cost forty thousand lire each. In each roll there are twenty, so there are almost two million. It is a present that I want to give you so that you may understand that I am not offended by the scene you made and that I am still your Mum who is so very, very fond of you.' But, as she said this, she placed the two rolls with a gesture that was at the same time bold, authoritarian, and consciously allusive, not on the bed, where there was all possible space, but right on my groin which, owing to her sudden entry, I had not had time to cover up with the edges of my dressing-gown.

I: What did you feel when confronted by this gesture, which you yourself have defined as bold and significant?

Desideria: A profound feeling, which in turn provoked a curious association of ideas. I was struck, more than anything, by the enormous weight, disproportionate to their volume, of those forty little coins.

I: Did they weigh a great deal?

Desideria: Yes, a great deal; and then it came about that I started to think of the motorists' saint, St Christopher, whose medallion is often set into the dashboard. St Christopher, as the name indicates, had carried Jesus, when still a child, on his shoulders, across a river. But in the middle of the stream Jesus had become so heavy that Christopher was almost drowned. Well, I had an analogous sensation of a huge weight, unendurable, universal, as though the weight of all the gold in the world were concentrated in those two little rolls of pounds sterling. And as though all the gold in the world had been placed there, on

135

my groin, in order to tempt me, in order to buy me, and, even beyond Viola's lesbian passion, in order to destroy me once and for all.

I: What did you do?

Desideria: In agreement, this time, with the Voice, I had the reaction of a pedantic schoolgirl who has recently read a manual of Greek mythology. Looking at the two rolls placed crosswise on my groin, I said slowly: 'Now tell me, Mum, d'you know the story of Danaë?'

I: Danaë?

Desideria: Yes, exactly, Danaë, whose picture I had seen some time before in a reproduction of the painting by Correggio. Viola looked at me and, still agitated by her own gesture, could not manage to speak, but shook her head in a negative manner. I went on: 'Danaë was a Greek woman, beautiful as the sun, with whom Jove had fallen in love; and Jove, in the end, in order to make love with her, transformed himself into a shower of gold coins, just like these that you placed on my belly. Danaë was lying on her back, just like me; her legs apart, like me; with her sex uncovered, like me; and then Jove, transformed into golden coins, rained down upon her, just like these little coins of yours, which you have now made to rain down between my legs. And d'you know what will happen next? In nine months' time there will be born a beautiful baby all of gold; and however strange it may seem, given that we are two women, he will be our son, yours and mine. This baby will be all of massive gold, he will weigh an immense amount, as much as all the gold in the world, he will have a body and a head of gold, eyes, nose, and mouth of gold, a golden backside and a golden member, everything, in fact, of gold. And since he will be worth a great deal – just think, all the gold in the world! – so that he shall not be stolen, we will put him in a safe rather than a cradle, perhaps even in Switzerland, where you have the greater part of your capital; and every now and then we will take a journey over to Geneva or Zürich, we will have the safe opened, and then we shall see that he has grown further, becoming

136

heavier and heavier. What do you say to it, Mum, don't you like the idea of having a son all made of gold, by me?' As I talked in this way I had broken the roll and had caused the coins to trickle gradually between my fingers onto my belly and between my legs.

I: And how about Viola?

Desideria: She was disconcerted; she did not understand whether she ought to consider the Danaë story as a piece of flattery or a repulse. Then the Voice made me shout all of a sudden: 'Don't you understand? You look at me with your big, stupid American eyes, you're all red on your neck and your cheeks, and you don't understand? What d'you think? That I told you the story of Danaë in order to say that I'm ready to make love with you? You think that, eh! Well, it's not like that; I told you the story so that you might understand the exact opposite: that all the gold in the world is not enough to buy me. Now do you understand?'

I: And she?

Desideria: Her reaction was unforeseen in a way which disarmed me.

I: What was it?

Desideria: She put on a more serious expression, bent forward, put out her hand, this time in a really maternal way and nothing more: then she picked up, one by one, the gold coins over my thin, hollow stomach, just as though she were taking them up from a fine silver tray, and put them down, all together, on one side, on the bed. Then, carefully, she pulled together the two sides of my dressing-gown, covering me up. Finally, she said humbly: 'Accept these coins as a present from somebody who is really fond of you. And now, my treasure, let us go and·eat; I think it's all ready, on the table.'

I: What did you do?

Desideria: The Voice pestered me to go on torturing Viola. I disobeyed the Voice and said that I would dress at once. Viola went out without adding anything more. I dressed hurriedly and joined her in the living room.

137

I: Did this story of the gold coins end like that? Or was there a sequel?

Desideria: There was a sequel. You remember that remark of the Voice during the scene: 'You're counting your gold that you've robbed from the people'?

I: Yes, a remark suitable for a rally, as I said to you. And then?

Desideria: That remark remained impressed upon my memory. In the end I said to myself that if it was true – as it could not help being true, seeing that the Voice had uttered it – that this gold had been robbed from the people, my duty was to restore it to the people. Here, however, a difficulty arose. With regard to the 'people', I only knew those of the so-called servant class. I thought it over; in the house we had six persons of this sort: the cook, Luigia, Viola's personal maid, the manservant, the chauffeur, and a boy 'factotum' who looked after the roof-top terraces, fetched and carried parcels, and helped the chauffeur to look after our two cars. On reflection I chose Luigia, as the one to whom I was most closely attached, who knew me best and would understand me. So one day I put the gold coins into a purse, went into the kitchen and said to Luigia that I wanted to speak to her alone. She followed me into my room. I brought her inside, turned the key in the door, and then pronounced, with an affectionate, promising air of mystery: 'Gigia, I want to make you a present.' There she was in front of me, plump and rotund, very like an elderly hen that has already hatched out many chickens, with her white apron over her prominent bosom, her little chubby hands, her clean, fat face like that of a benevolent nun. 'Desideria,' she said, 'what present d'you want to give me?' smiling – she in a truly maternal way – with the air of expecting some piece of rubbish or childish foolishness. Then I put my hand into the purse, took a handful of coins, and said to her: 'Hold out your apron.' Smiling and still not understanding, she obeyed. Perhaps she believed that I wished to give her some sweets, or else nuts; and I then dropped the gold coins, one by one, into her apron.

138

1: How did she react when she saw what kind of present you were giving her?

Desideria: For a moment she said nothing. I put my hand into the purse again, again filled it, and so on, three times more, until all Viola's gold was collected in the parlourmaid's apron. Then I looked at her. Her eyes were shining with a troubled, tempted look, with an ambiguous, perplexed light in them which, however, was extinguished all of a sudden. She asked softly: 'You want to make me a present of all these lovely little coins?' 'Yes, I want them to be yours.' 'But who gave them to you?' 'It doesn't matter who gave them to me, you must take them.' 'Who gave them to you, Desideria; if you don't tell me, I won't accept them.' 'Oh well, it was Mum; are you content now?' 'Yes, but I can't accept them.' 'But why?' 'Because they belong to your mother.' 'No, they're mine, Mum gave them to me.' 'One day your mother will ask what you have done with them, and what will you say to her?' 'That I've given them away, my goodness! So will you take them or not?' She still hung back for a little, then, seeing my determination, said all right, she would accept them; then she gave me a kiss and went away.

1: So, after all, she took them?

Desideria: No, wait a moment. All that day I believed that Luigia had accepted them and had perhaps even hidden them well away, sheltered from indiscreet looks, under her mattress, as avaricious, economical peasants were once wont to do. But I was wrong. That same night when I went to bed, as I turned back the covers I saw something shining; this was a coin, and then when I lifted the pillow the coins were there, the whole lot of them, in a glistening, yellow heap on the white sheet. Beside them was a note in which I immediately recognized Viola's handwriting. It said: 'Luigia has handed over this money to me and I am giving it back to you; it is yours. If you wish me to keep it for you, in the safe, at your disposal, you have only to say so. But if you say nothing, I shall understand that you have accepted it finally. Viola.'

I: She signed herself 'Viola' instead of 'Mum'.

Desideria: Of course: as Viola, that is, as a lover, she had given it to me and as Viola she was giving it back. But do you understand what had happened?

I: What?

Desideria: Either from fear of unpleasant complications (such as the accusation that she had stolen it), or from intuition of the real significance of this money, Luigia had finaͧly not accepted it.

I: And how about the Voice?

Desideria: The Voice told me to keep it. It might always come in useful, one never knew. And so I put it at the back of a drawer, among a lot of junk, beside the knife with which I had tried to kill Diomira.

I: What happened then?

Desideria: The Voice advised me to leave things as they were. In any case, the Luigia incident had not been without its use: if nothing else, it had served to make me realize that money is sacred not only for the person who has it but also for the person who hasn't it. Now, however, still according to the Voice, I must find another way of separating the paper or metal object that goes under the name of money from the sacred character which, so to speak, is stuck upon it like a thin, invisible membrane.

I: What way?

Desideria: The Voice thought about it for a few days and then came out with an extraordinary proposal.

I: What was the proposal?

Desideria: According to the Voice, I had made a hit, as they say, with Tiberi at the moment when I had burst into the study and had shouted my invective against the bourgeoisie. The Voice recalled that, while I was inveighing against Viola, he, Tiberi, not being impressed by it, enveloped me from head to foot in a cold glance of sexual appraisal. This look, according to the Voice, had taken in and, so to speak, photographed everything in his memory: the shape of my breasts, the flatness of my stomach, the size of my calves, the breadth of my shoulders, the slimness

140

of my waist, but above all – the Voice emphasized this point – the solid, aggressive, double superabundance of my buttocks.

I: Why especially your buttocks?

Desideria: There was no 'why' about it, said the Voice. It was a fact of which I ought to be aware: at the moment when, with a violent movement, I turned round to go away, giving a twist to my bust and vigorously swaying my hips, Tiberi's look was immediately aimed *there*.

I: Where was *there*?

Desideria: At my buttocks. Thanks to my movement, he was assessing their volume, their shape, their muscular consistency, their capacity to contract and to be distended, the possibility of penetration.

I: All that in one look?

Desideria: Yes, according to the Voice; and it went on to point out to me that I certainly could not have forgotten having seen Tiberi, three years before, stark naked, standing behind Viola, who was on all fours, just a moment before sodomizing my adoptive mother. This memory and that look proved that in three years Tiberi had not changed his ideas on the sexual relationship. Fortified by this persuasion, I should go to him and persuade him to withdraw, for my benefit, a huge sum of money from Viola's capital that he had the task of administering. He could do this without Viola being aware of it; he had the power of attorney and Viola trusted him. As to the argument that I should use to blackmail Tiberi, the Voice indicated it with a single word: brutally.

I: What word?

Desideria: My bottom.

I: The Voice, in fact, wanted you to seduce Tiberi.

Desideria: Yes.

I: Because it had noticed that he looked at your behind.

Desideria: Yes.

I: And it established a relationship of essential continuity between that look and the sodomitic relationship

141

between Tiberi and Viola that you had observed three years before.

Desideria: Yes.

I: Don't you think, however, that the image of three years before had been an emotional shock to you and had perhaps penetrated into your unconscious, and that consequently, without your being aware of it, you desired Tiberi to do to you what you had seen him do to Viola? And, in short, that the money which you wanted him to embezzle from Viola for you was no more than a pretext?

Desideria: It may be so, but the Voice said it did not matter. The important thing was to put the plan into action.

I: Always the Plan! But what did the Voice wish you to do with the money once you had obtained it?

Desideria: It made no pronouncement, at least for the time being. It said it would let me know at the right time and place.

I: And you did not have the feeling that there was something unreal about this project? A young girl of fifteen, even with an extremely beautiful bottom, going to her mother's man of business and managing to extract a few millions . . .

Desideria: Twenty million, to be exact.

I: Twenty millions in exchange for a few minutes of love?

Desideria: I had no experience of these things. I was at the mercy of the Voice. Which, as you know, knew everything, had done everything, and had no doubts about anything.

I: What did you do, then; or rather, what did the Voice make you do?

Desideria: I telephoned Tiberi, at the antique shop, and announced: 'I am Desideria.' I heard a kind of exclamation of satisfaction at the other end of the line – corrected, however, immediately afterwards, by a remark in an ironical tone: 'Desideria? What an honour! What can I do for you?' I told him in a great hurry that I must speak to him and that, if he didn't mind, I would come to his house,

142

as I thought that at the shop it would not be possible to be alone. Curiously, he did not show any surprise at the request, as one would have expected. After a moment's reflection, and speaking in a superior, drawling voice with his usual Roman accent, he gave me an appointment at his home, for the next day, in the early afternoon.

I: Where did he live?

Desideria: In a big building in the neighbourhood of Piazza Cavour; I had never been there, but I knew, from having heard Viola speak of it, that in his spacious flat, which occupied a whole floor, Tiberi kept a store of a great deal of furniture which he then gradually placed on sale in his antique shop, which was near Piazza di Spagna. Knowing these things, I was not too surprised, as I followed the old housekeeper who had come to open the door, to see everywhere fine antique pieces of furniture – fine and antique but, how shall I say? devoid of any sort of intimate, private character.

I: Intimate, private?

Desideria: Yes, that is, with the promiscuous, casual air of furniture in shops, placed together one piece beside another without any necessity beyond the solely mercenary purpose that characterizes the exhibition of any sort of object offered for sale. I had the strange impression that, at least as regards furnishing, Tiberi did not exist as a private person: even the bed in which he slept might be transferred, from one day to another, from his bedroom to that of a buyer. The housekeeper, a tall, thin, grey-haired woman dressed in black and lame in one leg, conducted me into the sitting-room, opened the shutters of the three windows, and went away, saying that Tiberi was busy, and asking me to wait a few minutes. I sat down and waited. The room was like the rest of the flat: big, dark pictures, furniture of every style, and, all the time, the just suspicion that it was the exhibition room of a shop and not the living room of a private apartment. Not knowing what to do, I rose and went to one of the windows; I opened it and looked out. The flat was on the second floor; one could see an ordinary

143

street of the Prati quarter, with tram wires, cars parked in a herringbone pattern, shops, entrance doors; on the pavement opposite there was a petrol pump, yellow and red, with a notice saying CLOSED; there was a fine drizzle and the cobblestones of the street shone in the calm white light of early afternoon. I was fascinated, looking at this street; I heard, or so it seemed to me, the opening of a door behind me; nevertheless, I remained leaning on the window-sill, without turning round; but, at the same time, I moved my buttocks, bending one leg and extending the other, as though tired of my position. Why I did it just then I did not understand; then I decided to turn round, and I saw Tiberi standing still in the middle of the room, and was sure, all at once, that he had come in some time before and had stopped where he was in order to look at me at his ease. There was a moment during which I recognized the truth of the Voice's observation about Tiberi's preference for the hinder parts of the female body. Then I was struck by the manner in which he was dressed.

I: How was he dressed?

Desideria: He was wearing a grey suit with a double-breasted jacket, a white shirt, a dark tie, shoes with thin soles and pointed toes. You remember the films of the thirties? Well, without realizing it, Tiberi had dressed in the same way as the actors in those films. He was, as they say, irreproachable, in the sense given to that word in certain military or bureaucratic circles. I noticed, with one look, this way of dressing of his, and I remember having an unfavourable impression of it.

I: Why unfavourable?

Desideria: Because I had a different idea of the fashions, and anyhow, without being aware of it, I attributed a particular significance to this kind of elegance.

I: What significance?

Desideria: Now, at this distance of time, I can say it; then, I would not have been able to say it; the significance was Fascist.

I: Fascist? But did you know what Fascism was?

144

Desideria: I did not know but the Voice did, as usual. For my part, as I said, I merely had a different idea of the fashion. That day, too, I was dressed in my own way and not in Viola's way, which was actually the feminine equivalent of Tiberi's Fascist way of dressing.

I: How did Viola dress?

Desideria: In clothes from the grand dressmakers of Milan, very expensive and not very personal. In a way, it could have been said that she was dressed in uniform. The uniform of the bourgeoisie of the Parioli quarter.

I: And you, on the other hand – how were you dressed that day?

Desideria: I was wearing a brown sweater, loose and out of shape, and blue cotton trousers, very worn and discoloured. Everyone wore them then; to me they seemed convenient and that was enough. In any case, I was very far from thinking that my clothes could be the sartorial equivalent of a revolutionary manifesto.

I: What was it that made you think, on the contrary, that your way of dressing expressed a message of revolt?

Desideria: Tiberi. Possibly to disguise the real reason why he had stopped to look at me as I was looking out of the window, he said: 'I watched you and d'you know what I thought? That in other times I would have taken you for a ragamuffin, but now I must consider you a revolutionary. Isn't it perhaps for that reason that you people dress in that way?'

I: And what did you say?

Desideria: I said lightly: 'What d'you mean by "you people"?'; and, without waiting for an answer, I went and sat down in one of a group of armchairs, slightly in shadow; Tiberi also sat down, at a certain distance. From the hip pocket of his trousers he extracted a long, flat, gold cigarette-case, flicked open the lid, and offered it to me; I refused; he took a cigarette, put the case back in his pocket, then lit the cigarette with a lighter which was also of gold, and breathed in a couple of times, blowing the smoke out through his nose and staring fixedly at me. Finally, he began

145

by telling me that he was pleased to see me; that there had been a time when he had thought of me as a daughter; that then, for reasons independent of his own wishes, he no longer visited our house and so had not seen me: and that now he was aware that I was no longer a child but, from every aspect, a woman. He spoke slowly, in the casual, good-natured way which is typical of certain bourgeois Romans; in his sing-song voice, slightly tinged with dialect, it would have been difficult to detect any sort of feeling; as he spoke he scratched the sole of his shoe with the nail of his forefinger, for he had crossed his legs and his foot was not far from his hand. His attitude, in fact, was extremely relaxed and tranquil. But at the same time a vivid flush, such as may be produced by a candle enclosed in the transparent paper casing of an Oriental lantern, seemed to be suffusing his whole face, from his chin to his cheekbones. I observed all this without, however, understanding very well what it meant. It was the Voice, as usual, which pointed out to me that Tiberi was troubled by my presence; and that I ought to increase this agitation by speaking to him of that famous night, now distant, when I had seen him standing, stark naked, sodomizing Viola on all fours on the bed. Of course I obeyed the Voice and said, in a tone that was suddenly confidential: 'Perhaps you don't know; but I became a woman, as you say, from every aspect, chiefly because of you.' 'Come, come; how was that?' 'Don't you remember, three years ago, that night when I burst without knocking into Mum's bedroom, and saw you, Viola, and the governess, as you were making love? Well, that discovery made me grow up in a moment. The day before I was still a child; the day after I was a woman.'

I: And what did he answer?

Desideria: For a moment, nothing. He was intensely red in the face, and was looking at me. Then he asked a curious question: 'But were you shocked because we were making love or because we were doing it in a certain way?'

I: And what did *you* say?

Desideria: My reply was dictated word for word by the

146

Voice! I was ashamed and unwilling. I answered him, smiling, calmly and slyly: 'Do you realize what it means to a child of twelve to see a man busily occupied in putting it up her mother's bottom?'

I: What had happened? A return to rude words? But didn't you say you had stopped making use of them?

Desideria: Yes, I had stopped. But one can see that the Voice had reserved the right, in special cases, to make me say them again. This was, indeed, a special case; I had to provoke Tiberi, and the best way was to make him understand that I was acquainted with what I may call his erotic speciality.

I: How did Tiberi take this relapse of yours into rude words?

Desideria: He became redder and for a moment I thought he was going to have a stroke. Slowly, and still picking at the sole of his shoe with his fingernail, he pronounced: 'Ah, so that's the way you young girls speak of certain things?' Unsuspecting and calm, I went on: 'Since that night, Viola has been nothing to me, all the less so because at the same time I learned that I am not really her daughter and that she is merely my adoptive mother.' At this point an extraordinary thing happened.

I: What was that?

Desideria: Tiberi began making love to me.

I: Did he lay hands on you?

Desideria: Not at all. He remained sunk in his armchair and said, with marked, self-satisfied slowness: 'Yes, I've always known that you were not Viola's daughter but a bastard, the daughter of a street-walker.'

I: Is that what you call making love?

Desideria: For Tiberi, yes. For him that insulting remark was equivalent to an introduction to sodomy. It was a form of verbal sadism. And in fact I was not offended. I felt, if anything, the embarrassment of a woman to whom a man suddenly declares his love.

I: Love?

Desideria: Yes, I felt that he could not love except in

147

that way and that at that moment, with absolute certainty, he loved me.

I: What answer did you give him?

Desideria: Nothing. I obeyed the Voice, which enjoined me not to speak; I waited, motionless and silent, for the sodomization to continue: 'Your mother was a street whore, and you're a whore like your mother. That *you* were a whore, I've always thought. Today I've had proof of it. D'you think I didn't realize that you had placed yourself at the window on purpose to make me look at the gaping backside of a worn-out prostitute? Don't come and tell me that you didn't hear me enter the room; I called you by name, loudly, and you, like a real harlot, instead of turning round, moved your backside from side to side, pretending to lean out and look into the street.'

I: At what point had the verbal sodomization arrived, with these words, in your opinion?

Desideria: Let us say that he had stripped me naked and was now contemplating the object of his desire.

I: How did you answer him?

Desideria: The Voice made me say, with feigned seriousness: 'It's not true that I moved on your account; I moved in order to get a better view of something in the street.' 'Of what?' 'I don't remember now. There was something that interested me.' 'I'll tell you what interested you. It interested you that I should have a really good look at your bottom.' 'Why d'you talk to me like this?' 'I talk to you like this because you are a whore and the daughter of a whore. How does one talk to whores? Like this.' 'Instead of repeating that I am a whore, why don't you ask me what I came to see you about today?' 'I suppose it's some whore's business.' 'But what, in your opinion?' This time he was silent for a moment, and then he said: 'Desideria, you're trying to provoke me, but I'm not having any. Tell me what you want of me and let's be done with it.'

I: What did you say?

Desideria: The verbal sodomization had by now reached a point when I could raise the question of the money with

148

a reasonable hope of obtaining what I wanted without submitting to physical sodomization. And so, without too much preamble, I said suddenly: 'I've come here because I need money.' 'You need money? Come then, I'll give you some money. How much d'you need? Would fifty thousand lire be enough?' 'No, I need twenty million.' My reply must have seemed so absurd to him that he did not even stop to discuss it. He said ironically: 'Twenty million?: And where am I to find them? If I had twenty million, I should be an aristocrat.' 'You don't have to lay down a penny. Hasn't Mum given you power of attorney? All you need to do is draw the money from her bank account. I've seen her account: she has two hundred and twenty million; so, if you take twenty, she'll still be left with two hundred.' 'I didn't know you were so good at mathematics.' 'These millions, in any case, are mine. They are part of my inheritance. It means that I shall have them in advance.'

I: How did you know all these things?

Desideria: As usual, the Voice knew them, and it was the Voice that suggested the whole affair to me, word by word. I knew nothing.

I: And Tiberi?

Desideria: As if to gain time, he asked: 'Relieve my curiosity; what d'you want to do with these twenty million?'

I: Rather a sensible question, wasn't it?

Desideria: Suddenly I felt bewildered. The Voice, as you will remember, had told me that it would inform me of the destination of Viola's millions at the right time and place; now, however, I had to give Tiberi an answer and I did not know either what the money would be used for or what I ought to make Tiberi believe. In a great hurry I asked the Voice what I ought to say; and I received this disconcerting reply: 'Tell him you need it to start a revolution.' 'But I can't say a thing like that to Tiberi.' It was silent for a moment, then it solved the problem by substituting the word 'revolution' with its Christian equivalent: 'Tell him: to do good.' I obeyed and said with sufficient conviction: 'To do good.' And all at once I realized that the Voice, with

149

didactic astuteness, had purposely placed me in an embarrassment so that I might become accustomed to considering revolution as being synonymous with good.

I: How did Tiberi receive your answer?

Desideria: He resumed his verbal sodomization.

I: You mean, he resumed making love with words.

Desideria: Yes. Slowly, as though he would have liked to slap me, leaving a pause between one slap and the next, he started talking: 'We are the daughter of a multimillionaire of the Parioli quarter, but we dress like a ragamuffin in a shapeless sweater and shabby cotton trousers. Thus dressed like a beggar, we go to see the multimillionaire mother's man of business, we waggle our bottom in front of his eyes and then ask him, as if in fun, for twenty million. To be drawn, of course, on her mother's account, thanks to her bottom and thanks to the power of attorney. Twenty million "to do good". But this good that you wish to do, my girl, I know what it is and have no difficulty in telling you. With those millions you want to do good, together with some group or other, to finance the so-called fight against the so-called bosses; in short, to start the so-called revolution. Don't deny this, you harlot – for that's what you are – don't deny it, because your clothes speak for you, your sweater, your trousers. All right then, but as for these millions, you must at least show, just to begin with, that you know how to deserve them.'

I: An obscure remark. What did he mean?

Desideria: Perhaps he didn't know that himself. He had lost his head; he was almost ready to pay twenty million for a few minutes of love-making; at the same time, he must have realized that it was too high a price; and perhaps he hoped to get everything without giving anything. Anyhow, he gave me to understand at once what he wanted, without much in the way of explanation.

I: In what way?

Desideria: Well, this was the way: still talking, he now rose to his feet, came up to me, and suddenly, making a dash, thrust his hand into my hair, grasped a big lock of it

150

in his fist, twisted it violently, making me almost cry out with pain, and compelled me to rise from the armchair. Meanwhile, he continued his sadistic speech, the verbal counterpart of the physical anal relationship. 'Get up now,' he said, 'don't say a single word, don't protest, don't breathe a word, you whore, whom I watched grow up under my eyes and, like an idiot, have respected because you were the daughter of the woman I loved, don't say a single word, otherwise I'll wring your neck; walk in front of me, go to the window again, look out as before, bend forward on the window-sill, yes, like that, lean well out, look in front of you, look at the petrol pump – isn't the pump beautiful, eh? isn't it beautiful? – and now thrust back your bottom, thrust it further back, thrust it back as far as you can and go on looking, yes, go on looking and go on thrusting out your bottom, yes, yes, yes, that's fine, like that, like that. And now open your legs, as far apart as you can, and go on looking at the lovely petrol pump – yes, like that; and now stand still, wait, stand still, bend forward and cry: 'Down with the revolution!''

I: Down with the revolution?

Desideria: Yes, that's what I heard him saying into my ear in a breathless voice, while, still holding me bent forward on the window-sill with that heavy hand twisting my hair in its fist and leaning on top of me with the whole of his body, he tried to pull down my trousers. Now, until that moment I had known nothing, absolutely nothing, of any revolution. It is true that the Voice, every now and then, came out with this word; but without explaining it, as though I already knew what it was all about, whereas in reality I was in the dark about the whole matter. In fact, I knew nothing of politics; but Tiberi, on the other hand, was convinced that I knew about all these things that he hated and feared, simply because I was dressed in a certain way, which in any case was the way generally adopted by boys and girls of my age. And so, to him, my sweater and trousers were like the banner of a hostile army. And he, in his sadistic manner, was making me deny this banner, sodomizing me and making me, at the same moment, cry: 'Down with the revolution.' Then, while I remained with my head bent forward and my bare bottom thrust out, my legs wide apart, my trousers fallen uncomfortably round my feet, and with that terrible hand forcing me to look down into the street, and his member, which he was meanwhile directing with the other hand, in search of the anal orifice between my contracted and stiffened buttocks, and the window-sill sawing into my chest, suddenly, hearing him bid me cry, 'Down with the revolution,' it came into my mind that, for the first time, I at last understood what the word 'revolution' meant, and that I owed this understanding not to the Voice, which never explained anything, but actually to him, the bourgeois conservative, the frightened sadist. Yes, it is to Tiberi that I owe my understanding of the true significance of the term 'revolution'.

I: By what means did he make you understand it?

Desideria: By doing again with me something he had already done with Viola.

I: What?

Desideria: D'you remember the remark he made to Viola, at the very moment when he was sodomizing her? 'Give me America.' He had asked me, on the other hand, at a similar moment, to cry, 'Down with the revolution.' Now, the two requests were identical. In both cases it was a question of 'putting it up the bottom', with Viola and with me. But Viola and I, at that moment, were two symbols, Viola of America and I of revolution. Which is as much as to say that, through Viola and me, Tiberi wanted to 'put it up the bottom' both with America and with revolution.

I: America? Why?

Desideria: Because America is powerful, and obviously he resented this power as a challenge, as a provocation.

I: Symbolism again, in fact, in the manner of the Voice.

Desideria: Yes, but with opposite aims. The Voice employed the symbolism of revolt, Tiberi that of conservation.

152

I: What was the result of this sudden illumination on your part?

Desideria: It was a lightning seizure of consciousness. While I was forced by Tiberi to remain with my head bent down towards the window-sill and was looking at the yellow and red petrol pump on the pavement opposite, beyond the wet, deserted asphalt, I remember that I thought, all of a sudden: Why, then I'm a revolutionary. This was a matter of a moment; then I asked the Voice what I ought to do and to my great relief, I heard it answer: 'Of course you must cry: "Long live the revolution!"' So then, in a subdued tone, as though talking to myself, and still looking at the petrol pump down in the street, I answered: 'Long live the revolution.'

I: And Tiberi?

Desideria: At the same moment, he could not contain himself any longer: desire was stronger than political hatred; he said nothing, but he bit my ear, not so much, one would have said, in order to hurt me as to keep me still, and almost at once he had an orgasm, but without penetration. I felt the warm, sticky flow of the sperm on my bare buttocks and tried to free myself, but he then grasped my ear with his teeth, emitting a low growl, just like an animal from which one seeks to snatch away another animal which it has just killed and which it is in process of devouring. I felt that if I moved again he was quite capable of really biting me, so I resigned myself to staying still, with him on top of me and that hand of his clutching my hair and keeping my head bent down over the window-sill, while the jerking movements of the orgasm followed each other rapidly and violently. In the end I felt him press against me for the last time; he let go of my ear and his feverish voice murmured: 'My love, stay still again, like that, I haven't had you yet, my love, stay still, my love, my love.'

I: He had changed his language, he was no longer sadistic.

Desideria: He had changed his language because he had changed his feeling. He had been sadistic as long as he had

153

wanted to make love; now he was tender because he was grateful to me for having allowed it.

I: What happened next?

Desideria: Tiberi detached himself from me and I still stayed for a moment in the position in which he had placed me in order to accomplish his sodomitic act: looking out of the window, with my trousers fallen down onto my feet and my bottom bare. Then, without turning round, I wiped myself as best I could with the tail of my chemise, stretched down, and pulled up first my pants and then my trousers, and fastened the belt: I did not want to turn round, I wanted to give Tiberi time to recover his composure. Finally, I did turn round. Tiberi was standing in the middle of the room, in precisely the position and the attitude in which I had seen him at the beginning of my visit; the only difference was a damp patch at the bottom of his double-breasted jacket. Then, without conviction and to please the Voice, more than anything, I said: 'Now you will give me my millions?'

I: Why without conviction?

Desideria: Because I had cried 'Long live the revolution,' instead of 'Down with the revolution'; and I was convinced that Tiberi would object that I had not kept to the agreement.

I: Is that what happened?

Desideria: No, strangely enough I was wrong about him, at least this time. He was looking at me and possibly because of the diminution of vitality that follows coitus, he appeared confused and humiliated. At last he said slowly: 'I could tell you that you don't deserve a single lira because you did not do what I asked you to do. On the other hand, I want to be sincere with you: you ask me something that I could not do for anybody, not even for a woman who was the mother of my children.' 'But that money is mine.' 'It doesn't matter, what you are asking of me is called stealing; and I prefer to break my word rather than to steal. An honourable professional man such as I claim to be does not steal.' 'Then you really don't wish to?' 'If I could do it, I would. But I cannot.' 'But you led me to understand that you

154

would do it if I showed you that I deserved it.' 'At certain moments one says all sorts of things.' 'You're a scoundrel, a turd, a coward.' He stretched out his arms and said with resignation: 'It may be so, but not a thief.' 'You can rely on never seeing me again. You disgust me.' 'If you want a little money – I mean, of course, my own money and not yours or Viola's – I can give it to you.'

I: What did you say?

Desideria: The Voice would have liked me to go away, slamming the door behind me. But I disobeyed it and asked, with sudden gentleness: 'How much can you give me?'

I: Why did you disobey the Voice?

Desideria: Because suddenly, at that moment when he refused to steal on my account, Tiberi appeared to me, if not entirely amiable, at any rate 'human'. Making *me* pay for the pleasure he had had with me was a manner of recognizing his humanity, of rewarding it.

I: Human, humanity: why?

Desideria: His profession is the point of greatest resistance in every man, and he, in resisting me on this point, had shown that he was no different from other men.

I: Did he give you the money?

Desideria: Yes, he put his hand into the inside pocket of his jacket and pulled out a little bundle of banknotes. 'This is a bundle of half a million in notes of fifty thousand,' he said; 'take these, they're neither Viola's nor yours, they're mine.'

I: Did you accept them?

Desideria: This time the Voice prevailed. It made me cry: 'What d'you want me to do with your filthy money?' As I said this, I took the bundle that he held out to me, broke the band, and threw the banknotes on the floor.

I: How did Tiberi react to your refusal?

Desideria: He didn't understand, he seemed surprised. Then, humbly and scrupulously, he went here and there bending down and picking up the notes scattered on the floor. He stood up, rearranged the notes in a single bundle, and placed them on the table; then he said: 'There is the

155

money. You asked me for it, now you don't want it, I don't know what you want: take it or leave it. I am going over there, I have things to do. You know the way out. If you want us to meet again, you have only to telephone me. Goodbye.'

I: He went out?

Desideria: Yes, he went out; by now he had recovered himself; upright and sure of himself, with the damp patch of sperm on his double-breasted jacket. He made a slight bow and left.

I: And you?

Desideria: I took the notes, put them in my bag, and then I too went away. When I was in the street, I looked up: Tiberi was standing at that same window on the sill of which, a short time before, he had made me lean during his love-making, and was looking at me. I waved to him, but he did not respond. Then I went off towards Piazza Cavour to find a taxi.

I: Why, in the end, did you take the notes?

Desideria: Because the Voice again changed its mind, as often happened. According to it, the part of the plan that concerned the desecration of money was concluded. I had proved to myself and to it that to me money was either nothing or was something other than money; I could now take Tiberi's banknotes without any scruples. In any case, the Voice concluded, the revolution had need not merely of twenty million, not only of half a million, but also of sums of a thousand lire.

I: Far-seeing and prudent, the Voice.

Desideria: Yes, like all fanatics. When I reached home, I put Tiberi's money in the same drawer in which I kept the knife I had threatened Diomira with, and also Viola's gold coins. For the moment I thought no more about it.

I: Did you go on seeing Tiberi?

Desideria: For some time I heard nothing of him. Then he decided to telephone me. He telephoned me several times, and every time I slammed down the receiver. Then one day, I remember, he telephoned me at a moment when

156

Viola was in my room. I said: 'Twenty or nothing,' alluding to the twenty million that he had refused to withdraw from Viola's account, and he remained silent, with a significant silence. So then I slammed down the receiver; Viola asked me who the person was who had telephoned me and what I had meant by that first remark: I answered: 'It's a joke between me and a boy friend.' Viola insisted on knowing what the joke was; I repeated: 'A joke with a boy friend. Nothing to do with you.'

I: Did Tiberi continue to telephone?

Desideria: No, he realized that there was nothing to be done on the telephone, and he changed his method. He took to waiting for me in his car, in the Parioli street where we lived. He knew exactly at what time I went out in the morning to go to school, so he placed himself a little farther down, around the bend in the street, with his car against the kerb, and waited for me there. I had to pass that way to catch the bus. When he saw me, he looked out of the window and called to me: 'Good morning, Desideria.' I pretended not to have heard him and went straight on, walking on the pavement at a normal pace. Then he would follow me slowly, in the car, and, like the first time, would start making love to me with words.

I: With words?

Desideria: Yes, uttering the worst obscenities that can be imagined, in that Roman bourgeois voice of his, well-brought-up, civil, traditional, never altering his usual drawling, good-natured tone.

I: What did he say to you?

Desideria: Why, I don't know. For instance: 'Come to my house, you whore, you affected slut, you harlot, you prostitute, come and give me your bottom again, come, I want to split your bottom with my big cock, I want to push my cock right up as far as your mouth, come and see me, you'll get down with your head on the sofa cushions and your bottom sticking up, and I'll push it into your bottom, I'll split your bottom open with my big cock, harlot's

157

daughter and harlot yourself, whore, prostitute, slut,' et cetera, et cetera.

I: In what tone of voice did he speak these words?

Desideria: In his usual voice, but with an undercurrent of tenderness, just like someone who is in love. Added to that, the desperate, passionate urgency of an unsatisfied and insatiable desire. He seemed like one possessed, for he spoke with an unchanging facial expression, without gestures, merely putting his head a little out of the window and being careful to regulate the pace of the car with mine. Sometimes he also made proposals that were, so to speak, practical. He said, for instance: 'Turn back, go back into the house, wait for me in the entrance hall. At this hour nobody goes out. We'll get into the lift, stop it between two floors, and you'll give me your bottom, whore that you are, and I'll shove it in standing up, well in, as far as it will go, and I'll pour it out inside you, then I'll set myself to rights, you'll pull up your trousers, and we'll go down into the hall again, and no one will be any the wiser. Come on, let's do that, come on, I have here in my pocket three hundred thousand lire, at the moment when I shove it into you I'll put it into your hand, come on, what's the matter, your bottom is well stretched by now, one cock more or less what does it matter? And you'll get three hundred thousand lire.'

I: A highly detailed programme.

Desideria: Yes, like all lovers he had already done several times in imagination the thing he had not yet succeeded in doing in reality.

I: Didn't you ever answer him, not even once?

Desideria: Yes, once the Voice said to me: 'Let's try and see whether he leaves off.' So I, obeying it as usual, stopped abruptly on the pavement. He also stopped, with a harsh screeching of his brakes. It was very early in the morning and there was nobody about; I looked to the right and left, then opened my skirt a little (it was one of those with a slit at the side, so that you could see the upper part of my thigh and the beginning of my buttock) and I gave myself a slap with the palm of my hand on my bare flesh,

158

saying: 'You see this? Let me have the twenty million and I'll give it to you.'

I: What did he do?

Desideria: He went red in the face, made as if to open the door, and make me get in. Then he thought better of it, started the car, and went off.

CHAPTER FOUR

I: So, in the end, you didn't really succeed in putting into action the desecration of money. Tiberi refused to withdraw the twenty million from Viola's bank account. But why twenty million and not a thousand lire? Had not the Voice always told you that the act of desecration was symbolic? If you had taken a thousand-lire note and wiped your behind with it, as you had already done for the desecration of culture with the page of Manzoni, surely money would have been properly desecrated, don't you think?

Desideria: The Voice explained to me that with money symbolism was impossible. Desecrating money meant desecrating a huge, a really huge sum of money. Money was quantitative not qualitative. A thousand lire, again according to the Voice, was not yet money; twenty million began to be.

I: In what way, according to the Voice, could twenty million be desecrated?

Desideria: By placing them at the service of revolution.

I: The Voice was now speaking freely about revolution.

Desideria: It spoke of nothing else.

I: What did it say about revolution?

Desideria: It said nothing, it simply said the word.

I: The word 'revolution'?

Desideria: Yes.

I: Without any further explanation?

Desideria: Without any explanation at all.

I: What was it? An obsession?

Desideria: Yes, something of the kind. It was always repeating remarks such as: 'You must become a revolutionary'; 'You must start a revolution'; 'The moment of revolu-

160

tion has come.' And so on. It was a word which acted in expectation of causing action.

I: What did you think of this word?

Desideria: I thought it was something irrational, fascinating, and obsessive.

I: But after all revolution doesn't start of its own accord. In what way, and with whom, did the Voice intend you to start a revolution?

Desideria: At this point other words began to intervene, words which formerly the Voice would never have mentioned to me, even though, no doubt, it already knew them and knew their meaning.

I: What words?

Desideria: For example, 'comrade'. For example, 'group'.

I: 'Comrade', 'group'? And did it tell you what they meant?

Desideria: No, as with the word 'revolution', it did not give any explanation. For it, at least so it seemed, the word was enough; later the thing would come of itself, without any explanations. In short, the word was the thing, and vice versa.

I: Here we have three words: 'revolution', 'comrade', and 'group'. The Voice at any rate organized them, connected them one with the other?

Desideria: Yes, certainly it connected them; for instance; in order to start a revolution I would have, together with other comrades, to form a revolutionary group. But the connection was not the result of any explanation; rather – how shall I say? – of the willpower that the Voice inspired in me with those three words.

I: The willpower?

Desideria: Yes, the willpower, in the sense of an obscure, consuming desire, that is, in the sense of something irresistible which comes not from the mind but from somewhere else.

I: From where?

Desideria: I don't know; from inside, from down below, perhaps even from the belly, from the sexual organs.

161

I: Did you have the willpower to start a revolution, the willpower to be a comrade, the willpower to form part of a group?

Desideria: Yes, it was more or less like that. With those three words, the Voice applied itself not so much to my mind as to another part of my body which I might even call the sex, if the willpower were localized only there. But it was a willpower diffused throughout my whole body, even if, fundamentally, it was physiological, sexual.

I: Diffused?

Desideria: In short, the Voice did not seek to persuade me but to make me feel.

I: To feel what?

Desideria: To feel revolution, to feel the fact of being a comrade, to feel the group.

I: And in what way did you feel them, these things?

Desideria: I don't know; let us say that it had given me an infatuation for revolution.

I: By now, then, the plan of transgression and desecration was abandoned. You had moved on to action, you were starting a revolution.

Desideria: No, on the contrary, the Voice wanted me to go right on to the end. As for revolution, I must, at least for the moment, limit myself to dreaming of it, to desiring it, to longing for it. As for the plan, on the other hand, I had to put it into action. And in fact the Voice now wanted me to desecrate human life as well.

I: What does it mean – desecrate human life? Kill somebody?

Desideria: Yes, or at least try to, seriously.

I: And you have tried?

Desideria: Since it was a question of an act that might have grave practical consequences, such as ending up in prison and staying there for many years, the Voice was satisfied that I should try, seriously of course; that is, that I should seriously have the intention. In fact, given the gravity of the desecration, it allowed me a symbolic margin that was wider than usual.

162

I: I understand. But if one knows in advance that the murder will be confined to mere intention, even if sincere, what becomes of the seriousness of the attempt? It is like an acrobat who performs a risky exercise with a net suspended below him; no one can believe that his life is really in danger; so in the end he is admired more for his ability than his courage.

Desideria: The comparison is just, but as often happens with comparisons, although it is just, it does not hold. In reality I wished, sincerely wished, to kill. Making use of the comparison again, it was as though the acrobat did not know that, beneath him, there was the net.

I: And who was the person selected for this sincere attempt at murder?

Desideria: Viola.

I: Quite logical, wasn't it?

Desideria: Why logical?

I: Because the murder of Viola, when all was said and done, was the true aim of the whole programme of transgression and desecration. The whole plan converged upon the physical suppression of your adoptive mother, adopted by the Voice as the living symbol of the hated bourgeoisie.

Desideria: Perhaps you're right. But things did not then go precisely in that way. I did not wish to kill Viola; I only wished to prove to myself that I was capable of it. Indeed, I did not hate Viola and I did not see in her what the Voice saw, that is, the living symbol of the bourgeoisie. Instead, the opposite happened during the attempt at desecration. I discovered that the Voice was right: Viola *was* the bourgeoisie and – even more important – I realized that she herself was conscious of it, that she knew it.

I: Conscious?

Desideria: Yes, Viola knew that she was the bourgeoisie. This was the discovery that I made on that occasion. She was conscious of it, even if, later, this consciousness remained inert and impotent. So, in the end, I found myself confronted by a person very different from the one I had previously imagined. A person who not merely justified the

163

hatred of the Voice; but also, at the same time, on my part, justified a return to former affection. Yes, Viola *was* the bourgeoisie, but the fact that she was conscious of it took from her that character of alienated, automatic social monster that she had hitherto borne in my eyes and made her, if not lovable, at any rate human.

I: Humanity again, as with Tiberi. And all this because you tried, even though without succeeding, to murder her?

Desideria: Yes.

I: The attempted murder brought you closer to one another?

Desideria: Not the attempt, but the sincerity of the attempt.

I: Always this sincerity.

Desideria: It was as if Viola had understood that I had wanted to kill her, as if she had thought that I was right to kill her, and in fact had desired that I should kill her.

I: Well, how did the Voice manage to bring you to the point of murder?

Desideria: Suddenly, without any preparation.

I: Suddenly?

Desideria: Yes, one evening, when I came in rather late from the local cinema, where I had gone with a girl friend, Viola announced to me that we had been invited to a party at the home of some people who had a villa on the Via Appia. In mad haste she explained to me that this was an 'important' invitation, that I 'absolutely must' come, that she would 'give me' five minutes to get dressed, that we 'must' be ready in not more than a quarter of an hour. She said all this breathlessly and half undressed, turning her back on me, standing in front of the cheval-glass, with her youthful back, as usual, in strange contrast to the mature image reflected in the glass. I answered her at once that I had no intention of going to her party; that I would stay at home and watch television. Viola was now running from one side of the room to the other looking for her dress, her shoes, her bag; meanwhile, she was explaining to me in a hard, didactic voice, just like an authoritarian, inflexible

164

mother, why these people were 'important'; why I 'absolutely must' go with her to the party. I replied with a shrug of the shoulders and made as if to go away; all at once, Viola was no longer the American mother, infatuated with social duties; she was the woman who loves and suffers from not being loved. In an anguished voice she asked me suddenly at least to accompany her in the car to the Via Appia and, later, to come and fetch her, because it was Saturday and the chauffeur had his day off and she was frightened of driving alone in the car on the Via Appia. Meanwhile, she was holding out her dress to me, begging me to help her slip it on. I said all right, I would go with her; I took the dress with both hands, slipped it over her head, and then pulled it down over her body, and inevitably, since it was a very tight and clinging dress, so that I had to smooth the folds over her hips and her legs, I touched her lightly with my fingers. Then, as if this casual, indifferent contact were intentional, deliberate, and caressing, she said to me in a low voice like a lament: 'Why aren't you more fond of me?' I answered her coldly that I *was* fond of her, that I had always been fond of her; she sighed, looked at herself almost coquettishly in the glass, then made a gesture typical of someone in love, taking my hand, raising it to her heart, and saying: 'D'you feel how it's beating? It's you who have this effect on me.' By way of a reply, I asked her whether she was ready; she said yes, took up her bag and her shawl, and we left the flat. In the lift she placed herself in front of the doors and, without turning, told me that I must come and fetch her at one o'clock. For some reason the Voice unexpectedly suggested that I should say something provoking to her, following its idea of flattering her and at the same time thwarting the usual oscillation towards maternal affection. So I said in a subdued voice: 'This dress suits you very well; apart from anything else, it shows off your best point.' 'And what is my best point, in your opinion?' I gave her a light slap on the buttocks, saying seriously: 'Your arse: that's your best point. If you know it, why d'you want to hear it said?' She shook her head and

165

replied: 'That's what you're like. You perhaps intended to say something nice to me, instead of which you said a rude word and gave me a smack on my behind.' In the midst of this skirmishing, the lift stopped at the ground floor and we went out into the street. Now, you must know that the garage was underground; it was at the bottom of a steep incline of cement, at the side of the building. I told Viola to wait for me at the gate and I myself went down the slope towards the garage. The roller-shutter was closed; I pulled it up and went into the garage, opened the door of the car, sat down at the wheel, put the key into the instrument panel, pressed my foot on the accelerator; the engine immediately started with a roar, followed by a rich, subdued metallic hum. I put it into bottom gear and the car started, went up the cement slope until it was right outside the garage; then I put on the hand brake, got out, and lowered the roller-shutter. Just at the moment when I was stooping to pull the shutter completely down, I looked up and caught sight, at the top, of Viola in evening dress, with her bag in her hand and her shawl over her arm, waiting for me beside one of the pillars of the gate – to be precise, the one on the left. Immediately the Voice said to me: 'Drive the car straight up the slope to within a metre or two of the gate, then swerve to the left, in such a way as to catch Viola with the wing.' It was a matter of an instant; and the Voice made use of that instant to warn me that, if I did not follow up its command, it would be the last time I should hear it. I said nothing; more dead than alive, I climbed back into the car, changed gear, pressed down the accelerator; the car went up the slope with increasing speed; at about one metre from the pillar I swerved to the left, felt the wing scrape against the stone of the pillar and then against something softer, Viola's leg. At once I stopped the car, pulled up the hand brake, and threw myself out.

I: Had you knocked her down?

Desideria: I had thrown her to the ground. I must say that, the moment I saw her, I was moved.

I: Why?

166

Desideria: She was on the ground, on her side, slightly bent over, with her face on the stone of the pavement. It had been drizzling and the pavement was muddy; Viola had her cheek pressed in the mud, she had her eyes wide open, staring, in fact, and she was groaning gently, like a beast in the slaughter-house as soon as it has been felled. Her black silk dress was muddied; the wing of the car had caught her on the thigh and there, in fact, the stuff appeared to be torn. I bent down and asked her whether she felt ill and whether she was able to get up; she answered in a very low voice: 'Leave me like this just for a moment; I still feel too ill.' So I did not touch her, but I was convinced it was not true that she felt ill, I thought she was staying there on the ground, with her face in the mud, in order to punish herself: in her, at that moment, the mother must have taken precedence over the lover. We remained like that, one of us standing and the other huddled on the ground, still and silent for quite a long time; I was looking at her, she did not move. Then she said in a very low voice: 'We can go now, help me.' So I took her by the arm and helped her to get to her feet. Then, with me supporting her and she walking with difficulty, one step at a time, we went back into the house and entered the lift. As soon as it started to rise, I said to her: 'I don't know how it happened, Mum, the car went to the left without my realizing it.' She raised her eyes towards me, her face confused and half dirtied with mud, and said softly and with difficulty: 'I don't know what your intention was, but in any case you don't need to justify yourself: it was my fault, I moved forward just as the car reached the gate.'

I: Intention? Then she had understood?

Desideria: Probably, yes. I said nothing; the lift stopped and we got out. She walked with an effort; I myself, rather than help her to walk, lifted her off the floor, holding her round the waist with one arm; so we reached her room and then I helped her to sit down on the bed, which she did with some difficulty and obvious pain. Then I busied myself in slipping off her tight, muddy dress from above, over her

167

head. She submitted, obediently; when I ordered her, she raised her arms and I took the dress completely off, pulling it away violently over the mass of her disordered hair. I threw the dress onto the armchair, knelt down and slipped off her tights; she herself, without my telling her, had taken off her brassière. She was naked now, sitting on the edge of the bed. She was bent nearly double, perhaps to conceal from me both her wrinkle-lined stomach and her flabby, pendulous bosom, and she looked up at me, as it were hopefully, as though I had undressed her not to help her but to make love to her. I told her dryly to lie down on the bed and helped her by lifting her legs, one after the other, by the feet. She did as she was told, then lay on her back on the bedcovers. Only the bedside lamp was lit. I asked her where it hurt her; she touched her right thigh, and I told her to lie on her side so that I could see; she did as I said, and then I saw that, from her knee right up to her hip, her thigh was reddened, scratched here and there, and with the surface as it were broken, with traces of blood beneath the skin, which had remained intact. Viola looked at me attentively while I was looking at her, then she said: 'You see what you've done to me?'; and I, standing beside the bed without saying a word, shook my head as if in sign of denial, as if to say: 'I haven't done anything to you; just a scratch.' But I could not manage to speak; then, suddenly, I became fully conscious of what had happened, or rather, of what the Voice had caused to happen. And I had a strange feeling, as it were of enormous relief at the fortunate result of a trial which might have been fatal.

I: Relief?

Desideria: Yes, I had come out of it cheaply. I had desecrated human life with homicidal sincerity and seriousness; but my good fortune had brought it about that I had not killed. The desecration had occurred inside me, with complete thoroughness and without after-effects; but in actual fact it had stopped symbolically at the scraping of the wing of a car against a leg. Such were my thoughts, and then I had – how shall I express it? – a sudden return of my former

168

affection for my adoptive mother, so unexpected and so afflicting that I could not help bursting into tears, with a bitterness and a violence that astonished me. I was in floods of tears, and as I wept, I stretched out my hand to place a timid caress on that long, reddish scratch on Viola's thigh. Then, with an effort, I said through my tears: 'It's nothing, Mum. Now I'll help you put on a dress, I'll dress myself too, and we'll go together to the party. It's nothing, just a graze. Now tell me what dress you want to put on and I'll go and fetch it out of the wardrobe.' I was crying; she gazed at me attentively; in the mean time, my hand, caressing her thigh, had reached up as far as her hip. Then, with surprising promptness, she seized it and, keeping firm hold of it on her thigh, she replied: 'I'm not going to the party now.' 'Why?' 'Because, in the first place, I don't think I'm capable of walking. And besides, I no longer have any wish to go.' 'Why haven't you any wish to go, you made such a fuss about going, you were pleased; it will certainly be a very lively party; why shouldn't you go? I swear that I should now like to go, too. Look, I'll go and fetch you the black velvet dress that suits you so well; I'll put on my red dress, your favourite, and we'll go and enjoy ourselves.' She was observing me as, hurriedly and rather haphazardly, I talked to try and convince her; she had an embarrassing expression of cold perplexity; finally, she said: 'Why, what d'you think? That I'm not aware of a whole lot of things?' 'Of what things, Mum?' 'All sorts of things. For instance, that parties are boring, absurd, intolerable. For instance, that while I was half naked and breathless and made you hurry, I was a ridiculous, foolish figure. For instance, that you looked at me as though you were looking at a madwoman. Of all these things I am perfectly conscious, and of a great many others, too. I know everything, do you understand, everything.' 'But what do you know, Mum? There is nothing to know.' 'I know everything, I tell you. I know that I am a person who is not worth anything, that I owe my appearance of existence to the fact of having a bank

169

account; I know that I shall never be a good mother or a good bourgeois lady; I know that what gives me the illusion of existing, apart from money, is being able to make love every time I want to and as much as I can, with men and women. I might even perhaps do it with animals – why not? Finally, I know perfectly well that I want to get you to make love with me and that I think I have a right to it because I bought you from your real mother and I cannot rid myself of the idea that you are an object belonging to me with which I can do whatever best pleases me.'

I: Very lucid, I should say. And you, how did you receive this species of confession?

Desideria: I asked her: 'If you know all these things and you don't like being as you are, why then don't you try to change?'

I: What did she say?

Desideria: She answered with an air that was unexpectedly melancholy: 'You know perfectly well that it is not possible to change. Besides, who says I don't like being as I am?'

I: Once again, very lucid.

Desideria: I looked at her, I must confess, with some astonishment. I had always considered her as a kind of monster entirely unconscious of her own monstrosity. And now, instead, I was discovering that she was fully conscious of her own situation, so desperate and yet so common, as a rich, lonely woman. But it must be a kind of consciousness, I went on to think, that was entirely powerless to modify the situation itself, even in the smallest degree. As if to confirm this reflection of mine, her eyes were lit up again with that ardent, impure flame that I knew so well; she went on pressing my hand on her hip; and she said in a subdued voice: 'Come here, sit here beside the bed.' I obeyed; and then she let go of my hand and stretched out her own hand to caress my face, saying: 'How beautiful you are, you know you're one of the most beautiful women I've ever known in my life?' Embarrassed, I lowered my eyes. I felt

170

her hand moving round my face, probing with her nails the pouting corners of my mouth, then encircling my chin with her caress, moving down my neck and very gradually slipping into the opening of my dress towards my chest. I took her hand gently and guided it back towards my shoulder; and she, at once, promptly replacing the physical with the verbal caress, went on: 'You're so beautiful that a short time ago I had a strange idea, while I was lying on the ground and you were standing in front of me, waiting for me to recover and looking at me. I imagined that you were the angel of death, and suddenly I was content to die by your hand. Yes, I was happy to have been run into by the car because it was you at the wheel, and you were so beautiful, so stupendously beautiful.'

I: What was this? A declaration of love?

Desideria: Yes, but complicated by the fact that Viola, as you know, alternated lesbian with maternal love and, somehow or other, nourished and reinforced the former with the latter. Indeed, she then added: 'I've so longed all my life to have a family, with a real daughter, a real home, a real education to impart, a real future to be lived with my little girl. I have so longed to be a woman like all other women. But I have not succeeded and, in the end, I have realized that all this fundamentally does not matter to me in the least, not in the very least, and I am only happy to be here with you who are so beautiful, and I only would like you to forget that I am your adoptive mother, that you should be conscious that there is no tie of blood between us and that henceforward we can be like two friends. Meanwhile, to prove that you want us to be friends, allow yourself to be caressed by me and caress me in turn, won't you?' She had now taken my hand again and was clasping it in hers. Then she raised it, carried it to her lips, kissed it, passed it across her cheek, and finally picked out the middle finger and put it in her mouth, sucking it and enveloping it with her tongue, as though imitating oral sex. I did not pull my hand away, but I said to her: 'If it gives

171

you pleasure, Mum, caress me then, there's no harm in a mother caressing her daughter, but not like that.' 'Why not like that? We are not in any way mother and daughter.' 'Then what are we?' 'We are two strangers who might become friends, even if you did try to kill me a short time ago.' 'It's not true, Mum, it was bad luck.' 'Well then, to prove to me that you're sorry and that you did not wish to kill me, kiss me here, here, and here.' She indicated to me, bit by bit, where she wanted to be kissed, and I stooped and touched with my lips the upper part of her thigh, from her knee up to her hip. You will ask me now why I obeyed her. My reply is that I was not obeying *her* but rather the Voice, which, for its own obscure reasons, wished me to encourage Viola's incestuous passion. My head stretched forward in a docile fashion, following her leg from the knee right up to the hip, then, still scattering little hurried, light kisses over the long, red scratch, it went down again towards her knee. At this point Viola must have thought that she could now persuade me to a bolder caress, for suddenly I felt her take hold of me by the back of the neck, as one does with a cat, and propel my mouth in the direction of her groin, of which the thick, black fleece was at this moment on a level with my eyes. Not without difficulty I freed myself with a jerk from her grasp, rose to my feet and said: 'Now I'm going to give you some whisky. You have had a really severe shock; tomorrow we'll call the doctor – provided you don't prefer me to call him now.' Viola replied in a bitter, disappointed voice: 'No, no doctor; if you don't want to caress me, all right, give me the whisky, but stay here with me while I drink it.' I said nothing but went to the other end of the room, opened a cabinet, took out the bottle of whisky and two glasses; then I went back towards the bed and said: 'All right, I'll drink with you. Only a little, however, because it disagrees with me.' I poured out the whisky, half a glass for Viola, a finger's breadth for myself. I gave her the glass and she took it eagerly, greedily raised it to her lips, and emptied it. She held out her glass again, and I filled it

172

again, three-quarters full this time. This also she drank hurriedly, with the manifest desire of getting drunk as quickly as possible; then, still looking fixedly at me in an obscurely embarrassing manner, held it out to me for the third time. She also emptied this third glass, with an effort pulled herself up to sit on the bed with her back against the head of the bed, and then frankly proposed to me: 'Why don't you sleep tonight with me?' I replied that, with that wound to her leg, she would have need of the whole of the bed; besides, I had to get up early to go to school. I saw her shake her head: 'Why don't you sleep with me? At Zermatt you slept with me, didn't you?' 'That was a different thing.' 'Why?' 'Because we had only one room.' 'Yes, but even so with a not very wide bed. You weren't aware of it, but there always came a moment during the night when you pressed up against me and embraced me closely. And I embraced you in turn and held my breath so as not to wake you and interrupt that embrace which gave me so much pleasure. During those nights you were my child again. I was your mother again. You were frightened at some dream you were having, and I held you close against me, as though to protect you.' 'Yes, but then it came to an end as it did.' 'What do you mean?' 'There's no harm in it, because we are not mother and daughter but two strangers who happen to live under the same roof. It came to an end when one night I dreamt you were touching me and I woke up and then realized that you were indeed touching me.' 'Who now wouldn't want there to be that relationship, so lovely and so healthy, of mother and daughter, between us?' 'But there is the truth, and you have forced me to tell it, with your insistence on asking me to sleep with you.' 'It's not the truth. The truth is different.' 'What is it?' Her eyes were shining in a new and so to speak naked manner, with a look somewhere between challenge and desire. 'The truth,' she said, 'is that we are mother and daughter, more mother and daughter than ever, and I love you just as much as, and even more than, if I had brought you into the world,

173

and at the same time I have fallen in love with you, but not as a stranger, rather as a perverted and unworthy mother who wants to make love with her daughter above all because she is her daughter.' 'I'm going away now; you're drunk and you don't know what you're saying.' 'I don't know what I'm saying? Look, I'm now going to touch myself in front of you, of my own accord; look at me, I'm doing it for you, you must look.' Suddenly she seized my hand again, with a nervous and authoritative force that surprised me; she put her other hand to her belly and proceeded at once to masturbate. I saw her palm flattened on her groin, then fumbling for a moment with a rapidity and expertise that seemed to denote long habit; then, as if having finally found what she was seeking, she plunged her index finger between her legs, while her thumb and middle finger remained outside, as though to delay the impetus of the masturbation. She began making an up-and-down movement with her arm, now plunging her hand forcibly inwards up to the wrist, now pulling it out almost entirely, now again fumbling deeply, and now readjusting her palm on her groin with renewed close contact; and all this with an air of curious impatience, as it were disdainful and hasty, as though she feared she would not be in time to achieve her orgasm before I freed myself from her other hand, which, with unchanging force, was holding me down against the bed. Meanwhile, she was looking up at me with a supplicating, and at the same time inebriated, expression; it appeared as if her attention was alternating between the voluptuous sensation of the masturbation and the anxious contemplation of my face. Finally, she must have felt that the orgasm was approaching, for she said suddenly: 'You wanted to kill me a short time ago, I know it, I'm certain of it. Well, kill me, yes, kill me, I'm not worthy to live, kill me, kill me, my love, my love, my love.' All at once I recollected that invocation: 'my love, my love, my love' had been previously heard by me when uttered by Tiberi, at the moment when he had ejaculated on top of me during his attempt at sodomization. This memory made me disobey

174

the Voice, which wanted me to be present at Viola's orgasm right to the end. With a wrench I freed myself from her hand and, followed by the feverish, imploring voice crying: 'Kill me, kill me,' I fled from the room.

Desideria: Now I must tell you of the last and supreme (for me at any rate) desecration, the desecration of sex. But before starting upon this last phase of the Plan, I wish to tell you of an episode which, in a way, was the introduction to it.

I: The introduction?

Desideria: Yes, because precisely on the eve of the desecration of sex, it so happened that I fell in love, and for the first time since it had made its appearance in my life, I seriously disobeyed the Voice.

I: What was it? It's almost as though, one fine day, Joan of Arc had replied to *her* Voice: 'No, I don't want to go on fighting against the English, I don't want to go on fighting for the King of France, I want to go home and make love with a young peasant of my village.'

Desideria: It was worse. It was as if Joan of Arc had fallen in love with an enemy, that is, to be precise, with an English soldier.

I: But in what sense did you disobey the Voice?

Desideria: I disobeyed it in two senses at the same time. First, in falling in love; and second, in falling in love with a bourgeois boy of my own neighbourhood.

I: How did the Voice react to your disobedience?

Desideria: It went away.

I: Where?

Desideria: Who knows where Voices go when they go away? It was certain that *my* Voice had really gone. It put into action the threat to abandon me which it made every time I seemed to hesitate to submit to its will. You will remember that this threat filled me with inexplicable, unspeakable terror, owing to which, as soon as there was any hint of it, I hastened to obey, whatever the thing it required

176

of me. Well, this time I overcame the terror and disobeyed. And then it went away.

I: What did the terror consist of?

Desideria: I was terrified at the idea of going back to what I had been before the appearance of the Voice – a piece of massive flesh even though endowed with frenzied physiological vitality.

I: Who was the man you fell in love with?

Desideria: A young man called Giorgio. He was a customer at the little bar in the quarter where our group used to gather.

I: What group?

Desideria: A group of boys and girls of my age, all of them living in the quarter.

I: What did you do in the bar?

Desideria: Nothing in particular. We used to meet there and chatter, make arrangements for going together to the cinema or on some expedition outside Rome or to some sporting event.

I: But were you really a friend of these boys and girls?

Desideria: I had one or two girl friends who went to my own school and with whom I went over our lessons; but I had no male friends. Giorgio was the first.

I: What was Giorgio like?

Desideria: What was he like? At that time he seemed to me extremely handsome. Now it seems to me that the definition which fits him better is that he had a face like a backside.

I: Why a face like a backside?

Desideria: Because the backside is the part of the body in which two apparently contradictory characteristics are united: perfection (the backside is often perfectly round or perfectly oval, with a colour that is also perfect, that is, of a uniform, even whiteness, without patches or sudden changes of colour), and lack of expression (the backside is a face lacking in the features which contribute to conveying expression, that is eyes, nose, mouth, et cetera). Giorgio, indeed, had a face like a backside. Otherwise, he was what

177

is called a handsome young man: blond, with pale-blue eyes, the strong neck and broad shoulders of an athlete, a well-developed chest, and firm, well-shaped legs. I recall that I especially liked his arms: muscular, with the muscles bathed in a sort of golden light, the gold of the hairs.

I: You were really in love with him?

Desideria: Not really, at least when I think back on it now. I had what may be called a physical infatuation for him; sex went to my head like a strong, bad wine and made me see things as they were not. At the same time there was in me a kind of return, in fact a backwash, of the masculine ideal, as I had thought amorously of it before the appearance of the Voice. It was above all this backward step which made the Voice lose its temper.

I: Masculine ideal?

Desideria: Yes, the type of man that seemed to me preferable to all others, before the appearance of the Voice.

I: What was he like, this type of man?

Desideria: Physically any sort of man between twenty and thirty, healthy, robust, and good-looking.

I: Healthy, robust, and good-looking. What was it then, the ideal of the sporting type of man?

Desideria: Let us say so. But the physical aspect, fundamentally, did not count; what counted was character.

I: And what did this character have to be?

Desideria: There are certain words which indicate that a given material, before being put on the market, has been subjected to treatment which has removed from it all toxicity and rendered it innocuous.

I: What words?

Desideria: For example: decaffeinated, denicotinized, disinfected, and so on.

I: Well, then?

Desideria: Well, the character of my ideal man must be like that.

I: Disinfected?

Desideria: Yes.

I: Of what germs?

178

Desideria: Of the germs of anxiety, of doubt, let us say.

I: But what made you realize that this ideal man had undergone treatment of this kind?

Desideria: The way of behaving that is called good breeding.

I: What d'you mean? Someone who did not act in a vulgar way, who did not use coarse language, et cetera, et cetera?

Desideria: Not exactly. It doesn't mean that good breeding today implies what once used to be called good manners. Times have changed. Good breeding today can perfectly well imply vulgar ways and coarse language.

I: Then what difference is there between good and bad breeding?

Desideria: It is, precisely, the fact that the well-bred person is disinfected, decaffeinated, denicotinized, while the ill-bred person is not.

I: But we had agreed that the fact of being disinfected was revealed by good breeding. Now you tell me that good breeding, in turn, is revealed by the fact of being disinfected. What is it? The snake which bites its own tail?

Desideria: Yes, that's how it is.

I: Let's go on. How did the disappearance of the Voice happen?

Desideria: It will seem strange to you, but it did not happen in a spectacular manner as its threat might have led one to expect. I simply realized, one day, that the Voice was no longer there.

I: In what way did you realize it?

Desideria: Giorgio and I were spending the time kissing and caressing and touching one another, in fact, doing the things that lovers do. I was excited all the time, as I told you, with my head full of sex; but even in the midst of this excitement I was aware of the presence of the Voice in a kind of mental reserve that came upon me, making me conclude that this was still not love; love was a different thing; this was an outlet of the senses. In short, the overflowing of that old masculine ideal of which I have spoken

179

to you had not yet taken place. Then, suddenly, I realized that I did not find any defect in Giorgio, that I saw him as being perfect, absolutely perfect, in every aspect. Giorgio seemed to me so lacking in defects that sometimes I found myself thinking: Let's see, let's pretend that he's not my boy friend but just some ordinary person; let's see, what objection can I have to him, what fault can I find in him?; and then I saw to my astonishment that I had no objections and no fault to find: he was good, intelligent, honest, able, well-bred, reasonable, sincere, loyal, perfect, in fact really perfect. Of course I did not conceal from the Voice my conviction that Giorgio was perfect; but it did not pay any attention to me, it seemed to wish to avoid the conversation, it was evasive or even silent. Until one day it burst forth in an unforeseen manner: 'Giorgio is perfect, that's fine; but you, alas, are not. And so, in order that both of you may be perfect, I'm going away. Yes, because your imperfection is due to my presence. Once I have gone away, you will be just as perfect as Giorgio, and so together you will make a perfect couple.' It was very calm, as it had never been on the other occasions when it had threatened to abandon me; I was wrong to mistake this calm for want of decision. I answered that it was not a question of my perfection but of Giorgio's. That it could perfectly well criticize Giorgio instead of going away. It could prove to me that I was mistaken, could point out the defects that I was incapable of seeing: I should be grateful, all the more so because Giorgio's perfection almost frightened me; it seemed to me, in some way, inhuman. The Voice replied to these words with a Sibylline remark: 'Why should I point out Giorgio's defects, considering that you are not capable of seeing them?' This happened, let us say, on a Monday. Next day, while I was in a car with Giorgio, and as usual, we were kissing, suddenly I felt, with great precision, that the Voice was no longer there; it had really carried out its threat and had abandoned me.

I: How did you come to be aware of this?

Desideria: Precisely in the way the Voice had foreseen

180

and predicted: not merely did I feel that Giorgio was perfect but, for the first time since I had been with him, I felt that I was perfect, too.

I: So what?

Desideria: That is, I felt – how shall I say? – that we were made for one another – isn't that what they say? And that his perfection was a faithful mirror in which mine was reflected, and vice versa.

I: Didn't you suffer from the absence of the Voice?

Desideria: Yes, I suffered very badly indeed.

I: How did you combine this suffering with your feeling of being perfect?

Desideria: I know it may seem extraordinary, but it was really like that: I felt perfect and at the same time I suffered from the absence of the Voice.

I: What kind of suffering was it?

Desideria: A suffering I had never felt before, like that of a terrible, insurmountable lack of security, comparable to that of a sleep-walker who wakes up suddenly and finds himself no longer in bed but in a corner of the room and gropes about in the dark and no longer recognizes the objects that surround him and feels an anguished sense of strangeness. Before the Voice, all I had done was to feel unhappy, but without in any way explaining my unhappiness to myself; now, on the other hand, this unhappiness assumed the aspect of a species of impotent, contemplative consciousness. It continually happened to me suddenly to stop thinking, in the middle of ordinary life, and to look round me and ask myself in alarm: 'Where am I? Who am I? Who is this man beside me in the car? Who is this woman sitting opposite me at table?' When there was the Voice, questions of this kind were impossible, I knew perfectly well who I was, who Viola was, who Giorgio was. But now my questions seemed to echo in a frightful void that repeated them *ad infinitum* without ever giving any reply. Or rather, in the end it was I myself who gave the reply: I was a holothurian, Viola was another holothurian, Giorgio was yet another, and so on.

181

I: The usual holothurians.

Desideria: Yes.

I: Haven't you ever tried to evoke the Voice? To call it back?

Desideria: Yes, when I remembered that I had heard it for the first time during masturbation, I tried several times to recall its presence by that means, but in vain. I went on titillating myself, stopping every now and again to listen, and then starting again, rather as one does with a car which one pushes for a short space and then stops abruptly so as to start the engine; but it served no purpose, the engine did not start. Inside me there was only silence.

I: What kind of silence?

Desideria: How can I describe it? A silence that was full, solid, massive, tightly crammed. As though the Voice had remained buried under an enormous, irremovable landslide.

I: How did you react to this feeling of absence and silence?

Desideria: I've already told you: by plunging more and more into sexual practices. I was excited all the time; but I knew that in the depths of this excitement there was desperation, and so, more and more often, it came about that I put the fundamental question to myself, the question that should never be put during love-making.

I: What question?

Desideria: 'What am I doing?'

I: One would think that you were not in love with this Giorgio of yours.

Desideria: Certainly I was not. But somehow or other I had reached an agreement with him such as can indeed exist between two people who do not criticize one another and who are reflected in one another's perfection.

I: Excuse the formal question: were you lovers or, as they say, engaged?

Desideria: We were engaged, I mean that we did everything, or almost everything, but not the main thing. To tell

182

the truth, I would willingly have given away my virginity, but Giorgio did not want that.

I: Why?

Desideria: He said he wished to respect me and to put off the complete sexual relationship until after marriage.

I: Had you decided to get married?

Desideria: Yes, as soon as he had taken his degree.

I: In what subject was he going to take his degree?

Desideria: In architecture.

I: Had you told Viola that you wanted to marry Giorgio?

Desideria: No.

I: Did Giorgio know that you were not Viola's daughter?

Desideria: Giorgio knew nothing about me.

I: You said you would have liked to give away your virginity. Why?

Desideria: Because this was one of the things that the Voice had always advised me not to do. To annoy it, to avenge myself for its disappearance. However, since Giorgio wanted me to arrive at marriage as a virgin, I found relief in kisses, caresses, contacts, et cetera. We used to go by car to some solitary place and kiss and caress one another for hours. I remember that my sex was always all benumbed and wet; I should have liked to make love all the time, day and night, partly in order to forget that the Voice had abandoned me. Meanwhile, between Giorgio and me, the discussion went on as to what we could and could not do in our love-making. He would have liked us to limit ourselves to kisses and caresses, above the waist, let us say; I, on the other hand, wanted at all costs to reach the stage of oral sex.

I: What sort of oral sex? On your part towards him, or on his part towards you? Or on both your parts to both of you?

Desideria: Do you mean whether I wanted him to kiss my sex, or whether I wanted to kiss his, or whether I wanted us both to kiss one another's, at the same time?

I: Yes.

183

Desideria: I did not wish to be kissed like that. I wished to be the one who kissed, I myself alone.

I: Why yourself only?

Desideria: Before doing it, I liked the idea of doing with one's mouth what one does with one's sex. Then, when I did it, I realized that for me oral sex was not a substitute for normal sex, but something else.

I: What was that?

Desideria: A prompt and rapid way of using my mouth to free myself from Giorgio, by extinguishing his desire, by castrating him.

I: Castrating him? How did you come to understand that?

Desideria: I became aware of it at once, the first time I overcame his moralistic resistance and succeeded in practising oral sex. It was in the car. Giorgio was willing and unwilling at the same time; in the end I threw myself upon him like a fury, with such an impetus that his opposition ceased and he let me do what I wanted. I bent down, pulled down the catch of the zip fastener, put my hand inside, and pulled out his penis and testicles all in a bunch; then I stooped and engulfed his member with such violence that I felt it reach almost into my throat. Then, while my head was going up and down, imitating the movement of the belly during coitus, I coldly asked myself whether I liked doing what I was doing, and I was forced to recognize that I was not feeling any appreciable sensation. I noticed that the penis was swollen, smooth, round, warm; I registered these feelings with precision, but that was all. And yet my head continued to go up and down and I strained my whole body towards the purpose I wanted to achieve: to provoke the orgasm, to make him ejaculate. Finally, he had the orgasm; a great gush of warm, sticky semen filled my mouth; once again I asked myself whether I liked it; and once again I had to admit that I did not feel any pleasant sensation but, on the contrary, if anything, a certain disgust. Motionless and with my mouth full of semen I waited until the jerking movements of the orgasm had exhausted them-

184

selves, then I felt distinctly that his member was no longer so swollen or so long but was softening and contracting; and then, to my surprise, I was conscious of feeling, for the first time, a kind of obscure satisfaction. I sat up, took a handkerchief out of my bag, and spat out the semen into it. As I was spitting, for some reason I looked up at Giorgio and saw him worn out, lying back in his seat, pale, exhausted, limp and deflated, like his penis, with his mouth half open and his eyes half closed; and from the sudden joy that I felt on seeing him so destroyed, I at last understood that, for me at least, the true pleasure of making love consisted in perceiving the effect of castration in the person of my lover. Yes, I was satisfied at having castrated him, even if only provisionally; and this was all the pleasure I derived from making love.

I: After that first time did you feel this sort of pleasure again?

Desideria: I felt it again, more and more strongly, it was a kind of vice: I made love orally; then, at the moment when I straightened up in order to spit out the semen, I contrived to throw a furtive look at Giorgio, and every time I again felt that strange, obscure satisfaction at seeing him exhausted, annihilated.

I: How did it all end up with Giorgio? After all, you didn't get married. And then what?

Desideria: The end came precisely because of, or rather on the occasion of, the oral love-making.

I: And how was that?

Desideria: Giorgio, at first, refused the oral sex for, as I said, moralistic reasons; but later he acquired a taste for it. So we did it more and more often, really almost every day. But we were not agreed with regard to the conclusion of this form of sexual relationship; I wanted to spit out the semen, he wanted me to swallow it.

I: Why?

Desideria: He said that, after all, oral sex was a substitute for normal sex; and so, in the same way that the semen, in normal sex, is swallowed up by the woman's belly, in

185

precisely the same way, substituting the mouth for the vagina, it should be swallowed by the stomach. And I am not saying that I would not have satisfied him. But semen disgusted me; I remember that once, unintentionally, I swallowed a little of it and I felt nauseated all day long.

I: But you did do it?

Desideria: One night we went to the cinema; then Giorgio accompanied me home; on the way he decided to stop amongst the shrubs and flower beds on the Foro Italico. I knew what he wanted: as soon as the car stopped I hastened to undo his trousers, to introduce my hand under his shirt, to pull out his member and take it in my mouth. At that same moment I heard Giorgio's voice saying to me: 'This time you must swallow it, if not, it's no go.' Incapable by this time of speaking, I nodded my head in agreement; but secretly I had decided not to satisfy him. Then I started this oral love-making with a violence redoubled by some kind of obscure rage; in a few seconds I caused the orgasm; suddenly I felt the usual gush of semen filling my mouth; I tightened my lips round his penis in such a way as to draw out all the sperm; then I sat up and prepared to spit out the whole lot on the floor, on the carpet of the car. But Giorgio was on the watch; when he saw me turn my head in the opposite direction to him, he quickly placed his hand over my mouth and started shouting into my ear: 'Swallow it down, swallow it down.' I shook my head in sign of refusal, but I was unable to spit now because he prevented me from doing so with that hand over my mouth. I heard him say to me again: 'If you really love me, you must swallow it down,' and then, all at once, I realized that I could not go on lying to him, as I had done hitherto, making out to him as an act of love what was in reality a secret, systematic death-wish. At the same time, suddenly, to my immense joy and in the most unexpected manner, I heard the Voice shouting like a mad thing: 'Vomit it over him, vomit it over him!'

I: So it had come back?

Desideria: Yes, it had come back. It had left me free to

186

see what there was at the bottom of Giorgio's perfection –
just like a good governess who knows that the best education comes from reality; and now it was with me again.

I: And what did you do? You obeyed it?

Desideria: Of course. Everything happened in an instant.
I tore myself violently away from Giorgio and had almost
immediately an attack of retching which filled my mouth
with a thick, warm, acid substance, a mixture of semen and
of partly digested food. Then I opened my mouth, bent
over towards him, and emptied everything I had in my
stomach over his trousers.

I: And what did he do?

Desideria: He gave a cry, pushed me away in a great
hurry, opened the door, and threw himself out. I saw him
go in front of the bonnet of the car, and look down at his
trousers in the light of the headlamps. He still had his penis
outside, soft and dangling and all plastered with vomit; his
face wore an expression of consternation and disgust. Then
he raised his eyes towards me and thus saw that I had seated
myself at the wheel and was on the point of starting the
car. He raised his hand as though to tell me to stop; but he
had to jump to one side since the car had started moving
and was on the point of running him over. I passed close
beside him, then drove at a great speed all the way to his
house, which was not far from my own home; I got out,
banged the door, and ran off homewards. In my mouth I
had the acid taste of the vomit, but I was happy; the Voice
had come back; and I had freed myself from Giorgio, my
perfect fiancé.

I: You disobeyed the Voice, you fell in love with a young man from Parioli, then you obeyed the Voice and vomited over him; what happened next?

Desideria: What happened was that everything was still to be done; I mean that the desecration of sex was still to be faced. Well, the Voice faced it.

I: In what way?

Desideria: In the simplest and most direct way. Who are the women who, practically at any hour of the day, desecrate sex? The prostitutes – isn't that so? I had therefore to prostitute myself or, at the least, to try and prostitute myself. Prostitutes prostitute themselves from necessity; I, on the other hand, would be doing it in order to put the Voice's plan into action. That's all.

I: That's all, yes indeed. Well, what did you do?

Desideria: I began thinking about it. My first idea, naturally, was to have recourse to Diomira. But I told myself that, after the fright I had given her with my knife, Diomira certainly would not want to have anything to do with me. Besides, I was in reality repelled by the idea of going back to that house of ill-fame: I had left my innocence there forever. So I decided to take as my model the common prostitutes, the street-walkers. I was urged to this choice by an obsessive longing for one particular aspect of this kind of prostitution.

I: What was that?

Desideria: It will seem strange to you, but my imagination had not been struck by the traditional characteristics, old as the world, of prostitution: the loud, tight dresses, the exhibition of the body, the techniques of enticement. No, what fascinated me was the fires that the street prostitutes light at their feet while they await the client who will take

188

them away in a car. Driving along certain suburban avenues, I chanced to see, here the figure of a woman standing in front of a fire whose flames trembled in the winter wind, there again a little pile of ashes and embers whose faint redness was dying on the deserted pavement. Sometimes I even slowed down the car to have a better look at these fires, so much so that it even happened that I was mistaken for one of these women and then followed almost all the way home by some determined driver.

I: Why did these fires fascinate you?

Desideria: I said to myself that the prostitutes lit these fires not merely to protect themselves from the cold, but also, and above all, to keep their own sexes warm. Like a beefsteak of red meat that should not be served cold, the part of their body that they put on sale should be offered, if not exactly ardent with passion, at any rate warmed by a reasonable semblance of wantonness. Otherwise, at the first contact, the client would realize all too well that he had bought not the whole, complete woman as he had hoped and as he deceived himself into thinking he had done, but merely the lifeless object of his own concupiscence. Furthermore, the dying fire on the deserted pavement gave me a waking dream of what was happening in some room or other in a third-rate hotel or modest flat at the very moment when the embers were blackening and disintegrating into ashes. In the same way as this fire, at that precise instant, it seemed to me that the amorous illusion of the client would be extinguished in his mind as he handed the agreed sum of money to the cold, exigent woman.

I: Curious reflections, indeed! Well then, in the end, what did you decide to do?

Desideria: I decided to go and take up my position, one evening, in an avenue frequented by street-walkers and their clients. The Voice explained to me that it was not necessary for me to make love with the client; it would be enough if I lit a fire, allowed myself to be approached, and perhaps even came to an agreement. I could even go so far as to get into the car, if my client had a polite appearance;

189

and then, under some sort of pretext, get out again without having done anything. Finally, if I really insisted on carrying out the experience to the very end, the Voice concluded, I could even do to my client what I had done so many times to Giorgio; castrate him with oral sex. It would suffice to get him to stop the car in that same avenue, a little way beyond the fire; everything would be finished quickly in a few minutes; and then the money that I should receive from it would guarantee that, for me at any rate, sex no longer had anything sacred about it. But the Voice, at this point, insisted upon the fire, which, in its judgement, sufficed to destroy the sacredness of sex. In fact, it said, in a didactic and educative tone, a woman can offer herself at the corner of an avenue and then make love and perhaps even get herself paid for erotism, even if it is a distorted and perverted erotism. But only the street-walker who wants to sell and resell her goods several times in the same night lights a fire between her feet and stands over it with legs apart in such a way that the heat of the flame rises up and thoroughly warms her private parts.

I: The Voice is always symbolical. But fire, once upon a time, was the symbol of virginity. The Vestals, virgins by antonomasia, had to keep it alight in perpetuity. For the Voice, on the other hand, fire became the symbol of prostitution.

Desideria: I told it exactly the same thing. I was fresh from my studies; I had read something about the Vestals in my book of Roman history that very year. D'you know what answer it gave me?

I: What?

Desideria: Every period has its Vestals and its sacred fire. We ourselves have the prostitutes and the fire on the pavement.

I: Come on, then, tell me how it went.

Desideria: One evening I went down into the street, slipped into Viola's little utility car, and drove to the end of the Viale di Tor di Quinto, a place where the humblest whores habitually took up their positions. I had noticed

190

that at the far end of this avenue, which is flanked by big plane trees, at the point where it turned at a right angle, there was an empty space where the prostitutes, who distributed themselves with their fires at a distance of every two or three plane trees, for some unknown reason never took up their positions. So I drove the car confidently towards the place previously studied and examined, parked it against a hedge of elder bushes, and prepared to light the sacrilegious fire, which I intended to make use of to desecrate sex.

I: Were you dressed in any special way for the occasion?

Desideria: The Voice had at first wanted me to go in my sweater and blue jeans like a young student; then, however, for some reason, it thought again and told me that I ought to put on an evening dress, or rather that type of shameless, tight evening dress which has always been the uniform of the prostitutes' army. This, however, raised a problem: I had no evening dresses, the Voice had made me dispose of them some time before. We debated the question, the Voice and I; then it was agreed that I should ask Viola for one of her dresses. I could have taken it out of the wardrobe without asking her at all, she would never have noticed; but it was part of the iconoclastic cruelty of the Voice to make me ask my adoptive mother for the dress that would serve me to attract men from the pavement.

I: What did you invent to Viola in order to get the dress?

Desideria: I told her that I would make use of it for a little party of boys and girls of the quarter. She believed it, though she was slightly surprised. She was even pleased at what she could not but consider a concession to the customary dress of our class. 'I'll give you my red dress,' she said, going immediately to the wardrobe; 'it may be a little short for you because you're taller than I am, but what does that matter? You have such pretty legs and it means that you'll show them.' I said nothing; I knew that such praise, with her, was a prelude, almost always, to awkward attempts, already regretted at parting, to give me

191

some kind of caress or to ask me to do the same. As she looked for the dress among the many others pressed together in the wardrobe, she went on: 'I'm pleased you should have understood at last that women ought to dress, first and foremost, as women, and, in the second place, to dress well, in such a way as to set off their beauty. Because, when all is said and done, women think about men far more than men think about women. And there is only one way of attracting a man: to put what pleases him right under his nose. What does please a man? Apart from a beautiful face, a beautiful body, above all a beautiful body. And what is the best way of putting this body under his nose? By dresses which, precisely, show it off. Sweaters and blue jeans are provoking for a short time, perhaps even for the precise reason that they don't let anything be seen, but in the end they become tiresome and confusing. And then one comes back to traditional dress. There it is, put it on at once, I want to see how it suits you.' I put it on, it was short for me, as I had foreseen. She took advantage of the dress to stroke my hips, with the excuse of pulling down the skirt and smoothing out the folds, and I let her do as she pleased. Then she drew back and clapped her hands with genuine joy. 'How well it suits you,' she said; 'really you seem a different person!' She looked at me, but now she seemed rather perplexed. Finally she said: 'There's something that doesn't go, and that's your pants. The dress is very tight and the pants show a little too much. Besides, without the pants, the hips and belly can breathe because the body is naked and free, without useless intimate garments,' et cetera, et cetera. The Voice was highly amused in pointing out to me that there was mighty little difference between these maternal recommendations and those of a professional procuress such as, for instance, Diomira. Without delay I put my two hands under the skirt, took off my pants and threw them haphazardly onto an armchair. Viola took the pants and plunged her face in them as if to kiss them. I pretended not to see, and crying: 'Goodbye, Mum, now I must really go,' I ran out of the house.

192

I: Dressed in red, you went to the Viale di Tor di Quinto, parked the car against a hedge of elder bushes, and got out. And then what did you do?

Desideria: I at once busied myself in lighting the mythical little fire of prostitution. At that point in the avenue there was a big heap of twigs and bits of paper and dead leaves. I took an armful of little dry branches and sheets of newspaper and carried it a little farther on, between the trunks of two plane trees. Then I fumbled in my bag and realized, alas, that I had neither matches nor lighter. A terrible rage came over me because, as I think I have made plain, I depended on the fire more than on any other element of this kind of profanatory rite. Without the fire, I felt, simply, that I could not do anything, I would have to put off the whole thing to another day.

I. You could have asked a passer-by for matches, couldn't you?

Desideria: In fact, that was what I decided to do. However, there followed something comic which only later on showed its serious side.

I: What was that?

Desideria: Desperate, and with the Voice showering reproofs upon me ('Fool, wretch, you will never be anything but a Parioli doll', et cetera, et cetera), I went on down the avenue and stopped the first car that came towards me. I must have looked very strange in that dress of Viola's which, in that place and in those circumstances, was obviously very different from and of too superior a quality to the street-walkers' rags; and indeed, from the big car that I had stopped there projected a head which looked at me with more curiosity than desire. I saw in a moment, with a sense of premonition, a face as of marble, like that of an archaic Greek statue, with black eyes that were clear and fixed as though made of obsidian, a straight, pointed nose, and a mouth with corners upward-turned, in a kind of involuntary, perpetual smile; then, as if I had not seen him and considered him to be a perfectly ordinary person, I said in an anxious voice: 'Please, have you any matches?' I was

193

out of breath, among other things, I had dirtied my skirt in transporting that bundle of sticks and papers. The driver looked at me for a moment in the way a statue does, that is to say, as if without seeing me, and then said, in the deep, guttural, vibrant voice of one who is oppressed by a sudden emotion: 'But what do you want matches for?' I answered impatiently: 'Why, to light a fire to warm myself by.' And he, still in that throaty, gurgling, strangled voice: 'But for the present at least you don't need a fire, since I'll take you in the car. Come on, get in and don't think about matches.' I was uneasy because, as I have said, I was counting on the fire both for its desecratory function, and because, with its symbolism, it would spare me erotic services which would otherwise be inevitable. So I replied stupidly: 'But I must light my fire.' In a reasonable tone, he said: 'You would have lit the fire to warm yourself while waiting for a client, wouldn't you? The client has arrived, it's me; and so, either you're not a whore, and tell me what you're doing in this neighbourhood, or if, on the other hand, you *are*, as everything leads one to suppose, what does the fire matter to you now? Come along, you shall light the fire when I bring you back here.' It was neither an objectionable nor a playful remark; there was not a shadow of irony in his voice. Without saying a word, partly because the Voice ordered me not to make any more objections, I walked round the car and got in beside him. He leaned across me to close the door, then pressed the accelerator, and the car moved gently. Driving slowly, almost at walking pace, he asked me: 'What is your name?' 'Desideria.' 'I'm called Erostrato. Well then, Desideria, how much do you ask?' 'Twenty thousand.' 'Twenty thousand, where?' 'What d'you mean, where?' 'In a car or in a room.' 'Twenty thousand in a car.' I had by now completely lost my head; in spite of the suggestions of the Voice, I was answering at random, profoundly troubled by some undefined presentiment. 'Twenty thousand in a car? You're expensive. And in a room how much do you ask?' 'I ask ... double.' 'Truly expensive. And if there is another person?' 'Another per-

194

son? What person?' 'I'm sorry, I meant to say another woman. How much do you want to make love with me and another woman?' Curiously enough, this question did not take the Voice unawares; it made me reply promptly: 'Then it would be once again double.' He was silent for a little, then he said slowly: 'Well, this evening I'm not organized. For this evening it will be only myself. But do you usually come here?' 'Yes.' 'One of these evenings I'll come and fetch you, I'll get you to meet a colleague of your own taste and then we'll go and make love, the three of us together. I'll give you twice the double. Is that all right?' 'All right by me.' 'But now, meanwhile, where shall we go? To an hotel? Or have you a room in this neighbourhood?' The car was moving slowly, following the same rhythm, one would have said, as our conversation. After a moment I answered, with an effort: 'Let's go to your place.' 'That's not possible.' 'Why?' 'Because I live in a boarding-house.' 'Well then, let me go, because I haven't a room and I can't go with you to an hotel because I'm a minor.' 'One moment – what's the hurry? – let's do this; I'll give you ten thousand lire extra and you'll take me to your home. You have a home, haven't you?' 'I told you to let me go.' 'Tell me whether you have a home to take me to.' 'I have a home but I don't take men there. Now will you let me go, yes or no?' 'Come on, let's do something in the car. We'll stop somewhere or other, I'll pull down the back of the seat, you'll let yourself be kissed *there*, and then I'll take you back to your fire. Is that all right? I'll give you ten thousand lire; that's no small amount, ten thousand lire for a kiss, even if it's not on the mouth.' 'Listen, if you don't let me go, I'll start screaming. You see that car over there, with the little blue lights on the roof. It's a police car; I'll scream and get you arrested.' This time he understood that I was being serious and he changed his tone: 'All right, I'll take you back to your car. For that is your little car against the hedge; don't say it isn't, I watched you while you were getting out of it. But before I leave you I want to tell you what I think about you.' 'Say what you like, as far as I'm

195

concerned, provided you let me go.' 'What I think about you is that you're not a whore, not the least bit. You're a girl of good family who, for reasons of her own of which I know nothing, wished for once to behave like a whore. Here you are; now you can go.'

I: He had understood everything.

Desideria: I should say he nearly had. I myself did not say a single word; my silence in some way confirmed the exactness of what he had supposed. I got out and ran to my little car. I saw he was continuing to drive up the avenue at the slow pace of a leisurely walk; I started off, went past him, then after a little I looked in the driving mirror and saw that he was following me, carefully keeping the same distance all the time between his car and mine. Then something happened that the Voice had not foreseen. I in turn started slowing down in such a way as to permit him to follow me. The Voice immediately became uneasy and encouraged me to go faster. I replied: 'I've had an idea. D'you know what I'm going to do now? I'm going to take him up to our flat, seeing that Viola is not there, and make love with him in Viola's room. Thus, at one stroke, you achieve the desecration of sex, of the family, of the family home, of the mother's room and of the parents' bed. What d'you say to it? Aren't you content now?'

I: A really complete programme. What did the Voice say?

Desideria: My idea was a failure. The Voice began shouting that this was too much for it to swallow; that I really liked this young man with the *homme fatal* look; that for me it was no longer a case of desecrating sex, but rather of an extremely bourgeois sudden infatuation, and so on. Yes, I had lost my head; I was behaving again like a hopelessly vulgar Parioli doll, and woe to me if I did not now drive fast and cause him to lose track of me. Then the unexpected thing happened; without hesitating I answered: 'Leave me, abandon me, but I shall do what I have decided to do.'

I: So now, for the second time, you placed yourself in

196

the position of being abandoned by the Voice, as had already happened with Giorgio.

Desideria: Yes, but this time I had a confused intuition that Erostrato, with his pallor, his emotional, guttural voice, his smiling face like that of an archaic statue, was someone very different from Giorgio. Someone for whom it was worthwhile to disobey the Voice.

I: Then the Voice was right. It was a sudden infatuation?

Desideria: The Voice was wrong, if by sudden infatuation it implied a sudden and complete falling in love. But it was right if it thought that Erostrato had made a particular impression upon me.

I: What sort of impression?

Desideria: A kind of presentiment that the thing between him and me would not come to an end there and then.

I: The thing? You mean love?

Desideria: I said the thing and not love. The thing – that is, the intercourse, the meeting, the relationship. Call it what you like, but don't call it love.

I: Very well: the thing. And it, the Voice, how did it take your disobedience?

Desideria: Curiously, it did not insist. All it did was to grumble in displeasure: 'So we're going to make love in your flat. But let it be a rapid affair without consequences, a token and nothing more.' 'What consequences d'you think there could be? Besides, who was it that wanted it, this desecration of sex? You or I?' Meanwhile, in the midst of this wrangling, I looked in the mirror and saw that he was following me closely. I drove along the whole of the Viale di Tor di Quinto, I crossed Piazzale Flaminio, I went up the Tiber embankment as far as the bridge opposite the obelisk of the Foro Italico, I crossed the bridge and started going up towards the Parioli quarter. He continued to follow me; and I felt a strong agitation, even though I knew it was not of love. I reached my own street, parked the car, and got out. He also parked, even though with some difficulty owing to the large size of his car; then he jumped out and came towards me. I waited for him on the threshold of

197

my door. As soon as he was close to me, I said to him:
'Let's go up to where I live.'

I: What did he say?

Desideria: In that deep, throaty voice, which for some
reason I liked so much, he asked: 'To do what?' I
answered quite simply: 'To do what whores do with their
clients, eh? By the way, have you the money? In my house
it will be fifty thousand lire.' I now preceded him across
the entrance hall, I myself tall and booted, in front of him,
small and dressed with all the correctness of a bourgeois
young man. We entered the lift; as I was shutting the doors,
he said: 'Do you really want to go on with this farce? Well
then, you must let me go down again at once, because I
haven't the fifty thousand lire.' 'How much have you?' 'I
have ten thousand lire altogether.' 'A Jaguar, and only ten
thousand lire in your pocket? And what would you have
done if I had accepted your proposal of twenty thousand
lire, there in the avenue?' 'I wouldn't have given you even
that much, because I had realized that you were not doing
it for money.' 'I admit there's another reason, but the money
is necessary just the same. Now listen, we'll manage it like
this: I will give you the fifty thousand lire; and I'll tell you
when and how you must give them to me. Thus, there won't
be any doubt that it is a token, neither more nor less.'

I: What does this mean? That you gave him the money
with which he had to pay you?

Desideria: Yes, it was a further idea on the part of the
Voice. So as to delude itself that I was keeping to the plan;
and so as not to admit that I was bringing him to the flat
because in some way I felt myself attracted by him.

I: Was Erostrato not astonished at your suggestion?

Desideria: No, not astonished, but certainly intrigued. In
an indefinable tone of perplexed complicity, he said: 'In
fact, you want to carry out this token affair at all costs. Very
well, all right as far as I'm concerned.'

I: What happened next?

Desideria: The lift stopped, we got out, and I took him
into the flat, saying in a low voice: 'Be quiet now, walk on

tiptoe, my mother's out but there are the servants.' I opened a door, pushed him into the passage, and led him into Viola's room. Pressing various switches, I turned on the bedside lamp, the one on the dressing-table and the one in the middle of the ceiling; then I announced to him: 'This is my mother's bedroom.' He gazed at me insistently, not in the least excited but, if anything, intrigued, as though he were faced with someone who, for unknown reasons, was behaving in an extravagant fashion. Then he asked: 'But haven't you a room of your own?' 'Yes, of course I have. But we're going to make love here.' 'Why?' I hesitated, then answered him in a light, evasive tone: 'Precisely because it's my mother's room.' 'Ah, I understand. And this is your mother?' He turned away from me and looked at the silver-framed photograph amongst the flagons and boxes on the dressing-table. In this photograph, which Viola had got Emilio to take, she and I were to be seen on a bare, rocky plain, leaning against a boulder, with the Matterhorn, all uneven and jagged, away beyond, remote against the sky. We were both of us wearing sports clothes suitable for the mountainous country, with ski-boots, thick woollen stockings, full knee-breeches, workman's blouses. I had my blouse unbuttoned over my chest; Viola was pressing against me, with her arm round my waist and her body twisted towards me in such a way that her hip clung to mine. Erostrato looked attentively at the photograph; he did not even turn round when I answered him that that was, in fact, my mother. Then he enquired: 'But where is your mother at this moment?' 'Don't worry, she went to a cocktail party a short time ago and she won't be back for a couple of hours.' 'And if by chance she came back earlier, how would you justify our presence in her room?' 'I wouldn't justify it, that's all.' 'Ah, I understand. But, d'you know, your mother's very attractive!' 'You think so? Her best point is her backside and you can't see it in that photograph.' He turned his back on me, looking at the photograph as though fascinated; I took my wallet out of my bag, pulled out a fifty thousand lire note, and said to

199

him brusquely: 'Well then, if you like, we can begin.' At last he turned: 'Begin what?' he asked. 'Begin what we came here for: to make love, in short.' To tell the truth, I expected that at these words he would throw himself upon me, for that was how I thought clients would behave with prostitutes; instead of which, he said, in his usual deep, vibrant voice: 'Clearly, for some reason I don't know, you want to act the part of a prostitute with me. So I'll tell you at once that prostitutes don't behave like this.' 'And how do they behave?' 'I may tell you that in the first place they do not take their clients into their mother's bedroom, except in a case of absolute necessity: they have the cult of the family, prostitutes do. Never mind, however. In any case, they undress, lie down on the bed, display themselves naked – in fact, they seek to excite the man.' 'But I don't wish to excite you, I merely want us to do something, as little as possible, and for you to pay me, or rather pretend to pay me, and then go away.' It was now the Voice that was making me speak in this brusque and disagreeable manner, for although I tried to reassure it, it had not yet given up its idea of a sudden infatuation. Erostrato's reply disconcerted me: 'As little as possible is equivalent, in our case, to nothing at all. So let us not do anything. This means that we now make an appointment, in two days' time, at the same hour and in the same place, and we'll pick up a whore that you like and make love, the three of us together. All right?' It was the same proposal, in a way mysterious, that he had made to me in the car; then, suddenly, as if evoked by a resemblance that did not seem to be casual, there came back into my mind, with all its attitudes and its colours, the picture which my eyes had registered once and for all: Viola naked and on all fours on the bed, Chantal naked, standing at the head of the bed, and Tiberi naked, on his feet behind Viola. This picture came between myself and Erostrato – just as an enormous, brightly coloured lorry might come between two people who were looking at one another from opposite pavements; it hid him from me for a moment; then it dissolved at these furious words from

200

the Voice: 'May I know what you are up to? Are you bewitched? Tell him you agree and let him go.' I shrugged my shoulders imperceptibly and once again I disobeyed. 'In two days' time,' I said, 'I don't know if I can. In the mean time, let's make love here, shan't we?' 'So you're quite determined to play the whore?' 'Yes, I'm set on it, even if it may seem crazy to you. But don't worry about me. In fact, behave as though I were the girl of good family that no doubt you think I am. What would you do with a girl like that?' 'I should make love, then I should say to her: "Introduce me to your mother." At least, then, I should be able to see you again without such a fuss.' 'All right, let's do it like that.' 'What, exactly?' 'You said it yourself, didn't you? We'll make love and then we'll go into the living room, I'll give you a drink, my mother will arrive, and I'll introduce you to her.' 'Perfect: you see how we understand one another, we two?' 'Now listen to me: I'll do everything you want. The only thing I ask of you is not to make normal love, because I am a virgin and I wish to remain a virgin. While we're making love, you must put into my hand that fifty thousand lire note folded in four. Then, when we're finished, we'll go and drink and I'll introduce you to my mother – all right?' I spoke these words with a persuasive humility proper to a woman quietly obsessed by a mysterious perversion of her own – which, according to all appearances, was what, at that moment, he thought I was. The Voice, in turn, cried: 'But why drink? Why introduce your mother to him?' And I replied to it dryly: 'What d'*you* want to know about it? Ask *him*.' Meanwhile, Erostrato had come close to me, had put his arm round my waist, lightly stroked my face; then he passed his hand over my neck, inserted it into the opening of my dress, and went on to feel my breasts – doing all the things, in fact, that a man does to a woman, even if she is a prostitute, before reaching the final embrace. Motionless and inert, I let him do as he wished, just as though I were one of those women I had taken as a model, a woman who, frozen by a long wait in the winter night, allows herself to be caressed without even

201

trying to simulate pleasure. Then he embraced me and, seeking my mouth with his, tried to kiss me. Again I let him do as he wished, but since the Voice shouted: 'Don't return his kiss, whores don't kiss their clients; woe to you if you return it,' my lips remained hermetically sealed beneath his. Then something unusual happened, unusual, I mean, in the comedy of prostitution that we were acting together. He said to me: 'Let's make love, then, but on one condition.' 'What is that?' 'That you will then tell me why you wanted to act the part of a street-walker and why you wished us to make love in your mother's bedroom.' 'All right, I'll tell you all you want.' Once again the Voice started shouting that this was not an encounter between a prostitute and her client, but between a girl who was in love and her lover; but I calmed it down by promising that in no circumstances would I speak of *it* and of our plan of transgression and desecration. In any case, the Voice was now powerless: it had wished me to carry out the plan to the point of prostituting myself; I had obeyed it; there was now nothing left for it but to accept that I should do things my own way, or rather, in the way of the client with whom chance had put me in contact.

I: Why? Was it a special way?

Desideria: Listen a moment. Erostrato, then, standing close against me, was caressing me for some time over my whole body, and I let him do as he wished. His hand lifted Viola's dress, and he discovered that underneath, as my adoptive mother had wisely advised me, I was naked. He paused for a moment at my loins, came forward again, stroked first one breast, then the other, pressed his hand down to my groin, and then went down between my legs . . .

I: Why do you describe the movements of his hand so minutely to me?

Desideria: To convey to you the impression of my perplexity or, if you like, of my curiosity. His insistent allusion to three-sided sex reminded me of the scene I had witnessed involuntarily in Viola's room. This recollection and that of Tiberi's sodomitic obsession had made me think that every

202

man (and of course every woman, too) had an erotic language of his own from which he could not escape and which could not vary in any circumstances, any more than his native language could vary. So I was now wondering what Erostrato's language towards me was, and to what exact, original communication the vague, casual caress of his hand was the insignificant introduction.

I: What happened next?

Desideria: I was standing up, pressed against him, my dress raised up in front and falling back behind against my calves; I felt upset and embarrassed, so I put out both hands as though to pull up my skirt and undress completely. But he gently stopped me and then, pushing me gradually, made me retreat to the bed and fall upon it flat on my back. I was afraid he might have forgotten my warning, so I said to him: 'Remember I'm a virgin and I want to remain a virgin.' He answered, with lowered head: 'Don't worry.' Reassured, I turned my head to one side and watched him with curiosity while he busied himself over me to prepare me for love-making, with movements that were rapid and precise and filled with a curious air of devotion, just like a priest hastily preparing an improvised altar before using it to celebrate a rite.

I: A rite?

Desideria: It really was a case of a rite; I understood this not merely from the reverence of the gestures with which he settled me but also from the fact that when, finally, he had arranged me quite naked from the waist downwards, with my dress carefully folded back over my belly and my legs well apart, he knelt down in front of me and, for a moment which seemed to me interminable, devoted himself to a kind of almost religious contemplation.

I: Contemplation?

Desideria: Yes, so much so that for a moment I expected that he would join his hands and start praying, like one of the faithful in front of the symbol of his own religion.

I: But what religion? I mean, in what way was what you

203

call religion different from the analogous religion of, let us say, Tiberi?

Desideria: Oh, it was really a very different religion. Tiberi was like someone who, in front of a closed door, tries to break it down in order to enter the house, bring devastation to it, and then leave it as quickly as possible. Erostrato, on the other hand, wished only to knock at the door, hoping that it would be opened to him, and deluded himself that he would be able to stay in the house for good.

I: This metaphor of the house remains obscure to me. What actually happened?

Desideria: He contemplated me for a long time, then, as though overtaken by giddiness, he very slowly bent forward, lowered his head, and gradually stooped towards my lap. But the slowness of his movement deceived me as to the nature of the giddiness that started it. I was expecting a gentle, gradual contact; instead, all of a sudden, the gentleness turned into fury; his forehead banged hard against the bone of my groin, with an angry, impotent violence, as of one who knows in advance that his desire is not going to be satisfied.

I: And then?

Desideria: Usually, in oral sex, only one of the lovers experiences the physical pleasure directly and corporeally; the other derives his enjoyment from the consciousness of causing his companion's pleasure. But in the case of Erostrato and myself, as I realized almost at once, this was not so. I felt that Erostrato was not seeking his own pleasure, even through mine and by means of mine, but something else which I could not succeed in defining.

I: Try and define it.

Desideria: Something obscure and painful, desperate and impossible. Then he, still without interrupting the kiss, started groaning with a strange lament, as though with a just and deeply felt desire which one knows, nevertheless, cannot be satisfied. And then, at last, I understood.

I: What did you understand?

Desideria: I understand that he was groaning like some

204

one who finds himself exposed to cold, to fear, to discomfort and solitude, and who knocks at a door and it is not opened to him. He wished to penetrate inside me, not in the way of a lover but as a new-born infant would penetrate or rather would re-enter, if that were possible, an infant who refused to live and desired to go back again into his mother's womb and to retrogress through the whole series of transformations through which he passed before being born, until he again became an embryo, a germ, nothing. As I have already said, this significance flashed across me when, after he had banged his forehead against my groin – like one who knocks frantically at a door that remains closed – he started groaning. In fact, it was not really a groan of pleasure, even if indirect and distorted, but a lament of mournful longing, of pining aspiration.

I: Longing, aspiration, for what?

Desideria: Longing for the time when he had not yet been expelled from his mother's womb, aspiration to re-enter it.

I: Did you have these thoughts at that moment or did you have them afterwards?

Desideria: I felt them at that moment and explained them to myself later.

I: But were you not feeling a pleasure too acute for you to be enabled to register your feelings with such exactness?

Desideria: I did not feel any pleasure, either acute or anything else, because I had decided not to receive it. But the pleasure of understanding Erastrato – that pleasure I certainly did feel.

I: What kind of pleasure was that?

Desideria: Try and understand me, on your side. Erostrato did really want to enter into me, through the very narrow orifice of my vagina, to enter, whole and complete, into my belly, to curl himself up inside in the foetal position and remain there for ever. That is, he wanted to flee from the world in which he found himself living since the day when he had been thrown out into it and abandoned by the very person who ought to have protected him and preserved him in the comfort of her own bosom. This wish for retro-

205

gression was at the same time, in a contradictory way, both desperate and full of hope. He knew perfectly well that it was impossible to retrogress to pre-natal nothingness; but I felt with precise certainty that, though he was conscious of this impossibility, he nourished the mad hope that the miracle would suddenly take place: suddenly my sex would open sufficiently to allow him to introduce himself into my womb and he would move backwards, through successive transformations, towards darkness and nothingness, by the same road that he had followed to come out into the light.

I: An unusual interpretation of oral sex.

Desideria: An interpretation confirmed by what happened next. At the very moment when I was on the point of having an orgasm, he slipped into my hand, folded in four, the fifty thousand lire note which I had lent him so that he might pretend to pay me. Then I realized all at once that this note, owing to his desperate wish for retrogression, was instantaneously transformed from the fee for the meretricious loan into the toll for crossing the threshold of the vast world, dark and protected, from which his mother, in bringing him into the world, had unconsciously expelled him.

I: What does all this mean? What was it, in your opinion: a refusal to live?

Desideria: Yes, let us say so; he no longer wanted to exist; and at that moment he turned to me so that I might cause him to escape from existence as quickly as possible and definitively. Then, while he redoubled his efforts as though hoping that his desire might be accomplished, I finally had an orgasm and I screamed like a woman giving birth in pain. Except that women bring their child, as they say, to the light; whereas to me it seemed that I was taking this child away from the light in order to restore him to darkness. It was a scream, in fact, that was in some way maternal; but that of a mother whose child has asked not to be born but to die.

I: A funereal sensation, wasn't it?

Desideria: I would say, rather, that it was an affectionate

206

sensation, as of one who receives a prayer and would like to grant it.

I: And then?

Desideria: And then we stayed for some time just as we were: I lying on my back with my legs apart, and he, kneeling, with his face on my sex. The first to recover was myself; he seemed incapable of it, he looked as if he were sunk in the disappointment of not having succeeded, in spite of his desperate efforts, in entering into me and staying there, whole and complete, for ever. I was still clasping the banknote in the palm of my hand, then I opened my hand and dropped it on the floor. I stretched out my arm so as lightly to push back Erostrato's head. Then, as though this gesture had finally confirmed that it was impossible for me to satisfy him, he rose to his feet and went and sat in front of me, on the stool from the dressing table. His face was reddened on the chin and round the mouth from rubbing against my pubic hair; otherwise, he appeared to have recovered his usual archaic statue-like expression, lucid, inhuman, and involuntarily smiling. I passed in front of him and went and shut myself in the bathroom. I washed in a great hurry, put on a dressing-gown of Viola's, and went back into the bedroom. He had remained as I had left him, seated on the dressing-table stool. He had lit a cigarette and was smoking. As I entered, he bent down to pick up the fifty thousand lire note off the floor and handed it to me between two fingers, saying: 'Here, this money is yours.'

I: And you?

Desideria: I was struck by the manner in which he handed me the note, as though unwillingly and in response to a half-hearted duty. And so, almost without thinking, I answered: 'Keep it yourself; after all, I wasn't capable of giving you what you asked for.'

I: Did he accept the note?

Desideria: Without any hesitation he put it in his pocket. Saying that he accepted it even though he did not understand the reason I gave it to him.

I: Pretty cool, eh?

207

Desideria: Cool, certainly. But it was also a way of carrying on the relationship between us, which otherwise would necessarily have been already at an end. And indeed I asked him in return: 'Can't you imagine why I've given it to you?' I saw him shake his head, not however from right to left but up and down – a manner of saying 'no' of which I understood the origin later, when I knew that he was a Sicilian. Then I resumed: 'You don't understand? You wanted something from me that I was not capable of giving you. On your side, however, you did what I asked you to do. Now you would like me to tell you what it was you wanted of me; you must know it, seeing that you asked for it with such great insistence. Anyhow, here it is: what you wanted from me was that I should make you retrace, backwards, the path that you followed to be born; to go back to being what you were before coming into the world; to go back to the nothingness that you were, that we have all been, before we existed. Do you understand?'

I: Had he understood?

Desideria: No, nor did it seem to me that he really wished to understand. Actually he seemed content to have fifty thousand lire more in his pocket; apart from that, as far as one could judge from his attitude of puzzled superiority, I believe he considered me, if not positively mad, at any rate seriously disturbed. Furthermore, I myself began gradually to get a clearer idea of him; or rather, of the things that I could say to him with the certainty of being understood and of those things which, on the other hand, it was quite useless for me to say to him, inasmuch as he would not have understood them.

I: What was the idea that you were forming of him?

Desideria: Perhaps I had been misled by his big, luxurious car, his way of dressing, which was sober and not without elegance. I had thought that he was a student or a young professional man, but one detail made me change my mind.

I: What detail?

Desideria: It was at that moment when I explained to

him that in reality what he wanted was to go back into his mother's womb. Obviously he did not understand what I was saying; but to give himself some dignity he raised the hand that held the cigarette to his lips. Then I understood something which the coolness with which he had pocketed the banknote of fifty thousand lire ought to have made me already suspect.

I: What was that?

Desideria: His hand was smooth, without knots or wrinkles or hairs, with rather short, tapering fingers, and oval nails that were almost white against the darker background of the skin. His forefinger and middle finger were yellow with nicotine. A gold ring with interlaced initials engraved on it, seeming to suggest the crest of a noble family, was on his fourth finger. All of a sudden, looking at this hand, I realized why he did not understand me and could not understand me.

I: Why? What sort of hand was it?

Desideria: It was the hand not so much of a bourgeois as of a proletarian superficially become bourgeois and therefore rendered fatally vulgar by the process. This hand, together with the car and the ease with which he had pocketed the money, suggested the idea of somebody who lived above his own means thanks to unexplained expedients.

I: What do you mean? That he might be a man who gets himself kept by women?

Desideria: According to the Voice, that is exactly what he was. But perhaps I haven't explained myself properly. What he lived on and what profession he followed did not matter to me fundamentally. I merely felt that he could not understand me because he was vulgar and that this vulgarity was due precisely to his hybrid nature, neither bourgeois nor proletarian, even though superficially it might seem both one and the other.

I: What, to you, is vulgarity?

Desideria: I should say, a form of intellectual impotence,

209

but without awareness and with a pretence of not being impotent – on the contrary.

I: In short, let me reassume: he did not understand you because he was powerless to understand; he was powerless to understand because he was vulgar; he was vulgar because he was hybrid, neither truly bourgeois nor truly proletarian: isn't that so?

Desideria: Yes, that is so.

I: How did he react to the allusion to his way of having oral sex?

Desideria: After he had taken in a mouthful of smoke and puffed it out again through his nostrils, he said slowly, in a curious tone, as though he were hesitating between showing himself offended or flattered: 'Explain to me more clearly what it means to retrogress ... how did you say?' 'I said: "retrogress into pre-natal nothingness."' 'Yes, exactly. What did you mean by those words?' Then I looked him straight in the face and said brutally: 'It means that, in my opinion, at that moment you wished to die.' He gave me a doubtful look, more offended now than flattered. Slowly he pronounced: 'I wished to die? But it's not true, I like to live, I want to live, what's this idea that I wished to die?'

I: He was offended?

Desideria: Yes, he was offended because he didn't understand; and because, at the same time, he understood that not understanding was, on his part, a sign of inferiority. I guessed all this and acted with him as one acts with inferior people in similar circumstances.

I: And how was that?

Desideria: I beat a retreat; I didn't persist in trying to make him understand; I gave a false explanation that did not offend his personal pride. 'I'm sorry,' I said, 'I didn't explain myself clearly. I didn't say that you always wanted to die, when you make love in that way; I only said that you wanted to at that moment, and that probably because it pleased you too much, it pleased you, as they say, to death. Is everything clear now?'

I: A fine lie. How did he take it?

Desideria: Very well. Reassured, he said: 'Ah yes, it's clear now. For me the greatest pleasure is to make love in that way. Yes, you're right, for a moment when I felt you were on the point of coming and your belly was going up and down more and more hurriedly and you were clasping my head tightly between your thighs and almost suffocating me, it seemed to me then that I should have liked to die – that is, that it would have given me pleasure to lose my senses together with you, at the precise moment when you came. To die together, that's what I should have liked.'

I: But wasn't he saying, fundamentally the same thing that you had wanted to say?

Desideria: Partly yes, but only partly. Now he was reassured and he looked at me with affection. Then the Voice said to me: 'Make him talk about himself, and then you'll be able to discover that he is a shady individual, a cheat, an adventurer.'

I: I seem to gather that the Voice did not much care for him.

Desideria: I don't know if it really disliked him. In any case, it did not wish me to fall in love with him.

I: But did you feel that you might have been able to fall in love?

Desideria: Absolutely not. However, I felt an affectionate, fraternal interest in him.

I: Fraternal?

Desideria: Yes, weren't we both of us of proletarian origin? Weren't we both of us badly adjusted to bourgeois society?

I: Yes, but you were conscious of it and wished to go back to your origins. He, on the other hand, at least as far as I seem to understand, disowned his proletarian origin and sought to hide it from himself and others.

Desideria: That's true; and in fact the Voice thought so too, and kept repeating to me: 'Why do you waste time with a type like that? You paid him for the service he rendered you; now kick him out.'

211

I: What did you feel?

Desideria: Try and understand me. I felt for him nothing that even remotely resembled an amorous feeling. There had been, it is true, the orgasm, but without abandonment and without real pleasure. Now, however, when the Voice advised me to send him away because I had paid him and he was of no further use to me, I did not feel like obeying it.

I: Why?

Desideria: I've already told you: because of some kind of strange, deep feeling that we resembled one another.

I: What then?

Desideria: Then, under a sudden impulse, I asked him who his father and mother were.

I: Why?

Desideria: Because it was the same question that had tormented me ever since the moment when I had discovered that I was not Viola's daughter. I had become aware that I did not belong to Viola's world, or rather, the Voice had made me aware of it, thanks to this discovery. Now I wanted to see whether there was the same awareness in him, too.

I: What did he answer?

Desideria: I noticed him hesitate, and, for a moment, I hoped very much that he would say to me: 'I'm the son of poor people; my father's a school caretaker and my mother a nurse.'

I: Was that the truth about his parents?

Desideria: Yes, as I learned afterwards.

I: And this truth – did he tell it?

Desideria: Naturally not. Otherwise, what would happen to his vulgarity? He took his time and then answered in a resentful, impatient tone: 'What does it matter to you to know who my father and mother are? Anyhow, here you are: my father is a baron, he's a Sicilian and a landowner: a despicable, extravagant man who has never done anything good in his life, either to himself or to anybody else; my mother is the daughter of a lawyer, she had a good dowry, my father married her for her money although she was

212

older than he; he made her produce four children and then he lost interest in her. Now she's an elderly, retired woman who lives for her family and goes to Mass every morning. Now are you content?'

I: This seems to me rather detailed news, as of people who really exist.

Desideria: They did in fact exist, but they were not his parents. They were the principal family of the provincial town in Sicily where his father worked as caretaker and his mother as a nurse. Liars of Erostrato's type do not go too far with their lies, partly because, at the origin of the lie, there is always something which is not entirely imagination.

I: For instance?

Desideria: For instance, to have desired, when he was a child, that 'those people' were his parents.

I: What next?

Desideria: Then I went on questioning him and he went on lying. I asked him: 'But you've studied, you've taken a degree?' and he said: 'I studied at Palermo and took my degree in Rome.' 'In what subject?' 'In economics.' 'And what do you do?' 'My father wanted me to go back to Sicily to help him administer our property. But I've no desire to bury myself in the provinces.' 'But he supports you?' 'In a sort of way; he pays my boarding-house bills.' 'However, you have a big, expensive car, a Jaguar.' 'It's an old box, I got it cheap, a bargain.' 'But what do you do, then?' 'In what sense?' 'You say that what your father sends you is not enough. So you must, somehow or other, earn the money you need.' 'Yes, I work in the cinema, I write scenarios.' 'What d'you mean by scenarios?' 'They're scripts for the making of the film. On one side you write the movements of the actors and the movements of the camera, on the other the dialogue.' 'And d'you earn much with your scenarios?' 'That depends.' 'Depends on what?' 'Depends on the production; there are expensive productions and there are cheap productions.'

I: Was this all lies?

Desideria: Almost all. But these lies allowed me to discern the reality of the man, what he really was.

I: The lie would be the truth?

Desideria: The lie is not truth but reality, that is so. The liar tells lies, but he is real. What I desired, more than to know the truth, was that Erostrato should be himself, should be, in fact, real.

I: Why?

Desideria: Because of an obscure, affectionate, fraternal compassion towards someone who was like me even though less fortunate.

I: Well, what happened now?

Desideria: I put a great many more questions to him about his family, his childhood, his adolescence, his studies, and so on. He answered without impatience and with a calm to which the deep, vibrant, guttural tone of his voice, the stillness of his black, clear eyes, and the emotional quivering of his curling nostrils added something authentic and some sign of past suffering. And so then I, faced with this mingling of untruth and authenticity, could not help recognizing once again that he was telling me the truth, or rather, *his* truth.

I: But what was it that made you think he was lying to you? After all, you had known him for barely an hour or two, you knew nothing about him.

Desideria: What made me think so, as I have already told you, was the vulgarity of the hand which he raised to his mouth every now and then in order to breathe in the smoke of his cigarette. I was looking with so much attention at this hand that he noticed it and asked me why I was looking at it like that. I replied hurriedly with the first thing that came into my head: 'I was looking at your ring.' 'It was given to me by somebody who was fond of me.' 'Will you let me look at it?' Without speaking, he took it off and handed it to me. It was of gold, very massive and heavy; on it were engraved, intertwined, the letters E.O., which he hastened to explain: they stood for Erostrato Occhipinti. Inside the ring I read the inscription: *To Eros,*

214

Aurora. Handing it back to him, I asked: 'Who is Aurora?'
'I've already told you: a person who was fond of me.' 'And
she calls you Eros?' 'Yes, she said that Erostrato was too
long.' 'Was it she who gave you the Jaguar?' He looked at
me for rather a long time, then replied in a distinct tone:
'No.' I went on: 'If we go on seeing one another, I shall
call you Erostrato. For Aurora you were Eros perhaps because you knew how to deserve this name. But for me you
are and will always be Erostrato.' He shrugged his shoulders, once again he did not understand; then he asked:
'Why deserved?' 'Don't you know that Eros was the god of
love? You must have given her the feeling that you loved
her.' 'It was not I who loved her, it was she who loved me.'
'It comes to the same thing, doesn't it?' Silence followed;
he smoked, looking at the end of his cigarette; finally, he
asked: 'When will your mother be back?' 'I don't know; in
an hour or two.' 'Then in the mean time you can keep your
promise.' 'What promise?' 'To explain to me why you
wanted for once to act the prostitute; and also why you
wanted to do it precisely here, in your mother's bedroom.'
'But it's a long, complicated business; to explain it I should
have to tell you the story of my whole life.' He remained
uncertain for a moment; it was clear that what really interested him was not I myself or the reasons why I was
behaving in this fashion; but something else which, for the
moment at least, I could not succeed in imagining. Finally,
without enthusiasm, he said: 'Your mother will come in an
hour or two. We have time, haven't we?'

I: Not a very encouraging remark.

Desideria: No, indeed. So much so that there came over
me a sort of sudden tiredness, partly also because of the
intensity of the experiences of that afternoon. The Voice
took advantage of this tiredness to return to the charge:
'Why do you have to tell the story of your life to this little
exploiter of women? Tell him you did what you did because
you are vicious and were excited by the idea of playing the
part of a whore, and send him off once and for all.' Suddenly rebellious and no longer tired, I said: 'I am not

215

vicious and I don't want to pass for vicious with the first man who has aroused a feeling of tenderness in me.'

I: Tenderness?

Desideria: In the end, it was really a kind of maternal tenderness that I felt for him.

I: So far you've been speaking of fraternal affection.

Desideria: When I thought of the similarity of our origins, it was fraternal affection. But when I though of his way of making love, it was maternal tenderness.

I: What happened then?

Desideria: Then once again I disobeyed the Voice and said to him: 'I am tired, and that means I shall tell you briefly why I act in this way, and then I shall sleep. But come here close to me, on the bed, lie down beside me, take me in your arms, then I shall feel encouraged to speak.'

I: What did *he* do?

Desideria: He had now taken the photograph of Viola and me from the dressing-table and was looking at it with close attention. Finally, he asked: 'But oughtn't we to go into the living-room and you'll give me something to drink and then introduce me to your mother? If your mother arrives early, what will she think when she sees us on her bed?' You know what impression his words made on me?

I: Well?

Desideria: That Erostrato did not so much fear the unexpected arrival of Viola as desire it.

I: And what was your answer?

Desideria: I wanted to put him to the proof, to see if my supposition was well founded. I said, in a weary voice: 'Very well, let's go into the living-room.' He immediately came over to the bed and said, in that deep voice of his, as though by a sudden inspiration: 'Make room for me,' and without more ado he lay down beside me. 'You're right,' he went on, embracing me, 'one's better off here. And then, we have plenty of time; come close to me, like that, there, that's good, now you can talk, I'm listening.'

I: Affectionate, wasn't he?

Desideria: Yes, affectionate, even a bit too much so.

216

I: Too much so?

Desideria: What would you think of a man who, at the very moment when he tells you he is listening to you, takes his member out of his trousers, grasps your hand, and makes you hold it? 'What are you doing?' I murmured. 'D'you mind?' he said. 'Like that I feel closer to you.'

I: And what did you do?

Desideria: I clasped it as he asked me; an idea had come to me and I wanted to see whether it corresponded with reality.

I: What was the idea?

Desideria: The idea had come to me that, in this exhibition of his member – which was, let me say in passing, of extraordinary proportions – there was something, how shall I say? of the professional.

I: Professional?

Desideria: Yes, he wanted me to be aware that he was well furnished by nature and that, from ¬the professional point of view, he was therefore capable of satisfying the most immoderate demands, of every kind.

I: What, in fact, did you think he was? A prostitute?

Desideria: That may be so. But I did not think so, I felt it was so, and I felt also that this exhibition did not concern me so much as Viola.

I: Viola?

Desideria: Yes, in the not entirely improbable case of her turning up suddenly and earlier than expected. In short, I felt that he wished to be 'seen' by Viola. That is, he wanted Viola to see his member.

I: So you were clasping what we may call the tool of his trade. And then what did you do?

Desideria: I told him the story of my life.

I: Fully and completely?

Desideria: Yes, I told him everything: the only thing I concealed was the existence of the Voice, although afterwards I realized that not to mention the existence of the Voice considerably lessened the efficacy of my story.

217

I: Why did you think it would be useful for Erostrato to know about the Voice? With what object?

Desideria: There was still that feeling that I have called fraternal which made me think like that. It seemed to me that if I mentioned the Voice I should have more authority over him.

I: What kind of authority? An authority such as that which Joan of Arc had over the feeble, ambiguous King of France?

Desideria: Put it like that, if you like.

I: Well, you told him the story of your life. From what point of view?

Desideria: From that of the Voice, naturally. How it had begun, how it had developed, how my rebellion against Viola and her world had asserted itself inside me.

I: Did you tell him that you were of plebeian origin and that Viola was not your mother but had adopted you?

Desideria: I said that very probably I was the daughter of Viola's husband and of a maid who afterwards had become a street-walker. And then Viola had adopted me.

I: Did you say that you had caught Viola making love *à trois*, with Tiberi and the French governess?

Desideria: Yes, and I especially dwelt on the fact that Viola selected the governesses not thinking of me but herself.

I: Did you say that you had let yourself be enticed by Diomira to that house of ill fame?

Desideria: Yes, but I kept quiet about the fact that I had called that complete stranger 'Mum'. I kept quiet because it was the Voice which inspired that folly in me and I could not speak about the Voice.

I: Did you say that, after being hostile to you for a long time, owing to your fatness, Viola fell in love with you as soon as you grew thin?

Desideria: Yes, I told him this, too; and for the first time Erostrato spoke. He asked me what proof I had of Viola's passion for me; in what way I had become aware of it; if there had been anything between us two. So I told him

218

about the night at Zermatt during which Viola had caressed me while I was sleeping.

I: Did you say that, on the day after that night, you worked out the plan of transgression and desecration?

Desideria: Yes, I said something like that, but I avoided saying that the plan had been dictated to me by the Voice. Instead, I invented the story that my original moral health as a girl of the people had rebelled against Viola's bourgeois corruption and, that, on this wave of indignation, I had decided to put into action a real, genuine plan of systematic revolt.

I: Did you tell him all the things you have done to actuate the plan?

Desideria: Not all, because, as usual, I felt that he would not understand. For example, I did not tell him that, in order to desecrate culture, I wiped my bottom with a page of Manzoni. Anyhow, what would have been the point of telling him? To him, I was sure, culture was certainly not sacred, so why tell him I had desecrated it? But I told him I had tried to kill Viola – that I certainly did; and that Viola had been aware of it and had taken it as a stimulus to her passion for me.

I: How did Erostrato comment on your story?

Desideria: In his own way.

I: In his own way? What does that mean?

Desideria: Not with any words, but all the time in a language which in him, it seems, is the only one that is not ambiguous or untruthful.

I: What was that?

Desideria: During the whole of my story I was clasping in my fist his member which, as I told you, was from the very beginning in a state of erection. But when I described my life as a child and my adoration for my adoptive mother, I felt that his member lost its hardness and stiffness and went back to being soft and short, in fact, was reduced to its normal proportions. I arrived at the (for me) fatal scene of the love-making *à trois* which I surprised from the doorway of Viola's room, and – strange to feel it in my fingers –

his member again swelled and stiffened. I lingered over the details of the scene: Viola on all fours, in the act of offering herself, Tiberi standing behind her, Chantal on her feet intent on looking at them; and then I could scarcely hold his member in the palm of my hand, so bulky had it become, protruding by at least two fingers' breadth. Then I dwelt upon the revelation on Viola's part of the fact that I was not her daughter and of the great distress that I felt; and his member returned again to its normal size. Then it swelled and stiffened once more when I described my incursion into the house of ill fame; to become small and soft when I gave an account of our life at Zermatt; to become stiff and swollen again during my description of Viola's first incestuous attempt; and so on and so forth.

I: I don't know if you realize that this pneumatic member which inflates and deflates itself in your hand, according to the things you are relating, has something comic about it?

Desideria: Sex is comic, or rather, one wants it to be comic because one does not know how to manage to speak seriously about it.

I: Well, how did the story come to an end?

Desideria: It came to an end with a flood of questions about Viola.

I: For example?

Desideria: Questions of all kinds. Especially on the matter of love-making *à trois*. In the end he asked me whether Viola had ever made a proposal to me.

I: In what words did he ask you that?

Desideria: 'Has she never given you to understand that she desired to make love with you and a man?'

I: Very clear, wasn't it? And what did you answer?

Desideria: The Voice made me answer: 'She must have thought of it, certainly, but hitherto she hasn't had the courage to propose it to me.'

I: And what did he say?

Desideria: He was silent for a moment and then he asked: 'Would you like it?'

I: And you?

Desideria: I said in reply, at the suggestion of the Voice: 'I should first have to know whether I should like to make love with Viola.'

I: Now you had faced the subject. How did the dialogue develop then?

Desideria: He asked me: 'You're right. Then you would like it?' I answered: 'That night at Zermatt it seemed to me that I liked it.' 'How did you manage to know that, if you were asleep?' 'Perhaps I wasn't asleep; I thought I was asleep. In any case, I let her do what she wanted.' 'You haven't yet told me whether you would like it?' 'But, yes, I have told you. I liked it that night; now, perhaps, I shouldn't like it, in that way at any rate.' 'What do you mean?' 'I mean that some new element would be needed.' 'For instance, a man as well as you two?' 'Yes, perhaps.' 'But why did you like it that night?' 'How can one tell? Let's say that I liked it enough to let her do what she wanted.' 'Tell me: did you like it because Viola was a woman?' 'Not particularly. But a little, yes.' 'Or because she was your mother?' 'Viola is not my mother.' 'I meant, your adoptive mother.' 'I don't know, perhaps this idea came into it. However, I should say that the chief reason was that Viola wanted it, and when a person wants something with such intensity, it then becomes easy to make other people want it, too.' 'You haven't yet told me, however, whether you would like to make love all three together, yourself, Viola, and a man.' 'One would have to see who the man was.' 'Tell me the truth: you think I'm proposing myself as the man?' 'Well, I'm sorry, but everything would make one think so.' 'On the other hand, that isn't so; I ask you that question because you're a strange girl and you interest me.' 'I interest you? Really one would say that the person who interests you especially is my mother.' 'You both interest me; but you interest me more, because you have something that the girls in your class usually have.' 'What is that?' 'Well, that so-called plan of yours, the fact that you've rebelled against your mother's world, your attempt to get away from home; all this is not

221

at all common. You're not a girl like other girls. Only, things have to be done, not merely said. You keep saying that you hate the bourgeoisie, you make out that you would be capable of goodness knows what, but in the end, what have you done? You hit your adoptive mother's leg with the wing of the car. As a revolutionary act, it isn't much.'

I: Were you expecting this deviation towards politics?

Desideria: No, not at all, and even less so the Voice, who regarded him as a little pimp. Indeed, it now cried: 'But this young man begins to interest me! Perhaps I was wrong about him.' Meanwhile, Erostrato continued: 'Revolution, too, is a matter of deeds, not words.' I asked him, humbly: 'In what way?' 'I don't know, there are so many ways; for instance, some people form a part of revolutionary groups which then act, in one way or another.' 'I'm only a young girl, what I can do is very little, for the moment at least; my school consists mostly of boys and girls, foreigners or Italians, who are not interested in politics.' 'And yet I think that you, with your rebellion, might be a useful element.' 'You think so?' 'It's an impression from outside, so to speak. After all, we've known one another for only a couple of hours; but all the same, it seems to me that you ought to do something more than – what d'you call it? – desecrate?' 'Yes, desecrate. And what ought I to do, in your opinion?' 'Well, I'm a member of a recently formed group. I could introduce you. Would you like that?' 'I certainly should.' 'If you would like it, quite soon one of the committee should be arriving. The group was formed in Milan and I represent it here in Rome. When this comrade arrives, I'll introduce you and you can come to an agreement with him; and then you'll begin to understand that causing a revolution doesn't mean teasing one's own mother,' et cetera, et cetera.

I: Why et cetera, et cetera?

Desideria: Because in retrospect this dialogue seems to me a whole tissue of commonplaces.

I: Commonplaces?

Desideria: Yes, the cultural commonplaces that precede

or follow the sexual act. In our case, revolutionary common-places.

I: The Voice – what did it now think of Erostrato?

Desideria: It was at the highest point of exaltation. It explained to me that one can perfectly well be at the same time both a prostitute and a revolutionary. Which was as much as to say that, though it still retained its original con-tempt for Erostrato, it now thought that I should be able to utilize him in some way on the political plane.

I: How did all this come to an end?

Desideria: The end of it was that the Voice made me ask, with a certain anxiety: 'But supposing you introduce me to the group and I become a member of it, what kind of action shall we carry out then?' He replied, with the greatest indifference, almost negligently: 'A bit of everything, from bank robbery to attempted murder.' He looked at me fixedly while he spoke, with those black, clear, obsidian eyes and his unconscious smile with the upturned corners of his lips; he was at the same time both unbelievable and convincing. But the Voice, by now completely conquered, let itself go in a revealing remark: 'You must do all that is both pos-sible and impossible not to let him escape you. Even if it is necessary to make love *à trois*, with him and Viola.'

I: As for the Voice, it had lost its head.

Desideria: It's understandable. The Voice and I had been talking about revolution for years, and here was some-one who proposed that I should really put revolution into action. Our exaltation was justified.

I: *Ours?*

Desideria: Yes, I too let myself be carried away by the enthusiasm of the Voice. So much so that in the end, filled with gratitude and zeal, I sat up, bent over him as he lay on his back, with that extraordinary member erect, and started, with gratitude and passion, to pay back, in my turn, his oral caress.

I: Did he have an orgasm?

Desideria: No, he stopped me in time, seizing the back of my neck with two fingers of iron and forcing me to open

223

my mouth. We were almost in the dark; there was nothing but a small lamp enclosed in a red glass shade on the night table. He was clasping my neck and I was left in suspense, so to speak, with my mouth open and my lips wet with saliva above his erect penis, which the reddish light made to look positively purple. Well, do you know . . . ?

I: What?

Desideria: That penis was, so to speak, excessive, that is, too bulky, too rigid, too swollen, too red. And this excess was translated, in my eyes, into vulgarity. It was like his hand, in fact; and I thought, as I looked at it, that it was indeed the vulgarity of the proletarian ill-adjusted to the bourgeois world. It gave the impression of being a penis suited for making love with peasant women, from whom he had withdrawn it in order to offer it for sale to bourgeois women. Then he relaxed his grip on the back of my neck and said: 'Enough, that's enough, I don't want to come.'

I: Why, do you think, he didn't want to have an orgasm?

Desideria: I also wondered about that. Later, when I knew him better, I understood that he was able to control his own member at will, just as one controls the use of a delicate and precious tool of one's trade. The account of my relations with Viola had excited him enough to allow the oral caress; but not enough to reach the point of an orgasm.

I: But why this control just at that moment?

Desideria: I only guessed that later, when Viola finally arrived. But let me finish. I was feeling very sleepy now; I curled up against him and murmured to him, with an effort, almost, as I was gradually dozing off: 'When is the comrade from Milan coming?' 'Soon.' 'But when?' 'Perhaps in a fortnight's time, perhaps earlier.' 'Why shouldn't we go together to Milan to see him? Even tomorrow morning.' 'These things can't be done like that. One must first come to some agreement. Also we should risk not finding him.' 'Why? Does he go about much?' 'I should say he does.' 'Is he one of those who carry out bank robberies and attempted murders?' 'You have a strange idea of revolutionary action. Let us say, then, that he is one of those.' 'Once I'm a mem-

224

ber of the group, will you make me act?' 'Of course; otherwise what would you be doing?' 'Shall I have a pistol? Will you give me a pistol?' 'Certainly, if necessary.' 'You promise me so many things; and then you won't keep your promise.' 'That's not true; I'm a person who, when he makes promises, keeps them.' 'Come on, I've understood you by now. You promise to introduce me to the group so as to persuade me to make love, the three of us together, with you and Viola. All the afternoon you've been playing about with this idea. Perhaps you like Viola better than me, you've never stopped looking at her photograph; perhaps you like the idea of making love with a mother and daughter; or even of seeing mother and daughter making love together. But we're not mother and daughter, we're strangers to one another.' 'What are you saying, what d'you mean?' 'I'm convinced that you're a prostitute; but it doesn't matter, even a prostitute can be a revolutionary.' 'Now listen: if you introduce me to the group and let me take part in action, I promise you we shall make love, the three of us together, you, Viola, and I,' et cetera, et cetera.

I: Et cetera, et cetera again; what does it mean this time?

Desideria: It means that the conversation proceeded rather like that between a mother telling a fairy story to her child to send him to sleep and the child who listens to the story and gradually dozes off. The story was that of the revolutionary group, armed with pistols and machine-guns, carrying out bank robberies and murderous attacks, shooting, killing, fleeing. The mother, in this case, was Erostrato; the child dozing off was myself. In the end I think I repeated, in a muddled, uncertain voice, very quietly: 'If you introduce me to the group, the three of us will make love; otherwise nothing.' Then I don't know what happened. It was as though I had taken a powerful sleeping draught; I fell asleep and Erostrato took care not to wake me up. But later on I learned from Erostrato himself how his first encounter with Viola went.

I: With Viola?

225

Desideria: Yes, with Viola. Erostrato stayed awake and looked at me as I slept curled up against him, with his member still clasped in my fist. Suddenly Erostrato had the feeling that he was no longer alone in the room: there was somebody looking at him; he was conscious of a presence. Then he raised his head in the direction in which he noticed this mysterious presence and at the same moment was dazzled by an intense and very brief flash of light. When he ceased to be dazzled, he saw Viola standing in the doorway, in the act of drawing from her Polaroid camera the photograph she had just taken. Erostrato, when he told me the story of his encounter, said that for a moment he had feared that Viola had taken the photograph for some purpose of hostile evidence; but, immediately afterwards, the look that Viola turned upon him over the top of her camera reminded him of what I had told him of my adoptive mother's incestuous passion for me; and thus he understood that she had simply wished to photograph me asleep in the arms of a lover, with the latter's member clasped in my hand – a spectacle both new and fascinating to her. Then, as I went on sleeping, Erostrato and Viola gazed at one another in profound silence, and understood one another more completely and intimately than they could have done with words. This was for the space of a moment. Then Erostrato, it seems, at the end of this prolonged look, made an eloquent gesture to Viola: he pointed to the space left empty on the bed, beside me, as if inviting her to occupy it. It was an invitation to love-making *à trois*; since the photograph Erostrato knew that he could now do what he wanted with Viola. Tempted, Viola hesitated, looked fixedly at Erostrato, then finally shook her head in sign of refusal, turned her back on him, and disappeared. Erostrato immediately freed himself from my embrace and rushed after her.

I: What happened between Erostrato and Viola?

Desideria: Erostrato caught up with Viola outside the room, in the connecting passage leading to the hall. It is a very wide passage, with shelves and mirrors and old prints.

226

Viola was now frightened by the obvious invitation to sex *à trois* proffered to her by Erostrato when he pointed to the empty space on the bed beside me. Who was this unknown man who knew all about her, even including her most confidential dreams, even including her passion for me? Terrified as though by a diabolical intervention (Erostrato with his pallor, his black hair, his shining eyes had, at that moment, something demoniacal about him), Viola had a sharp return to her role as a mother; not trusting herself, she decided to run away from the flat. She put down her camera on a shelf, took up her bag which she had deposited when she came in, and ran towards the end of the passage, intending to reach the hall. But Erostrato pursued and caught up with her. Viola suddenly felt herself clutched by the hair, pushed by a blow of a knee in the back towards the door leading into the living room, guided towards a sofa, and flung head downwards onto the cushions. Then everything happened with irreverent but subservient violence. Viola indicated to her aggressor the manner in which she preferred to be penetrated; Erostrato promptly obliged; very soon Viola's troubled breathing was changed into a regular groaning; finally she gave a prolonged howl and then collapsed exhausted, sideways on the sofa, still panting and with her eyes capriciously closed, the upper part of her body distended with turned-back clothes, the lower part naked and bent double. Erostrato sat down beside her and looked at her coldly: from her his eyes moved towards the door leading into the hall. Then he noticed that while he was pushing her towards the sofa and she was struggling, her bag, which had flown open at the moment when he laid hands on her, had shed all over the floor the many small objects it contained: key-ring, handkerchief, wallet, lighter, lipstick, cigarette case, compact, and so on. These objects, scattered over the floor like the leavings of an army in flight, confirmed Erostrato in the conviction that he had achieved a complete victory: Viola had been defeated in her role as a mother, had been constrained, perhaps once and for all, to keep to her erotic function, without any

227

further possibility of an alternative of different character.

I: What happened afterwards between Viola and Erostrato?

Desideria: After a long pause of silence and stillness, it appears that Viola slowly got up and recomposed herself as best she could, while Erostrato watched her and smoked in silence. In the end, nevertheless, they spoke. Viola is stated to have said: 'Now it would be better for you to go away,' and Erostrato to have replied: 'I think so, too; but when shall we see each other again?' Viola then had a moment's hesitation, as though wishing to refuse and not having the courage to do so; then she is stated to have said: 'Come to lunch tomorrow.' And he: 'Will Desideria be there, too?' 'I think so' was Viola's answer. After this, still according to his own account, Erostrato went away.

I: Why do you say 'is stated to have said'?

Desideria: Because Erostrato, when he gave me an account of the conclusion of his encounter with Viola, lied to me. In any case, the absurdity of that invitation to lunch would be enough to make one realize it.

I: So what?

Desideria: In reality Viola and Erostrato, after making love, remained together for at least two hours. It seems they made love a second time, then they talked about many things, laying the foundations, as they say, of a relationship far more complex than the one there can be between a woman and the man who has raped her.

I: What then?

Desideria: Erostrato's instinct drew him towards Viola and me for three different reasons. The first, that of eroticism. The second, what I shall call ideological–political. The third, that of material profit. With me he had made some progress on the first two paths. And now with Viola he set out decisively upon the third.

I: What was he aiming at? Getting himself kept?

Desideria: Yes, certainly, but only in what may be called a subordinate way. What was important to him was to put

228

down roots into Viola's life, to make himself necessary, indispensable.

I: What did they talk about – business?

Desideria: Yes, about Viola's business affairs.

I: What came out of it all?

Desideria: What came out of it was that Viola was dissatisfied with Tiberi; that she was convinced that Tiberi, to avenge himself for having been sacked as a lover, had purposely contrived to make her lose money in his role as administrator; and that an administrative employment for Erostrato would be an effective means of concealing and at the same time cementing their newly formed relationship. It also came out that Erostrato was just the man that was needed in Viola's situation: holder of a degree in economics, an ex-bank employee, an ex-administrator of an estate in Sicily.

I: Was this true?

Desideria: None of it was true, it was all lies, but Viola wanted to have confidence in Erostrato and she believed him.

I: And what then?

Desideria: Then they came to an arrangement to have an examination of Viola's balance sheet, directly after lunch the next day.

I: Wasn't all this rather rapid?

Desideria: In cases of this kind, rapidity is, so to speak, the substance of the case itself. Erostrato did not wish to lose the opportunity afforded by Viola, a unique opportunity of its kind, and therefore acted in haste and with decision; but for Viola, also, Erostrato was a unique opportunity, not to be missed on any account. Just imagine: a man whom she had caught embracing me, and who, immediately afterwards, had thrown himself upon her; how could she fail to see, in this succession of events, the scheme, so often nourished and longed for, of three-sided lovemaking? And this, into the bargain, with me and my lover? In the relationship between Erostrato and Viola, rapidity was closely tied up with the fact that they both had the same

229

end in view and they both realized that they found themselves, at that moment, in the best conditions for achieving it.

I: What else happened between Viola and Erostrato?

Desideria: Viola accompanied him to the door; Erostrato said goodbye and went away. Viola put back the displaced cushions on the sofa, picked up, one by one, the objects which had fallen out of her bag, then went into the passage to fetch the Polaroid, which had remained there on the shelf, with the photograph she had taken hanging out of it like a mocking tongue. She detached the photograph and looked at it for a long time: there was I, Desideria, curled up asleep, holding Erostrato's member in my hand; there was Erostrato turning his face towards her, and already he had in his eyes the look of professional complicity that is so much to her liking. It was, so to speak, an important, a positively historic, photograph. Then Viola took the Polaroid, came back into her own room, seated herself, without making a sound, at her dressing table, and photographed me two or three times more as I slept. Finally, at one of the magnesium flashes, I suddenly awoke.

I: How do you explain this mania of Viola's for her Polaroid?

Desideria: I don't know: something like a form of existential voyeurism, the idea of snatching existence at its most ingenuous and most intimate moment. But Viola had always been a good photographer, she had always gone in for taking photographs. The Polaroid was her last discovery and she was always taking photographs of me: it was her way of loving me. Once she photographed me stark naked, lying on my back with my legs open: she said I had the most beautiful sex she had ever seen in her life.

I: You allowed her to do it?

Desideria: I would not have wanted to do so, but I had to obey the Voice, whose point of view, as you know, was that I must do everything possible to prevent Viola returning to her maternal role.

I: In what way did she persuade you to let yourself be photographed with your legs open?

Desideria: Really, she played a trick on me.

I: What trick?

Desideria: She said she wanted to photograph the whole of my body, piece by piece, in a number of separate photographs. She said she would put all these photographs into an album and would entitle it *Desideria's Body*. So, in the end, she was able to get the photograph of my sex without letting me guess her real aim.

I: And what was this aim?

Desideria: Precisely, to possess a photograph of my sex.

I: Did she then compile the album?

Desideria: Yes, she did; but she did not put this particular photograph into it; she had it enlarged and wanted to hang it up, framed, in the bathroom, on the wall in front of the bath. I pointed out that the servants would see the photograph and would derive matter for reflection about her relationship with me. So she attached it in a place where it was possible for her to see it whenever she wished without anyone knowing.

I: What place was that?

Desideria: You remember the safe hidden behind a panel of the bookcase in her so-called study? Well, this enlarged photograph of nothing but my sex was stuck up with adhesive tape by Viola on the inside surface of this panel. She herself showed it to me one day, when she opened the panel in my presence. While she was dialling the numbers to open the safe, she said, in a carelessly coquettish way: 'You see, this is you; it might be any woman, but I know it's you.' She gazed for a moment at the photograph, with an indefinable expression, half charmed and half self-satisfied; then she opened the safe, took from it a little bunch of banknotes, closed the steel door again, touched her lips with the ends of her fingers, and deposited a light kiss on the photograph, saying finally, with a sigh: 'Inside here I keep my treasures' – a sibylline remark; I did not understand

231

whether it alluded to the money or to the photograph or to both of them.

I: So you woke up and saw Viola taking a photograph of you; what did you do then?

Desideria: I made a movement of childish annoyance, looked at her for a moment, inert and awkward, and then, seeing that she was holding the Polaroid, I stuck out my tongue at her. At the same moment the flash of light dazzled me. Viola carefully removed the photograph from the camera and then said: 'Your friend has gone away. As you were asleep, he did not want to wake you and asked me to say goodbye to you.' I said nothing, I had no desire to speak; I was sure, suddenly, that Erostrato had not thought he ought to put off until tomorrow, for motives of simple decency, something that he knew for certain he was in a position to do today. But the idea that, immediately after having made love to me, he had done it with Viola, nevertheless aroused in me a subtle, obscure disgust: once again it was his vulgarity that expressed itself in this avidity: I felt a sort of pain in again recognizing its unmistakable symptoms. In some way my displeasure must have become visible, for Viola, after waiting in vain for me to speak, said: 'You're annoyed at not having been able to see him again, but you'll see him again tomorrow, don't worry; I've asked him to lunch.' 'I'm sorry, I shan't be here, I have an engagement.' 'Did I do wrong to invite him? He gave me to understand that he wanted to see you again.' 'You did right, only I shall not be there.' 'But what's wrong? Are you offended?' '*You* can't offend me.' This last remark escaped me unawares; its banality at once made the Voice cry out that all this was grotesque; now I was jealous of Viola; evidently I was still the usual sentimental, lascivious doll from the Parioli quarter, et cetera, et cetera. But my displeasure was tenacious; and so, when Viola objected, brutally: 'Perhaps I can't offend you, but it seems that I can make you jealous. What are you afraid of? That I should rob you of your boy friend?' – I answered her with violence: 'He's not my boy friend, he's nothing, in fact. I'll

232

hand him over to you – is that all right?' 'I'm sorry, but I don't understand you, I thought I'd done right to invite him and now, there you are, beside yourself, at the highest degree of rage.' 'Well, we'll talk about it later, I must go now.' 'No, wait, come here, come closer, there's something I must say to you.' 'I'm here, you can speak, I'm listening.' 'No, come closer, there's something very simple that I must say to you.' 'What is it?' 'I wish to say that we two must no longer consider ourselves as mother and daughter, but as two friends.' 'This very simple thing I've already heard on other occasions. All right, we're two friends, so then?' 'Then there could be the relations between us that there are between two women friends. That is, every kind of relationship.' 'Yes, but don't squeeze me like that, you make me lose my balance.' 'You'll be my best friend, won't you?' 'A friend of the type of Chantal?' 'Why, what d'you mean, Desideria?' 'Goodbye, Mum, I really must run away, goodbye, goodbye.'

THE GROUP AND THE ORGY

I: Next day, Erostrato came to lunch at your house. You were not there, were you?

Desideria: Yes, I was there.

I: You had said you didn't wish to be there. Did you change your mind at the last moment?

Desideria: It was the Voice that made me change my mind. It said that if I were not present, I should be showing that I was jealous, that is, I should be confirming its suspicion that I was in love with Erostrato. So I remained.

I: What happened during lunch?

Desideria: Nothing particular. Erostrato seemed very sure of himself; one could see perfectly well that it was not the first time he had found himself in a similar situation. Viola had gone back to being the American lady of the Parioli, the affectionate, mature mother with a beautiful grown-up daughter. At the end of lunch I said I had things to do and I went away.

I: What happened during the following days?

Desideria: What happened was that Erostrato, gradually, took the place of Tiberi.

I: What did that imply?

Desideria: Before their alleged rupture, Tiberi used to come to lunch with us two or three times a week: Erostrato started coming too, on some days. After lunch Tiberi would shut himself up with Viola in the study to go through the documents of her business affairs; Erostrato did the same. Tiberi and Viola would go out together in the evening to a restaurant, to the cinema, to the theatre, to a nightclub; Erostrato, in turn, also accompanied Viola to these places. The only novelty was that in Tiberi's time I was still a child and so I stayed at home in the evenings, whereas now I was grown-up and Viola, who was in love with me, insisted that I should go with her and Erostrato.

I: And you accepted?

Desideria: I had to. The Voice wished me to and I obeyed the Voice which, after all, amongst so much confusion and obscurity, was the only clear, stable, and coherent thing in my life.

I: Where did they make love, Viola and Erostrato?

Desideria: At the delicatessen shop.

I: Why, what d'you mean? What delicatessen shop?

Desideria: It was a flat contrived within a pork-butcher's shop. Erostrato, with imperceptible moralistic irony, actually called it the delicatessen shop. Viola had rented this flat after I had caught her at her love-making *à trois*, with Chantal and Tiberi. You will remember that on the following morning Viola had sacked Chantal and ceased to invite Tiberi to the house. With me she pretended that she had broken off all relations with Tiberi and even that she no longer made love with women. These were a couple of falsehoods, she was lying; actually, she had rented the delicatessen shop and had continued to make love *à trois* there, with Tiberi and various women in rotation as third partners.

I: Who were these women?

Desideria: Street-walkers, call-girls, models, shop-girls, secretaries, whatever the streets provided.

I: Who procured them?

Desideria: Tiberi, I think. But with my own eyes I've seen her, on part of the Tiber embankment, stop in her car in front of a street-walker and, after a brief negotiation, make her get in beside her. And at least on two occasions I have heard her telephoning to a so-called masseuse with financial arrangements to fix an appointment. At such times I have been struck by her voice, hard, exacting, the typical voice of the client who pays and wants something in exchange for the money.

I: Was Erostrato still living in the boarding house?

Desideria: No, he was living in the top-floor flat.

238

I: What top-floor flat?

Desideria: As I've already told you, Viola invested her money in restorations or constructions of small, expensive flats. Apart from being a way of saving her money from the erosion of inflation, these investments were also, and perhaps above all, a way of occupying herself and of exercising her own will and power on all those who were taking part in these building activities: architects, builders, overseers, joiners, contractors, workmen, artisans of various kinds, and, in addition, lawyers, administrators, notaries, and so on. Recently Viola had had built, up above our own flat, a top-floor flat consisting of a very large studio and a small bedroom. Plus the usual offices, of course, as well as an immense terrace all around the studio, from which one could see the whole panorama of Rome. I had helped Viola to decorate it; the original idea was to let it furnished. But one day, at table, Viola informed me casually, in the presence of Erostrato, that he would be coming to live in this top-floor flat.

I: Why on earth did Viola and Erostrato meet in the flat at the delicatessen shop, seeing that there was this top-floor flat?

Desideria: After the surprise of that night six years ago, Viola had discovered, so it seems, that her promiscuous eroticism was known in the quarter. Hence her decision no longer to receive her lovers in our building.

I: Was Viola now keeping Erostrato?

Desideria: Everything led one to suppose so. She was paying him a salary. She said she had taken him on as secretary.

I: And did you make love again with Erostrato?

Desideria: I, no. Why should I have done so?

I: Did you hate him?

Desideria: Not in the least. I certainly did continue to feel a kind of fraternal sorrow, melancholy and impotent, at knowing him to be corrupted and seeing it happen.

I: Did the Voice approve of this sorrow?

239

Desideria: It disapproved. It said I was an incorrigible sentimentalist.

I: Did you avoid being with him or not?

Desideria: I tried to be with him as much as possible. He had promised to introduce me to the revolutionary group; the Voice said that, corrupted or not, Erostrato must be courted at least until the day when he kept his promise.

I: Did the Voice think you would even be able to accept love-making *à trois*, provided you were introduced to the group?

Desideria: To the Voice, if the end was revolution, all means were good.

I: As for Erostrato, did he try to make love with you again?

Desideria: Yes.

I: In what way?

Desideria: It will seem strange to you; but especially by talking to me about his relations with Viola.

I: In what way did he speak of that?

Desideria: He spoke ill of her to me.

I: Why so, do you think?

Desideria: Probably because he thought that we ought to arrive by degrees at love-making *à trois*. He had been able to become Viola's lover at the first attempt; now he wanted to resume our relationship at the exact point at which it had been interrupted on the day of our first meeting. Then, later on, he would unite and fuse together the two relationships, the one with me and the one with Viola, in three-sided love-making, and the trick would be done. In the mean time, however, he was careful to represent his relationship with Viola as something professional and self-interested, and his attraction to me as something sentimental and disinterested. All this will perhaps seem to you rather calculated and premeditated. But it was not so. Erostrato made no calculations; he simply lived with instinctive naturalness in a situation that was congenial to him.

240

I: Do you mean that he was not conscious of what he was doing?

Desideria: Why should he have been? He had no need to be. Erostrato, superficially, was a prostitute who got himself kept by a woman he did not love, whom, in fact, he probably hated. At the same time, his feeling for me, desperate and lifeless as it was, was expressed superficially in his manner of making love orally. Thus, even if his aim was to achieve sex *à trois*, there really was in him something similar to love, for me, and to hatred for Viola.

I: But what, in fact, did he say?

Desideria: He did not say much, for he was rather laconic, as I think I have indicated to you. But he let it be understood that he felt nothing for Viola, that his feeling was entirely for me, that we two were made for one another, that we ought to act together against Viola.

I: Against Viola?

Desideria: Yes. For the moment merely to speak ill of her and perhaps even to make love, just the two of us, and later on – there was no telling.

I: But then he loved you?

Desideria: Not really: he wished above all to knock again at the door of my sex in order to achieve the pre-natal nothingness, like the first time. And he wanted me not to consider him a prostitute – as in fact I held him to be – and not to despise him. All this cannot yet be called love.

I: But what, in short, did he say about Viola?

Desideria: That she was selfish, hard, greedy, moralistic, foolish, boring, exacting. Above all, exacting.

I: Exacting, in what way?

Desideria: He gave me to understand that she was exacting in every way. From making him accompany her in the evening to a restaurant or a show, to what we may call his professional services.

I: What fault did he find with Viola as regards his 'services'?

Desideria: He did not say precisely; even his discretion, come to think of it, was a professional feature. But I seemed

241

to understand that Viola insisted on his going right to the end in the sexual act; he, on the other hand, wanted to spare himself, for he knew his own potentialities and did not desire to overstep them.

I: On his going right to the end? To what end?

Desideria: That he should have an orgasm every time they made love, which happened almost every day. For this reason also, he preferred me to Viola; that one time when we had made love, I had asked nothing of him, I mean nothing that concerned his own body. In short, the kind of sexual relationship that he preferred was one in which he could make use of his member in a limited, incomplete manner, more to arouse pleasure in the woman than to feel it himself. Carried away by confidence, or rather by the desire of inspiring confidence in me, he spoke to me of confidential matters on this subject, some of them amusing, some embarrassing; and all of them, always, I do not hesitate to say, strictly professional.

I: For example?

Desideria: Viola wanted him to sodomize her, for that was the kind of sexual relationship that she liked best. In this position, she could not look him in the face. And so, while he was on top of her and penetrating her, he would make faces at her and put out his tongue. Then he would start puffing and groaning noisily, although he was feeling practically nothing. Finally, he would cry out, bite the back of her neck, fix his nails in her shoulders to give her to understand that he was having an orgasm.

I: Did Viola believe him?

Desideria: Sometimes she did, sometimes she didn't. Erostrato explained to me, still with that professional tone of his, that Viola was so constituted that she felt, in front, little or nothing, but behind, a great deal, in fact, very much indeed. With regard to this, he told me that sometimes he amused himself by pressing her anal orifice lightly with his finger; at once he would see her fall into his arms with her eyes upturned to show their whites and her mouth half open. These details seemed to him curious, as elements of

242

that mysterious machine, the female body, which he knew as an expert and in which nevertheless he chanced continually to discover new and unexpected aspects. It was to this extraordinary sensitiveness of her hinder erotic zones that he attributed the fact that Viola, transported by ecstasy, often failed to notice that he was acting so as to avoid having an orgasm. But on other occasions she was aware that Erostrato was controlling and sparing himself, and then there were scenes that were at the same time both painful and ridiculous.

I: What sort of scenes?

Desideria: She informed him harshly that he ought to ejaculate inside her, for that semen was hers, her own property, and she had already paid for it in advance. Erostrato said that these scenes exasperated him, partly because, in the end, he was forced to satisfy Viola's demands, although he had no wish to do so. Erostrato described one of these scenes to me with what I may call a technical realism which, in him, did not seem to be accompanied by any moral judgement. He told me that one day when he, after crying out falsely for a feigned orgasm, had thrown himself down on her shoulders pretending to be breathless and exhausted, Viola, all of a sudden, turned quickly over and seized his penis, which was dry and still swollen and stiff, had squeezed it, pointing out that not even one drop of sperm was coming from it; then, in a burlesque authoritarian manner, calling him in English: 'my dear boy' and in Italian 'carino mio', had invited him to do his duty as a male. As she said this, she had again thrown herself on all fours, and had again offered him her perfect, superb buttocks. Then, while he was hanging over her and working feverishly and without warmth to penetrate her again, Erostrato had seen Viola deliberately close her eyes as she waited for the renewed pleasure of genuine sodomization; but at the same time her face retained the rapt, determined attention of one who listens to a faint and distant sound; and he had realized that she wanted to be sure that he would not again pretend but would truly comply with his

243

duty as a prostitute. In the end, full of impotent rage at the thought that his own precious semen was going to be lost in Viola's voracious intestine, he had had an orgasm and had seen Viola's face with an expression of reassured satisfaction as she followed, with minute and expert attention, the gradual flow, in her rectum, of the warm stream of the ejaculation. Then, after he had withdrawn, with his penis reduced to a small rag of wet flesh, Erostrato had the humiliation of her patronizing praise: 'This time it went well. Bravo, you see that when you like you can do it extremely well.'

I: You have said that his confidences were sometimes amusing, sometimes embarrassing. This technical description of intercourse no doubt belongs to the category of amusing confidences. Let us now speak of the embarrassing ones.

Desideria: Yes, there were also embarrassing confidences due to the fact that, in the candour of his vulgarity, he believed in all good faith that I was on terms of such complete agreement with him that I would not feel any repugnance for certain details.

I: For instance?

Desideria: For instance, the fact that Viola, sometimes, had not taken the trouble to empty her intestine, so that, when he withdrew after the real or the pretended orgasm, he would find his penis all speckled with yellow marks of excrement.

I: What effect did such information have upon you?

Desideria: It disgusted me, naturally.

I: But did you give him to understand that it disgusted you?

Desideria: That is the point: no. I continued to have a feeling of fraternal, loyal compassion for him, not so very remote, after all, from the complicity in which he would have liked to involve me. Among the embarrassing confidences I must also include one which referred to a physical anomaly of Viola's, which, incidentally, partly explained her preference for anal intercourse.

244

I: An anomaly?

Desideria: It appears that, if Viola let herself be penetrated in the normal manner, as the movements of her stomach and Erostrato's stomach quickened, she became steadily filled with air, like an energetically wielded pair of bellows. Then the orgasm would occur, her stomach muscles would relax, and so the air would be released with the disagreeable and, in a way, obscene, noises usually produced by air issuing from the intestine. Erostrato told me that every time they made normal love and Viola, at the end, abandoned herself in his arms with all the signs of the most complete amorous transport, it seemed to him that the sound of the flatulence issuing from her womb was mocking him and reminding him of his own state of mercenary inferiority. He would have wished Viola at least to apologize for making these involuntary mocking noises; he was especially irritated by the fact that she did not say she was sorry, that she behaved just like a mistress with a servant who has to put up with anything and to whom no regard is due.

I: Did these confidences finally to some extent modify that feeling of yours for Erostrato that you call fraternal and compassionate?

Desideria: No, on the contrary, they deepened it and made it more heart-rending.

I: But not to the point of making you want to make love with him? Or was it so?

Desideria: No, for me the amorous relationship began and ended on the afternoon of our first encounter. I had made use of him and I did not desire to repeat the experience, absolutely not. Also, because I had no need of it, to feel myself close to him.

I: What do you mean?

Desideria: Of the oral love-making that I had had with him I had retained only and definitively his desperate and entirely unconscious desire for death. I had no need to repeat the relationship in order to confirm to myself the

245

impotent compassion which my intuition of it aroused in me.

I: Let's talk of something else. After stealing your lover, did Viola cease to pursue you with her attentions?

Desideria: Far from it, she was on top of me more than ever. Anyhow, it's not exactly true that she had stolen my lover – or rather, she did not think so.

I: What did she think?

Desideria: Apparently, that she had taken a step forward towards her final aim, which, for her as for Erostrato, was love-making *à trois*. Furthermore, I understood that Erostrato, for some reason, made her believe that he and I were continuing to make love together. So it was rather natural that Viola should think, not so much that she had stolen my lover, as that she was sharing him with me. This made her hope that some day, instead of our seeing Erostrato each on her own account and separately, we should become united all three together, in the triple orgy which was her favourite manner of making love.

I: But you – why did you not contradict this lie on Erostrato's part?

Desideria: The Voice did not wish me to. In any case, it was not as if Viola spoke to me openly about her relations with Erostrato. She kept, as they say, to the conventions: Erostrato was the secretary, she the giver of work. Rather in the same way that I was the daughter and she the mother.

I: But, since she believed that you and Erostrato were lovers, how did she fail to think that you were jealous of her?

Desideria: She thought, on the contrary, that I was content to share my man with her.

I: Why?

Desideria: Probably because she wanted it to be so.

I: You said that she persecuted you with her attentions. Give me an example.

Desideria: They were strange attentions. Possibly they

246

were inspired by the memory of that night when I tried to run her over with the car.

I: What d'you mean?

Desideria: She wanted me to hurt her.

I: Hurt her in what way?

Desideria: Physically.

I: What had she become, a masochist?

Desideria: No, she was in love, and since I had shown myself stronger than her, being, as you say, a masochist was for her simply the most natural manner of demonstrating her love.

I: What did she ask of you? To beat her?

Desideria: Yes.

I: In what way?

Desideria: She included me in her continual, depressing, oscillating movement between maternal affection and incestuous love. One day we went in the car to a restaurant, she, Erostrato, and I. I was sitting at the wheel, she beside me, Erostrato behind. Then, as I was driving, I felt her hand being placed on my thigh and then sliding down towards my groin. I said between my teeth: 'Don't do that,' in a very low voice so that Erostrato should not hear. She immediately withdrew her hand; afterwards the evening passed normally. We had dinner, we went to see a film, we went back home, we went to bed, each one on his own. I was already in bed when the door opened and Viola came in without knocking, in a long white nightdress, moving erect and upright with chest thrown out like a sleep-walker, with her hair loose and hanging over her chest, her eyes fixed in front of her and her arms dangling. Naturally I thought she wished to resume the caress she had started in the car; I asked her, rather annoyed, what she wanted, what was the matter, why couldn't she let me sleep in peace? She approached, looked at me for a moment, and then said: 'This evening, in the car, I touched you and I saw that, if Erostrato had not been there, you would have slapped me. Well, I have come to receive that slap. Eros is not there now and you must give it to me.'

247

I: Must?

Desideria: Yes. I noticed that word, too, and I answered her: 'There's no "must" about it.'

I: What did she say?

Desideria: She begged me: 'Give it to me; look, I'll sit down here, on this chair, and you'll give it to me. I'm an unworthy mother: you must punish me.' So I answered her rather brutally: 'In asking me to give you a slap, you continue to be an unworthy mother. To you, the slap would be a caress. What d'you think – that I don't understand you?' D'you know what she did?

I: What?

Desideria: She realized that I did not wish, as she said, to punish her; then she changed her method. She provoked me. She drew herself up and exclaimed in her most puritanical voice: 'You're a liar and you're insolent; how can you permit yourself to talk like that to your mother?' She added other remarks of the same kind; then, in a typically awkward and clumsy manner, she tried to slap me. The slap, not in the least violent and perhaps restrained for fear of hurting me, caught me between nose and cheek and would have left me indifferent if she had not had, on her middle finger, a sapphire ring with a very massive, protruding platinum setting. The ring hurt me in precisely the way she wished to avoid; all at once, partly from exasperation at her insistence, I lost my head, jumped off the bed, and slapped her seriously and with all the force I was capable of. Immediately afterwards I realized that I had done exactly what she had asked of me. And in fact, as it were to confirm this, she seized my hand, carried it to her lips, covered it with kisses, licked it, and soaked it with saliva and tears.

I: With tears?

Desideria: Yes, she was crying, partly perhaps from the pain of the blows. The whole affair, in any case, lasted a very short time; then Viola rose and went away with a sprightly air, saying to me from the doorway in an enigmatic manner: 'Sleep well, my child,' as though she wished,

248

with these words, to make fun both of herself and of me. But I was upset.

I: Why?

Desideria: Because it was the first time that I had struck her. A mother's cheek, even an adoptive mother's, is not like other cheeks.

I: Were there other similar episodes?

Desideria: Yes, many of them. I want to tell you about another one just to make you understand that this was not a casual, occasional thing but continual and obsessive. You must know that Viola, apart from the Italian newspapers, read every day an American paper to which she subscribed. One day after breakfast she was reading this paper and suddenly she handed it to me, saying: 'Read this.' I took the paper and read. It was the story of a crime: a man had enticed a photographic model into the desert in the neighbourhood of San Francisco, California, and, with the excuse of taking some unusual photographs, had tied her up in such a way that the poor girl, after many hours of agony, had ended by strangling herself. The police had arrested the murderer and had found the roll of photographs in which the maniac had captured the various phases of his victim's cruel death. I read the notice and then said: 'What a terrible thing, poor girl, how she must have suffered.' Viola answered: 'She kept calm to the end; the photographs are a witness of it. She talked, she tried to convince the man, she tried to delay her death by holding her legs in such a way as not to tighten the cord. In the end, however, her legs straightened out and she slowly throttled herself. In the mean time, he was taking photographs of her, in all the phases of her death.' Viola was silent for a moment, as though overcome by a sudden agitation. Then she went on in a low, laboured voice: 'Listen, I would like you and me to do the same thing in fun.' At these words I looked at her in astonishment and then recognized in her face the impure, burning blush which in her rose from low down and moved upwards; from her stomach, it seemed, steadily up over her bust until

249

it overspread her neck and her face, and which was a sure sign of the sudden awakening of her senses. I started laughing, rather cruelly, and said: 'You want me to strangle you? In that case, it's easier to do it with one's two hands.' 'With your hands it would cease to be a joke: either you would really strangle me or you wouldn't do anything to me.' 'But why do you want me to do what that maniac did to the model?' 'Don't know.' 'Don't know isn't an answer.' 'I would like you to tie me up and then take some photographs: the fun would consist entirely in that.' 'Always photographs; why d'you so much like taking photographs and being photographed?' 'Once upon a time one looked at oneself in looking glasses, but one was never natural. Now we have photographs to look at ourselves and see ourselves as we really are. What is there strange about that?' 'All right, let's do it then. Where d'you want to be tied up?' 'I don't know; wherever you like – here, even.' But we were in the living room and I replied: 'Not here, you're crazy; if someone came in, what would they think? Anyhow, I'm no good at doing the sort of tyeing-up process that's described in the paper. All I can do is to tie you to something like a post or a pillar, like St Sebastian, and then take the photographs.' 'An idea! Tie me to the balustrade on the landing of the top-floor flat. No one is likely to come and see Eros and today he's out to lunch and won't be back so very soon.'

I: But why did you lend yourself to this game?

Desideria: It was the Voice again, with that idea of preventing Viola from getting back into her maternal role. In the mean time, Viola, infatuated with the idea, went out and came back a moment later with a long nylon rope which she had found somewhere or other. We took the Polaroid and went out of the flat. From our landing a wooden staircase led to the top-floor flat. We went up as far as the door and then discovered that – better still than the balustrade, which was too low – our purpose would be served by a rectangular window situated near Erostrato's door and protected by a very complicated, robust grating. This win-

250

dow, which opened from inside the studio, was always closed; but the distance between the grating and the shutters allowed room to pass the rope through. Moreover, it was high enough for Viola to be tied to it without her being forced to go down on her knees, as would have been necessary if I had tied her to the balustrade. So Viola stood on the landing with her back against the window, and I passed the rope between the bars of the grating. Viola had taken off her jacket and remained with her arms bare right up to her armpits; I made her stretch them out to the full width of the window and, after a few mistakes and reconsiderations, succeeded in tying her to the bars. Then I wound the rope round her neck and tied this also to the grating. From her neck I brought down the two ends of the rope as far as her waist, passed them twice round her stomach, then passed them between her legs and fixed her sides to the grating with two very tight knots. Viola played her part in the game with great seriousness; evidently it pleased her that I should be acting the part of torturer; perhaps she hoped that I would become excited, too. I finished tying her up and made as if to fetch the Polaroid, but she stopped me, saying: 'In the newspaper article it said that the murderer, before photographing the girl, kissed her on the mouth. You must do the same.' I answered that this was not part of the game, at any rate as she had hitherto put it to me. She then uttered this ambiguous phrase: 'You see, you're not the affectionate daughter that you say you are. You don't even want to give your mother a kiss.' I replied dryly: 'All right, all right, but let it be really a kiss from a daughter to her mother,' and I went up to her to satisfy her. She was truly in the attitude of the crucifixion, with her arms spread out, and she was tied to the grating not only by her wrists but by her neck, her waist, and her sides. The inside part of her round, youthful arms was turned outwards, the effort making the veins visible, blue, and prominent; the rope that I had wrapped three times round her neck made her face look swollen, and gave her a congested, childish look. I was struck by the absurdity of this game; but the Voice re-

251

torted: 'Eroticism is always absurd. The further you take her in this direction, the better it will be.' I looked up towards Viola and then, to my surprise, saw that she was weeping with exactly the same sort of tears that she had shed in my room when I had slapped her; tears not so much of pain as of exasperated, unsatisfied, and therefore painful, desire. Raising my hand and wiping the tears from her cheeks with my fingers, I asked her: 'Why are you crying? I'll take a photograph of you now and then untie you.' 'No, don't photograph me, untie me at once; I think the game is really over.' This reconsideration roused the temper of the Voice as though, at the last moment, Viola had escaped by instinct from some kind of trap. 'Untie her then,' it cried, 'but first kiss her on the mouth, yes, stick your tongue into her mouth, right inside, before you untie her.' I did not dare entirely to disobey the Voice, but I did not wish the kiss to be a kiss of love such as it had suggested. I said to Viola: 'As you like, but don't cry; look, I'll give you a kiss now,' and I planted a dry kiss on her lips. I heard her murmuring: 'Give me a real kiss, give me your tongue,' but I pretended not to hear and busied myself in undoing the knots of the rope. Finally, she came away from the window, rubbing her arms and her neck, which were paining her. 'We're a couple of real lunatics,' she said, in a tone of confused but intense complicity and as if speaking to herself.

I: So she did not wish you to photograph her crucified against Erostrato's window. Why was that?

Desideria: I suppose because at the last moment she recollected that after all she was my adoptive mother.

I: But then she implored you to give her a kiss which was not precisely filial.

Desideria: For the same reason but the other way round: she had become tired of the role of mother almost at once, and wanted to return to that of lover.

I: With her remark: 'We're a couple of real lunatics,' Viola gave it to be understood that you were now little less than lovers. On the other hand, however, you have told me that she had never yet explicitly suggested love-making *à trois* which, according to her intention, was to be the supreme expression of your lunacy. In the end, then, had she suggested it to you or had she continued to circle round it? In short, were you really 'a couple of lunatics' or not?

Desideria: Yes, she did suggest it to me.

I: Explicitly?

Desideria: In the frankest way.

I: So I am to believe that the question of sex *à trois* was finally raised between you and Viola. And how did you resolve it?

Desideria: We didn't resolve it, we experienced it.

I: What d'you mean?

Desideria: That in life there are no problems, that is, objective and external choices; there is only the life which we do not resolve as a problem but which we live as an experience, whatever the final result may be.

I: Then, I should like to know, how did you experience the question of sex *à trois*?

Desideria: It was Viola who forced me to experience it. One evening I came home a little after midnight, having been to the cinema with friends, and I saw that there were lights in the living room. I looked in and saw Viola sitting all alone on a divan, in front of a table upon which I noticed – objects for me significant – a bottle of whisky and a glass half full. I greeted her from a distance and was on the point of leaving; but she stopped me, raising her hand and moving her forefinger, in the confidential and even slightly sinister manner which is equivalent to such a re-

253

mark as, for instance: 'Hey, you, my dear, come here for a moment, there's something I must say to you.' I realized, from this gesture, that she was drunk, and that probably she had made herself drunk on purpose to say or perhaps even to do something which otherwise she would not have had the courage to say or do.

I: Why, was Viola shy?

Desideria: No, but there was that continual oscillation in her between the role of mother and that of lover: alcohol allowed her to halt the pendulum on the side of incestuous passion.

I: What then?

Desideria: Then I took one or two unwilling steps forward; but she now, with the almost teasing distraction of the heavy drinker, had lost interest in me and was occupied in pouring whisky into her glass which was again full. Then, without raising her head, she said between her teeth, 'Why don't you come closer? What are you afraid of?' I took another step forward; I was quite close to her now; and then, all of a sudden, she sprang at me like a wild beast from its ambush in the grass; and there I was, suddenly, seized hold of by my dress, pulled down onto the divan, flung violently on my back with her on top of me; and she, as a man might do, put a frantic hand under my skirt and tried to strip me naked. Then my skirt was pushed back at one stroke over my face; muffled up and blinded, I felt Viola's teeth fix themselves in my groin with a strange violence which was at the same time both voracious and prudent and which again reminded me of an animal, a cat for instance, which seizes its kitten with its teeth and transports it to safety. In reality, as I understood, Viola seemed greedy, not so much to bite me as to fill her mouth with flesh and hair, as though she were hungry for me, or rather for that part of my body which excited her desire at that moment.

I: What did you do?

Desideria: My reaction was somewhere between fear and surprise, as if I had slipped and fallen to the ground. I freed myself forcibly from the skirt, which muffled my head, pushed Viola away with a kick, and jumped to my feet.

I: And Viola?

Desideria: She sat down again and, as though nothing had happened, bent forward to pick up her glass from the table. Then she began to speak without looking at me, her head bowed, her eyes lowered, the glass in her hand: 'I've been waiting for you since ten and it's now nearly one. I've been waiting for you here, all alone, for almost three hours.' 'I didn't know you were waiting for me, Mum.' 'I've waited for you for three hours but I would have gone on waiting longer because I absolutely must speak to you.' 'What is it, Mum?' 'There's an impossible situation between us two which absolutely must be cleared up.' 'What situation?' 'Don't pretend you don't understand. You know perfectly well that there's an impossible situation between us two which must be cleared up, you know it, so why d'you ask me what the situation is?' 'I don't understand you, Mum.' 'Don't call me Mum, you know that we're not mother and daughter. For a long time we've been strangers and now we're something different, something very different from mother and daughter.' 'But what d'you mean, Mum?' 'We're lovers, whether you admit it or not. But since you pretend not to know it, I want our situation to be cleared up. I want this absolutely. D'you see? I want it absolutely, really absolutely.' She repeated this 'absolutely' with her head down, like a real drunkard, which she was. With some embarrassment: 'Yes, I understand, or rather, I don't understand.' 'In the first place, don't call me Mum, call me Viola.' 'Yes, Viola.' 'In fact, call me Violetta.' 'Violetta?' 'Yes, Violetta is the name Eros calls me by. You must call me Violetta, too.' 'I don't understand you, Viola, or rather, I mean, Violetta.' 'You don't understand me, eh?' 'I don't understand you; I think it's late and we ought to go to bed.' 'No, no, not before the situation between us two is cleared up.' 'All right then, let's clear up the situation. Speak, then.' 'I'm speaking, who says I'm not speaking? I'm speaking and I'm telling the truth. And the truth is that you are

255

Eros's whore and at the same time you're my whore. And so, seeing that you're Eros's whore and my whore, I don't see why you couldn't be the whore of both.' 'I'm sorry, Viola, but I don't understand at all. I'm not your whore. I'm not Eros's whore, I don't wish to be the whore of you two nor of anybody else.' 'Listen, you see that I was right, you don't want to admit that between us two there is a love relationship, a very tender, very beautiful, very profound relationship. On the other hand, there *is*, and that's why I tell you that the situation must be cleared up. Yes, absolutely cleared up, fundamentally. Everything ought to be clear between us, no more play-acting, no more pretences. Everything ought to be clear: you, Eros and I must break down the barrier of hypocrisy that divides us and everything must be clear, absolutely clear once and for all.' She continued with her drunken talk, her head lowered all the time, the glass in her hand. I felt sorry for her, I put out my hand to her, gave her a caress, and said to her: 'Don't you see that everything is clear and that there's no need for anything to be cleared up? Didn't you say that between us there is something very beautiful, very tender, very profound? Well, let's stop at that and go and sleep.' 'So you admit that you are my whore!' At these words I turned round and hurried out of the living room.

I: Did you go to bed?

Desideria: Yes, but I didn't sleep. I lay awake most of the night.

I: Why?

Desideria: Because the worst row we have ever had broke out between the Voice and me.

I: What about?

Desideria: All at once there appeared to me – as they used to say once in serial stories – an abyss or, if you prefer a scientific term, a black hole into which the Voice was preparing to cast me down headlong; but I dug in my heels, refusing to fall in.

I: Apart from the metaphor, what did you reproach the Voice for?

Desideria: For having brought me, by degrees, under the pretext firstly of desecration and then of revolution, to become my mother's lover and my mother's lover's lover.

I: That was the abyss, otherwise the black hole; how did you manage to dig in your heels so as not to fall in?

Desideria: First of all, for some time I went back in memory to what had happened between myself and Viola that evening. I was desperate; I realized that I was neither the honest girl to whom a suggestion such as Viola's turns out to be incomprehensible, nor yet the cunning revolutionary that the Voice would have liked me to be. My desperation came from the consciousness of my weakness in the face of Viola's passion, which, instead of arousing horror in me as I should have wished, upset me and in some way tempted me.

I: Tempted you?

Desideria: It seemed to me that I still felt in my groin the bite that Viola had given me there; in the silence and darkness of my bedroom this sensation appeared to me as though detached from the person who had provoked it and, for that reason, to be somehow acceptable and innocent. But almost at once I recalled Viola sitting on the edge of the divan, bent double, in the act of repeating, with a drunkard's obstinacy, that our situation must be cleared up; and I realized that it was actually she who had given me that bite, she who was my adoptive mother, and that the sensation of the bite was not separable from her.

I: What was the result of this recollection?

Desideria: It was that I suddenly said to the Voice: 'That's enough, I don't intend to pay any more attention to you. You've made me believe a lot of rubbish, but now that's enough.'

I: What was the 'rubbish'?

Desideria: Everything: the plan of transgression and desecration, dictated at Zermatt with such solemnity and afterwards reduced to a few acts of demonstration that were entirely insignificant; the revolution which, according to the Voice, I should have put into action with the help of

257

Viola's support. Everything. 'In reality,' I concluded, 'I am merely a modest bourgeois girl who does not get on with her adoptive mother. You know what this girl ought to do? In my opinion, she ought to throw aside all the rubbish of her so-called Voice, rent a little flat of two rooms and a kitchen, and go and live there alone. That's all.'

I: A speech full of good sense. And how did the Voice react?

Desideria: With lucid, rational calm: first of all, it confirméd its idea that the plan had been just and necessary and now could not be halted in the private sphere but must logically pass on into the public. Furthermore, it recognized willingly that the situation between me and Viola had reached a dead end. It was necessary that it should be released by something exceptional and violent, which the Voice at once designated by the term 'revolutionary action'. But this action depended, unfortunately, upon Erostrato, upon the seriousness of his promise to introduce me to the group from Milan. For some time, however, Erostrato appeared to have forgotten his promise. According to the Voice, I must refresh his memory, compel him to keep his promise, in short, put him to the proof. By what means? At this point the Voice made me an extraordinary proposal.

I: Viola had made you a no less extraordinary proposal. And what was the Voice's extraordinary proposal?

Desideria: Still calmly and reasonably, the Voice explained to me that, in order to put Erostrato properly to the proof, I must raise my sights, that is, make my requests more exacting. Hitherto, it had been merely a question of being introduced to the group from Milan. Now I must insist on Erostrato organizing a kidnapping.

I: A kidnapping?

Desideria: Yes, a political kidnapping, full-scale and with the usual ritual: seizure, custody in some 'people's prison', demand for ransom, et cetera, et cetera.

I: And who was the person whom the Voice thought of kidnapping?

Desideria: Viola, of course.

I: Viola? Desideria, at this point you can't hope that I'll believe you.

Desideria: Yet it's the truth. The Voice said precisely this: 'Very well, we'll make a last attempt to make Erostrato come out into the open. We'll suggest to him that he should organize the kidnapping of Viola.'

I: I didn't explain myself. I believe you when you tell me that the Voice expressed itself in this way. But I cannot help thinking that such an idea could only come into the mind of some lover of fairy-tales in the grip of a lucid but uncontrolled delirium.

Desideria: Why, I protested immediately that it was madness. That I wouldn't have anything to do with it, on any condition. That it should not even be mentioned.

I: And yet, in the end, it seems, you yielded.

Desideria: Yes.

I: Why, seeing that it seemed to you madness?

Desideria: To bend my will, the Voice had recourse to exceptional and unforeseen means.

I: What means?

Desideria: It provoked in me something like the convulsion of one possessed.

I: Possessed?

Desideria: Judge for yourself: after rejecting the plan of the kidnapping I turned over in bed, determined to go to sleep. But then I felt suddenly invaded by an uncontrollable anxiety. I threw off the bedclothes, threw away the pillow, opened my eyes wide in the darkness, took my head between my hands and listened. Then I heard the Voice whispering to me in the dark: 'You're all tied up, you're in a trap, you're in a cage; you must free yourself, you must regain your liberty, you must do this at all costs.' These words were followed by a violent crisis, like an epileptic fit. I went into convulsions, I gnashed my teeth, I shook my arms and legs, I struggled with extreme violence as though fighting against someone or something that tried to keep me still and imprisoned. My nightdress embarrassed me, I tore it off, I was naked, I scratched my breasts and my belly, I

259

pulled at my pubic hair, I laid hold of the hair of my head and struck my head against the bed post with such force that I lost consciousness, fell down onto the floor, and remained there, stupefied and exhausted, my whole body ravaged, in an inert, obtuse half-sleep which lasted until morning. At dawn (probably) I rose and got back on to the bed and lay curled up, without bedclothes, quite naked, and plunged into the depths of a sort of lethargy. When I awoke it was midday and I immediately understood that the Voice, by fair means or foul, had been right about my resistance. I now no longer thought of leaving home to live on my own; the kidnapping of Viola appeared to me not only just but also inevitable. An event of that morning proved that the Voice was right.

I: What was the event?

Desideria: While I was drinking my coffee in the kitchen as I am accustomed to do every morning, the manservant looked in and told me that there was a girl out in the hall who wished to speak to me. I asked him who it was and he replied that she did not wish to give her name. I got up and went into the hall. The girl was standing in front of the console-table mirror and for a moment I saw her only from behind. She was wearing the usual youthful uniform of those years, a sweater and blue jeans, the garments that I myself was wearing at that moment, but one look was enough for me to see that hers were a special sweater and jeans – imitations, I mean, that were almost parodies and anyhow expensive, tailored for a type of clientèle that was desirous not so much of getting things cheap as of being in the fashion. The sweater was very short, of very fine black wool, glossy and bulging; the blue jeans, without patches or rents, came up almost to her chest and were held in at the waist by a high leather belt with a brass buckle, and they had a piece of red embroidery in the shape of a heart on the left buttock. The girl was broad-shouldered, with a narrow waist, ample hips, and long legs. I don't know why it occurred to me that I had seen that back and those legs before. Then she turned; and I realized who it was.

I: Who was it?

Desideria: It was myself. The same chestnut hair, bright and smooth; the same kind of face, rather long and with Germanic features; the same strong, muscular neck; the same overserious, almost touchy expression. I noticed that she wore her sweater over her bare skin, like me; and for a moment I had the strange feeling that her breast was my own and that the wool of the sweater was rubbing and hardening not only her own but my nipples. Then the girl spoke with a voice that was not mine, with a foreign accent; and indeed, as I came to know later, she was Austrian. Holding out her hand to me, she said: 'My name is Brigitte. Really I ought to have spoken to your mother, but I prefer not to see her. You are called Desideria, isn't that so? Well, Desideria, go to your mother and tell her that I left my driving licence in her flat yesterday. Tell her that she must give you the key of the flat, and no nonsense about it. Then you must come with me; I'll fetch the licence and then bring you back home.'

I: But what flat is this?

Desideria: Obviously the one in which Viola and Eros-trato meet, with the call-girls.

I: And what did you say?

Desideria: I said nothing. I looked at her and was still struck by her resemblance to myself. This resemblance troubled me, just as one's own image in a looking glass can trouble one, when seen suddenly and as a surprise. Brigitte mistook my silence for an attitude of hostility and made an unmannerly and impatient gesture as though to imply that I must obey her: 'Come on, what are you looking at me for? I'm a girl like you; what is there special about me that you should look at me like that?' Bewildered, I said: 'I see that you're a girl like me. I'll go at once and fetch the key.' I turned round, left the hall, and ran to Viola's bedroom. I found her still in bed, reading the newspaper, holding it spread out in the air in front of her eyes. In one breath, I said: 'Brigitte is there. She says she left her driving licence in your flat. You must give me the key; I'll go with

261

her and she'll fetch the licence and then bring me back here.'
I: What did Viola say?
Desideria: Very little. At that moment she was a hundred per cent American, with even the cruel sensuality that goes with Puritanism but without even a shadow of Italian sentimentalism. With a movement of her hand she indicated the chest of drawers, still keeping her eyes fixed on the newspaper. 'The key is in my bag,' she said, 'and my bag is in the top drawer. You'll see, it's a key with a label on which is written; VIA GAETA.' I went to the chest of drawers, opened the drawer and then the bag, and immediately found the key. Viola suddenly went on: 'There should also be in the bag an envelope with some photographs in it. Give it to me.' I did as she asked; she opened the envelope, took out some photographs, and examined them one by one, then gave me two of them, saying: 'Give Brigitte also these two photographs, from me. Tell her I'll telephone her as soon as possible.' I took the envelope and went out. In the passage I opened the envelope and looked at the photographs. In both of them could be seen Brigitte and Erostrato, naked, in two different positions: in the first, Brigitte was on all fours, Erostrato, standing, was penetrating her from behind; in the second, Brigitte was kneeling and was making oral love to Erostrato, who here again was on his feet. In both photographs Brigitte could be seen entire; of Erostrato, on the other hand, only the middle part of his body, without either feet or head. But all the same I guessed it was he, from the hand with which he was pressing Brigitte's head against his stomach – that hand which seemed to me so vulgar and which had, on its ring-finger, the ring with the intertwined ciphers engraved on it. I reflected that Viola had given me these photographs on purpose for me to look at them and recognize myself not only in the physical person of Brigitte but also in her function as the girl 'on duty' in the love-making *à trois*. I replaced the photographs in the envelope, put it in my pocket, and went into the hall. Brigitte was awaiting me, still standing but leaning against the console table. She had

262

lit a cigarette; when she saw me she threw it on the floor and crushed it with the point of her boot. Without saying anything, I opened the door and led the way out. In the street, Brigitte overtook me, making for her car. She walked in front of me, with long steps on her long, strong, elegant legs, putting into her movements a haughty energy which gave prominence to the muscles of her buttocks. She was truly a splendid creature, endowed in a high degree with the hard, severe beauty which Viola seemed to admire so much in me. But at the same time I was aware that this hardness and severity, which in me were spontaneous and disinterested, in Brigitte had to be considered as a precise and conscious erotic speciality that she offered for sale to her clients. She got into a small utility car, I took my seat beside her, and we drove off. After a little, as she drove with her eyes fixed on the road, I asked her: 'Have you been just once into this flat, or several times?' She raised a hand with four fingers outstretched: 'Four times.' 'How did you come to meet Viola?' 'A friend of mine introduced me.' 'Had she also been in the flat?' 'Yes, several times.' 'How did you come to know that Viola had a daughter and that I was called Desideria?' 'She told me so herself. She said I looked like you; she talks about you all the time. But tell me . . .' 'What?' 'Your mother hasn't by any chance developed an infatuation for you?' 'She's not my mother, she's my adoptive mother.' 'Now I understand. It does happen. I, for instance, have made love with my stepfather.' 'Did you meet someone called Eros in the flat?' 'Yes.' 'Did you like him?' 'I neither liked him nor disliked him; I was indifferent to him.' 'Viola told me to give you these photographs. It's Eros, the man with you?' I placed the photographs on the steering-wheel; she cast a rapid glance at them and said: 'Yes, it's him. But I don't know what to do with the photographs. Keep them in memory of me.' 'Memory of what?' 'Of me, of my legs, of my body. A little time ago you looked at me in a certain way. With that photograph you'll be able to go on looking at me.' 'My mother said that she would telephone you as soon as

263

possible.' 'As far as I'm concerned, she can telephone as much as she likes; she won't see me again.' 'Why, what has she done to you?' 'Why, this fixation that she has with her Polaroid; I don't mind being photographed, but there's a limit. And then, she's violent, your mother; she laid hands on me, then she wanted me to slap her, and in her opinion I didn't do it so very well. In the end I should have had to get myself called Desideria and to say to her: "Yes, Mum, no, Mum." No, no, too many complications, it doesn't do, for me.' I hesitated as she spoke: should I tear up the photographs or keep them? The Voice intervened: 'Keep them, they'll come in useful for Erostrato.' 'Why, in what way?' 'To blackmail him and compel him to introduce you to the group.' Always the group! I put the photographs in my pocket. Brigitte said: 'D'you know, I like you? There's something about you that pleases me very much.' I made no answer; and so we remained silent until we reached Via Gaeta. In Via Gaeta Brigitte parked the car in front of a small door of light-coloured wood, with a well-polished doorknob and lock. Beside this very new-looking door was to be seen the shutter of a shop, of the old type, made of corrugated iron, all rusty and dusty, lowered right to the ground and fixed with a big padlock. With a sudden air of sympathy and without moving, the key already in her hand, Brigitte said to me: 'Will you come up too, into the flat?' I thought that this was a curious manner of displaying her benevolence and said uncertainly: 'If you like; I have never been there.' She looked at me with her liquid, transparent, glassy-blue eyes, then said in a quiet voice: 'I like you, really I do, perhaps because we're like one another. Come up, we'll make love, I'll make you pay only a little, the least possible. But we must be quick, because I'm expected in another place.' I was struck by the spontaneity wholly devoid of awareness that appeared in this offer; I could not help thinking that beauty and unconsciousness made Brigitte into a kind of animal not so very different from a very beautiful racehorse or a magnificent highly bred dog. So it was with just the tone of regret of a

264

connoisseur who finds himself short of money that I replied: 'Not now; possibly another time.' 'As you like.' She opened the door, jumped out, crossed the road, and disappeared into the door opposite. I sat still and as if stupefied, looking at the long, narrow street with its few modest-looking shops, its large number of dreary, insignificant houses, and, at its far end, what appeared to be a workshop: one could see a man in blue overalls busying himself about a car with an open bonnet. Then, all of a sudden, the Voice cried: 'Eureka! I've found the place where we will hold Viola once we have seized her.' 'And what is this place?' 'Why, here, in this same flat that she has rented to carry on her orgies.' 'Are you mad?' 'No, I'm not mad; there's logic in all this. We'll transform the vulgar bourgeois *garçonnière* into a people's prison, we'll purify the flat, we'll so to speak re-consecrate it.' 'Oh, so there are sacred things even for you.' 'Of course, all that has to do with the revolution is sacred. This flat is a brothel; by placing Viola in it after kidnapping her, we shall re-consecrate it as a human dwelling.' It continued on this note, partly elated and partly demonstrative; what it termed 'logic' went to its head like an excessively strong wine; and then suddenly the door opened again and Brigitte came out into the street. She got back into the car, closed the door, started the engine, and asked me if I wanted her to take me back home. As she spoke she handed me the key, with a detached air as if to say: 'Everything is over between us even before it began.' I was silent for a moment; a strange, mad idea had come to me. Brigitte resembled me, she was ready to do, for money, all the things I did not feel like doing for any reason; why not suggest to her that she should take my place both inside and outside the house, with Viola, with Erostrato, with Tiberi and the whole lot of them? With her, doubts would vanish; the revolution would be finally put on one side; sex *à trois* would no longer be a problem; the kidnapping would come to nothing; the Voice would go away definitively, goodness knows where, just like the whirl of dust and bits

265

of paper driven by a sudden gust of wind at the far end of the street. But the Voice brought me back to reality just as an officer, faithful to his duty, would bring back a deserting soldier to the front line: 'Don't be under any illusions. You are what you are and you cannot change places with someone else. Perhaps that morning, at Diomira's, you might still have been able to become someone like Brigitte. Instead, you chose me, once and for all, and now all that is left for you is to go forward with me along the road that you started out upon that day, even if it frightens you.' All this happened in an instant. Then I told Brigitte that I had something to do in that neighbourhood and I hastily got out of the car.

I: So the Voice made you finally accept the idea of kidnapping Viola, as the only thing it remained for you to do?

Desideria: In a way, yes.

I: But did it seem right to you to kidnap your adoptive mother?

Desideria: It had nothing to do with me; it seemed right to the Voice.

I: By the way, admitting that the kidnapping was successful and that Viola paid the ransom, what did the Voice intend to do with the money thus obtained?

Desideria: It had given me to understand that it would serve Erostrato's revolutionary group or any other group of the same kind.

I: But was it really certain that Erostrato formed part of a group? And that the group really existed?

Desideria: No, it wasn't at all certain. To be sure of it I telephoned Erostrato one morning and told him I wanted to talk to him, but not at home or in the top-floor flat. So we made an appointment for midday, at Villa Borghese, where I went sometimes to take my dog for a walk.

266

CHAPTER THREE

I: What sort of a dog did you have?

Desideria: An extremely ugly mongrel that I had taken from the municipal kennels at Porta Portese. The Voice had wanted me to have a mongrel as a sort of challenge to the highly bred dogs which, when they were taken for walks, could be seen running about, up and down the lawns, with their smart, well-dressed masters from the Parioli quarter. I had named him Bico, and in the end he became much attached to me.

I: Why Bico?

Desideria: From *bicolore*, two-coloured. He was a kind of wolf, with a body divided exactly into two parts of different colours: the forepart very dark, the hinder part very light.

I: So you put the dog in the car and went to Villa Borghese. What happened then?

Desideria: I parked the car near the horse-jumping hurdles, under the trees. The dog jumped out and immediately ran down the slope towards the lawns. I clambered over the hurdles and followed it, holding the dog's lead. I at once saw Erostrato, who came to meet me, and I looked at him as we walked. Then I noticed a physical feature which for some reason had hitherto escaped me.

I: What was that?

Desideria: I saw that he had crooked legs, as the Japanese sometimes have when, as children, they have been carried astride by their mothers. After his hands, after his penis, this was the third physical detail which, in some inexplicable way, gave me the impression of his vulgarity. And this time too I again had the sense of fraternal solidarity as of one plebeian to another. Then I recalled the obsessive, stupid remark that Viola had repeated so many times two

267

evenings before: 'We must clear up our situation'; and I said to myself that I must really clear up my relations with Erostrato, not in a drunken way, like Viola, but as an affectionate and rational person. Yes, I had to put him to the proof by the drastic means of the kidnapping; but above all, I had to provide him with the opportunity – the last – of getting himself out of the lie in which he had become involved. I thought of these things; although the Voice disapproved, I was moved and felt much relieved.

I: The Voice disapproved?

Desideria: Yes, the Voice considered Erostrato to be no more than a means to attain a certain end. Everything else was sentimentality and served no purpose.

I: What did Erostrato say to you when you met?

Desideria: I was standing on a grassy mound with a whole lot of dead leaves, yellow and red, heaped round me; it was the middle of December and autumn was finishing. Erostrato climbed up to me, slipping on the grass, and, when he reached the top of the mound, he said to me, in his deepest and most emotional voice: 'You know, this morning, when I heard your voice on the telephone, I was so pleased that afterwards, while I was shaving, I caught myself singing' I had a sudden feeling of irritation at the thought that he always spoke in this emotional tone, whatever he was saying; and I answered him dryly: 'I must speak to you and that's the reason why I asked you to come here. This is not a case of an appointment just to see one another; it's a matter of something very precise.' 'Precise? And what is that?' 'It's that I can't wait any longer.' 'Wait for what?' At that moment the dog came back up the mound with a dry stick between his teeth for the usual game of getting the stick thrown and then bringing it back to me; I took the stick from his mouth and threw it a long way off; and then I said: 'Waiting for your comrade to arrive from Milan. Anyhow, what does your comrade matter? We can start to act by ourselves; when he comes, he'll be pleased to discover that we haven't been idle.' 'But to act in what way?' 'As you're always telling me, on a revolutionary

268

level.' He pretended not to notice the irony and said: 'We can certainly act on a revolutionary level without having to wait for the comrade. But first of all, I should like to know what our action would consist of.' 'Do you know an Austrian girl called Brigitte?' At that moment Erostrato was looking at the lawns with the dogs running over them this way and that and their owners walking slowly up and down on the misty slopes, under trees with bare branches pointing in all directions in gestures like those of consternation and appeal. He was silent for quite a long time, then finally he replied: 'I know her; what of it?' 'Yesterday she turned up at home and asked for Viola. She said she had left her driving licence at the flat in Via Gaeta where you, Viola, and she had met the day before. I made Viola give me the key, got into the car with Brigitte, and the two of us went together to fetch the licence. Then, after she had gone up to the flat, an idea came to me while I was waiting for her in the street.' 'What was the idea?' 'Viola's doing her best to make me take Brigitte's place next time, at Via Gaeta. Don't protest, for that is so. Well, the action that I propose to you would consist in this: we go, all three of us, to Via Gaeta, and when we're there, we two attack Viola, tie her up very thoroughly, and shut her up in a room; then we write to the family, that is, to myself, and ask for a large sum as ransom. I take the letter to Tiberi, who has Viola's power of attorney. Tiberi draws the money from the bank and hands it to me. When the comrade from Milan arrives, we give him the money as a contribution to the financing of the group; and then we'll see.' 'And Viola?' 'Viola returns home where I, that is, the family, await her with open arms.' 'And supposing she reports us?' 'She won't report us, don't worry. In the first place, she won't know, and besides, even if she did know, she wouldn't report us. She didn't report me when I tried to kill her: all the more reason why she won't report me for relieving her of a few million lire.' This time he said nothing, he stood still and silent looking at the lawns and the dogs and the dogs' owners, his hands plunged in the pockets of his overcoat. The dog came back with the

269

stick in his mouth; I took it from him and threw it far away again; then I said to Erostrato lightly and quietly: 'You'll gain from it, after all. I'll give you, let us say, ten per cent of the sum we shall derive from the ransom.' Again he said nothing; then, with sudden decision, he moved and started to go quickly down from the mound. The Voice then shouted to me: 'You see, he's running away! He's a coward, a liar; the group doesn't exist, nothing exists except his own enormous member and the money that he makes out of it. Tell him the truth to his face once and for all, tell him!' I don't know why, but this time the incitements of the Voice inflamed me. Erostrato was now a few steps in front of me, but I ran and caught up with him and started talking to him hurriedly and with vehemence. He hastened his step, like someone who tries to take shelter from a sudden shower; so I started to run again beside him. We must have been a curious pair, he, small, walking as hurriedly as he could, his hands thrust into his short coat; and I tall, bigger than he, in sweater and blue jeans, running beside him and talking to him without pause; and the dog which, thinking it was all a game, ran around us and barked cheerfully.

I: You must indeed have been a curious pair. And I should like to know what you said to him.

Desideria: This is more or less what I said: 'Coward, liar, I came here with the intention of being sincere with you and of acting in such a way that you should be the same with me. I don't love you even if on the day of our first encounter we made love; I don't love you and I shall never love you; but I have a feeling of affection for you such as a sister might have for a brother. And you know why? Because I am a foundling, a bastard, a daughter of the people sold by her mother to a Parioli lady and introduced forcibly and without her consent into this filthy bourgeoisie, and I know also, mind you, that in spite of all the fibs you've told me, I know for certain that you're like me, you're a proletarian, a son of the people plunged up to your eyes in the bourgeoisie bog. But the difference between you

270

and me is that I not merely know all this but I also accept it, whereas you do not accept it and by dint of not accepting it you almost convince yourself that you're ignorant of it. I came today in order that there might be truth between us, simply the truth with its courage and its light, and instead, what have I found? A coward who doesn't speak and doesn't answer and runs away like a sewer rat driven from its hole. Yes, you're a liar, I can't prove it, but I know it for certain; it's not true that you're the son of a landowning Sicilian baron, it's not true that you have a degree in economics, it's not true that you're kept in Rome by your father; nothing is true. You're a son of the people, but the shame of being so, the mania that devours you to be a bourgeois, have made of you a vulgar man, a dubious character, a boor. Instead of rebelling you adapted yourself, you lied to yourself and to others, you sold yourself, you prostituted yourself. You're utterly corrupt, right to the marrow of your bones, you're a real, proper shit and that's all you want to be. As for the group, as for the revolutionary action and all the rest of the rubbish, it's clear that you invented everything, just in order to deceive me, to get me to take part in love-making *à trois*, as Viola wants me to do, Viola, whose slave you are, whose kept man, whose procurer. Now you will wish to know how I come to be so sure that you're a liar, a coward, and a shit, and I reply that I know it because I have understood you from the moment of our first encounter and have penetrated your secret, just as though you were transparent and I had read you through and through. And what is your secret? Your secret is that, after all, even you have a conscience, even though it's buried under a mountain of shit, and this conscience consists in the fact that you know you're corrupt to the marrow of your bones, and since you know it, you wish to die, no longer to exist, to go back to being what you were before you were born – which is to say, a foetus, an embryo, nothing. And do you know how I became aware of this? I became aware of it from the manner in which you made oral love that day. As I was lying on my back with

271

my legs spread out and you were kneeling in front of me and kissing my sex, I felt quite precisely that you were not seeking your own pleasure but that you wished simply to die, yes, to die inside my belly which for you, at that moment, was your mother's womb – that is, to retrace backwards the road that you had already travelled in coming into the world, to curl up inside me like a foetus, with your arms folded and your eyes closed, and then to regress back and back, return to being an embryo, a mere clot of life, a nothingness. Yes, this is what you asked of me with the consciousness of asking the impossible; in fact, you gave a sad, despairing groan which moved me, because in it I felt the whole of your horror of life and the whole of your longing for death. It moved me and aroused in me the fraternal feeling that made me come here today to propose the kidnapping of Viola. Yes, because this is your last opportunity to pull yourself out of the mud and be a man and lose that longing for nothingness and to love life. If you carry out this kidnapping with me, even if there's no group and it does not exist, as I'm convinced it does not, you'll be doing something that will save you. But if you reject my proposal, then there will be nothing more to be done, you will be lost without remedy, and will continue to knock at the doors of nothingness between women's legs, to attempt the impossible, and naturally the doors will not be opened to you, and therefore you will go on till the very end as a coward, a liar, a vulgarian, a prostitute, and a boor.'

I: You said these things to him?

Desideria: Yes, and a lot more, too. He sought to escape from the hailstorm by quickening his step, but I kept up with him without effort, having longer legs than he. And so, with him running and keeping silent, with me running and talking, with the dog jumping round us and barking, we crossed the big misty lawns, amongst the dogs and the dogs' owners, and came back again to the hurdles. Erostrato's large Jaguar. dusty and dented, was parked just at that point; he ran desperately to the door, opened it, and slipped inside: but I was quick to run around the car and get in

272

beside him. I shut the door violently and cried to him: 'Answer, speak once and for all, say even that I'm not right, that none of it's true, confirm that you *are* the son of a Sicilian baron, that you have a degree in economics, that you are a revolutionary, that the group does exist, that you don't in the least want to die, that you like being alive: say whatever you like, but speak.'

I: And he?

Desideria: Then something terrible happened, at least for me. He answered me in such a way as to allow me to realize that he took my words seriously, also the anguish that shone through them and the fraternal affection that inspired them; but at the same time I was sure, in a definite and final manner, that he did not understand me and would never understand me.

I: And so?

Desideria: I don't know how to define the truth of the scene. Myself, on one side, moved, sincere, and vehement and, at bottom, passionately affectionate; he, on the other side, precise, cold, controlled and ... totally uncomprehending, just like someone who finds himself confronted by a foreigner and is under the illusion that he comprehends his language whereas he doesn't understand it and answers him with words which show that he does not understand him.

I: In fact, what did he say?

Desideria: Suddenly he decided to answer me. He lit a cigarette, raised to his lips his extremely vulgar hand with its nicotine-yellow fingers, and then said: 'Now I'll answer you in order. Point one: I do not wish to die, I do not wish to go back into my mother's womb, I know absolutely nothing of the pre-natal state and I do not want to regress to it, I like life, I like living, I wish to live. Point two: I'm sorry, but I can only confirm what I have already said about my origins: I *am* the son of a Sicilian baron and landowner and of a mother who was the daughter of a lawyer. Point three: the revolutionary group of Milan exists, it has a name and a programme and I take part in it regularly.

273

Point four: I have nothing against the idea of a possible kidnapping of Viola, but we cannot do it on our own, without first consulting with the people at Milan. For this we must await the arrival of the comrade who is on the steering committee. Point five: the comrade arrives in a week's time, or ten days at most.'

I: It was all lies, wasn't it?

Desideria: That's the point. Some of it was lies, as, for instance, the part that concerned his family: some of it was truth, which, however, was truth only for him, like the part that denied his unconscious desire for death; other parts again were half-truths, such as the fact that he had no objection to the kidnapping of Viola. Finally, there were truths, falsely objective we may call them, such as the affirmation that the group existed and that the comrade from Milan would arrive in ten days' time. Possibly the group did exist and the comrade would really arrive, but this in no way meant that Erostrato was a revolutionary. If anything, the existence of the group and the arrival of the comrade were in connection with his aspiration to be something that he was not. Anyhow, what importance did the truth have? What mattered to me at the moment was not so much that Erostrato should tell the truth as that he should be real, even by means of lies.

I: I have heard you say that before.

Desideria: I shall always say it; and in fact, after he answered me in this fashion, thus reiterating all his lies, I understood that the feeling I had for him was justified and could be none other than it was.

I: What feeling?

Desideria: The obscure, heartrending feeling of a powerless brotherhood, of an inert compassion.

I: So your meeting served no purpose. Things remained at the point where they had always been.

Desideria: To me it served no purpose. But to the Voice it did. It now knew for certain that the group existed, that the comrade was arriving, and that the idea of the kidnapping was, generally speaking, accepted. All the rest

274

didn't matter a damn. You know what it said of my reflections on Erostrato and on the difference between truth and reality: 'You're incorrigible; when you don't give way to sentimentality you do something worse, you go in for psychology.'

I: Well, what answer did you give Erostrato?

Desideria: None. I merely said: 'If things are as you say, and I have no reason to doubt them, we'll await the arrival of the comrade from Milan.'

I: And he, what did he say?

Desideria: He confuted me with an unexpected question: 'Meanwhile, what am I to say to Viola?'

I: Truly unexpected. What did you reply?

Desideria: I replied that he must not say anything to her. I added: 'Besides, what has Viola to do with it?'

I: Did he explain to you what Viola had to do with it?

Desideria: He was silent for such a long time that for a moment I thought that he was not going to explain anything to me. Finally, he said: 'Viola knows that you asked to see me. She was there with me when you telephoned. I realized from the start that you wanted to talk to me about the Milan group; but I made her believe, on the other hand, that it was a question of her and myself and the flat in Via Gaeta. So she's now waiting for me to come back and tell her yes or no.' You see? Viola was waiting for me to say yes or no to the question of love-making *à trois*. It occurred to me suddenly that there was a parallel situation between Viola and myself, in our relations with Erostrato. We were both dragging Erostrato, one from one side and the other from the other, towards something that was of importance to us: to Viola, the orgy, to me, the group. Erostrato was in the middle and seemed to be influenced now by one and now by the other.

I: It seems to me that he was influenced mainly by Viola, wasn't he?

Desideria: Not so very much. In the first place, he did not love her, perhaps he actually hated her. Then, the very fact that the group really existed and that he took part in it showed that, in theory at least, he was influenced by me. Moreover, I had confirmation of my theory about the parallel situation between myself and Viola in relation to Erostrato almost immediately. To his question as to what he ought to say to Viola on my behalf, I answered instinctively: 'And you, what d'you think I ought to say?' Then something unforeseen occurred. He was silent for a moment and then he said: 'You think I would wish you to answer with a yes. But you're wrong. As far as I'm concerned, you can answer with a no. You don't know me, I'm not what you think.'

I: Unforeseen, certainly.

Desideria: Then he went on: 'You think I came to this appointment on account of Viola. Once again you're wrong. I too, like you, came to the appointment in order to be sincere, to tell you certain things that I have at heart and that I have never yet told you.'

I: You must have been surprised, weren't you?

Desideria: Yes, and there even came to me a kind of hope that he, at last, would withdraw, somehow or other, from the lying image of himself which he had so far offered me. But I did not trust myself; I said, as a precaution: 'What would the things be that you have never told me and that you wanted to tell me today?' I saw him puff the smoke out through his nose in a decisive way, and then announce: 'Your idea of kidnapping Viola so as to get money out of her is simply crazy. Yet you will have noticed that I did not breathe a word against it, that I accepted it at once. And you know why? Because I think as you do about Viola.' 'What is that?' Instead of answering this question, he turned towards the back seat and took up a book which lay on the seat. 'To make you understand what I think of Viola,' he said, 'I brought this book.' He handed me the book, I took it and with some surprise saw that it was an album of photographs of tne revolution in China, by Cartier-Bresson. I knew this album extremely well; Viola had bought it a couple of years before and for a long time I had seen it in the living room, together with other books;

276

then it had disappeared, and now it turned up again in the hands of Erostrato. I could not help exclaiming: 'But this book is ours!' 'Yes,' he said, 'I took it from the living room up to the top-floor flat to look at it. In it there is a photograph which struck me and which I should like you to look at.' I opened the album; he put out his left hand while he raised his cigarette to his mouth with his right; and with that one hand searched in the book, on my knee, for the page he wanted, and indicated it to me. I looked. It was a photograph taken actually on the day before the entry into Shanghai of the Communist troops in 1949. It showed a row of Chinese who, packed close together and with faces strained with the effort, clasping to their chests documents or savings books, were struggling to reach the doors of a bank as quickly as possible with the object of withdrawing their money and fleeing before Mao's army occupied the city. I examined the photograph, then looked up towards Erostrato and gazed at him questioningly: 'They're the bourgeois Chinese withdrawing their savings from the bank, before Mao arrives. So what?' He shook his head and replied with unexpected ingenuousness: 'Why, that's what I should like to see here in Rome.' 'What d'you mean?' 'I mean a row of bourgeois struggling to withdraw their money from the bank, and among them Viola with her savings book clasped to her chest. And meanwhile, the troops of the revolution are occupying the city.' 'Was it to tell me this that you brought the Cartier-Bresson album?' 'Yes, so that you'll be convinced that I think like you.' 'But what do you, in fact, think?' He took his time and then he answered: 'That photograph has made me understand so many things. The day when the troops entered Shanghai was, so to speak, the boundary line between two epochs. Before that day there was capitalism, the bourgeoisie, banks, people like Viola; after that day everything was changed for the good, there has been no more capitalism or bourgeoisie or banks or people like Viola. Well, I should like that day to come.' He was not looking at me but, stubbornly, as he smoked, at the windscreen; and I, although I was so much younger

277

than he and so much less experienced, felt like a mother in front of her child, a child that is expressing, with immature, approximative words, an obscure feeling of its own.

I: You felt superior to him at that moment?

Desideria: As always, because I understood him and he did not understand me.

I: But did you ever ask yourself why you understood him and he did not understand you?

Desideria: Certainly. I understood him but he did not understand me because I had the Voice and he had not.

I: Who told you that he did not have a Voice too, a Voice all of his own, a personal Voice, exactly like yours?

Desideria: I was told by the fact that he did not understand me.

I: Well, well, the snake that bites its own tail . . . What did you say to him, then, in your indulgent and affectionate tone, like a mother questioning her child?

Desideria: I asked him: 'You – on which side do you see yourself while Viola struggles to withdraw her money from the bank: on the side of the revolution or on Viola's side?' 'On the side of the revolution.' 'But would you not be afraid that, once Rome was occupied by the revolutionary army, they might accuse you of having been a bourgeois, a capitalist, and would finish you off?' 'I a bourgeois, a capitalist, what nonsense you talk.' 'Well, if not exactly a bourgeois and a capitalist, someone who got himself kept by a bourgeois, capitalist woman.'

I: Were you so frank with each other even about the fact that he got himself kept by Viola?

Desideria: Yes, we were frank about that, as about so many other things. Too often I had seen him, at home or in restaurants, receive money from Viola so that he could maintain, in front of me, the fiction of the salaried secretary. And then this frankness formed part of our complicity in relation to, and against, Viola. Finally, I put him at his ease one day by saying to him: 'You and I are alike in this way too: that we're both of us kept by Viola, you as a lover and I as a daughter.'

278

I: Was he not disconcerted by your prophecy that the Communists would finish him off?

Desideria: Oddly enough, he didn't protest; somehow or other he accepted my point of view. After a moment's reflection, he said: 'I would not run away with Viola, I would stay in Rome in any case. They might then, perhaps, even bring me to trial, they might perhaps even finish me off; but I should be content just the same because the revolution would have taken place and people like Viola would no longer exist.'

I: He was really angry with Viola!

Desideria: He was and he wasn't. I asked him: 'But why are you so keen that Viola should be swept away in the throng of bourgeois people struggling to get to the doors of the bank?' He reflected for a moment, then replied: 'I don't know. I suppose that now and then I get angry with her just because she is a rich, selfish woman who really loves nothing beyond her own money. And then I forget that even she has qualities and that sometimes it even happens that I am fond of her and would like to know that she had departed, had fled, together with her jewels, her furs, and her gold to goodness knows where, forever. After she had gone, there would be the revolution and everything would be new and the world could at last breathe.'

I: What did Viola represent to him? The bourgeoisie?

Desideria: I should say so. That is, the feminine equivalent of the emblematic picture of the capitalist in the caricatures of the end of the last century, in a top-hat, white waistcoat, tailcoat, and with a diamond ring on his little finger. Out of curiosity, I asked him: 'Are you in fact fond of Viola or do you hate her?' 'At certain moments,' he said, 'I am fond of her. Not, however, when she gives me presents or money. Nor even when she starts weeping on my shoulder and tells me she can't endure life any longer and would like to die. But at certain other moments I really hate her. The other day she was underneath me and I was on top of her, and she was holding her buttocks wide open with both hands so as to make herself more easily entered,

279

and I – I'm telling the truth – was tempted at that moment to put out my hand to the night table, where there was a bronze candlestick, and split open her head with one single blow. She would not even have been aware of it, because she had her eyes shut and her face buried in the pillow.' He remained silent for an instant as though overcome by feeling, then he added: 'In the end I'm sorry for her because she is unhappy. The chief reason for her unhappiness, however, is you, to be precise. With me she makes love: but in your case, she loves you, and since you reject her she is unhappy. I've never seen her cry on my account. But when she speaks of you, her eyes always fill with tears and she begins to stammer and then starts weeping.' 'Has she ever told you why she weeps when she speaks of me?' 'She hasn't told me, but I know.' 'What d'you know?' 'She weeps from exasperation. She weeps like someone who wants something at all costs and doesn't manage to get it. If you like, that's a selfish reason, but the tears are real, so much so that at such moments she really makes me pity her.' For a moment he remained thoughtful, then suddenly he resumed, with a curious return to his professional role: 'You asked me what I would like to be able to say to Viola on your account. I'm not asking you to make me give a definite yes or no. But she's so unhappy, she wants it so badly, that it would be enough for you to send me to say that you want to take time. That you want to get accustomed to the idea.' 'What idea? The idea of taking the place of a call-girl in the Via Gaeta flat?' He was not upset; he said: 'The idea that you are not mother and daughter but two friends and tomorrow perhaps even something more.'

I: How did the meeting at Villa Borghese come to an end?

Desideria: The end of it was that, when I looked at my wristwatch, just like any ordinary girl who has lingered chattering to a so-called acquaintance, I exclaimed: 'Why, it's late; Viola asked me to go with her to lunch at some embassy or other'; and I jumped out of the car, with a hurried: 'Goodbye, goodbye.' The dog, which had taken

280

up a position under a tree to wait for me, at once jumped up to meet me, barking; I ran to my own car and left immediately. At home I found Viola already dressed to the last detail and awaiting me with impatience; I rushed to change in my own room and a little later we went out together.

I: Did you learn later how Viola had received the information that you wished to 'get accustomed to the idea'?

Desideria: Yes and no, because I did not wish to enquire into what Erostrato might have told her. He lied continually; and I knew it. He might have told her that I wanted to 'get accustomed to the idea'; just as he might have told her that I was already accustomed to the idea and was ready to meet him and Viola in the Via Gaeta flat. However, that he had spoken to her was certain, because Viola, that same evening, at the restaurant, made a gesture of gratitude that alluded to it. Erostrato had risen to go and pay the bill; she put out her hand to give me a caress and said: 'Thank you for what you sent Eros to tell me.' I should have liked to ask her what Erostrato had really said; but the Voice, which, as usual, wished me to encourage Viola to become more and more the lover and less and less the mother, suggested to me instead this remark full of Sibylline coquetry: 'Don't thank me; you know that I'm fond of you' – a filial remark which, however, in the context in which it was made, might also pass for amorous. The same night I had a dream which I want to relate to you.

I: A dream connected with Viola?

Desideria: Yes; now listen. It seemed to me that I was in the so-called delicatessen shop in Via Gaeta. I was lying on the bed, on my back, my hands joined at the back of my neck, and I was waiting. I was waiting for Viola and Erostrato to arrive; I had accepted the idea of love-making *à trois* and was ready to do it, convinced that by now it was inevitable. While I was waiting, I happened to look beyond the bed to the far side of the room, and to see that the whole of that wall was occupied by a big black sofa; and that on this sofa was lying a naked body of a bright pink colour which stood out against the black in a way that was attractive, even if in some way almost obscene. I jumped down off the bed, went across, and saw that it was Viola, entirely naked, bound with a rope which, starting from her neck, crossed her chest, tied her two wrists together, was twisted several times round her legs, and bound her ankles together. Viola could not speak on account of a gag of adhesive tape which was stuck over her mouth; but the tape and the rope spoke for her: it was clear that Erostrato and I had enticed her, under the pretext of sex *à trois*, to the flat in Via Gaeta; we had attacked and bound her; and I myself was now on guard. In fact, as further proof, there was a tommy gun lying on the chair beside me: my own tommy gun since I was now a skilled guerrilla. But there was something lacking in this pretty exact and ordinary picture of a kidnapping with a political aim; and that was the feeling of hatred that I ought to be feeling for Viola. Not merely did I feel that I did not hate her; somehow or other I had the opposite feeling. What feeling was it? It was a confused, profound uneasiness, in which were combined my quality as a guerrilla; the fact that I was the daughter of the woman I was guarding; and finally the consciousness of the incestuous passion of that woman for myself. I looked at the bound and gagged body; then, after looking round to make sure nobody was watching me, I came to a decision. I bent over Viola; very slowly, so as not to hurt her, pulled the adhesive tape from her mouth; and joined my lips to hers in a long, passionate kiss. The kiss lasted a long time; it was so voluptuous that I lost all notion of time; then suddenly I had the uncomfortable feeling that someone was standing behind me and looking at me. I turned and there I saw my tommy gun held in mid-air, aimed at me by the figure of a man standing there. Who was this man? Someone whose head I could not see because it seemed to be hidden by a black shadow; but I knew for certain that it was the so-called Milan comrade whose forthcoming arrival Erostrato had announced to me during our meeting at Villa Borghese.

I felt a terrible fear; I knew that he was going to shoot, to kill me; the hour of my death had come, I knew, and I gave vent to a long, bitter, pitiful groan . . . and I awoke.

I: It seems to me a very obvious dream.

Desideria: Yes, perfectly obvious. But the Voice pointed out to me that it was, in fact, a dream. It meant that, in life, I did not act; I confined myself, though with great precision and complexity, to dreaming.

I: What did the Voice mean by that?

Desideria: That it was time that I acted, that I had a duty to act.

I: What happened during the week – what we may call the decisive week – between your meeting with Erostrato at Villa Borghese and the arrival of the 'Milan comrade'?

Desideria: What happened was that, the day after the meeting with Erostrato at Villa Borghese, Tiberi telephoned me very early in the morning, when I was still asleep, and asked me to go and see him because he had something important to tell me.

I: Had you seen Tiberi again, recently?

Desideria: No, for some time he had disappeared out of my life. For a long time he had not been coming to the house; when she had to consult him about her business affairs, Viola used to go and see him at his own house or at his antique gallery. From time to time, but less and less often, he would wait for me in his car in the street and follow me at walking pace, driving close to the pavement and uttering his usual brothel obscenities in a calm and gentlemanly voice. But it was obvious that he now did this more for his own private satisfaction than because he expected that I would decide to pay him any attention.

I: Did you agree to go?

Desideria: Yes, he reassured me by saying it was a question of things that particularly concerned Viola. So I told him I would come and see him that same day, in the afternoon.

I: Did you go to his house or to the gallery?

Desideria: To the gallery.

I: Where was the gallery?

Desideria: It was in an old palazzo in the neighbourhood of Piazza di Spagna.

I: Was Tiberi an important antique dealer?

Desideria: Yes, one of the biggest in Rome.

284

I: How ever did he manage to be Viola's man of business?

Desideria: Viola's husband had been his partner; he, in turn, had been Viola's lover. Then Viola's husband died and Tiberi continued to administer his mistress's fortune. Moreover, Viola had invested money in Tiberi's antique gallery.

I: You arrived at Piazza di Spagna and went straight to the gallery. What happened then?

Desideria: I went up two flights of a great white staircase with gold decorations, and rang the bell at an elegant white and gold door in the Empire style. The door was opened at once by an elderly assistant who knew me and bade me come in without asking me what I wanted.

I: The assistant knew you. So you went often to the gallery?

Desideria: In the past, yes. Viola used to employ me to take papers to Tiberi; I was more or less her messenger. Sometimes I would stop and have a chat with him.

I: When you took the papers to him, how old were you?

Desideria: Thirteen, fourteen . . .

I: And he had never given any sign of his passion for you?

Desideria: No, perhaps because I did not yet dress as a hippy but like any ordinary bourgeois young girl; and thus the blue jeans and the sweaters had not yet made him think that I was a dangerous revolutionary to be defeated through the act of sodomy.

I: You went into the gallery and what did you see?

Desideria: A long gallery with a polished floor. On one side a row of tall windows veiled in white, on the other, pieces of furniture exhibited for sale. At the far end I spied Tiberi accompanying a pair of elderly customers, a fat, red-faced, white-haired man in a tight blue overcoat, and a woman, also red-faced and white-haired, bulging like a barrel and with thin legs. Tiberi, as usual, reminded one of a film actor of the thirties: double-breasted jacket of grey cloth, white shirt, dark tie, black shoes. The married couple

285

walked slowly along the row of furniture; every now and then they stopped in front of a piece which struck them; then Tiberi stopped too and spoke. I watched this scene for a moment, then walked in a leisurely way along the whole of the gallery, from the door by which I had entered to the door at the other end, which, as I knew, led into a small room which served Tiberi as an office. As I went past Tiberi and his two customers, I threw him a glance of understanding and he in turn made me a sign, as much as to say that I was to go into the office and wait for him there.

I: What was Tiberi's office like?

Desideria: It was very small, a prolongation of the gallery, from which it was separated by a partition. There was a desk in the Empire style, no doubt also for sale; there was a big sofa of light-coloured leather, and two armchairs. I sat down on the sofa, and for a moment, mechanically, I looked round, without however fixing my eyes on anything in particular. Then my glance came to rest on the desk and I noticed that it was free of papers except for one thin green folder. I looked round again and saw that in one corner there was an old safe, very like a refrigerator, and in the other, opposite corner, a steel filing cabinet, suitable for an office; and I reflected that Tiberi probably kept his business papers in these two pieces of furniture. But my eye was drawn irresistibly to the green folder. All at once I rose, went and sat down behind the desk, and opened the folder. It contained a few typewritten sheets: I looked at the first line and read: 'Object: report on Occhipinti Erostrato.' Then I went on reading.

I: What was written there?

Desideria: I don't want to tell you now, because, shortly afterwards, Tiberi revealed it himself. In order to understand what happened between me and Tiberi that day, it is better that you should come to know it at the moment when Tiberi spoke to me about it. Two things, however, I can tell you: the first is that it was a question of a police report on Erostrato, with the whole of his life related, so to speak, from the judicial point of view, from his adolescence until

286

today. The second thing is that, although it related a quantity of things that I did not know, I had the impression that, somehow or other, I had always known these things.

I: What do you mean?

Desideria: I mean that, from the very beginning, I had had a precise intuition of the way in which Erostrato's character was made up.

I: And that was?

Desideria: It was that, in the same way that I was divided between myself and the Voice, in the same way that Viola oscillated between the role of mother and that of lover; so Erostrato was torn between the exigencies of lying and those of the truth, between the reality of corruption and the aspiration towards revolution. In any case 'torn' is perhaps an inappropriate term. It would be more correct to say 'balanced'.

I: I see. What happened then?

Desideria: I read the police report carefully, from the first to the last line. Then I put back the folder on the desk and went back again to sit on the sofa. I waited five minutes longer and Tiberi came in.

I: In what state of mind were you then, after reading the police report on Erostrato?

Desideria: In the state of mind of a spectator who knows the play and knows what the actor on the stage is going to do and say.

I: Anything else?

Desideria: Yes, I realized that, since my reading of the report, my feeling for Erostrato was modified.

I: In what way?

Desideria: I recognized that the balancing mechanism seemed to be too strong for me, I mean too strong for the feeling of fraternal solidarity that I had felt for him since our first encounter. I was rather desperate, I thought that only a miracle could save him.

I: Save him from what?

Desideria: From himself, that is, from the mechanism.

I: What happened then with Tiberi?

287

Desideria: He came in and immediately assumed an attitude that was in no way confidential or even merely friendly, but formal and bureaucratic, as of someone receiving a person for official reasons and in his office. He said hurriedly: 'Hullo, Desideria, sorry I kept you waiting, but there was that couple, boring and very long-winded, but serious and, in fact, they ended by making up their minds. How are you? Glad to see you.' Then he sat down at the desk, put on his spectacles, considered the folder for a moment but without touching it, looked up towards me and informed me: 'This is a police report on that man Occhipinti Erostrato with whom your mother and you have recently formed a relationship – a very complex relationship, it seems. If it had been only what I may call a sentimental relationship between Occhipinti, your mother, and yourself, it would never have entered my head to take any notice of your friend. But from certain remarks that your mother has dropped, I have understood that it is not so. Between you there are also relations of an economic order, and so, in my capacity as administrator of your mother's affairs, I felt that I ought to do something. I went to see a superintendent of police who is a good friend of mine and asked him to carry out, on my behalf, a little enquiry regarding Occhipinti. The result was these pages that I have here in front of me. I shall not read them to you, it would be too lengthy. I will recapitulate the salient points.' Tiberi looked down again at the folder, then thought again and looked up at me. 'I warn you that I have taken steps to inform your mother of the contents of this report, for the reason that, fundamentally, the report chiefly concerns her. You yourself come into it, of course, but I sincerely hope only in an indirect way.'

I: What did he mean?

Desideria: To put it plainly, he was hoping that I, too, should not be put to shame by Erostrato.

I: Let us hear the salient points.

Desideria: There were many of them; it might be said that the whole report was a salient point. Tiberi was now

288

reading without speaking, his eyes lowered, and then he raised his eyes towards me and resumed: 'The information that Occhipinti usually provides about himself had come to me through your mother. Occhipinti, then, according to Occhipinti, is supposed to be the son of a Sicilian baron and landowner, with a mother who was the daughter of a lawyer; from their marriage were born two sons and two daughters. Our hero (let us call him) is said to have attended a school run by priests for upper-middle-class boys at Palermo, then he entered the faculty of economics in the university of that city and obtained his degree with full marks. After taking his degree, he is said to have administered, under his father's direction, a very large estate of theirs (two thousand hectares), and then, finally, with the agreement of his father, who had consented to maintain him till he had succeeded in maintaining himself, he came to Rome, where, since then, he has worked in the cinema as a scriptwriter and scenarist. As I said, this is Occhipinti according to Occhipinti. But the police depicted a very different character. In it, Occhipinti is the only son of a school caretaker and a nurse and lives in a small town in western Sicily, in his parents' house. The baron and his wife, daughter of a lawyer, exist; there are also the four children; but they are the principal family of the place. Occhipinti did not go to the priests' school for middle class boys but to an ordinary secondary school in the town; he did not go to Palermo or enter the university; all he did was to pass the school-leaving examination and then he abandoned his studies. Meanwhile, he was employed by the baron as a clerk, or something of the kind, in the administration of the estate. At this point comes the first of a series of financial–sentimental–political episodes that regularly punctuate Occhipinti's life. The baron was old and in poor health and remained almost always at Palermo; the baroness, still young, had a passion for occultism; she frequented sorcerers, astrologers, wizards, held spiritual sessions, interrogated the souls of the dead. Occhipinti – no one knows how – reveals considerable knowledge in the field of occultism; he helped the baroness in her meta-psychic activities and, naturally, became her lover. The baroness lived alone on the estate with one of her daughters. The two sons and the other daughter lived at Palermo with their father. Occhipinti – whether with the mother's knowledge or not is not known – became the lover of the daughter, too. Everything went on for a little without any incidents worthy of note, what with spiritualist séances, love affairs, and also activities of an economic kind, for in the mean time the baroness had raised Occhipinti from the rank of clerk to that of her private secretary; then, through secret information, the baron came to know that something was not going right with his estate; he arrived unexpectedly from Palermo, sacked Occhipinti, and reported him for embezzlement. However, rather mysteriously (but it is a mystery that I will clear up shortly), judicial action did not follow; the baron withdrew his accusation. Occhipinti, safe and sound, left his little native town and transferred himself to what Sicilians call "the continent". A year passed and we find Occhipinti again, at Perugia. Here again he is linked by a sentimental relationship with a mature woman, a widow with one daughter. The widow is very religious. Occhipinti enters into a relationship with her through religion, that is, by means of a priest who makes use of him as a kind of aide to look after twenty or so children entrusted to the parish by their mothers. Occhipinti was supported in the same task by the widow's daughter, a young teacher who instructed the children in the first rudiments of religion. Occhipinti promptly became the lover of the teacher as well, and at the same time poked his nose into the affairs of her mother, who ran a household-goods shop in Perugia. Everything went well until, suddenly, everything went wrong: the daughter attempted to commit suicide with barbiturates; the mother sacked Occhipinti and reported him on account of a consignment of aluminium saucepans which had never arrived at the shop even though she had paid for them. Again this time, however, Occhipinti got away with it; the accusation was merely filed. Occhipinti left Perugia and transferred himself to Rome. This time there was a gap of barely six months and then we see Occhipinti again in what we may call his usual, typical situation. The setting was the Rome of suburban villas, of speculators in building sites; the couple, mother and daughter: Aurora Zendrini, ex-actress of the thirties and wife, in fact, of a builder, and her daughter Emanuela; ideology: Fascist. Thanks to their sharing of political ideas, Occhipinti became, first of all, a friend of Aurora's two sons; the two brothers introduced him to their mother and sister. This time the usual order was reversed: Occhipinti became first the lover of the sister and then, with the pretext of getting her work in a film of which he had written the script, the lover of the mother. Meanwhile, he was frequenting a group of the extreme right, was making speeches, taking part in demonstrations. Then, the usual collapse: the sons discovered that the film in which Aurora was to be presented to the public again after ten years' absence did not exist; that Occhipinti was carrying on with both their mother and their sister; that an expensive car, a Jaguar, had passed from their mother's possession into that of Occhipinti without plausible reason. The usual things followed: expulsion of Occhipinti, accusation, filing of the latter.' Tiberi, at this point, replaced the folder on the desk and looked at me: 'What do you say to all this delightful news about your friend?'

I: Well, what did you say to him?

Desideria: The Voice advised me to 'cover' Erostrato, that is, to reply that they were all inventions of the police because Erostrato was of the Left. Of course, the Voice knew perfectly well that the police report was telling the truth, but that did not matter: the comrade from Milan was shortly to arrive; Erostrato had accepted the idea of the kidnapping of Viola; at all costs I must be on Erostrato's side. So I obeyed the Voice, but not without some ambiguity: 'I say they are all things that I knew already.' 'But how?' 'Erostrato himself told me of them from the very first time we met.' 'Oh, so that's so, he told you of them, but

291

I am sure he did not tell you everything.' 'What d'you mean?' 'I mean that the mystery of the filing away of the denunciations hides a very simple truth.' 'What truth?' 'That Occhipinti, ever since the time he lived in Sicily, has been in the confidence of the police, that is, he is a paid spy with a regular salary.' I was silent for a moment, then I said intrepidly: 'I know that, too, he told me that too. But he has not been that for at least a year.' 'Yes, he is no longer that, but d'you know why? Because the police got rid of him owing to his poor productive efficiency. He himself would have asked nothing better than to go on being a spy. But since he produced nothing, they fired him.' 'Was this what you wanted to tell me?' 'Yes, nothing more, but I think it's enough, isn't it?' I made no answer; I rose to my feet.

I: In the report which you read, were there really all the things that Tiberi related to you about Occhipinti?

Desideria: Yes, all of them; he hadn't added or omitted anything.

I: Even the fact that, ever since Sicily, he had been a police agent?

Desideria: Yes, even that.

I: And while he was telling you these things, what did *you* think?

Desideria: I thought I had already known them for some time, for a long time before having read the report. My thinking was focused on two aspects of the report.

I: Which were they?

Desideria: The first was that two women, mother and daughter, kept occurring; that there was always an ideological justification (occultism, Catholicism, Fascism and, lately, in my case, the far Left); and finally, that there was never lacking some sort of financial complication (the embezzlement at the Sicilian estate, the affair of the saucepans at Perugia, the Jaguar with the Zendrinis, the secretary's salary with Viola). The second aspect that struck me was that he had ceased for a year to be a police agent. That is, for some months before our meeting.

I: What did this mean, in your opinion?

292

Desideria: It might mean that they had really sacked him for poor productive efficiency. But it might also mean that, somehow or other, he had perhaps begun to have an attack of conscience about the reality of his situation. And this made me again have hope for him.

I: What did the Voice think of these two different hypotheses?

Desideria: The Voice didn't care a damn; it was not interested in psychological profundities.

I: Well, then, what was the conclusion of your interview with Tiberi?

Desideria: It ended at once. Tiberi appeared disconcerted, one could see that he did not know what to say or do. But he looked at me with unchanging desire, his pink samurai face redder than ever. I said dryly: 'Goodbye,' stretching out my hand to him, and he, with a gallant, old-fashioned gesture, raised it to his lips. 'Desideria,' he said, 'one of these days I'll come and wait for you outside your house at the time when you go to school.' 'To say what to me? That I'm a whore, that I ought to give you my bottom?' He was not in the least disconcerted at the brutal reply suggested by the Voice. With a curious reticence, he said: 'No, it's something different, but before telling you I want to think it over.' 'Think it over as long as you like.' I went out by a small door and found myself unexpectedly on the main staircase.

I: What happened then? And, first of all, did you speak to Erostrato about the police report?

Desideria: Yes, that same day. He had come to lunch with us, and Viola had not yet arrived; I found him reading the paper as he waited in the living room and told him everything.

I: What was his reaction?

Desideria: He listened to me right to the end without interrupting me, with his usual impassive air, and then he gave me an explanation characteristic of a minor delinquent of the plebeian class.

I: What was that?

Desideria: Speaking in a reticent, evasive, shifty tone and choosing his words with care, he said that Tiberi, for obvious reasons upon which it was useless to dwell, was angry with him; that even in the police he had many enemies; that, in fact, he was the victim of a conspiracy; and so on, on that line. In the end, nevertheless, he did admit that there was 'something' of truth in the police report, but it was a matter of things without importance, of 'errors of youth'. So then I tried to press him closely with precise questions about his past. He listened to me attentively without moving a muscle of his face, without changing his fixed, inexpressive look for a single instant. In the end his nostrils twitched as though with a gust of emotion, and in his deepest and most vibrant voice, he uttered this remark: 'I have no intention of answering you this time. What I had to say, I have already said. You won't get a word more out of me.'

I: How about his rebellion against the bourgeois? And his aspiration for a total palingenesis which would sweep away everything, himself included? And the Cartier-Bresson photograph?

294

Desideria: Nothing; everything forgotten, removed, wiped out. At this point the Voice said to me that I must not insist on verifying the reliability of the report. It was now a matter of waiting for ten days, then the comrade from Milan would come, and so it would be seen whether Erostrato could still be of use to us or not. I obeyed the Voice, as usual. And so, while waiting for the arrival of the comrade from Milan, we took up our normal life again.

I: What was it like, normal life?

Desideria: What was it like? It wasn't.

I: What d'you mean?

Desideria: It was neither normal nor abnormal. It wasn't a life.

I: Explain yourself more fully.

Desideria: I mean that it wasn't a life because I felt it to be provisional from beginning to end, while awaiting the arrival of the Milan comrade, that is, awaiting action, in other words, the kidnapping of Viola.

I: Then what did you do?

Desideria: Nothing particular. Erostrato now came to lunch every day. He would come down from the top-floor flat, where he worked all the morning at a so-called film script of his, sit down on the sofa, and read the papers. Then I would arrive from school, greet Erostrato briefly, take possession in turn of a newspaper, and become absorbed in reading it. The last to arrive would be Viola, who went out every morning on business or to do shopping. She looked in for a moment, greeted us with a cordial 'Hello, children,' then went out again, went to her room to take off her coat; shortly afterwards made an incursion into the kitchen to see that everything was proceeding smoothly; and finally came back into the living room and poured herself a whisky as an apéritif. Meanwhile, since she had already looked through the papers in bed, with her morning coffee, she chatted with us about nothing in particular. The morning was the time when Viola was most the mother, the Parioli lady, the mistress of the house, the native American. She kept up this role all day long; but gradually, as the hours went by, she acted it with more and more fatigue and more and more effort. So that, when evening came, it was perfectly natural to her to abandon it and to enter into the role of the incestuous lesbian.

I: What happened at lunch?

Desideria: Nothing. While we were eating we talked little, not because we were embarrassed, but rather because we were people of the same family who have no need to talk in order to stay together. Anyone who looked at us through the window, let us suppose, would certainly have thought that we were a mother, a son, and a daughter; or else a mother, a daughter, and the daughter's husband. A family group, in fact, of the most normal kind.

I: How did the lunch finish?

Desideria: Like all the lunches in this world. We rose and went to take our coffee always in the same corner of the room. After coffee I would go away without saying goodbye, and shut myself in my room to study (I had to take the school-leaving examination that year) or to read. Sometimes I went out in order to go and study at the house of a friend. In short, I did not see Viola and Erostrato again until evening.

I: And they – what did they do during the afternoon?

Desideria: I don't know; really, I never asked myself. Nothing particular, I suppose. Except for the days when they went to make love *à trois* in the Via Gaeta flat.

I: Did they make love *à trois* during the afternoon?

Desideria: Yes, never at night, which instead was devoted to me. In any case, the call-girls, like all those who practise a fixed trade, work usually from morning till evening and keep the night for their private lives.

I: In those ten days of a life which was 'neither normal nor abnormal', did Erostrato and Viola make love *à trois* in the Via Gaeta flat?

Desideria: Certainly they did, at least once.

I: How did you come to know this?

Desideria: I knew it one day at dinner from a red, circular mark on Viola's neck, as if from a kiss accompanied by a prolonged sucking; from the devastated look of her face, which was haggard and yet still excited; as well as from two black rings of sexual fatigue round her eyes, which contradicted their distant, authoritative expression.

I: You said that during the whole day Viola acted her part as a mother more and more wearily, and then, as night came on, she abandoned it and entered decisively into the role of uninhibited sex-maniac. Can you give me an example of this lack of inhibition?

Desideria: Yes, during those same days something happened of the kind of thing you want to know. But in order to understand what happened at night, one must go back to something that happened during the day, at lunch.

I: At lunch Viola must have still had the sulky, puritanical American expression, I suppose, seeing that she abandoned it only after sunset.

Desideria: Yes, indeed. But have you ever thought what puritan moralism can be when applied to the muddles of eroticism? Anyhow, this is how it happened. I came back from school, found Erostrato reading the newspaper while waiting for lunch, and greeted him; I also took a newspaper and started reading; then at last Viola arrived. She responded briefly to my 'good morning' but did not sit down; from the doorway she made a sign to Erostrato, to ask him to leave the living room as she wished to speak to him alone. Erostrato rose, joined Viola in the hall, and left the door open. I pricked up my ears, hearing that they were whispering; then this whispering was transformed into a rather harsh discussion; Viola's voice was urgent, even though low; Erostrato's equally low though reticent. Finally they came into the room again, Viola's face strained with furious discontent, Erostrato, as always, impassive. We went to dinner and the first course was served. Viola refused it, remaining still and silent, her bust very erect, the very image of puritan severity. The manservant left the room and Viola said suddenly: 'Now give me back that money, seeing that it serves no purpose.' Erostrato said nothing; he put his hand into the inside pocket of his jacket,

297

brought out and handed to Viola some banknotes folded in four. Viola did not take the money, but she fixed Erostrato with eyes that seemed to be rendered almost black by anger (in reality, her eyes were greenish-brown), and she said slowly and disdainfully: 'Keep it, then. You had some trouble, after all; keep it as a tip.' Erostrato said nothing but put the money back in his pocket. Viola went on: 'Your speciality, according to the police report, is evidently mother and daughter. A mother and daughter in Sicily with fraud and spiritualist séances. A mother and daughter at Perugia, with fraud and religion. A mother and daughter in Rome, with fraud and Fascism. But now things are not going quite so well for you. You have found the mother but not the daughter. Or rather, there is a daughter, it's Desideria, but Desideria is a hard nut to crack, she's a woman who knows what she wants and what she doesn't want, and among the things that she doesn't want is to act as third woman with you and me. Certainly Desideria from time to time asks you for some service because you're expert and well-endowed by nature, but this does not mean giving in to the matter of love-making *à trois*. As I told you, Desideria is a hard nut and there is nothing to be done – or rather, there is something to be done so that at least I may find some pretty girl to do with us what Desideria does not want to do, and apparently will never do. But you are a twopenny-halfpenny kept man even though you consume a lot of money and don't even know how to make a telephone call or two, how to propose a compensation or how to hand over a few notes secretly. I had told you that I wanted a certain thing, I had given you the money, and you had a duty to find me this thing at all costs. Instead, you come back with your tail between your legs, you tell me that Brigitte was absolutely unwilling, that she threw the money back in your face, and other absurdities and lies of the same kind. It's not true, Brigitte is a girl who sells herself, she's on sale from morning till night, just as a piece of meat with a price label is on sale from morning till night on the butcher's counter. If she was unwilling, it means that

298

you didn't know how to manage things. And don't come and tell me that she was unwilling because I gave her a slap; you know perfectly well that the slap was included in the bill and paid for in advance. No, you didn't want to make arrangements with Brigitte because she despises you and lets you see it and perhaps even tells you so, and then your precious sensitiveness is wounded and you prefer to have nothing to do with her. But I don't care a damn about your sensitiveness, I wanted to see Brigitte this evening, at all costs, I had given you all the money that was needed and you were unwilling to arrange the meeting because you hate Brigitte. But what does all this matter to me? I buy you and I buy Brigitte; this is my right, seeing that you are both of you for sale, and, once I have bought you, you must do what I want, you the procurer and she the whore!'

I: A pretty scene, I must say. What was Erostrato's reply?

Desideria: He made no reply. He waited until Viola had finished, then he put down his napkin on the table and went away.

I: But what had really happened?

Desideria: You know already: Erostrato evidently procured for Viola the third woman for their meetings in Via Gaeta. The last, in order of time, had been Brigitte, the call-girl who looked like me. Just because she looked like me, Viola had taken a fancy to her, but during their last meeting Viola, for some reason, had slapped Brigitte and so Brigitte, although Viola, through Erostrato, had sent her a large sum of money (I think there were five notes of a hundred thousand folded in four), did not wish to have anything more to do with her.

I: What happened that day?

Desideria: Nothing particular. I did my studies at the house of a friend. When I came home, I found Viola and Erostrato sitting in the living room as though nothing had happened. Viola was already dressed to go out; she told me to be quick, for it was late; we must go as quickly as possible to the restaurant so as then to be in time to see a certain film. From a kind of hesitation and encumbrance in her voice, I knew at once that Viola was drunk. The bottle of whisky stood on the table in front of her; she held a glass in her hand, and after having told me to be quick, she raised the glass and, with a wink, gave Erostrato a toast, and he, in turn, raised his own glass and reciprocated the toast. I thought quite logically that they were reconciled, and without saying a word went to my room to change.

I: So then you went out together. What happened at the restaurant?

Desideria: You mean what happened in the car, because that evening we never arrived at the restaurant. A little later, then, we left the flat and got into Erostrato's car. He took his place at the wheel with me beside him and Viola behind. As soon as the car moved, Viola stretched forward, twined her arm around Erostrato's neck, and started kissing him in his ear. Erostrato said, between his teeth: 'Keep still, otherwise I can't drive and we shall have a smash.' Then she, like a real drunkard, cried out: 'I don't care, I made you a present of this car, it cost ten million, I have the right to embrace you.'

I: Didn't he have the old Jaguar that Aurora Zendrini had given him?

Desideria: No, it was a new car, a Mercedes still being broken in, that he had driven for the first time barely two days before. He answered her: 'Yes, you have the right to embrace me, but not in the car, or we'll very soon lose control.' For a short time she was silent, huddled on the back seat, sulking, then she cried: 'Stop then, I want to come in front. You've shut me in here behind, I want to be in front, too.' The car stopped, Viola got out, opened the door, threw herself impetuously upon me before I had time to get out and make room for her, and, crawling over me in an obviously intentional fashion, as though for a prolonged caress of her body against mine, slipped in between Erostrato and me. He started the car again, and then there began between her and Erostrato a scene of sexual aggression on her side and of disgusted resistance on his. Tipsy but

300

nevertheless precise in her gestures, which were a testimony to a prolonged habit, she started caressing his groin with one hand, without looking at him, sitting erect in her place with her eyes fixed on the windscreen. I saw Erostrato keeping one hand on the wheel and trying two or three times with the other to seize Viola's hand and seeking in vain to push it away. This game went on for a little, until the moment when she judged that she had succeeded in her intention, which was, technically so to speak, to cause Erostrato to have an erection. Then the second phase began: Viola sought to open his zip fastening; Erostrato, once again, opposed her. In the end, however, whether it was that she was more expert (she was using both hands now, bending towards him), or whether it was that his excitement got the better of him, Viola succeeded in pulling down the tab of the zipper and in getting his trousers wide open. I looked at her out of the corner of my eye and saw her, with movements that were furtive, greedy, and yet full of delicacy and respect, introduce her hand into the opening, gently fumble, and then, gazing into the air as though seeking to reconstruct, in imagination and memory, the exact position of his genitals, finally extract, cautiously, the whole bunch of living, swollen flesh. There followed, then, a scene of admiration and devotion, which were in a way religious and, fundamentally, devoid of eroticism. Erostrato's member stood straight up beneath the steering-wheel: Viola, fascinated, started stroking it, tremblingly, lightly, barely touching it with her fingers; and meanwhile she was saying: 'Isn't it beautiful, isn't it the most beautiful thing one could ever see, isn't it the living incarnation of the beauty of the world?' Her eyes were sparkling, she moved her hand all round his member as though she were seeking to give it a shape, with the gestures of a potter giving a shape to his vase; in the end she clasped it in a ring formed by two fingers to see it swell up and then, with a swift, fugitive movement, held her hand to her nose, greedily sniffing its smell. This sexual smell, to her delicious and intoxicating, overcame her last restraint; she threw

301

herself sideways, with the blind decisiveness with which one throws oneself from a very high springboard, and immediately started going up and down with her head above Erostrato's belly. I thought for a moment that, as usual careless of my presence, she wished to carry through this oral love-making to its end. I was wrong; in reality, it was a question of a kind of preparation for something more complicated and more unapparent. Viola's head went up and down not more than two or three times; then she sat up with a jerk and turned towards me; I had barely time to catch a glimpse of her face in the light of the street lamps when she grabbed me by the hair and pulled me towards her, or rather towards Erostrato. 'Now it's your turn,' she cried; 'you'll drink my saliva and I'll drink yours, we'll both drink his semen so that there will be a bond between us stronger than any other, for good, and we shall be united, all three of us, for life, and all three of us will together adore the beauty of the world.' She said this and many other similar things; meanwhile, she was pulling me by the hair towards Erostrato's member, which was still standing straight up under the wheel, in shadow. I managed to free myself with a jerk, and I sat up, dishevelled, and cried to Erostrato: 'Stop, stop!'; he obeyed, and the car came to an abrupt halt. Then, to my vague surprise, I saw Erostrato, in turn, throw himself upon Viola, seize her by the hair, and throw open the door on her side. There followed a painful, agonizing scene of terrible violence. Erostrato was trying to pull Viola out of the car; Viola opposed him with all her strength and all the time begged him: 'No, don't do that, I swear I won't do it again, let me go, please, let me go.' I watched but kept still. I pitied Viola, but the Voice did not wish me to intervene. In the end Erostrato jumped out into the street and, from the pavement, started pulling Viola by the arm, trying to get her out of the car. She continued to struggle, and was clinging with both hands to the steering wheel. Then the Voice said to me: 'Come on, help Erostrato to throw this bitch out of the car.' Like an automaton, I too threw myself upon Viola and seized her with both hands, just as if it happened by chance, and pushed her towards the door; on his side, Erostrato redoubled his efforts: Viola was thrust half in and half out of the car, and I saw the moment coming when she would fall onto the pavement. But quite suddenly she let forth a piercing, heartrending cry that froze my blood; across her our eyes met and Erostrato said: 'She won't get out. So we'll get out; come on, Desideria, let's go.' These words had a calming effect. I got out of the car. Erostrato took me by the hand and we went together towards the white and violet advertising lights of a more important street, leaving the car and Viola in the darkness of the dark side-street. We walked in silence; the hand with which Erostrato clasped my hand moved me; again it seemed to me that somehow or other I should manage to achieve my purpose – to save him from himself. We had not gone far before, in an open space, we found a taxi; we got in and Erostrato gave our address. Once we were at home, when we reached the landing of the top floor, Erostrato said to me: 'Won't you come up?' indicating the little staircase that led to the little flat above. I hesitated; it would have been the first time I had been in the top-floor flat. 'I must show you something,' Erostrato added. I said nothing, but followed him up the stairs, and we entered the studio. I sat down on the sofa, in front of the fireplace; Erostrato went to the bookshelf, took down a book, turned over the pages for a moment, then handed it to me open, pointing with his finger at the beginning of a paragraph. Before reading it, I looked at the outside of the book and with some surprise saw that it was the Bible. Then I read: 'And when Jehu was come to Jezreel, Jezebel heard of it; and she painted her face, and tired her head, and looked out at a window. And as Jehu entered in at the gate, she said, Had Zimri peace, who slew his master? And he lifted up his face to the window and said, Who is on my side? Who? And there looked out to him two or three eunuchs. And he said, Throw her down. So they threw her down: and some of her blood was sprinkled on the wall, and on the horses, and he trod her underfoot. And when he was come in, he did eat and drink, and said, Go, see now this cursed woman, and bury her: for she is a king's daughter. And they went to bury her; but they found no more of her than the skull, and the feet, and the palms of her hands. Wherefore they came again, and told him. And he said, This is the word of the Lord, which he spake by his servant Elijah the Tishbite, saying. In the portion of Jezreel shall dogs eat the flesh of Jezebel: and the carcase of Jezebel shall be as dung upon the face of the field in the portion of Jezreel; so that they shall not say, This is Jezebel.' I read the passage of the Bible, then I asked: 'Am I to go on?' 'No, that's enough. You know why I made you read the episode of Jezebel? Because Jezebel for me is Viola and Jezebel's death is just what I sometimes wish Viola's might be.' 'Sometimes? This evening, for instance, when you tried to throw her out of the car?' 'Yes, like this evening.' 'You came to our appointment at Villa Borghese with the Cartier-Bresson photographs of China; and this evening you make me read the Bible. I should like to know what it is you want to convince me of.' 'That I am not what you believe, that I think as you do.' 'I don't believe anything – or rather, I do believe one thing.' 'What?' 'That in some way, that is, in your own way, you are a moralist.' 'A moralist?' 'The moralist is one who hates himself in other people, who condemns himself in other people, who kills himself in other people. He pardons himself, but precisely for that reason, he doesn't pardon others. Actually, you would like to die, to go back to nothingness; but you're not conscious of it and so you want to make Viola die. Even, perhaps, by throwing her from a window, like Jezebel, and having her eaten by dogs.' 'This is your usual nonsense. It's not true that I hate myself, and it's not true that I hate other people; it is simply that Viola sometimes makes me desire to kill her.' 'Very well, as you like, don't get angry; but tell me how you come to read the Bible.' 'I read it as a boy, it was one of the few books that there were in the house.' 'What was it that urged you to read it?' He hesitated, then said:

'As a boy I was very religious. I prayed, I commended myself to God, I frequented the priest of my parish, I even served Mass.' 'How did you then lose your faith?' 'I didn't even notice. I thought of other things.' 'Of occultism, for example?' 'Yes, of occultism.' 'And then again of religion, and then of Fascism, and now of Communism. Since when did you become a police agent?' 'I have already told you that I prefer not to speak of my past.' 'Well, with me you can now speak of anything, can't you?' 'I began to have dealings with the police at the age of sixteen. However strange it may seem, I didn't become an agent from motives of interest.' 'From motives of idealism, then?' 'You're making fun of me, but it is true. As a boy I was all for order, for morality, for authority. I hated the Mafia, which in Sicily is so powerful and which seemed to me to be at the root of disorder. I spent hours imagining the best way of exterminating the Mafiosi. I thought that if I were to become a minister or chief of police, I would assemble all the Mafiosi in a courtyard and would then open fire with machine guns and kill the lot of them. Finally, I would send to tell the families that they should come and take away their dead, and thus the Mafia would no longer exist. Since I believed that the police were against the Mafia, I was pleased to collaborate.' 'But were the police really against the Mafia?' 'You're joking! No, they were not. They perhaps pinched the smaller ones, when they really couldn't help it; but the big boys they left alone. In the end they themselves realized that I was unproductive and so they sacked me.'

I: How did your evening end?

Desideria: In an unexpected manner. Suddenly we heard a key turning in the lock and Viola came in, quiet, serene, sure of herself. She said casually: 'Ah, you're here. I looked for you down below and didn't find you; I thought you had run away together. But if there's a question of running away, then let's run away all three of us. D'you want me?' We were left rather embarrassed: was this then Jezebel, thrown out of the window and eaten by dogs? She

305

gave us no time to answer, but sat down and suddenly said:
'Listen, children, I want to make a suggestion. Italy bores
me and frightens me, too: too much disorder, too many
strikes, too much terrorism, too many kidnappings. So I
am suggesting to you both that you should go away with
me: let us go around the world.' There was a silence, and
then I ventured: 'Round the world in how long?' 'It's an
old plan of mine that I've been studying for some time; I
had a detailed plan made for me by a travel agency: in the
longest time possible, seeing that our object is not to stay
in Italy – two, three, five years. The money's no problem;
I have my bank account in Switzerland. Let's go; and in the
first country that we like, we'll stop. Then we leave and
arrive in another country which also arouses our curiosity;
we stop again and so on. I have here the list of countries.
Listen for a moment: Greece, Turkey, Egypt, Syria, Iran,
Afghanistan, India, Nepal, Burma (for Burma, however, it's
not certain), Thailand, Malaya, perhaps Communist China,
Hong Kong, Japan, the Philippines, Hawaii, Polynesia,
Australia, the United States, Mexico, and, finally, Europe.
We can go also to Africa and Latin America. We can go
where we like.' She recited her geographical rigmarole in a
nonchalant, light-hearted way, as though she had a globe
on a tripod in front of her and made it revolve at her
pleasure with a few slight taps of her hand. After a moment
she resumed: 'There are marvellous places: Bali, Tahiti,
the Seychelles, where one can lead a natural life, with the
sea, the sun, the beaches, the palm-trees. I am sure that in
those places we shall be happy. We will live naked, we
won't read the papers, we won't listen to the radio, we
won't watch television. We'll be all day in the open air,
we'll sleep in a hut. Don't you like this idea? I do, I can't
stop thinking of it.'

I: The earthly paradise.

Desideria: Yes, even if provided by tourist agencies.

I: And you two – what did you reply?

Desideria: I said I wanted to think it over, that I had to
take my exam and therefore, for some time yet, I could not

leave Italy. Erostrato said nothing. Suddenly I rose, said I was sleepy and was going to bed. Viola exclaimed: 'But you haven't dined, let's dine now; we'll go out to the restaurant. Or dine at home.' I replied that I was not hungry and went away.

CHAPTER SIX

I: I should say that at this point things come to a crisis. Or am I mistaken?

Desideria: No, you're not mistaken.

I: All the characters in your story are moving towards a final encounter. Viola wants to leave for a tour round the world. Erostrato announces the arrival of the comrade from Milan. You, or rather the Voice, wish to stay in Rome to prepare for the kidnapping of your adoptive mother. By the way, what did the Voice say of the tour round the world?

Desideria: It said that it served to indicate that Viola, somehow or other, had got wind of the danger that threatened her.

I: You, in fact, had the choice between sex *à trois* and kidnapping.

Desideria: Yes, between an orgy and the group.

I: I often hear you speak of the orgy and the group. What did you mean then by the orgy and the group? And in the mean time, you give the impression that you put the orgy and the group on the same plane – isn't that so?

Desideria: No, that isn't so. This was the same accusation that the Voice made against me. I considered them two different things, that is all. For the Voice, however, the group was the opposite of the orgy, exactly as good is the opposite of evil. I did not think of it in this way.

I: What did you think?

Desideria: As usual, I didn't think anything, I felt. Well, I felt that beyond the orgy there extended a whole world to which the orgy itself served as entrance, as introduction.

I: A whole world?

Desideria: Yes, the world of eroticism. But understand me: it was not a question of making love *à trois*; but of transforming my body into an alchemistic crucible in which the fire of desire would fuse all the values by which I had lived hitherto, and would create others.

I: What others?

Desideria: Feeling has not the habit of defining itself; all it does is to present itself. What values? Obviously, values different from those of the Voice, at least to judge by its furious reaction.

I: And the Voice's values, what were they?

Desideria: They were those of the group.

I: And the group – what was it?

Desideria: The dream of a heroic community.

I: Heroic?

Desideria: Yes, heroic. But, curiously, I was conscious of this heroism as something indivisible from defeat. What I mean is, heroic action was heroic not merely because it was dangerous but also because it was dedicated to certain failure.

I: Meaning what?

Desideria: Meaning that the heroism of a revolutionary group consisted in making a revolution though knowing perfectly well that, in the end, the revolution would not change the world.

I: Orgy, on the other hand, did not intend to change the world, did it?

Desideria: Orgy intended to escape from it.

I: It seems to me that, after this preamble on the difference between the orgy and the group, the moment has come to talk about the comrade from Milan whose arrival had been announced by Erostrato. This comrade from Milan was not, so to speak, a mysteriously emblematic figure for you at that moment, was he?

Desideria: Yes, he was; how did you manage to guess? I said to myself: 'The comrade from Milan.' And certainly the sound of these words made me indulge in daydreams. I saw him as an important, fatal, decisive figure; but I did not manage to fit him with a face. It was as though I were awaiting the man of my life, without, however, knowing who he was or what he was like.

309

I: The man of your life?

Desideria: That's what one says, isn't it? Perhaps it was the Voice which crowned these words with a halo of expectation that was almost mystical. But, for once, I was in agreement with the Voice, partly because I remembered that the Voice had made me promise not to part with my virginity until I had come across a man worthy of it. Well, I hoped, I really hoped that the comrade from Milan would be this man.

I: Then did he arrive or not?

Desideria: Yes, Erostrato and I went to meet him at the station.

I: How did Erostrato appear on this occasion?

Desideria: Perfectly calm, as always.

I: Didn't it seem to you odd that he should be so calm, when you knew that he had been a police agent?

Desideria: Evidently he trusted me, and he was right. And then he was always calm, perhaps from lack of imagination. Or perhaps because he was always ready to meet the discovery of one of his lies with another bigger lie.

I: In your opinion, did the Milan group know that Erostrato had been a police agent?

Desideria: I had asked him that and he had answered no, adding the usual things: that these were things of the past, errors of youth, and that anyhow they had no importance for the group.

I: Well, you went to the station, the train arrived, what happened?

Desideria: At first something happened inside my head. At some distance, between the platforms, under the station roof, in the darkness, I saw the two enormous luminous eyes of the locomotive lights approaching slowly, and I thought, for some reason: A train! As in a nineteenth-century novel; but today revolutions are made by jumping from one aeroplane to another, from one airport to another. A train! But what kind of a revolution will this be?

310

I: So you no longer believed in the mythical 'comrade from Milan'?

Desideria: On the contrary, I was conscious of irony because I believed in him more than ever; for me that was the most fatal moment of my life, in which I should at last meet – let us use the word from the Song of Songs – 'my spouse'. This is so true that, as soon as the train stopped, amid puffs of steam and whistlings and the banging of doors, as soon as the passengers had begun to get out, as soon as Erostrato had said to me: 'There he is,' I thought I recognized him in somebody who was coming towards him with outstretched arms.

I: What was this man like?

Desideria: D'you remember Humphrey Bogart in the film *Casablanca*? This was a similar type, only younger. I ran to meet him, all at once he smiled at me and I felt that there was something unreal in this smile, because I had never seen the 'comrade from Milan' and he had never seen me. Then a young blonde woman in a short fur coat popped out from behind my back and threw herself into the arms of the young man, and with a feeling of acute disappointment, I realized that it was not he.

I: What was he like then, this famous 'comrade from Milan'?

Desideria: The word 'comrade' coupled with the word 'Milan' had suggested to me what was, after all, a fairly plausible image: in Milan there are tall, thin, dark men with marked features like those of Bogart. But the real 'comrade from Milan' had nothing whatever to do with Bogart.

I: What was he like, in fact?

Desideria: He came towards us, greeted Erostrato, and the latter introduced us to one another. Then, as he went off towards the exit, I looked at him attentively. He was a young man of about thirty, not so very tall, but thickset, with almost no neck, so that his head seemed sunk into his shoulders, which were broad, muscular, and as though padded like those of American football players. He had a

311

white, colourless face, deep-set eyes of pale blue; a straight nose, short and so thin that it gave the impression of being nothing but cartilage covered with skin; a curiously shaped mouth, at the same time fleshy and flat and as though crushed. I was struck by the fact that, at a time when, among his contemporaries, especially those of the extreme Left, the fashion was for long hair and beards, he was perfectly clean-shaven, with very short hair, in the manner of the Germans during the years of Nazism. He had small hands and feet, a long body, and short arms and legs. I saw at once that he wore entirely new clothes, even though they were ready-made and of poor quality: a leather, or rather, artificial-leather, jacket; mustard-yellow trousers; shoes with thick rubber soles. His jacket was too short for him, his trousers too tight over a hard and prominent behind that stretched the material. From his hip pocket there half protruded a long, narrow, black notebook, of the kind that are used for recording addresses and appointments; over his shoulder he carried a very swollen bag on which he held a protective hand. The last touch to this image of the 'Milan comrade' was given by the remark with which he greeted Erostrato.

I: What did he say?

Desideria: He said: 'Hello, chum.'

I: Why did that greeting seem to you so significant?

Desideria: It was the last I should have put in the mouth of a revolutionary. To call Erostrato 'chum' implied something provincial, the absolute opposite of revolutionary. And then there was in this word a presumption of superiority, even if possibly of an affectionate kind. But after I had looked at him, I saw that I was mistaken: there had been no affection for Erostrato in that 'Hello, chum'; it was merely an automatic slang phrase.

I: Then how did your meeting with the 'Milan comrade' continue?

Desideria: It continued in this way. We came out of the station and got into the car; Erostrato placed himself at the wheel, Quinto (that was the name by which Erostrato had

312

introduced him to me) beside Erostrato, and I behind. From the very beginning, I don't know why, Quinto behaved in such a way as to exclude Erostrato from the conversation and give his whole attention to me. So, while Erostrato kept silent as he drove, in every possible way like the driver of a taxi, we two, Quinto and I, talked as though we were alone.

I: What did you say to each other, you and Quinto?

Desideria: It was like a kind of interrogation: he interrogated and I answered: 'Do you live alone?' 'No, with my mother.' 'And your father?' 'No, my father is dead.' 'What did your father do?' 'He was a builder of houses.' 'Did he build luxury houses?' 'Yes, I would certainly say so.' 'Did he speculate in building sites?' 'I don't know, but it is probable.' 'You're very rich, eh?' 'My mother is, I possess nothing.' 'People always say that; the rich one is somebody else. And where do you live in Rome?' 'In the Parioli quarter.' 'The bosses' quarter. And what do you do?' 'What you see: I go to the station to meet the comrade from Milan.' 'That would be me, I suppose. But you, what are you? Erostrato's girl friend?' 'No.' 'What d'you mean, no?' 'I said, "No".' 'Oh well, well. Then you're engaged.' 'No.' 'Again, no? But you go to bed with somebody, you're not a nun, surely?' 'Who says I'm not a nun?' 'You, with that face and with that figure. Come on, I wasn't born yesterday!' 'I, on the other hand, was. In fact, I can tell you exactly when I was born: four years ago.' By this I meant that I had really come into the world from the moment when the Voice had begun speaking to me; but he interpreted it as a piece of coquetry and exclaimed: 'Are you really a little girl of four years old, with those tits? Well, as a little girl, you haven't wasted your time.' And so on and so forth . . .

I: What did Erostrato say in the mean time?

Desideria: He said absolutely nothing. Meanwhile, we had crossed half of Rome and I saw that the car was directed towards Parioli. I asked Erostrato: 'Where are we going?' And he, with a curious accent, as of a chauffeur

313

who is answering a question of his master: 'We're going to Via Archimede.' 'To Via Archimede – where?' 'Home. To the top-floor flat. For the time that he will be in Rome, it is best that Quinto should stay with me.' I said nothing: Quinto asked me: 'D'you know Erostrato's flat?' in the unsuspecting, idle voice of one who knows nothing; and I answered almost without thinking: 'I should think I do know it. He lives above us. It's the property of my mother.' 'And do you often go to the top-floor flat?' 'I went there for the first time yesterday; Erostrato wanted to show me a book.' 'A book, what book?' 'The Bible.' 'Does your mother go to the top-floor flat to see Erostrato?' 'Ask him. I know nothing about it.' 'Ah, now I begin to understand, your mother and Erostrato see one another in the top-floor flat.' 'I've already told you to ask *him*.' 'And you're jealous of your mother or you're annoyed that I should be coming to stay in your house?' 'I'm not jealous and I'm not annoyed.' 'But from the way you speak to me one would say that you don't like me.' 'On the contrary, in fact, I've been waiting for you for I don't know how long. The comrade from Milan. For me you had become a positive obsession. Ask Erostrato if that's not true!' 'Is it true, chum?' Erostrato, without turning round, confirmed: 'Yes, it's true.'

I: But was it still true, now that you had seen him, that you found him so different from what you had imagined?

Desideria: It was still true in the sense that my obsession had changed into its opposite. So long as I hadn't seen him, I had obsessively idealized him; now, on the other hand, he inspired in me a repugnance which was also obsessive: I went on looking at him, seeking the reason for this repugnance; I did not find it and yet the repugnance persisted.

I: And what did the Voice say about Quinto?

Desideria: The Voice had an entirely different feeling. It said: 'He may be what he is, but he's the real thing.'

I: What did it mean by the 'real thing'?

Desideria: The revolution, I suppose, the revolutionary spirit.

314

I: So you arrived at Via Archimede. What did you do then?

Desideria: No, I haven't finished yet. We did not arrive at Via Archimede. We were still in the car and we found ourselves in the neighbourhood of Valle Giulia, a region of trees and shade. Then, while I was talking to Quinto, bending forward towards him from the back seat, and Quinto in turn was talking to me, turning round towards me from the front seat, and Erostrato was driving, Quinto let his arm dangle against my knees. We crossed an area where it was light; then the car turned off into a secondary road that was flanked by thick, low trees and was very dark. Then Quinto moved his arm with a sudden jerk, like a lever, inserting it between my legs and separating them abruptly. Instinctively I closed my legs, so as to stop him; but the Voice hinted to me: 'Open your legs, let him do as he wants. D'you really wish to ruin everything?' 'But he's behaving like any spoilt bourgeois child!' 'He's behaving like any ordinary man!' 'And why shouldn't I react?' After a moment's thought, the reply was: 'Because he's your man' – a remark apparently simple but actually ambiguous and obscure. So I let him continue, as the Voice commanded. No longer held back by the tightening of my thighs, his hand crept up as far as my groin, inserted itself between my pants and my private parts, and a finger was introduced into my vagina. At the same moment, for some reason or other, a political discussion started between Quinto and Erostrato.

I: In which you also participated?

Desideria: No, I was upset and more or less paralysed by Quinto's caress. I was in no state to speak.

I: What did you feel?

Desideria: The horrified agitation of someone who, in spite of himself, has a voluptuous feeling that is odious and repugnant.

I: What were Erostrato and Quinto discussing?

Desideria: Still owing to that horrible voluptuous feeling, I didn't understand very well what was the subject of

315

their discussion. It was a political argument, that much is certain. And it is equally certain that Quinto was finding fault with Erostrato.

I: Finding fault with him? What d'you mean?

Desideria: He interrupted him, pointing out certain mistakes in political terminology, correcting him, telling him the exact word, or the word which he himself considered exact.

I: Political terminology, but what?

Desideria: That of the extra-parliamentary Left. The difference between Erostrato and Quinto was that the latter seemed to have learned to speak that language, whereas Erostrato tended to say things in normal language and if anything to adopt political language by putting it, as it were, in inverted commas, as though he were translating from a foreign language. This knowledge of the lingo of the Left gave Quinto superiority and placed Erostrato in a position of inferiority.

I: Give me an example of Quinto's fault-finding.

Desideria: Oh well, I don't know. At one point their discussion was concentrated on certain groups in the north who descended upon supermarkets, took what they wanted, and went away without paying. 'Seizure of goods,' said Erostrato. And immediately, promptly, Quinto corrected him: 'Proletarian expropriation.' Then Erostrato, speaking of the houses in which the victims of political kidnappings were held, used the word 'Apartment' and Quinto corrected him: 'People's prison.' Finally Erostrato alluded to a director of the Fiat company, calling him 'Head of department' and Quinto said: 'Slave of the multinational.' And so on and so forth.

I: Erostrato let himself be found fault with without protesting.

Desideria: Yes, he seemed to think that Quinto had that right. On the other hand, Quinto did not put any particular tone of rivalry into his fault-findings; he made them in a casual manner, almost like a schoolmaster indifferently correcting a pupil.

316

I: D'you really remember them all, these fault-findings?

Desideria: I remember them all because all the time there was that disgusting voluptuous feeling which the Voice compelled me to experience; and so, in some way, each of Quinto's fault-findings acquired, in spite of myself, an erotic character, even though it was an eroticism that I wanted to resist, to ignore.

I: What d'you mean?

Desideria: Well, Quinto's political superiority served, in reality, to make his sexual aggression calm and skilful. And vice versa.

I: What was the end of all this?

Desideria: It ended badly, at least for me. I did not wish, and at the same time I did wish, to reach an orgasm, but when we reached Via Archimede, there was our house; the political discussion ceased, Quinto removed his hand, Erostrato parked the car. We got out, went into the house, and entered the lift. I still felt the raging pain of the voluptuous pleasure which I had at the same time both resisted and accepted, the humiliating frustration of not having carried it through. I felt so nervous and so tense that in the lift I closed my eyes and when Erostrato asked me what was wrong with me, I answered with violence: 'What is wrong with me is that Quinto has been masturbating me the whole time – that's what is wrong.' From the silence that followed I deduced that the two of them were now looking into one another's eyes in a way that was questioning but without rivalry, accomplices, now, in considering me little less than mad. The lift stopped, we got out; Erostrato said that he would now settle Quinto into the top-floor flat. Without saying a word, and in a great hurry, I opened our front door and then banged it in his face. I ran into my own bedroom; with anger and violence I threw myself at full length on the bed.

I: What did you do, did you go to sleep?

Desideria: I would have liked to go to sleep but I felt too nervous, divided between disgust at that pleasure that I hated and the need to have the orgasm which I had not had

317

time to achieve. Then the Voice suggested to me that I should masturbate in order to have the orgasm on my own account and so get rid of my nervousness. According to the Voice I ought, however, to masturbate thinking of Quinto; he was 'my man', it was he who had started the caress, and I ought to think of him as I concluded it. At that moment I hated the Voice from the bottom of my heart; nevertheless I obeyed. I stretched out my hand to my groin, closed my eyes, and began thinking of Quinto.

I: In what way did you think of him?

Desideria: With the same feeling of horror and attraction with which I had submitted to his caress in the car. I concentrated my thought on his mouth and started titillating my clitoris.

I: Why his mouth?

Desideria: Because, while he was masturbating me, I had been struck by his smile, a strange, meticulous, victorious smile. Almost at once I had an orgasm; suddenly somebody said: 'That's fine, go on, go on then, once is not enough, you must start again, do it a second time, a third time.' Then I opened my eyes and saw Viola standing at the end of the bed, looking at me with her arms folded. I quickly sat up, composed myself as best I could, and said that I had just come back and had dozed off while waiting to go out to the restaurant with her and Erostrato. It was the first thing that came into my mind in the confusion of my surprise. Viola answered immediately: 'No, we're not going to the restaurant. If you like you can dine with me here at home. Or we can go to the restaurant, just we two, without Erostrato.' I could not now help realizing that something new must have happened between her and Erostrato and, not without annoyance – for quarrels between them were frequent – I asked: 'What is it now, with Erostrato?' And she, as though she had only been expecting this question, at once sat down on the edge of the bed and, looking at me fixedly, said solemnly: 'Everything is finished between myself and Erostrato.' 'Everything is finished? That's something I've already heard on other occasions.' 'No, between me and Erostrato everything is *really* finished. Today, after lunch, we had an explanation. You must know that for some time he has been insisting on my taking the power of attorney away from Tiberi and giving it to him. However, ever since Tiberi gave me the police report on Eros to read, I have kept my eyes open and observed him carefully in his way of behaving towards me. It doesn't matter to me that a man should be a Fascist or a Communist or whatever; it doesn't even matter to me that he should be paying court to my daughter; but I cannot endure the idea that he should be after my money and should pretend to love me because of this interest in my money. Perhaps if he had not kept on worrying about that power of attorney, I might have passed over his many defects. But his insistence on the power of attorney has decided me. It's like that with me: I accumulate without even realizing it, and then all at once I explode. Suddenly, almost in spite of myself, I reached the limit. I told him that not only had I no intention of giving him the power of attorney but also that he must consider himself dismissed as secretary, as lover, as everything. That I did not wish to see him any more, that everything was finished between us. And that meanwhile he must vacate the studio as soon as possible.'

I: The power of attorney? But had you and Erostrato not agreed that it was the right thing for Tiberi to keep it so that he should then be in a position, after the kidnapping had taken place, to pay the ransom?

Desideria: Yes, and for that reason I was left speechless, for a moment, from surprise. It seemed to me suspicious, not so much that Erostrato should wish to replace Tiberi as holder of the power of attorney, as that he should not have spoken to me of it. And yet, as I understood, his so-called 'insistence' on the power of attorney had been going on for some time. Viola resumed: 'I notified him of his dismissal, then left the room at once; I came down here, wanting to speak to you, but you were not here; then, all alone, I started reflecting on the situation that has finally been created between us two, and in the end I took a certain number of decisions.' 'Decisions?' 'Yes, my dear: decisions or, if you prefer, measures. The first of these decisions is that from now on I shall renew all my confidence in Tiberi, who is a trusted friend and a skilful administrator. The second, that from now on we shall be truly mother and daughter, *only* mother and daughter. Through Erostrato's fault, we have perhaps recently let ourselves go rather too far, we have behaved like a couple of friends and even something more than friends. Well, all this must absolutely come to an end. The third is that within about ten days you will be nineteen. In order to emphasize that everything between us, from now on, is changed, I will give a party for your birthday and will invite all those who for some time, through Erostrato's fault, I have neglected. Finally, the fourth decision concerns you especially. From now on you must not only behave towards me like a beloved and affectionate daughter, but you must also go back to being the girl that you were two or three years ago, before you took to frequenting a certain mob of people.

I: Whom was she alluding to?

Desideria: To the boys and girls that I saw at school and out of school.

I: Did these boys and girls know Erostrato?

Desideria: No, they were two separate things. Erostrato, at least until the arrival of Quinto, had been, so to speak, the revolution. These boys and girls were what, later on, was called the 'contestation'.

I: And you – what did you answer?

Desideria: I said dryly: 'I don't know any "mob", I don't know who you're talking about.'

I: And what did she say?

Desideria: She shook her head and replied: 'You know perfectly well who I'm talking about. I'm talking about Camillo, about Renzo, Livia, Gianni, Vera, Serena, Giulio,' et cetera, et cetera.

I: Who were they?

Desideria: They were, indeed, my present friends, at school and in the quarter. Viola had become aware that after having frequented, until I was fifteen, a group of boys and girls of the type of my ex-fiancé Giorgio, I had changed my circle of friends from the moment when the Voice had begun speaking to me. Previously they had all been the children of rich parents and were, as they say, non-political, that is, of the Right; now they were all the children of parents of modest condition and were all more or less 'politicized', that is, of the Left. All this, as I said, had not escaped her notice because she had an acute sensitiveness for class differences, and naturally, it had not pleased her at all, although, with me, she had pretended not to be aware of it. But now, in view of the reforms that she intended to bring into action in her life, the whole question came to the fore.

I: Reforms?

Desideria: Yes, that was the word with which the Voice at once designated the whole of the 'measures' which Viola, that afternoon, had decided to take. But d'you know from what I realized that she had opted for these reforms?

I: From what?

Desideria: From a physical detail.

I: A physical detail?

Desideria: Yes. As I've already observed, Viola oscillated continually between the role of mother and that of lover; between permissiveness and repression. In some way this oscillation was reflected in an analogous oscillation between her two national components, the Italian and the American. Of Italian parentage but American by birth and upbringing, Viola revealed herself as Italian when she chose the role of lover, and American when she chose the role of mother. Now there was one object, the use of which on her part indicated to me in which direction her existential see-saw was tending. In some way, even if she had wished to hide her sudden changes of state of mind from me, the presence or absence of this object would have spoken for her.

I: What was this object?

Desideria: An elastic girdle or belt – actually of American type – with which, certainly by instinct and without any consciousness, she compressed her stomach and her hips whenever the repressive tendency prevailed in her life. This girdle compressed her bottom, which, as I have remarked before, was the most beautiful and most youthful part of her body and at the same time the part of which she made use, in preference to other parts, to take her pleasure. When the permissive tendency prevailed in her, then the girdle disappeared and her body breathed freely and happily, and her buttocks moved impetuously and with unconscious provocation.

I: Was Viola wearing the girdle that night?

Desideria: Certainly she was, and I could not help looking at it all the time, while she was announcing what I have called her reforms.

I: What was it like, this sheath?

Desideria: Viola was wearing a blouse and a skirt. The skirt, inspired by the fashion of 1950 or even earlier, was very tight and clinging down to her knee; then, below the knee, it widened and had an opening behind, so that you could see her leg. Without the girdle, a tight skirt of this kind would have revealed the shapes and movements of the body; with the girdle, on the other hand, it appeared to be stuck to a tube or cylinder, as it were, of metal or plastic. To such an extent that, when Viola came close to me as she was speaking, and when she knocked her hip against a chair, I was almost surprised that this knock was not accompanied by the sound of a stone or metal object hitting against the wood.

I: Really!

Desideria: She came close to me and still remained standing with her hands in the pockets of her skirt; then she resumed, in a cold, calm, carefully articulated voice which, curiously, betrayed a marked Anglo-Saxon accent: 'You must stop frequenting these presumptuous, idle ragamuffins; you must go back to seeing the boys and girls of your own circle, of your own class. When I see you with those characters, my heart fails me. I ask myself whether this has to be the result of all my efforts to give you the best education that money can buy in this country.'

I: What answer did you give her?

Desideria: None. I looked up at her, I watched her and noticed so many other things that confirmed what, in its own mute language, the sheath had already told me: the hostile hardness of her eyes, as of one who has taken a final decision and is irritated in advance at the sole idea that it may be rejected; the fact that the features of her face had become cold and pale and, so to speak, dismantled, features which, in moments of eroticism, reddened and grew warm and seemed, as it were, to be sustained by the impure flame of passion, but which now, on the other hand, appeared slackened and limp, with an opaque pallor in which were visible the red marks caused by her almost maniac habit of prodding and squeezing her skin. Finally, the tone of her voice, distant and calculatedly casual, a tone of the American middle class rather than of the Roman bourgeoisie, with inflexions and accents, as I have already remarked, that were positively Anglo-Saxon.

I: And then what?

Desideria: Then, at this point, I had to pay attention to the Voice, which was shouting to me, as if beside itself with hatred: 'A real, genuine restoration of bourgeois values; that's what this imbecile of an adoptive mother of yours is trying to bring about. A party in honour of your nineteenth birthday! In what year does she think she's living? In 1930? You must immediately demolish it, this monolith of bourgeois idiocy, and you know very well how to do it: suggest love-making *à trois* to her. You'll see how she collapses!' 'But seeing that she's sacked Erostrato . . .' 'She's dreamt of sacking him.' 'Love-making *à trois* – but when, but where?' 'Today, tomorrow, as soon as possible. In the top-floor flat, at Via Gaeta, wherever you like. And immediately afterwards: the kidnapping. And if the kidnapping is not enough, kill her.' 'Kill her?' 'Haven't you already tried to kill her? But now the attempt must succeed and I guarantee that it will succeed.'

I: The Voice was in a great hurry!

Desideria: Yes, in a great hurry, that's the word. What in the past had been a symbolic attempt at homicide was now already becoming the thing itself, that is, real, genuine homicide.

I: What did you answer?

Desideria: Nothing. I was in agreement with the Voice on the question of the restoration of values. Apart from that, I did not want to think of it. I looked up towards Viola, and in the end, I said: 'As I seem to understand, you intend to invite to my birthday party all those with whom, in your opinion, I ought to be on friendly terms from now on. I bet you've already written out the list of guests. Well, let me see it.'

I: How did you come to know she'd already written it?

Desideria: I was well acquainted with her, and I knew that she had been thinking for a long time about this project of a party for my nineteenth birthday. And in fact she replied to my request simply by handing me a sheet of paper folded in four which was projecting from the pocket of her skirt. I took it in silence and began running through it. And then I could not help thinking that the Voice was right when it spoke of 'restoration'. They were all there, the whole lot of them!

I: All – who?

Desideria: All those whom I had so hated ever since the day when the Voice had manifested itself inside me: the rich and powerful of my quarter, those gentlemen and well-dressed ladies whom I was accustomed to see every Sunday morning at Mass in the church in Piazza Ungheria. And, together with the parents, the children, once my friends in the bars and cinemas and sporting clubs. Yes, they were all there, a column of names on Viola's list: the generals and the admirals, the presidents and the directors, the builders and the bankers, the entrepreneurs and the stockbrokers. All those whom the Voice had been for years pointing out to me as enemies to be avoided and hated. I ran through the list and at the same time listened to the Voice, which

324

commented, raging with indignation: 'Viola has made a list of Fascists, yes, veritably of Fascists. And she intends, with this party of yours, to make you solemnly and finally re-enter the ranks of Fascism!'

I: But you told me that, when there was an analogous reception years before, absolutely nobody had come. What had happened? Had the situation changed in the mean time?

Desideria: The neglected reception went back to the beginnings of Viola's social career. Later, through the years, she had succeeded in getting herself accepted by that same society which, at the beginning, had rejected her.

I: So you saw that in the list there was 'everybody'. What did you do?

Desideria: My first impulse was to tear up the list and throw it in her face. But the Voice pointed out to me that my aim should be to put an end not so much to the party as to the 'restoration' of which the party was merely one aspect and perhaps not even the most important. So once again I obeyed and, looking up towards Viola, I said: 'I want to keep this list and see whether I ought to add a few names. But listen – what have you done? I see you entirely changed, so to speak.'

I: An abrupt change of tone and of subject. What did *she* say?

Desideria: As though she were offended, she repeated: 'Changed, in what sense changed?' 'I don't know; move, turn round. Ah, now I understand: you've put on that American girdle that suits you so badly.' 'Suits me badly? I don't think so. Anyhow, it makes me slimmer.' 'Turn round, move; but don't you see that your sides are transformed into a tube, a cylinder?' 'What d'you mean? A tube? But it suits me extremely well.' 'It suits you extremely badly. You have the figure of a girl of twenty, with the most beautiful behind in the world. It's your best point and you conceal it with this horrible girdle. The girdle says: "I am a mature woman, I am a severe woman, I am a woman who has renounced love." On the other hand, your behind says:

"I am young, I am beautiful, I want to enjoy life, I want to be admired, caressed, loved." ' I introduced an almost affectionate accent into these words, not only because the Voice wished it so, but also because I did not find any difficulty in producing such an accent: I had loved Viola so much and now I could always pretend, to order, that I loved her still. My calculation turned out to be right. I saw her look at me, tempted and moved; then, almost by instinct, she looked at her own image in the wardrobe looking-glass. Feebly, she said: 'Everyone wants to be loved; but we ought to know how to say so with our mouths, not with our behinds.' Then the Voice intervened: 'Say something brutal to her, break her resistance once and for all.' Obedient as always, I said with an effort: 'But your behind says something which it is difficult to say with your mouth.' 'What is that?' 'Put it up my bottom.' I saw a sudden redness rise from her neck to her cheeks, and I did not doubt, for one moment, that I had, as the Voice said, weakened her resistance. Almost sincerely, she exclaimed: 'But, Desideria, what are you saying? Do you forget that you are speaking to your mother?' 'You know perfectly well that we are not mother and daughter but a couple of strangers, even perhaps a couple of friends or, if you still desire it, a couple of lovers.' 'What are you saying, are you mad?' 'Yes, a couple of lovers, here, or even better, at Via Gaeta. With Eros, naturally. Today, tomorrow, as you like. But meanwhile, come here and let me take that horrible girdle off you.'

I: And so you let her know that you were ready for three-sided love-making. Why?

Desideria: Because the Voice wished it.

I: And how did she react?

Desideria: How does a tree react to the lightning that strikes it? By falling to the ground, the whole of it, with its foliage shattered, its roots in the air. My words had the effect on Viola that lightning has on a tree. In silence she came close to me, looking into my eyes; and I, in imagination, saw her just like the tree struck by lightning – thrown to the ground, incapable of rising. So I stretched out towards her, lifted up her skirt, put my hands up to seek the upper edge of the girdle from below, my palms sliding over the smooth, taut surface of the elastic material. I found the edge, pulled it down, but the girdle, tight and clinging, resisted; I redoubled my efforts and realized that it was yielding and was coming down over her sides; then I gave a last, energetic tug and felt that her buttocks were, so to speak, joyfully exploding with the whole force of their compressed rotundity, and were acquiring again, in a moment, their natural shape. Steadily, more lightly and easily, I pulled down the girdle from her thighs to her knees and from her knees to her shins; obedient, now, like a child being put to bed by its mother, Viola stepped out of the girdle, first with one foot, then with the other. I took the girdle and threw it onto the head of the bed, with the cruelly satisfied gesture of a soldier throwing away his defeated enemy's arms. Then I muttered between my teeth: 'Now turn round.' She obeyed, and I smoothed out her skirt in such a way that it clung without folds to her hips, adding with feigned satisfaction: 'Yes, that's better now! We have liberated the most beautiful bottom in the world, we have removed its gag and it can speak as much as it likes.' Viola said nothing, she was silent and still; no doubt she was waiting for me to throw her down on the bed and throw myself on top of her. I pretended not to notice; I rose to my feet and said casually, 'Make an arrangement with Erostrato, won't you, for us all three to meet at Via Gaeta.' I saw she was looking at me with wide-open eyes and, at the same time, perhaps under the illusion that I did not notice, she pretended to pass her hand over her forehead: in reality, she made a tiny sign of the cross between her eyes, as some people do when they get into an aeroplane or go into the water at the seaside. Then she stammered: 'You want us to go tomorrow?' 'Yes, tomorrow's all right.' 'At six o'clock?' 'Six o'clock is all right for me.' 'D'you want us to meet here, all three of us?' 'No, I'd prefer that each of us should go there on his own account. And go away now, because I have things to do. By the way . . .' 'Yes?' 'By the

327

way, it's agreed that you throw your list of guests into the waste-paper basket and do nothing more about your absurd party.' 'But, Desideria . . .' I went up to her rapidly and gave her a kiss on the mouth, a light kiss, but with the penetration of my tongue, which I caused to dart inside for an instant. She tried to detain me, to prolong the kiss, but I pulled myself away. 'Then it's agreed about the party.' 'Yes, my love.' She went out walking almost backwards, like a slave leaving the presence of his master.

I: And you?

Desideria: I went into the bathroom, spat into the basin, rinsed out my mouth with toothpaste to take away the taste of Viola's mouth. Every love has its own taste. Incestuous love has it, too.

CHAPTER SEVEN

Desideria: That night Quinto slept in the top-floor flat and went out very early together with Erostrato, so early that when I telephoned to the flat from Piazzale Flaminio (I did not wish to telephone from home, knowing that both Viola and the servants listened to my telephone calls) a little before going into school, no one answered, they had already gone out. This disappointment, I don't know why, provoked in the Voice a violent feeling of rejection as regards the school: 'You're on the point of seizing your adoptive mother to kidnap her and if necessary to kill her; and off you go, as though nothing were happening, as good as gold, to sit on a school bench and listen to a pedantic, boring lesson about Racine. Why, what are you? A monster of unconsciousness? A total lunatic? A madwoman?' I was struck by this accusation of madness because hitherto I had always thought that reason was on my side, and the touch of madness which had involved, among other things, the formulation of the transgression-and-desecration plan, on the side of the Voice. I retorted: 'It's you who are the madwoman. I have to take my school-leaving exam, and I absolutely cannot, for any reason whatever, allow myself to miss a single lesson.' 'But the school-leaving exam, the real, decisive one, *that* you will pass today, at Via Gaeta.' 'That may be so, but this morning I'm going to school.' 'What for?' 'To listen to the lesson on Racine.' 'You're mad, mad, mad . . .' It went on shouting itself hoarse, yelling that I was a madwoman, when I was already going into the school. I listened to the lessons, left the school, and went home again at the usual time. I felt calm and tranquil, as it were, suspended motionless in a great, silent, astonished solitude. I went into my room, combed my hair, and went on into the living-room. There I found Erostrato, who

329

was, as usual, reading the newspapers. The Voice, seething with impatience, immediately made me ask: 'Have you spoken to Quinto?' 'What about?' 'About Via Gaeta.' 'About Via Gaeta?' 'Yes, about the operation of proletarian expropriation at Via Gaeta.' 'But what expropriation?' 'The kidnapping of Viola. All right now?' 'Ah yes, I have spoken to him about it.' 'And what did he say?' He looked at me for a considerable time before answering, as though he did not recognize me and did not understand my question; finally, he replied: 'He's against it. He too, like me, thinks it would be a crazy thing.' 'Why crazy?' 'Because these things are not done in that way.' 'And in what way are they done?' 'I don't know how they're done, but certainly not in this way, and that's that.' 'Then I must be a madwoman.' 'No, why?' 'Because anyone who makes crazy suggestions must be mad.' 'What's wrong with you? You seem to be out of your mind.' It was true; the Voice, hearing itself called mad, after having that same morning called me a madwoman, had got into a terrible rage. I looked at Erostrato; the eyes were mine but the look was that of the Voice, sparkling and deadly; he threw me a sideways glance and resumed, conciliatingly: 'In any case, we've decided to go at three o'clock today to examine the flat together and see what can be done.' 'I'll come, too.' 'What for? For the present this is an affair between myself and Quinto. Besides, haven't we an appointment with Viola, again at Via Gaeta, three hours later, at six? It's better that we should meet at six.' I looked at him with hatred; the fury of the Voice was so apparent in my face that he was again frightened and added: 'I should like to know what's wrong with you this morning.' Then I exploded: 'What's wrong is that you two, you and Quinto, agreed together last night to treat me as a madwoman, to be held at bay, and meanwhile to exploit us for love-making. What's wrong is that you want me to go to Via Gaeta at six in order to make love with you and Viola, the three of us together, and so take the place of Brigitte and perhaps even to get photographed like her, on all fours, with you penetrating me from behind. What's

330

wrong is that you don't want me in the group, you want me to become my adoptive mother's whore. What's wrong is...' I broke off abruptly, because Viola had suddenly appeared at the door, saying in a shrill voice: 'Hello, children, take your places for lunch, it's ready, I'll be with you at once'; and then at once she disappeared in a puppet-like manner, just like a marionette that appears on the scene for a moment and is then pulled back by the puppeteer. Still foaming with rage, I rose and went and sat down at the table. Erostrato followed me and said, in turn, before sitting down: 'Very well, then come with us at three o'clock to see the flat. We shall find Quinto in the bar down below.' 'I'll come. But take heed of this: if the kidnap doesn't take place, I'll show Quinto the photographs of you with Brigitte. Viola has given them to me. So he'll know you're a prostitute and get you turned out of the group.' He was silent a moment and then he replied sententiously: 'We're organizing a revolution against capitalism, not against sex.' 'And then I'll tell him that you're a police agent. I hope that at any rate you will organize a revolution against the police.' Now he gave me a lingering look and then said, with a strangely quiet and at the same time threatening air: 'In your place I would not do it.' The Voice immediately screamed: 'Before he was a police agent, he was certainly a Mafioso. This is the tone of the Mafia, unequivocal, precise, exact, clear as sunshine.' At that moment Viola came in.

I: What happened then?

Desideria: Erostrato did not say a single word during the whole of lunch. As for Viola, she chattered away, or rather, delivered a voluble monologue; there was visible in her joy, now without either remorse or reserves, at the prospect of love-making *à trois*, at six o'clock in Via Gaeta. She had slept on it; she had completely thrown off the terror which, on the previous evening, had induced her to make the sign of the cross; she was truly – I could not help thinking – reminiscent of a celebrated line of Racine to which my teacher had drawn particular attention that morning:

'Vénus toute entière à sa proie attachée.' Now and then, however, desire appeared to overcome her felicity, and then her joyous monologue broke off and she would turn upon me a glance full of heavy, anxious agitation, which I sought to avoid by looking obstinately in another direction. I sat still, my hands joined under my chin, staring vacantly, not eating, but listening to the Voice. What was it not able to say during that atrocious half-hour! It was attacking me now: 'You are not, you never will be, anything but a little bourgeois whore, long-winded, cowardly, decadent . . .'

I: Decadent?

Desideria: Yes, recently 'decadent' had become its favourite epithet in its invectives against me.

I: What did it mean?

Desideria: According to it, I was totally lacking in proletarian genuineness, I was an irremediable bourgeois, confused and weak-willed, mingling eroticism and revolution. In short: decadent.

I: And what else did it say?

Desideria: It said that Erostrato was an utterly vulgar Mafioso and prostitute; his pretended revolutionism served as a covering for the corruption in which he wallowed like a fish in its own element. Regarding Quinto, it said that he was a bureaucrat of terrorism, a bourgeois of revolution. He and Erostrato were different, but in one point they resembled one another: in considering me a madwoman, in excluding me from the group, in confining me to my role as a Parioli whore, et cetera, et cetera. By then we had reached the fruit course. Then all of a sudden the Voice gave me this strange, terrible piece of information: 'D'you remember that night when you had a kind of epileptic fit? D'you remember how ill you were? Well, either you contrive, today, to lock up your adoptive mother at Via Gaeta; or I shall cause you to become, forever, what you were on that one night.' 'Meaning what?' 'Meaning a woman possessed, possessed by the devil, a real, genuine madwoman. Not just for a single night but for all your life!'

I: Once it threatened to abandon you, not to make itself

332

heard any more, to restore you to your primal state of sexual object, of holothurian. Now, on the other hand, it was making an opposite threat: never to leave you alone, to precipitate you into madness and death like the swine in the Gospel fable when the devils went into them. Why this change?

Desideria: I don't know. I only know that I suddenly had a feeling of desperate, impotent terror and that, for no apparent reason, I thrust my fingers into my hair and grasped my head in my hands until I felt pain in my temples.

I: How did the luncheon end?

Desideria: With a toast.

I: A toast?

Desideria: Yes, Viola, in her joy, had that morning bought a cake in a pastry cook's shop in the neighbourhood. The manservant came in with this cake. We helped ourselves, and it was only then that I realized that, beside the usual glasses for wine and water, there were today some long, narrow goblets for drinking champagne. The manservant went aside to a small table and busied himself in uncorking the bottle of French sparkling wine. The popping of the cork was heard and then the wine was poured into the goblets. With a casual, cheerful air, Viola said: 'I don't know why, but I had this idea of the cake and the champagne. We have nothing to celebrate, as far as I know, yet I could not get rid of the idea that we ought to drink a toast. So I bought the cake and the champagne and I propose that each of us should drink to the success of something that is particularly close to his heart at this moment. But no one must say what that thing is that he is so eager about. All right?'

I: She was thinking of the appointment at Via Caeta.

Desideria: Certainly.

I: And you, of the kidnapping.

Desideria: Yes: or rather, it was the Voice that was thinking of it.

I: And Erostrato – what was he thinking about?

Desideria: I suppose – alternately and without being

able to decide – now of the kidnapping and now of the orgy.

I: How did the toast go?

Desideria: It was ambiguous and fierce. While we raised our glasses with one hand, with the other, so to speak, we grasped a knife, under the tablecloth, to cut each other's throats. We clinked our glasses together, calling each other by name: 'Eros', 'Erostrato', 'Desideria', 'Viola', 'Mum'. Viola emptied her glass at one gulp and had it refilled again; I scarcely wetted my lips, put out my cigarette in the cream of the cake, and rose to my feet. I said to Viola: 'Then we'll meet at six.' Erostrato, taken unawares, put down his half-full glass on the table and hurriedly followed me.

I: Did you find Quinto at the bar?

Desideria: Yes, he was sitting at a little table, writing something in his narrow black notebook. We all three got into the car: this time I placed myself in front beside Erostrato, who was driving, and Quinto got in behind. The car started off. Then, from the very first words that we exchanged, I understood, or rather, I felt precisely, that whereas on his arrival Quinto had excluded Erostrato from the conversation between him and me, so he was now excluding me from the conversation between himself and Erostrato.

I: How did you come to feel this?

Desideria: As soon as we had moved out of my street, the Voice, anxious and violent, made me immediately attack the subject of the kidnapping. 'Tell me, Erostrato has spoken to you about our plan?' 'What plan?' 'The kidnapping plan regarding my adoptive mother.' 'Ah, your plan for giving her a nasty shock?' 'Yes, but you must say "our" plan, mine and Erostrato's, because we devised it together.' 'Let's put off everything now until we have seen the flat. What kind of flat is it?' Then the Voice screamed in exasperation: 'Now you see, they've come to an agreement behind your back. Erostrato has explained to Quinto that you are a madwoman who hates her adoptive mother and, with a political excuse, wants to give her a "nasty shock" in order to avenge herself for the wrongs that she imagines have been done to her. Quinto believed him. The proof of all this is that he hasn't even described the flat to him; yet they've had all night to talk about it. Don't you realize that they're leading you by the nose? Don't you realize that this visit to Via Gaeta is nothing but play-acting in order to take you in and to keep you quiet?' I told it to keep calm. 'And you,' it said, 'are in agreement with them to bring the whole plan to nothing.' It was the first time that the Voice had accused me of being in agreement with someone against it. From this you can judge of its fury.

I: How did the conversation between Erostrato and Quinto continue?

Desideria: Erostrato appeared, though in a scarcely perceptible manner, to be slightly embarrassed; after a fit of coughing he said, as he drove, 'It's a rather special flat; in a certain way it seems made specially for this purpose.' 'Why?' 'Because it's secret.' 'Secret?' 'I mean that it's arranged in such a way that it's difficult to know what's going on there, who is there and who isn't and so on.' 'But what purpose does the flat serve at present?' 'It serves for meeting women there, for making love. In fact it's what is usually called a *garçonnière*.' 'I've heard that word before. Isn't it also called a love-nest? But who does it belong to?' 'It belongs to someone I know. This person would let it to us, if you agree.' 'And who is this person?' 'A ... an old man.' 'An old man, eh? And he went there to make love with women!' I was listening, my heart filled with anguish: the old man was Viola; Erostrato was talking to me, through Quinto. After a moment's reflection, Quinto resumed: 'It's all the same to me, it pleases me to visit a *garçonnière*, just to look at it. Anyhow, let it be understood; a *garçonnière* is always better than a car for making love, especially if it's a case of a small utility car, because you can't manage to get down to business without acrobatics, or else you have to get out and do it in some suburban meadow among tin cans and shit.' Erostrato said nothing. I exclaimed angrily: 'But they're disgusting places, these *garçonnières*, they're private brothels, hothouses for prostitution.' 'Now don't speak badly of prostitutes. What should we men do without prostitutes? One doesn't always want to look for a girl friend! So, when I feel that the pot's going to boil over, I go off to a certain avenue, get hold of a nice street-walker, and unburden myself. Unfortunately, it is necessary to do it in the car and, into the bargain, with a contraceptive, so that one hardly feels anything. That's why I say that these so-called *garçonnières* would sometimes be really convenient for me.' 'But are you married?' 'Me – married? Tell me, have you ever looked inside the pay-packet of a workman? D'you know what the cost of living is? I mean, the cost of living of a family. But of course, you have a rich mother, rich enough to be kidnapped, and what do you know about certain things? No, families are for the bosses. They have the money to set up families. We proletarians, we have only what's required for the Saturday evening street-walker.'

I: You must have been content now. Quinto was excluding Erostrato and conversing with you.

Desideria: I should think so indeed, that he was conversing. I was sitting in front beside Erostrato and Quinto was sitting behind on the back seat, in the opposite positions to those we had occupied the day before. Suddenly, seeing that he was continuing to chatter with Erostrato and to exclude me from the conversation, I turned round, let my arm dangle down, and made with my fingers a sort of gesture of summons, such as one makes to a dog or a cat to make it approach. Quinto saw the gesture; he understood and moved forward, leaning his arms on the back of my seat. So I stretched out my arm between his legs and took hold of his member. It was at that moment that he finally decided to speak to me.

I: Why did you do that?

Desideria: It was the Voice that ordered me to do it. I did not want to. It said: 'Now turn round and grasp his cock.' I answered: 'But why d'you make me do such a thing? I have a horror of Quinto.' 'Because Erostrato and

336

he have come to an agreement against you and you must contrive to come to an agreement with him against Erostrato.' 'But neither one nor the other matters to me.' 'He is a revolutionary and Erostrato is not. You must win him over at all costs.' 'A revolutionary! But what kind of a revolutionary! To me he seems bourgeois, exactly like Tiberi.' 'In fact, if by bourgeois you mean a man of order, he is a bourgeois, but he's a bourgeois who wishes to change the world, whereas bourgeois like Tiberi wish it to stay as it is. You've got a wrong idea of revolutionaries. They are often in every possible way like the bourgeois, except in one point: that they want revolution whereas the bourgeois do not.'

I: Cynical, the Voice, isn't it?

Desideria: The Voice was not cynical, but it wanted revolution.

I: At all costs, eh?

Desideria: One wants revolution at all costs or one does not want it at all.

I: Well, what was the end of your counter-offensive on the basis of masturbation?

Desideria: It ended with Erostrato suddenly saying very quietly: 'We're there.' Then I withdrew my hand and Quinto threw himself back. The car drew up beside the pavement and stopped.

I: And what happened then?

Desideria: We all got out; Erostrato went over to the freshly painted door beside the rusty, dusty roller-shutter of the ex-delicatessen, opened it, and we went in. Erostrato closed the door and for a moment we were in the dark. Then he turned on the light and said: 'Behind the roller-shutter next to this door there was once a delicatessen. The place was very lofty. So they divided it into two rooms with rather low ceilings, one on the ground floor and one on the first floor. But they kept the shutter so as better to conceal the flat. The two rooms don't have real, proper windows; they get their light from two long, horizontal slits which once looked out from the façade of the house, in the place where the shop sign was. So the slit in the ground-floor room is on the level of the ceiling and that of the first-floor room is at floor level. The shutter, of course, is fixed; behind it there is a normal brick wall. Now take a good look at this door and this staircase: the door opens into the ground-floor room, which is furnished as a study; the staircase leads to the first floor, where the bedroom is. Let us look first of all at the study.'

I: Why was Erostrato so meticulous, seeing that, according to you, he did not want to carry out the kidnapping and had convinced Quinto that you were a madwoman?

Desideria: It was a continuation of his ambiguity, an ambiguity that was in some way sincere and even perhaps welcomed. He did not want the kidnapping, yet at the same time he liked to behave as though he did.

I: What was the room like, that was furnished for use as a study?

Desideria: It was a very severe-looking room, characteristic of certain rather old-fashioned professional men: there was a big brick chimneypiece with a shelf of travertine that carried an incised Latin phrase. There was a baroque writing-desk, with a bronze lamp and a parchment lampshade, which also had Latin inscriptions. At the two sides of the chimneypiece there were bookshelves, with rows and rows of books with red, green, or brown backs ornamented with gilt decorations and letters. In front of the fireplace there were two twin sofas covered with bottle-green ribbed velvet. Finally, some large, dark pictures hung on the damask of the walls, which was also green.

I: All fake stuff, from secondhand dealers, wasn't it?

Desideria: No, on the contrary, they were all very fine antique, genuine pieces. I recognized Tiberi's taste. Probably it was he who had furnished the flat.

I: Quinto – what did *he* say?

Desideria: He seemed intimidated and incredulous. He said: 'But what used the old man to do in this study? Was he studying?'

I: What did Erostrato reply?

338

Desideria: He replied by describing, with punctilious meticulousness, the manner in which Viola, in all probability, proceeded with the call-girls whom she imported to Via Gaeta for love-making *à trois*: 'No, he didn't study there,' he said in his throaty voice, in which there was a curious mingling of the impersonal tone of the information and that of an emotion in some way involved, 'he received the call-girls here before going upstairs with them, into the bedroom, to make love there.' 'The call-girls? But how many of them came? More than one?' 'Yes, two.' 'What did he do, did he choose the better one and send away the other?' 'No, he kept them both.' 'To do what?' 'To make love.' 'With both of them?' 'Yes.' Quinto at this point moved his lips as though he wished to ask some other questions; but then he fell silent, realizing no doubt that he had already shown too much curiosity. Erostrato continued by saying that the old man was already there as much as an hour before the call-girls arrived. As he waited, he would try to control himself, to preserve his usual respectable, even haughty, air; but as time passed, he succeeded less and less in mastering the anxiety which devoured him. At first he would try to keep still, sitting on the sofa in front of the fire, with an illustrated magazine and a glass of whisky within reach of his hand. The fire would be crackling in the fireplace, some classical music would be coming from the record player with the volume turned low, and anyone who saw the old man at that moment would have thought that he was resting at the end of a day's work, calm, relaxed, and without worries. But it was not so. The old man would pour himself a drink and would drink more and more frequently; he would turn the pages of the magazine violently and almost without looking at it; in the end, unable to succeed any longer in mastering his own restlessness, he would do something or other just for the sake of doing something: he would go to the floor above to see if the room was in order; or he would take a rag and with maniacal care dust, one by one, all the pieces of furniture in the study; he would poke the fire and put two or three

339

more logs on it; he would regulate the lights; he would change the record on the record player; and so on. But the time did not seem to pass quickly enough; the old man was for ever consulting his wristwatch to see the time and meanwhile would be coming and going, up and down the study, just like the animals at the zoo at meal times, with the same hungry impatience, the same frenzied monotony. In the end it might happen that he would open the front door to cast a rapid if useless glance into the street; or he might climb up on a chair and, looking through the horizontal slit that served as a window, take a prolonged, vain peep at the pavement opposite. Sometimes the time of the appointment would go past without the call-girls appearing; then the old man, exhausted and anxious, would get down off the chair, seize the telephone, and enquire, at the girls' home, how long it was since they had gone out, whether they were coming together or separately, whether they had a car or were coming by bus, and other similar things which, somehow or other, either directly or indirectly, might have caused their lateness. Finally, there would be the long-awaited ring at the bell, the old man would examine himself in the looking-glass for a moment, then, assuming his usual air of formal detachment, he would go and open the door. The two call-girls would go into the study, looking round with an air both jaunty and embarrassed: they were accustomed to paying visits of this kind but did not yet know whom they had to deal with. With a casual, evasive, severe look, the old man would invite them to sit down on a sofa in front of him. The girls, who had been expecting a prompt, perhaps even a shameless welcome, were astonished when the old man, instead of laying hands on them, proceeded to ask the same kind of questions that bourgeois ladies put to servants before engaging them: how old they were, where they were born, where they lived, what their parents did, and so forth. But when the old man, still in that same lordly tone, went on to questions regarding their imminent erotic services, they then understood that the authoritarian distantness was deliberate and calculated as

340

an extra element of excitement. This supposition was confirmed, at any rate, by the change that the two call-girls could not help observing, at this point, in the demeanour of the old man. Hitherto he had been calm and cool; suddenly he enquired whether they had already made love *à trois*; and then they saw him blushing and noticed that his voice was no longer so firm. In fact, as he gradually plunged into the details of his erotic preferences, it seemed that the old man was no longer able to control his own agitation; he had recourse to words whose brutality was not now tempered by an objective tone; his voice became slow and hesitating; he had sudden bursts of blushing; he moved about on the sofa with increasing restlessness. The call-girls, put at their ease by this confusion, answered with frankness, also had recourse to the language of the brothel, laughed and exchanged allusive looks and words. But suddenly there was a further change : the old man announced that he was now going to fetch his camera; all they must do was to uncover those parts of their bodies as he indicated them : to be able to photograph them as much as he wished, he was ready to pay a supplementary amount. His tone was now relatively calm and distant again; it might have been thought that the camera, with its technicalities, replaced in the old man the overthrown capacity of reason; that it again placed a distance between his desire and the bodies of the call-girls. But it was not so – or at least it was not *only* so. In reality, the camera was incorporated by the old man into the erotic game and became an indispensable element in the two phases of sex *à trois*. In the first phase, the camera brought it about that the call-girls undressed without, so to speak, being aware of it, uncovering, obediently and amused, first one part of their bodies and then another, according as the old man pointed out his objective; in the second phase, which took place in the bedroom on the floor above, the camera was used to force the girls, now naked, to make love in the positions which the old man successively invented and suggested. Thus, in the first phase the camera assumed a certain welcoming composure like that of a

341

mistress interrogating a servant girl before engaging her, combined with the technique of photographs in erotic magazines. But in the second phase, this same technique was no longer sufficient, for it was contradicted by the participation, now completely uninhibited, of the old man, who had himself photographed by one of the girls while he was making love with the other, or threw aside the camera, now useless, and devoted himself frankly and without the pretext of photography to the complicated, acrobatic erotic relationship which was both one-sided and tripartite.

I: Why, do you think, did Erostrato want to describe, with such exactness and meticulousness, all that happened between himself, Viola, and the call-girls at Via Gaeta, during the three-sided love-making?

Desideria: I imagine, from an unconscious impulse of sado-masochistic self-punishment. He, like the call-girls, was prostituting himself to Viola; in the call-girls, he saw himself; in the old man, Viola. So on the one hand he hated himself; on the other, Viola. The result of all this, however, was not active revolt, as it was with me: the two hatreds balanced one another out, produced that apparent impassiveness of his which in reality was a powerlessness to act, to get out of the situation in which he found himself entrapped.

I: What was Quinto's comment on this tale of Erostrato's?

Desideria: Both disturbed and envious, he asked: 'How do you come to know all these things?' Erostrato replied that he knew one of these call-girls and she herself had told him.

I: And then what happened?

Desideria: With a sudden sincerity, evidently caused by his troubled senses, Quinto said: 'It will seem to you strange, but I feel more deeply conscious of injustice in this kind of thing than, for example, in culture. Anybody can provide himself with a culture; the money to buy books can always be found. But expensive tarts in a flat like this – that's what the bosses get hold of and there's nothing to be done. How much would these call-girls cost the old man?' 'Never less than a hundred thousand lire; often two hundred or three hundred thousand; sometimes half a million; it depends on the quality.' 'You see, that's actually the pay of the director of a factory.' Talking in this way, we left the study. On the narrow staircase leading to the upper floor I had proof that I had now succeeded, as the Voice wished, in attracting Quinto to my side and pitting him against Erostrato.

I: What made you realize that?

Desideria: We were going upstairs in this order: first went Erostrato, then I myself, and then Quinto. Suddenly Quinto slipped his hand in under my sweater, found that underneath it I was naked, turned my body round with his hand, and started caressing one of my breasts. I turned back abruptly, to bid him keep quiet; he stared at me with sparkling eyes, then withdrew his hand and cocked a snook in Erostrato's direction.

I: What did you do?

Desideria: For the first time I had a presentiment, an anguished, frightened presentiment, of what was going to happen.

I: What was going to happen?

Desideria: I'll tell you. We reached the landing, found ourselves in front of a small door, which Erostrato opened; and there we were in a tiny passage all lined with mirrors, ceiling, walls, floor. I saw my reflection multiplied a hundred times in all these mirrors and it made me almost dizzy. Erostrato walked in front, and, opening doors, showed us behind the mirrors a bathroom, a small kitchen, a lumber room from which, by means of a small corkscrew staircase, one could go down into the courtyard and come out thence into a street parallel with Via Gaeta. Erostrato commented: 'In fact, a very useful safety exit in case one wished to transform the flat into a people's prison.' Quinto then asked: 'But the bedroom – where is it?' Erostrato replied: 'I'll show it to you now as the old man sometimes looked into it – for, by the way, he was also a voyeur and liked to spy upon the call-girls while they were making love.' As he spoke these words, which without doubt alluded to one of Viola's erotic habits, he pressed the brass button of one of the mirrors, which opened like a little door and revealed a peep-hole of the kind in the front doors of houses. Invited by Erostrato, Quinto put his eye to the peep-hole and gave an exclamation of admiration: 'Not at all bad! A very suitable bedroom for making love!' Erostrato asked me whether I wanted to look, too; I shook my head; I felt an oppressive uneasiness which prevented me from speaking; he then opened a door camouflaged by mirrors and showed us into the bedroom.

I: What was the bedroom like?

Desideria: Again I recognized the origin of the furniture: Tiberi had more or less specialized in furniture of the sixteenth and seventeenth centuries, Italian, Provençal, and Spanish. The room had a dark red fitted carpet, and on the walls a damask of a lighter red. There was a canopied bed, very high, with twisted pillars; there was a cupboard studded with bosses; there were big chairs of Cordova leather; there was a big baroque lectern with a Bible or a missal open upon it. Here again there was a fireplace, with a hood of majolica tiles; as a shelf, there was an old beam upon which was a row of brass and pewter vessels. Light came from the horizontal slit at floor level: the same type of slit which, in the room below, gave light at the level of the ceiling. Quinto said: 'And so, on that bed, the old man made love with the expensive call-girls,' in a curiously conclusive tone in which moral condemnation mingled, it might be said, with egalitarian envy. Then, inspired by the Voice, as an actor is inspired by the prompter, I asked him abruptly: 'You would like, wouldn't you, to do what that old man did, at least once in your life?' There must have been some special accent in my voice, some flattering, provoking tone, for he answered at once: 'I think that everyone has a right to everything. The bosses have intercourse with half-a-million lire call-girls in *garçonnières*; well, the proletarians also have the right to have intercourse

344

with the very same call-girls in the very same *garçonnières*. Is that clear? And now, tell me, would you like to act as a call-girl for once? I was disconcerted because I did not expect this unconscious allusion to my acting the part of a street-walker in accordance with the Voice's script for revolt. But I did not have time to answer him, because Erostrato, in an entirely unforeseen manner, intervened with a strangely antagonistic aggressiveness, just like someone who sees a friend taking excessive liberties with his woman.

I: But you were not his woman.

Desideria: No, absolutely not. That's why I said his aggressiveness was strange.

I: What did he say?

Desideria: He said, between his teeth but looking straight into Quinto's eyes: 'Come off it; you'd better say whether you'd like to put your eye to the peep-hole and look at the girl while she's being had by the boss. The boss did that, too. As a proletarian, you ought to claim the right to act the voyeur, too, oughtn't you?'

I: Quite aggressive! What did Quinto reply?

Desideria: He was silent for a moment, then he remarked: 'Eh, chum, what's the matter with you? If there's a voyeur here, it's certainly you.' 'But answer me, would you like it or not?' 'It's you who's the voyeur, so much so that Desideria and I will have intercourse right on this bed and you can look on through the peep-hole in the passage.' 'If I were you, I wouldn't talk like that.' 'I shall talk as I please; if you like, you can even masturbate while you're looking at us.' 'A comrade doesn't talk like this to another comrade.' 'I'm not taking any lessons from you, chum! And now clear out, get out of the way, d'you see? Get out and go and watch.'

I: What did Erostrato say, or rather, what did he do?

Desideria: I told you that Quinto had a short jacket, which came down barely to his belt. He and Erostrato were near the door, I myself beside the bed. I saw Quinto make a rapid gesture, putting his hand inside his jacket and then

345

drawing back his arm. But I realized that he had taken out his pistol and was now pointing it at Erostrato only when the latter, calm and impassive as always, started backing towards the door. Then Erostrato said: 'Very well, but it takes two to have intercourse. Maybe Desideria might be asked whether she wants to do it.' Quinto half turned, in such a way that I should not see the pistol, and replied: 'Desideria wants to do it. You tell him, Desideria, to go away and act the voyeur and leave us in peace.' To tell the truth, I was on the point of crying out: 'No, no, I don't want to.' But the Voice intervened: 'You must do what Quinto wants, otherwise you'll lose us both, both him and me.' 'Even if he takes my virginity?' 'Even if he takes your virginity.' Then I raised my eyes and answered in a clear voice: 'I've made my choice, I stay with Quinto and you must go away.' Erostrato looked at me for an interminable moment, then he said: 'Very well, I'll go. Quinto, you know where to find me. Goodbye, Desideria.' He went out; Quinto put his pistol back in his jacket pocket and turned the key in the door.

I: So the supreme moment of your life had arrived; you were about to lose your virginity.

Desideria: Yes, that was so, the moment had arrived.

I: If it had not been for the Voice, probably you would not have let Quinto take your virginity.

Desideria: Certainly not.

I: You didn't like Quinto, did you?

Desideria: Didn't like him is putting it mildly. I had a horror of him.

I: Horror – why?

Desideria: Because, in some obscure and inexplicable way, I felt that he was a murderer.

I: A murderer?

Desideria: Yes, I felt it as one feels that a wild beast is savage. To such an extent that, in the car, I had looked at the thumb of his left hand.

I: His thumb? Why?

Desideria: I had read in a book on chiromancy that

346

murderers have thumbs 'like billiard-balls', so to speak, that is, with the last phalanx *round*. And he had this. And now my supposition was confirmed by the way in which he had terminated his dispute with Erostrato.

I: Then what happened in the room in which the old 'boss' had intercourse with the half-million lire call-girls?

Desideria: In view of the circumstances nothing really extraordinary happened. It's true, I was aware that it was an important and, in a way, a fatal moment; but as for Quinto, one could see perfectly well that he considered what was going to happen as something casual and, above all, normal: a Milan comrade liked a Rome comrade, and vice versa; what was there strange about their making love?

I: Yes, indeed.

Desideria: So everything went off as one might reasonably have foreseen. Quinto took off his jacket, hung it carefully over the back of a chair, then came towards me, clasped my breast with his two hands, pushed me back towards the bed, and made me fall there on my back. Now he was on top of me with his whole body and he started swiftly to undress me, but only just as much as was necessary for the sexual act, a confirmation, if one was needed, of the small importance that he gave to the act itself. He turned up my miniskirt over my belly, lowered my pants over my legs, and was then about to pull it down over my feet; but here he encountered the difficulty of my boots. The Voice ordered me brutally: 'Come on, take off your boots,' and I hastened to comply. Now I was naked from the waist downwards; I obeyed the Voice, which was dictating every movement to me, opening my legs as much as I could; and he threw himself into the middle, holding in his hand his member which, in the mean time, he had extracted from his very tight trousers – not without difficulty, because of his erection. He moved a little to one side, alert and intent, seeking with his member the opening of the vagina; then, when he had found it, he pressed his whole body forwards and penetrated inside me. I felt a quick, sharp pain, as though from a pointed blade; at the same time Quinto, sure now of having thoroughly penetrated, threw himself upon me and started going vigorously up and down with his body on mine. At the same time, he squeezed my breasts, covered my cheeks and my neck with kisses; finally, he thrust into my mouth a big, rasping tongue, a tongue, I could not help thinking, that was truly proletarian, handed down, in its bigness and its simplicity, from father to son, like the hunched stiffness of the peasant or the fixed look of the workman accustomed to the assembly line.

I: At that moment, did you really think this?

Desideria: Yes. So much so that the Voice was astonished and enraged: 'What, you think of these things at the moment when you are giving your virginity to the revolution? More than anything, this shows your irremediable class-consciousness.'

I: What did you say?

Desideria: I didn't answer. You know what I felt I was? Not the revolutionary of which the Voice spoke, but the young girl who, at the end of a long, boring, exhausting Sunday spent in trailing round the streets and the public gardens, lets herself be violated, more from weariness than from love, by some casual companion of hers, in a field on the outskirts of the city.

I: Did Quinto have an orgasm?

Desideria: I think so, because he stayed inside me, but not moving any more, with his face pressed against mine. He had had a sort of quiver followed by a deep sigh, and then nothing more.

I: Were you not afraid of being made pregnant?

Desideria: I did think of it and realized that it didn't matter to me in the least.

I: What happened next?

Desideria: We dozed off, both of us, in each other's arms, Quinto with his chin on my shoulder and I with my chin on his. Quinto was the first to fall fast asleep and he started snoring; I myself had the following dream. I thought I was on the edge of an immense plain, I was standing up, quite still, holding by the hand a man whose face I did not see,

348

because actually I saw myself and my companion from behind, black figures erect on the edge of an abyss of light. It was dawn and we were waiting ecstatically for the sun to rise and flood us with its beneficent light. The sun, indeed, rose, red as blood, with strange paler veinings, as if it were not made of solid, but of fluid, liquid matter; and as if this matter were contained in a transparent envelope like the yolk of an egg. Nevertheless, my companion and I continued to look ecstatically at the horizon. In our attitude there was devotion, admiration, expectancy, hope. The egg-yolk sun rose, still red and still of a strange soft, clear consistency, it rose and flooded the earth with an unreal, purplish light, and then, suddenly . . . it broke. Yes, it broke, as the yolk of an egg breaks if it is not absolutely new-laid; it broke, and from the breaking there came forth streams of something liquid and red that I had no hesitation in recognizing as blood. The sun was inexhaustible, one had no idea of how much blood it contained; very soon, at the horizon, the immense plain appeared inundated with blood, and this blood, like the high tide of oceans, was advancing towards us, was slowly unrolling itself like an endless, liquid carpet. Then finally I became aware of the danger that threatened us; without turning round, I said to my companion that we must run away, otherwise we should be swallowed up; then I turned towards him and, with a profound feeling of frustration and disappointment, discovered that he was no longer there, that I was alone. At this point I awoke. Quinto was still close against me but he was awake. He raised himself, from his stomach upwards, above my supine body, and looked at himself disconcertedly, his hand covered in blood. I expected that he would say: 'Why, you were a virgin'; but that was not so. Instead, Quinto burst out in an angry exclamation: 'Hell!' He was silent for a moment and then, looking at his hand, he resumed: 'Hell take it, you might have told me that you had your troubles!' Caught unawares and, into the bargain, having been commanded by the Voice not to reveal the truth, all I could do was to stammer: 'I did not know I had them. Now and then I have little haemorrhages, it might have been one of these.' 'Hell, now my trousers are all stained with blood. What shall I do? They were new ones, put on for the first time only today. Hell, what am I to do now, with all this disgusting blood of yours on my trousers? You know, you're an absolute turd not to have told me before.' There was in his voice precisely the fury of an orderly, mean man of the lower middle class who, faced with damage to one of his belongings, loses his head and gives vent to an ancient, angry feeling of frustration. Once again this thought struck me: How different everything is from what I imagined; and then I could not help saying: 'What a lot of fuss over a little spot of blood! Why, d'you start a revolution with your trousers?' Evidently my innocent, mocking remark caught him on the quick, as though I had passed my hand roughly over the wound of some unconscious feeling of guilt on his part; for suddenly there was let loose in him a blind fury, just the kind of fury that projects onto others the hatred that one feels for oneself. He slapped me violently, bang bang, first on one cheek and then on the other. 'Don't you dare speak of revolution,' he said, 'you who have just betrayed your man, you bourgeois whore! We shall start a revolution, don't worry, a revolution against you, too.' Then he rose from the bed, holding up his trousers with both hands, grumbling confusedly that he was going to the bathroom to wash off the stain; then he left the room.

I: So you were left alone. What did you do?

Desideria: I still had the burning sensation, wide and flat, from the slaps on my cheeks, and that other subtle, sharp pain, as of a razor, in my sex; I rose mechanically to sit on the bed and looked round. My eyes rested first of all on Quinto's jacket, which, at the moment when we had come into the room, he had hung over the back of a chair. I bent forward and hastily felt it; I felt the pistol in the inside pocket; for some reason I wanted to be sure that it was still there. Then I looked down and on the floor; on the carpet I saw the long, narrow black notebook which, at the time of our first meeting at the station, I had noticed sticking out

350

from the back pocket of Quinto's trousers. Evidently it had fallen out while we were making love. I picked it up, opened it, and turned its pages with sudden curiosity. What I saw at the first glance induced me to examine it more carefully.

I: What was there in this notebook?

Desideria: I looked at the handwriting and discovered, to my surprise, that it wasn't in handwriting at all.

I: What d'you mean?

Desideria: The whole of the book, from beginning to end, was written in block capitals, rather as is done on telegraph forms. Then I noticed that it was a very, very orderly notebook. Every day there was a complete account in which, under headings of various kinds, there were some which recurred and were repeated with regularity. First of all, restaurant bills. It seemed that Quinto ate in a restaurant once a day; it could be seen that at the other time he ate at home. The bills were minutely detailed: everything was written down. Here is an example: *pastasciutta al sugo milanese*, salad, apple, coffee, quarter litre of red wine. You won't believe it, but there were also criticisms of the quality of the dishes: mediocre, bad, very bad. Under one bill, still in block letters, was written: TODAY I ATE SHIT.

I: Meticulous indeed.

Desideria: Of course there were other expenses: clothes, cigarettes, toilet objects, cinema, taxi, car. And then there were also the prostitutes, the famous street-walkers whose praises he had sung.

I: Prostitutes?

Desideria: Yes, indicated by four letters: PROS. On some pages there were not merely the four letters but also criticisms of professional efficiency. For instance: expert; not worth anything; old; very expert, etc. etc. Of one he said: see her again, gives her bottom.

I: But what was this notebook? A journal, a diary?

Desideria: Not exactly; but almost.

I: Apart from the prostitutes, was there anything else?

Desideria: No, nothing else.

I: Not even telephone numbers?

Desideria: No, later I discovered that this was the rule to which somebody like Quinto, who was part of a group, had to keep: observe: not to keep on him addresses, telephone numbers, names, or other similar indications. But, all the same, I again had the impression which Quinto had given me from the very beginning.

I: What impression?

Desideria: That he was a murderer.

I: Why?

Desideria: That orderliness typical of a mean, meticulous lower-middle-class man, combined with the idea that he was a revolutionary: in all this I felt there to be a contradiction which it seemed to me could be explained in only one way – that is, that by vocation and temperament Quinto was a murderer.

I: What did the Voice say about the notebook?

Desideria: It was of no importance. The Voice was more than ever convinced that Quinto was a revolutionary and that I absolutely must not let him escape me. The Voice said to me – just imagine: 'You must link your destiny with that of this man; you must implicate him in the kidnapping of Viola, you must go and live with him and become his woman.'

I: And you – what did you reply?

Desideria: I replied that Quinto was repugnant to me, for the precise reason that I knew for certain that he was a murderer. And the Voice said, with a laugh: 'Maybe he is. Don't you know that the time of murderers has arrived!'

I: Bloodthirsty, eh, the Voice!

Desideria: I should say so, certainly. At this point Quinto came back.

I: Did he see the notebook in your hand?

Desideria: Yes; in fact I purposely held it open and said to him with an indifferent air: 'Interesting, your notebook.'

I: And he?

Desideria: He had washed his trousers; he had a damp mark in front but no trace of blood. He seemed more relaxed now that he was reassured about the state of his cloth-

352

ing. 'Give it to me,' he said, but without violence, as it were, casually. I reflected that he had cleaned off the blood; but I myself now felt this same blood spurting forth again from my sex and making the inside of my thighs sticky, so that I had to hold them as close together as possible. Forcing myself to put some vigour into my faint voice, I said: 'What will you write in your notebook now? "Desideria, a passable piece." If that's what you're going to write, I warn you that it would not be correct. You know what you ought to write: "Desideria, a wretched piece, a virgin, trousers ruined." '

I: You told him the truth, after all!

Desideria: It was the Voice which imposed this upon me; after explaining to me that, fundamentally, it did not know whether I ought to mention it or not.

I: So even the Voice, after all, sometimes had doubts?

Desideria: Yes, it had, but always of a practical kind, about the suitableness, or not, of doing things. On the question of revealing my virginity, was it suitable to tell or not to tell? The Voice argued like this: if I did not tell him, he would get rid of me as soon as possible. If I did tell him, since he was a man of the lower middle class, there were two probabilities: either he would get rid of me just the same, as a genuine slut; or else he was a sentimentalist, like all the lower middle classes, and would feel it his duty to 'make it up to me'. After explaining its doubts to me, the Voice, in the end, decided that I should tell him.

I: How did Quinto take it?

Desideria: He made the remark that I expected. He looked at me, a little disconcerted, then he asked: 'So I was the first?'

I: What did you say?

Desideria: 'I think so, certainly,' I said, but he did not seem entirely convinced. I saw this from his suspicious look. He asked: 'Tell me, you're not telling me this in order to catch me out?' Then, even before the Voice could order me to keep quiet, I answered him disdainfully: 'Well, with a mother who's a millionaire, I ought really to trap you – you who have only one pair of trousers.' I saw him give me an ugly look; evidently the trousers were important to him, one way or another. I hastened to add, on the urgent suggestion of the Voice: 'However, perhaps you're right after all. There was an intention of catching you out, but not in the way you think.' Again he looked at me with suspicion, I now felt an almost frantic need to go to the bathroom and wash myself; but the Voice nailed me down, to discuss the future with my seducer; and I obeyed it: 'I know you're thinking goodness knows what, but don't be afraid: I'm not asking you to marry me. I'm merely asking you to take me to Milan and introduce me to your group and let me share in whatever action you have in mind to undertake. And in the meantime, to collaborate in Erostrato's and my plan for the kidnapping of my adoptive mother.' It was quite a lot that I was asking of him; but it could be seen that a possible request for marriage on my part frightened him more than my wish to participate in revolutionary action, for he said in a quiet voice: 'As for the plan, we'll talk about it. But what is preventing you from coming to Milan? Come then.' 'But shall I be part of your group?' 'That is something that does not depend on me.' 'On whom, then?' 'I can only tell you that it doesn't depend on me.' At this point, what with the urgency of going to the bathroom and the insistence of the Voice, my nerves gave way. I jumped to my feet, pulled up my skirt, showed him my pants stained with blood, and cried: 'Look, this is my blood, it was shed for you, for all of you. And you stand there, weighing the pros and cons in your head, fool that you are.' I became immediately conscious that this was an absurd remark; but in that absurdity was expressed everything that I was suffering at that moment: the rebellion planned by the Voice which seemed now to be leading to nothing; the loss of virginity, which I had considered for years as the symbol of that rebellion; my own disappointment; my despair. More, apparently, than my words, their tone had an effect on Quinto. He said slowly, with some embarrassment: 'I understand you and I appreciate your revolutionary feeling. But now I must give myself time to reflect, to think it over.'

354

I: Did he seem to you to be sincere?

Desideria: No, not in the least. It was clear that my violent, absurd remark had merely served to convince him, once and for all, if there was still need of it, that I was a madwoman who should not be taken seriously but flattered and satisfied with words. Since, however, I could no longer resist my need for cleanliness, I said, though still violently: 'Reflect, reflect as much as you like; I'm going to the bathroom, I feel all sticky with blood'; and I went out. I locked myself in the bathroom, took off my pants and threw them into the rubbish bucket; then I washed myself, squatting on the porcelain, in a position that was inconvenient and, in my circumstances, somewhat mortifying because it made me acutely conscious of the subdued and humble normality of what you called the supreme moment of my life. I turned on the tap and rinsed myself until I saw the water, at first red, then pink, become transparent and colourless. Finally, I got up, dried myself vigorously, took a little cotton-wool from a small cupboard, made a tampon, and fixed it inside. Meanwhile, I was listening to the Voice, which was talking to me uninterruptedly – rather like the radio in a taxi, I could not help thinking; and one never knows whether the drivers really listen to it or leave it turned on so as to have company in their solitude.

I: What, in the main, was the Voice saying?

Desideria: It was beside itself at the idea that I had lost my virginity for nothing. It, too, thought that Quinto regarded me as a madwoman; according to it, I ought to give up the journey to Milan and compel Quinto to 'make it up to me'. This should consist in his collaborating in the kidnapping of Viola. The Voice, in short, aside from the revolution, thought of the situation like any Sicilian or Calabrian mother whose daughter had been violated. Quinto had seduced me and now he owed me reparation.

I: And what did you yourself think?

Desideria: I wanted to go to Milan. Oddly enough, I felt more inclined than the Voice to believe in Quinto's seriousness. Perhaps the atavistic tendency of every woman to at-

355

tach herself to the first man, to the initiator, was active in me.

I: You finished washing, you left the bathroom and went back into the bedroom; what happened then? Did Quinto turn out to be a sentimental lower-middle-class man or a swine?

Desideria: Neither one nor the other. It may seem strange to you, but after so much vulgarity and brutality there came forth a practical man, divided between attraction and diffidence. In fact, something very mediocre and very normal.

I: What exactly do you mean?

Desideria: I went into the room and found him sitting on the bed, as though plunged in deep thought; I went over and said to him: 'Well then, you've thought it over?' He raised his head, pointed to a chair, and began: 'Sit down there and listen carefully. Erostrato, who certainly knows you better than I do, tells me that you're a hot-head, with a screw loose' – and here he tapped his temple with one finger. 'This may be so, in fact without doubt it is so. But that does not take away from the fact that you were a virgin; that I was the first; that I like you; and that there's something in you that interests me, I don't yet know what it is, possibly the fact that you're a bourgeois girl and that in spite of that you think as we do. So I've thought it over and I say this to you: I agree, you'll come to Milan with me and we'll try living together. Of course, you'll give up all idea of your mother's money. You'll live with me, in a house where there is also my mother. You'll have to be content to take us as you find us. Well then, it's yes or no. If it's yes, we'll leave together tomorrow morning, let us say. If it's no, I'll say goodbye to you and go back alone to Milan.'

I: In the end, it was a matter of a real, genuine 'reparation'.

Desideria: Yes indeed! But you'll notice that, at the same time, he did not have a single word to say about the kidnapping of Viola in Rome or about the group in Milan: it was a matter of partial reparation. Infuriated, the Voice started screaming: 'There, so that's that; he persists in tak-

356

ing you for a madwoman. Not to such an extent, however, as not to continue making love with you; but enough to keep you carefully away from serious things: the bourgeois relationship, in fact, traditional between man and woman.'

I: What was it, was the Voice a feminist?

Desideria: It was everything. As it suggested to me, I immediately answered: 'I thank you, but before going to Milan we must lay the foundations for our plan, Erostrato's and mine, here in Rome.'

I: What did he say?

Desideria: He asked dryly, with an expression that was already hostile: 'Why, what plan?' The Voice willed me to give a brutal answer: 'You know perfectly well what plan: to kidnap that sow of an adoptive mother of mine, and to make her cough up a good deal of her money.' The effect of this remark, contrary to the calculations of the Voice, was counter-productive. Quinto replied reluctantly, like someone waking from a long sleep: 'Ah yes, the kidnapping plan; we talked about it, Erostrato and I, last night: for the present, at any rate, it's not possible.' 'Why is it not possible?' 'Because you want to make use of this flat. Now this flat, on the other hand, won't do.' 'What is there that won't do about this flat? It seems made on purpose.' 'It won't do because it's a brothel. Revolutionary quarters can't be sited in a brothel. It would be against our rules.' 'And what are your rules?' 'Our rules are that the place where we live, where we meet, where we prepare for action must be proletarian.' 'And that means?' 'It means that it must not be a brothel.' 'But tell me at least what it must be?' 'Haven't you ever seen a workman's house where the wife is a good housewife? Go and look at one. The proletarian home is modest, simple, perhaps even poor, but like the face of a respectable woman – clean. This house, on the other hand, has the face of a whore.' 'But don't you realize that by making it a proletarian house we should purify it? In a sort of way we should re-consecrate it, as a church is re-consecrated after there have been soldiers in it who have defiled it?' 'You may even be right, I don't say you're not. But these are

357

the rules and we must observe them. You and Erostrato must look for another house, then we'll see and discuss the matter.'

I: What answer did you make? Or rather, what did the Voice answer?

Desideria: The Voice shouted: 'He continues to regard you as a madwoman. He wants to take you to Milan, keep you at his disposal as a whore in his mother's house and then; when he's fed up with you, he'll get rid of you. But you must try at all costs to frustrate him. To break his link with Erostrato and draw him over to your side. You have an infallible means and you must make use of it.'

I: What means?

Desideria: 'You must reveal to Quinto all that you have come to know about Erostrato through the police report. And above all that he is a police agent.'

I: Terrible, the Voice! But in any case it was some time since Erostrato had been an agent, though he had been formerly.

Desideria: That was what I tried to make the Voice aware of. Answer: 'Once a spy, always a spy.'

I: And then what?

Desideria: Then I obeyed, as usual. Without preparation, I said to Quinto: 'You and I will look for the house together, but not with Erostrato'. 'Why?' 'Simply because Erostrato is a police agent.'

I: You said it like that?

Desideria: Yes, just like that. He looked at me, really in astonishment this time, and said: 'Why, what d'you mean?' 'It's the truth, he's a pimp, a Fascist, a police agent.'

I: A full-size denunciation, in fact. How did he take it?

Desideria: With bureaucratic seriousness. He rose unhurriedly from the bed, took a chair, sat down astride it, and said to me: 'Sit there,' pointing to the bed where he had hitherto been sitting, as though to signify that he had now become the accuser, the inquisitor, and I the accused, the interrogated. Then he resumed: 'This is a very serious piece of information, which must be carefully weighed and evaluated. You must realize that you cannot make a statement like this without bringing proofs.' I was struck by the transformation that had taken place in him. Shortly before he had been a man of the lower middle class preoccupied with the state of his own trousers; now he seemed to have become – what shall I say? – a police inspector, a secret-service colonel, a personage, that is, somewhere between military and political. The light that penetrated through the slit parallel with the floor, scanty and flattened as it was, left the room in half-darkness. Quinto rose, twisted the lamp on the bedside table in such a way that the light fell full on my face, then sat down again astride the chair with his arms folded on the back, but a little outside the ray of light, in such a way as to have his own face in shadow.

I: What was it? A third-degree interrogation?

Desideria: In a way it was, yes. But more than anything a way of behaving.

I: Of behaving? Then, according to you, Quinto was an actor?

Desideria: No, he was what he was convinced of being: a revolutionary; but he knew by instinct that to be a revolutionary the first and most important thing was to behave like a revolutionary.

I: The interrogation, then, really took place?

Desideria: Indeed, did it *not*!

I: What did he ask you?

Desideria: Practically everything. To begin with, how I came to know that Erostrato was a Fascist and a police agent. Then I told him, or rather, the Voice made me tell him (it took control from the very first moment, because, it said, it did not trust me and feared that I should not be hard enough on Erostrato) – I told him the whole story of the relationship between Erostrato and Viola, saying nothing, however, of the way in which I had met him and of the fact that we had made love. Apart from this, I concealed nothing; I said I had taken Erostrato home and he had immediately laid hands on Viola. That Viola was my adoptive mother and that she was in love with me and that, once

359

she had become Erostrato's mistress, she was anxious that I should make love *à trois* with her and Erostrato. That Viola, before Erostrato, had had another lover, Tiberi, who was also her man of business. That she and Tiberi enlisted call-girls and made love *à trois* in that same flat. That Erostrato had to a great extent supplanted Tiberi, not only in the sexual relationship with Viola but also in matters of business. That Tiberi, jealous of Erostrato, had had an enquiry on the latter carried out by a chief inspector of police who was a friend of his. That from this enquiry it had come out that Erostrato was a swindler, a Fascist, a police agent, as well as a vicious character not new to three-sided erotic relationships. That, finally, Tiberi, to avenge himself on Erostrato, had shown me the police report.

I: What was Quinto's reaction to all this?

Desideria: He said urgently: 'Where is the police report?'

I: That was what was most important to him?

Desideria: I should say, only that. I replied that I didn't have it, that it had remained with Tiberi.

I: And he?

Desideria: He spoke again, still with the same urgency: 'It's absolutely necessary that you should let me have it as soon as possible.'

I: What was his tone of voice? Frightened, preoccupied?

Desideria: Neither frightened nor preoccupied but, so to speak, exclusive: at that moment, for him, nothing mattered but the report.

I: Did you not ask him why he was so determined to have it?

Desideria: Yes, I did ask him. He answered reluctantly that the accusations must be proved. Then the Voice made me cry: 'So you don't believe me, you believe that I'm mad, that I'm inventing the whole thing. I should like to know *why* I should be inventing. What does Erostrato matter to me? I am warning you that he is a police spy because I believe in revolution.' 'I'm not saying that you invented the fact that he is a police agent. I'm saying that proofs are re-

360

quired.' The Voice, at this point, cried: 'Show him the photographs; show him that he's a prostitute.' It was alluding to the photographs taken by Viola during the lovemaking *à trois* at Via Gaeta; I still had them in my bag; I took them out and handed them to Quinto, saying: 'Meanwhile, look at these photographs. Erostrato gets paid for these photographs. He's a kept man, a prostitute. Look at them, tell me if a revolutionary would allow himself to be photographed in this way.' Quinto took the photographs with diffidence and visibly made it a point of honour to cast as rapid a glance as possible at them. Giving them back to me at once, he said: 'They don't interest me. What I need is proofs that he is a police agent. These photographs prove nothing.' The Voice then cried out: 'Ask him what they will do to him if there is a trial and the accusations are proved.' I obediently said: 'But what would you do to him if you discovered that he was really a police agent?' I saw Quinto hesitate; then he replied, with diffident reticence: 'That we shall decide when the time comes.' The Voice exclaimed: 'He's not telling you, he doesn't want to tell you because he doesn't trust you. To him you're not a comrade, a revolutionary, but a madwoman to be made use of but kept at a distance.' Then, in a didactic but furious tone, it explained to me that they would commit Erostrato to a so-called people's tribunal, would condemn him to death, and would finish him off with a blow to the back of the neck. That was the end of spies, it concluded; thus also, thank God, it would be the end of Erostrato!

I: It was bloodthirsty, the Voice!

Desideria: Yes, it was in a state of excitement that was both catastrophic and indiscriminate; it hated everybody and condemned everybody.

I: And then what?

Desideria: I said to Quinto: 'If you're so eager to have this report, I can telephone to Tiberi and get him to give it to me.' He immediately rose to his feet in great haste: 'Telephone. We'll go there now; by fair means or foul we'll make him hand it over.' The Voice, seeing this urgency on the part

361

of Quinto, commented: 'So the existence of the group wasn't an invention of Erostrato's. You see how determined he is to have the police report.' I looked round, but there was no telephone. Then I remembered having seen a telephone apparatus in the bathroom. I told Quinto I was going to telephone and left the room. I went into the bathroom, turned the key in the door, dialled Tiberi's number, and placed the receiver to my ear . . . and then fell to the floor in a faint. I must in some way have fallen gradually, for when I came round, after a time that I cannot calculate, I was lying on the floor with my feet in the basin of the shower and my head underneath the telephone. Quinto was knocking at the door, loudly but not impatiently, at regular intervals; between one knock and the next, there came to me, from the receiver dangling over my head, the signal of the telephone. Gradually I raised myself, with an effort, to my feet and cried: 'Wait a minute.' Then I dialled Tiberi's number again. He came to the telephone at once; I did not give him time to speak but said in one breath: 'This is Desideria, I'm coming in a moment to fetch the report.' 'What report?' 'The police report on Occhipinti.' There was a rather long silence, then he asked: 'But of what use is it to you?' A mysterious thing happened then, which can be explained only by the in some way hysterical desire of the Voice to make me into a revolutionary. Hurriedly I lied: 'It's of use to us in the group, to make an accusation against Erostrato in front of a people's tribunal, and eventually to condemn him.' 'Condemn him to what?' 'To death.' At the other end of the line I heard Tiberi's voice utter an incomprehensible exclamation; then, in his usual Roman accent, drawling and refined, he said: 'But, Desideria, what are you saying? Have you gone mad? I don't want to get mixed up in these things, they're your affair and you must deal with them.' The Voice, too, at this juncture, realized that, without meaning to, but drawn on by the revolutionary myth, it had made me go beyond the limit of Tiberi's erotic dependence. So it suggested to me this emendation: 'Of course these are theoretical condemnations, since we haven't yet started the

362

revolution. In practice, we shall tell him to keep away from us.' 'Desideria, I have realized for some time that you were a member of a group, but to the extent of . . . no, no, I'm not getting mixed up in it and I don't wish to be.' 'Come on, I'm coming to fetch the report and then I'll go and look out of the window, as I did that day when I looked at the yellow-and-red petrol pump opposite your house.' This time there was a profound and interminable silence; in the end, with a kind of strange sigh, he said: 'Come, but be quick.' I hung up the receiver, opened the door, and found myself face to face with Quinto. To him I said: 'Why are you knocking? I've telephoned, the report is there. He's expecting me at his house.' 'Let's go, then.' 'Wait: Tiberi has made a condition: in exchange for the report I shall have to . . .' I stopped for a moment; the Voice wanted me to tell the whole matter, that is, the act of sodomy which for Tiberi was at the same time both irresistible and symbolic; but some sort of modesty made me finish, instead: '. . . to make love with him'; and then I saw Quinto look at me with an air almost of boredom, as though he considered that this was my affair: he himself had need of the report, absolutely; and little did it matter to him that I had to pay for it in this way. I don't know why, but at that moment I hated him as if he were not the perfect stranger that in effect he was, but a much loved and much esteemed husband who, unexpectedly, showed himself to be, on the contrary, nothing but a perfect stranger. I said to him brusquely: 'However, I absolutely don't want to make love with this man. Let's do this; you give me your pistol and wait for me at the front door. I'll go up and ask him for the report. If he lays hands on me, then I'll show him the pistol.' 'No, not the pistol, I won't give it to you, don't even mention it.' 'But I'm now a member of the group, am I not?' 'You're a part of it inasmuch as you're with me; but the pistol, no.' 'You want to make use of me, you want to have me again for a little and then to get rid of me.' He said nothing, he raised his hand and clasped my two cheeks with two fingers of iron, forcing me into a ridiculous and painful grimace. Then, articu-

363

lating by syllables, he said: 'Well then, are we going?' In those small blue eyes of his there was a pitilessness that made me think once more of an inborn homicidal vocation. Not being able to speak on account of those two fingers that were clasping my cheeks, I nodded my head. He relaxed his grasp, immediately turned his back and walked off to the door at the end of the passage as though he were sure that I would now follow him.

I: What did you do, did you go to Tiberi's?

Desideria: Yes, we went up Via Gaeta as far as the station square, we stopped a taxi and I gave Tiberi's address. The Voice now – it is the only word for it – was in a delirium. It did not believe in Quinto's promise to introduce me to the Milan group; with growling, unrestrained exasperation it repeated to me without ceasing that Quinto considered me a madwoman or little less; that only my beauty and the attraction which my beauty exercised over him had prevented him from leaving me in the lurch immediately after he had taken my virginity. That was how it was, muttered the Voice as the taxi moved through the streets of Rome, that was how it was: my destiny was not to flow out with the muddy stream of my revolt into the great limpid sea of revolution; but to be agitated, without relief and in vain, in this same revolt, as in a foul marsh from which I could not escape. Yes, I might perhaps go to Milan, I might perhaps establish a conjugal life with Quinto in his so-called proletarian house, but the group would remain a mirage, and in the end I should have to come back to Rome. Here everything would recommence as before, as in the past; with this difference, however, that my foolish aspirations to rebellion would no longer have the symbolic, planned character that it had been able to confer upon them in the past; they would be nothing more than what they were in the now everyday, accepted reality – to be precise, nothing more than disordered, ineffectual aspirations. And I would never again be able to escape from the accursed, bewitched circle of my class, that class which determined my existence and every aspect of that existence, including

364

my rebellion; and into which I had been integrated, in spite of myself, once and for all, by Viola, with the fatal act of my adoption. I had been bourgeois, I was bourgeois, I would remain bourgeois, for ever. As if this delirium of rebellion and impotence had not sufficed, Quinto suddenly intervened to confirm the predictions of the Voice. He turned towards me and said: 'You get him to give you the report now and I shall leave for Milan immediately, but alone.' 'Why alone?' 'Because if you come away with me, Erostrato will realize that something has gone wrong. You must stay here.' 'What for?' 'To do the things you've always done. When d'you think you'll see Erostrato?' 'Today, at six.' 'Well, at six I shall take the train for Milan, while you see Erostrato.' 'I have to see him with Viola.' 'See him with anyone you like, the important thing is that he should not suspect anything. You must tell him that I've gone back to Milan temporarily because I telephoned and my presence is needed there. To confirm this, I'll leave my little bag and my pyjamas in the top-floor flat.' 'But then you'll come back?' 'Of course, in two days at most. Meanwhile, you must not change your life in any way, nor your relationship with Erostrato. You must give him the impression that nothing is changed between you.' I remained silent at this juncture; partly because the Voice was by no means silent and I was bound to listen to it.

I: What was the Voice saying to you?

Desideria: As you can imagine, it was triumphant, in a bitter, hysterical way. 'Now my predictions are confirmed,' it said; 'he's going to Milan without you, he won't come back again. And, into the bargain, he's instructing you, though unconsciously, to keep the appointment with Erostrato and Viola and make love *à trois*. And not to change anything in your life, neither today, nor tomorrow, nor ever.'

I: Perhaps the Voice also told you what you ought to do to solve this situation of yours?

Desideria: It did indeed tell me.

I: And what was it?

Desideria: It said: 'There is no way of escape from your situation unless you have recourse to the pistol that Quinto has in his jacket. A pistol is "always" a solution.'

I: The Voice was out of its mind. What was it alluding to: suicide, murder, or both?

Desideria: It didn't specify.

I: Why didn't you ask?

Desideria: I didn't want to ask, I was afraid of its being more precise. Besides, I didn't have time. The taxi stopped and we had arrived.

I: What happened then?

Desideria: We got out of the taxi, quite close to that yellow-and-red petrol pump which Tiberi had once forced me to look at from the window while he tried to sodomize me. Then the question of the pistol came up again: the Voice wished me to get Quinto to give it to me under the pretext that I could make use of it to threaten Tiberi: with equal and even greater obstinacy Quinto refused to give it me. We were standing on the pavement close to the petrol pump; all at once I looked up casually and saw, up on the second floor of the building opposite, at the window, Tiberi, motionless, looking at us. Vehemently I said: 'Don't you understand that that man is mad about me and won't give me the report unless I make love with him? Don't you understand that it is immoral, on your part, to ask me to do something like this, something that is profoundly repugnant to me? Come on, give me the pistol and let's have done with it.' I looked up again at the window of the house opposite to see if Tiberi was still there. Quinto followed my look and then asked: 'Is it that man who's looking at us out of the window?' 'Yes, that's him.' 'I'm not giving you the pistol. But it's not necessary that you should make love with him. If he's mad about you, a little cajolery will be enough. Let's start, then. I'll go up with you to the floor below his and wait for you there. You'll go to the floor above, get him to hand over the report, and then rejoin me. Is that all right?' I said nothing; I walked off towards Tiberi's front door. Meanwhile, the Voice was screaming:

366

'Idiot, we're ruined! Without the pistol we can't do anything.'

I: What did it mean by those words?

Desideria: It meant that I could not solve my own situation. By now, in its delirium, it saw no solution except in violence.

I: What did you do then?

Desideria: We got into the lift, I pressed the button for the first floor; we reached it and Quinto got out. Then I pressed the button again and I myself, in turn, went up to the second floor. I paused for a moment standing motionless in front of Tiberi's door: I was sure that he was on the other side of the door and was looking at me through the peephole. In fact, I had barely rung the bell when I heard his hands moving to undo the chain. Then the door was thrown open. Tiberi was standing there on the threshold, serious, perhaps even frightened, nevertheless red in the face from his usual agitation. He was holding his arm extended in an unnatural manner, rather distant from his body; I looked down and saw that he was clasping in his hand a small, flat, black pistol. This had a curious effect because it contrasted with the old-fashioned, unwarlike elegance of his double-breasted suit; besides, he was clasping it as one clasps an entirely new object whose utility and whose use are unknown to us. He caused me to enter hastily and cast a glance onto the landing, then said: 'But you were with somebody.' 'Yes, I found someone to come with me.' 'But who is it, one of your group?' 'No, it's a boy who is a friend of mine.' 'A boy; he looked like a man of about thirty.' 'I call all men boys.' 'Anyhow, I took up this pistol, for some reason.' 'Eh, what a lot of precautions!' In the meantime, we had proceeded into the broad, dark passage; I looked round and again, as on the first occasion, at the thought that all these pieces of furniture might be sold at any moment, I could not rid myself of the impression, disconcerting as it was, that I was in a shop rather than a private house. Tiberi was a short distance in front of me. I said to him: 'It's useless to take me into the drawing-room. I've come to fetch the report; give it to me and I'll go away at once.' He did not turn round; he was walking in a curious, listless manner, holding the hand with the pistol in it at some distance from his side, as though the pistol were a dirty thing; he was silent for a moment, then he stopped in front of the drawing-room door and said: 'Do you remember that, last time you came here, I informed you that I had a certain thing to say to you? Well, let us sit down now and I'll tell you.' He opened the door and we went into the big, gloomy, furniture-crowded drawing room. I looked round and saw that something had been changed. The whole of the far end of the room was occupied by a strange, incongruous object: a complete church altar all made of wood, of antique, yellowish wood, which gave the impression of being light and crumbly and worm-eaten. The altar was in Renaissance style, with Corinthian pillars, a pediment, and three niches with three statues also of wood, on one side Saint Joseph, on the other the Madonna, and in the middle the crucified Christ. There was a straight shelf with small pillars, also Corinthian. There were vases and a monstrance of silver. There was a short flight of steps leading up to the altar. Seeing that I was looking with curiosity at this unusual piece of antiquarianism, Tiberi said: 'Beautiful, isn't it? I had it put here; there was no room in the gallery.' 'Who's going to buy an altar?' He did not answer, but took me by the arm with sudden violence: and so we found ourselves both standing in front of the altar. He was silent for a moment and then, looking at the altar and without turning towards me, he said: 'You want the report, and what are you giving me in exchange?' As he spoke he seemed absent-minded, with his thoughts elsewhere. But the heightened colour of his face and the force with which he squeezed my arm made me think that he wished to barter the report for the price of a sexual service of the kind he had extorted from me the other time I had come to see him. The Voice was of the same opinion; 'He's a sadist. Now he is going to make you kneel with your head on the altar steps, he'll uncover your behind and sodomize you. Of course, being

368

on the altar gives it more zest.' I said simply: 'In exchange? I'm not giving you anything.' He echoed me, in a questioning tone: 'Nothing?' He did not move but seemed to be reflecting; then he resumed: 'I'll give you the report and also many other things, but now you must listen to me.' 'I am listening, but I warn you at once that if, in exchange, you want to make love, you can get the idea out of your head.' 'No, I want to do something else and I am not making it a condition; I'm only asking you to listen to me, that's all.' 'I'm listening, I'm not doing anything else.' 'Well, the thing that I told you the other day that I wished to say to you is this: "I want you to become my wife." '

I: So at last it came out. Fairly foreseeable, wasn't it?

Desideria: He did not give me time to answer, but went on inflexibly as though talking to himself: 'I am – and I'm proud of it – a Catholic, an Apostolic, a Roman. To me this altar, at this moment, is not a piece of antiquarianism; it's something sacred. Don't say anything to me now; I shall pray for a moment, like a good Catholic; in my prayer I shall ask that your reply may be positive. Be quiet and wait until I've finished.' He let go of my arm, put down the pistol on the shelf, joined his hands; then he started moving his lips, looking straight at the altar.

I: Was he really praying?

Desideria: Yes, he was praying. I watched him in silence, with surprise. Not so much because he was praying – I had already seen him praying in church at Mass on Sundays – as because he was praying at that moment and for me. Then the Voice, furious, violent, beside itself, made me jump: 'Imbecile, don't you realize that it's always the same thing?' 'Why, what thing?' 'Don't you realize that he wants to put it up your bottom again this time, but seriously and for good?' Meanwhile, Tiberi had finished praying and bade me, in an authoritative tone, as though I had already accepted his proposal of marriage: 'Now let's kneel down. You must tell me solemnly, yes or no.' He took me by the arm again, exerted some force as if to compel me to kneel; and then, suddenly, the fury of the Voice spoke through my mouth:

369

'I was surprised: you haven't tried to sodomize me like last time but now I realize that that is still your idea, only now you want to put it up my bottom for good, definitively. Because if last time you had succeeded, I should have then shrugged my shoulders, washed my behind, and that would have been that. But if I become your wife, you'll put it in from behind once and for all, from now until the day of my death. And as for your altar, what would a promise of marriage be worth when exchanged in front of a few pieces of dusty, worm-eaten wood? Nothing, less than nothing; today I would give my word, tomorrow I would spit on it. So sell your altar to some rich man who believes in it, give me the report and let me go.'

I: Always that report!

Desideria: I was there for that, at least as a pretext. For the first time since I had known him, I saw Tiberi turn pale, really pale, just as if someone had blown out the flame which, against the light, made his red face like a lighted lantern. 'I haven't got the report,' he said; 'it's at the gallery.' 'Then let's go to the gallery and then you can give it to me.' 'I'll give it you tomorrow. But now listen.' 'What is it?' 'You remember that day, the first time you came here? You were looking out of the window into the street. I was standing behind you and you were looking at the petrol pump, and everything was so fine.' 'Let me alone, you're hurting me.' He was twisting my arm now, as if to compel me by force to kneel down; this time, however, as I understood, not to pray with him and to tell him that I agreed to become his wife, but to force my body into the right position for the act of sodomy. He had gone red in the face again; he was biting his lower lip; as he twisted my arm he peered at me with a curious, intent look from the oblique slits of his eyes, as though to measure the intensity of the pain that he was causing me. It happened in a moment. I pushed him away, seized the pistol that lay on the shelf; he noticed this and gave an ugly twist to my left arm, which he was still grasping; then I, owing to the sharp pain, pressed the little lever of the weapon with my first finger – a spontaneous, simple,

370

easy thing to do. There was an explosion, sharp and loud; then he relaxed his grasp and bent forward, seeming to kneel on the steps of the altar; finally, he fell sideways, hunched together, and remained there, crumpled up, like a poor man who, his strength exhausted, sleeps on the steps of a church. Then I threw down the pistol and ran away.

I: Where?

Desideria: Almost without noticing it, I ran along the corridor again and rushed out onto the landing. But I remembered that Quinto was waiting for me on the floor below, so I closed the door gently and started going slowly downstairs. Quinto emerged at once, before I had finished coming down. He asked me in an impatient tone of voice, seeing that my hands were empty: 'And the report?' 'He has it at the shop and will give it to me tomorrow.' The lift had remained stationary at this floor. I went past Quinto, who was disconcerted at my attitude, opened the lift doors, went in, and, before he could enter in turn, closed the doors in his face and pressed the button. The lift began to descend very slowly; it was of an old-fashioned type, swaying and tinkling with panes of glass. I saw Quinto shaking a threatening fist and then throwing himself down the stairs, flight after flight, racing against the lift. Then, as he appeared and disappeared, flight after flight, I sat down on the old threadbare red velvet bench and listened to the Voice. In a calm and reasonable tone it said to me: 'You did very badly to throw Tiberi's pistol away, very badly indeed. Now at all costs you must get hold of that tiresome Quinto's pistol, to resolve the situation once and for all. You already know the way, I don't need to repeat it.' I nodded; it was perfectly true, I knew the way, and if I had sat down, it was because I had felt a sudden dizziness, possibly because of the blood I had lost. The lift came to a stop, I remained seated and looked up at Quinto, who was opening the doors. My look must have had such a murderous glitter that he certainly thought I was really mad and he remained silent before speaking. I said harshly: 'Were you afraid I should run away – but where? Maybe to go round the world as my mother would like to do? But don't you know that deflowering is a trauma for a woman? Don't you know that a virgin, immediately after she has been raped -- for you did rape me -- can even have the right to feel ill?' With these words I rose to my feet, came out of the lift and preceded Quinto into the hall. We walked in silence along the street; at Piazza Cavour, close by, we found a taxi rank. Quinto gave the driver an address that I did not know; but I remembered that it must be in the neighbourhood of Piazza San Giovanni. I asked where we were going and he replied that we were going to the house of a comrade. During the whole long journey we did not speak at all. Quinto looked attentively out of the taxi, at the street; and I was thinking only of the best way of stealing his pistol and to be in time to arrive at six o'clock at Via Gaeta. I looked at my watch and saw that it was nearly five. I calculated that even if I succeeded in extracting the pistol during the first five minutes that we were in the comrade's house, I should not be in time to arrive at six o'clock at the appointment with Viola and Erostrato. But it was true that they would keep one another company and that in any case they would wait for me, perhaps even for the whole night: passion is not sparing of time.

I: So you arrived at the comrade's house. What happened?

Desideria: The taxi came to a stop in a street of modest old houses, of the kind that were built for the working classes at the beginning of the century. There was no lift; we went up three floors of a squalid, dimly lit staircase. I remember the lights with shades in the shape of soup-plates painted blue and white; the grey-speckled tiles on the landings; the iron bars of the banisters. I looked at these details with the irritation of impatience: I longed to be in the flat, to get hold of Quinto's pistol, and to hurry to Via Gaeta. The door was of a blackish colour, like pitch, and there was no name-plate; we went in in the dark; then Quinto turned on the light and I looked round. I at once saw that it was a very modest and scantily furnished flat; but what struck me most of all was the disorder, the care-

372

lessness, the lack of cleanliness in the four little rooms that composed it. In each room there were one or two camp beds; the sheets and blankets were disordered, as they had been left at the moment of awakening; there were garments left about here and there on chairs, crumpled newspapers on the floor, a few dog-eared books, a pair of shoes under a bed. We went into the kitchen. Here again there was the same disorder, but even more repugnant owing to the accumulation of dirty dishes in the sink. The Voice, which hitherto had been silent, suddenly spoke in a fury, as if this filthy and untidy flat had constituted a provocation: 'Ask this imbecile whether this is the proletarian home whose cleanliness he was boasting of a short time ago. Ask him and let's hear what he answers.' Quinto had now taken off his jacket and hung it over a chair; he was sitting at the marble table in the kitchen and consulting a railway time-table. I went to the window, threw it violently open, and said in a voice distorted by anger: 'Would this be the famous proletarian home that you mentioned to me a short time ago?' I noticed that he turned round and gazed at me with an uncomprehending stare, looking down his nose at me. 'It's a house that we have in common,' he said, 'where we know that we can go and find a bed for a night.' 'Answer my question. Is it the proletarian house or not?' 'Yes, it is; but what's the matter with you?' 'You said that the proletarian home is like a face without make-up. But you did not say that this face is never washed and is disgustingly dirty.' This time I saw in his look a change from astonishment to perplexity: at first he had been surprised, now he was wondering whether he ought to take me seriously. He said: 'Of course the comrades went away in a hurry and didn't make the beds. In any case, this house serves above all as a dormitory.' 'Oh yes, but in the mean time there's a stink to take one's breath away, and all these dishes have been dirty for a week.' He now pushed back his chair with decision, got up and came over to me: 'Now look,' he said, 'what's the matter with you? Are you ill, or what?' It was not precisely the tone in which one enquires after a person's

health. And in his eyes could be read his cold determination
to bend me to his will. In fact, he added: 'If you feel ill,
that's one story. But if you're angry with me, I advise you
to drop it at once. I shall stay here now until nine o'clock
because the train leaves at ten. If you like, you can keep
me company; we might even have dinner together, later
on. But if that doesn't suit you, it would be better for you to
go away at once. D'you see?' I looked over his shoulder at
the chair on which his jacket was hanging, I thought of the
pistol in its pocket, and I said humbly: 'It's true, I don't
feel well. If you like, I'll keep you company until the time
when you leave, but first I want to lie down and rest
for a little. Be kind enough to go in there and tidy up one
of the beds, and I'll lie down and sleep.' He looked at me
a little less harshly, and I went on in haste: 'As soon as you
summon me, I'll come to Milan, I'll live with you and your
mother, I'll keep your proletarian home in order, I'll be your
comrade.' 'Comrade – we'll see about that.' 'I meant, your
wife.' 'Ah, comrade in that sense, yes.' However, he did
not seem all that convinced. The Voice said: 'But don't you
see that more than ever he goes on considering you to be
mad? He's a man of order, even if of an order that is yet to
come. What have you got to do with a man like this?' I
lifted my hand and stroked his face: 'Neither a comrade,
nor a wife, isn't that so, Quinto? Then I'll be your whore,
is that all right? And now, say with me: "Long live the
revolution"; come on, say it to please me.' He gave me a
hasty look, then said hurriedly: 'Long live the revolution,'
in a reticent tone as though he were ashamed. He added:
'Now I'll go and arrange the bed for you.' And he went out.
I immediately went over to his jacket and pulled out the
pistol from the inside pocket. It was very different from
Tiberi's little flat pistol; more massive, heavier, with the
magazine and the butt of yellow wood. I took it up by the
haft, carried it to my lips, and pressed a light kiss upon
it before slipping it into my bag: it was again the Voice
which, to my profound astonishment, made me act like this.
Then, stepping lightly, I went out into the hall. The front

door of the flat was there, close by; but the door of the room in which Quinto was making the bed was wide open and he immediately saw me. He came into the doorway and asked: 'Why, where are you going?' I replied (the Voice was speaking through my mouth and acting through my movements): 'Ah, I was forgetting that I have something here for you'; at the same time, I plunged my hand into my bag, seized the pistol, and aimed it at him. This time the explosion was much louder than that of Tiberi's pistol, less sharp, and, as it were, echoing. I knew that I had struck Quinto because I saw him stagger, put a hand to his stomach, and then, like an actor leaving the stage, disappear from the threshold, probably to go and fall onto the bed which he was preparing for me. I dropped the pistol into the bottom of my bag, opened the door, and ran down the stairs. Once I was in the street, I started walking unhurriedly in the direction of the church of San Giovanni, away against the background of the black sky, with its great gesticulating statues on the top of the crudely floodlit façade.

I: What did you do? Did you go to Via Gaeta? It was late: did you telephone that you were delayed, or did you take a taxi and go straight there? What happened, in short?

Desideria: Nothing happened, nothing happened any more.

I: Nothing?

Desideria: Nothing; my story is finished and the moment has come for us to part.

I: Your story is not finished.

Desideria: Why, what else d'you want to know?

I: You stole the pistol from Quinto; the Voice pointed out to you that the solution to your problem lay in this pistol; that is, that you ought to kill your adoptive mother and her lover, as you had already killed Tiberi and Quinto. It would seem that this ought to be the conclusion of your story.

Desideria: But it's not true. Life has not, and cannot have any conclusion; I shall continue to live even after what you and the Voice call the solution of my problem, and so

375

then my story would never come to an end. But what does the story matter? What matters is myself, and now you know enough of me to understand, and to make others understand, who I am.

I: It's true, I know who you are, I have known it from the beginning. But, all the same, I should like to know what you are going to do now, beginning from the moment when you started walking towards San Giovanni. What you are going to do might modify the idea that I have of you, might throw light upon a new aspect of your personality.

Desideria: It isn't so. I can only be what I am, both yesterday and today and tomorrow. For that reason: good-bye.

I: Wait, you can't go away like that; you yourself have admitted that you haven't finished yet.

Desideria: At Hiroshima, after the explosion of the atomic bomb, there remained on a wall the imprint of a human body, as the print of a foot remains on the sand; that is, a shadow rather darker than the plaster, with a head, a body, and legs. The body that left this imprint was devoured, annihilated by the blast. So it is with me. Your imagination has burned, has consumed me. Finally, I shall no longer exist except in your writing, as an imprint, as a somebody.